# INSIDE THE CIRCLE

*Kate Strauss, 1937*

# INSIDE THE CIRCLE

## Kate Strauss, 1937

## A novel by Paul Berge

This is a work of fiction. All incidents and dialogue are fiction. Except for obvious historical and public figures too dead to speak for themselves, all characters in this book are creations of the author's imagination and are not to be construed as real or imitations of real persons living or dead, and any resemblance to persons living or dead is entirely coincidental.

"In Flanders Field" by Lt. Col. (Canada) John Alexander McCrae

ISBN: 978-0-9728150-3-1

Ahquabi House Publishing, LLC
11872 G58 Hwy
Indianola, Iowa 50125

To Joe Pundzak…
…and, no, there's no connection between the Joe
with the Travel Air 4000 in this book and that Joe
Pundzak.

*The author would like to thank the following friends (in alphabetical order) for their inspiration and assistance (whether they knew it or not) in this project or simply their devotion to the notion that life is better with wings:*

*AAA/APM (Antique Airplane Association and Air Power Museum and Library), Vernon L. Ackerman, John Barcus, James F. Berge, John Bower, Theresa Byers, Richard Coffey, Susan Curtis, Rick Durden, Emily, Thad and Mary Fenton, Ila Fox, Kevin Garrison, Mikey Harbater, Ken Hanscom, David Ho, Iowa Aviation Museum, Jim OTW Jones, Kathy, Curtis Kelly, Bob and Jodi Mathews, Gary Miller, Nash Field Pilots, Lee Ann Nelson, The 99s, Harry Omensetter, Ann Pellegreno, Hal Reynolds, Jim Rosenow, Doug Rozendaal, Bruce Russell, Lorenzo Singer, The Taylors, Sean Tucker, The 1978 Watsonville Airport Pilot's Lounge crew, Wayne Whitfield and the many pilots I've met flying around this country over the years....*

*Honi soit qui mal y pense*

# Chapter 1

# Southern Iowa, 1937

K ate looked over the cockpit rim past struts and wires laced between upper and lower wings. The runway was 1500 feet of grass—500 uphill, 500 level and 500 sloping away toward the river with a slight dogleg at the end.

She pulled the power back. The radial engine popped, exactly as expected. Airspeed—a little fast and altitude a little high, so she squeezed the throttle even further against its stop and banked with the stick while adding opposite rudder beneath her feet.

The yellow biplane with its black checkerboard stripe stenciled down the fuselage resembled a flying taxicab. It slipped into the turn, the ball rolling down the inclinometer on the instrument panel. It was exactly as she knew it would be, having made the approach a thousand times, two thousand, who knew? She gave up counting years ago.

With her left hand on the throttle and her right squeezing the joystick toward her lap, she watched the runway and felt the wind slap against her cheek as the sky drew away.

1

"God, I love it," she said, her heart rather than her mouth speaking.

The biplane fell toward the ground in a gentle slide, her instincts alone judging the distance to the turf. A soft wind lifted a wing tip, and she corrected.

She gunned the engine as though clearing her throat, and the biplane rose momentarily with the extra thrust.

Telephone wires, like guitar strings, stretched between the poles along the road. A green, open-top 1923 Nash two-door roadster sped down the gravel road, swirling gray dust behind it. She saw Daryl behind the wheel. Head below the windshield, his brown fedora pulled low across what she knew were blue eyes, and she knew his foot held the gas pedal to the floorboards.

The biplane skimmed the wires. The Nash took the turn from the gravel road, almost tipping onto the dirt path to the airfield. Daryl clung to the wheel, and she saw him glance over his shoulder at her abeam him crossing the runway's threshold. It was a *Ben Hur* race—she slowing, he swerving toward her.

The car bounced onto the runway, which was little more than a hay field, green from the spring rains and the best surface for landing airplanes. The drought that withered the rest of the Midwest hadn't arrived this year.

The biplane touched. The stick shook. A gust of wind tried to upset her but Kate easily corrected. The grass slapped against the wheels, and she felt the tail settle with a soft jolt and the familiar rumble. It was a short roll to the top of the grade, where, without brakes, she turned and taxied back.

Daryl was out of the car before she reached the shack. He walked toward the faded red gas barrel stand and climbed the short ladder to get the hose and jumped down again. When she swung the tail around he grabbed his hat and closed his eyes against the dusty propeller blast. She killed the engine, and the world fell thunderously silent.

"You're late," he said as he maneuvered a wobbly stepladder beside the airplane's nose. From a worn metal cabinet, he grabbed a funnel with a chamois cloth stretched across the wide opening. It was there to filter out water and crud, but was so old and cracked Daryl wondered if, instead, it was disintegrating into the fuel. He climbed the stepladder and inserted the funnel into the tank.

Kate slipped the white leather helmet from her head and shook out her hair. Dark, like her eyes, it spread in unruly waves across her collar, and she brushed a strand from her forehead.

"Headwinds," she said. "I've been watching the cars pass me all the way." She stood in the cockpit, swiveled and lifted one foot at a time over the rim and then onto the wing root. "I think I even saw a hay wagon pass me at one point."

"Your sister called," Daryl said.

She pretended not to hear and dropped to the ground, where leaning over she touched her toes and gave a soft groan. Her hair draped like a brown waterfall past her knees.

"Your sister called," Daryl repeated.

She stood but still ignored him by asking: "Did we get the new load?"

"Of fuel?"

She nodded her head and walked around the lower wing, absently running her fingertips along the leading edge and around the bow. "Miller said our credit was good, and he'd bring it out today, didn't he?" She looked up at him. "Isn't that what you told me this morning?"

Daryl stared into the funnel, watching the fuel slosh and sift through the chamois. *Liquid money*, he thought.

"Did you call him?" she asked.

"Your sister called."

"Did you call about the gasoline?" She tossed her helmet onto the wing and climbed the ladder to the fuel storage barrel. It stood high enough for gravity to work. She rapped it with the side of her fist.

*Bong!*

"Empty," she muttered. "Why didn't you call him, Daryl?"

He hated when she said his name in those two drawn-out syllables, "Dah-ruhl." It always meant she was annoyed. He adjusted the funnel in the filler neck and lifted the hose over his shoulder.

"Squeeze every drop out," she sighed and stepped off the ladder. She walked to the biplane and stood beneath him. He said nothing, so she asked, "What are we going to do?"

Daryl lifted the funnel away and squinted to see inside the tank. "I think I got about eight gallons in there."

"That won't do." She climbed onto the stepladder and stopped beneath him. Her waist pressed against his hip, and she tried to climb past him toward the filler neck; the old ladder about ready to splinter. Daryl lifted his eyes and turned toward her.

"Eight gallons won't be enough," she repeated. "I came in on faith and..."

"Yeah, 'and fumes,'" he finished for her. "That's a bit cliché, don't you think?"

"I try not to think; I'm a pilot. I pay mechanics to think."

"I get paid?" and he laughed before saying, "I'll call Miller again."

She pressed her head against his body, and he reached for her. "Why bother?" she asked in a way that wasn't really a question. "He knows we're broke."

She touched his hand. It was strong with light red hair on the back and calloused palms from wrenching airplane motors and digging fence posts. The fence posts paid two dollars a day, when work was available; the wrenching he did for nothing.

"I could sell the car," he offered.

"You'd rather sell me."

"The car might bring more."

"Better body," she said disparagingly.

"Says who?"

"Says me."

"And what do you know?" he asked. "You're just a girl." He smiled, and she squeezed his leg. "Here, let me get down."

She jumped from the ladder and took the hose from him. He stepped off the ladder, took the hose back from her and hung it on the storage tank.

"Eight gallons'll get me started," she said. "I'll get the rest somewhere. Somehow."

He pushed his hat back on his head and slipped his arms around her waist. She pressed herself against him and closed her eyes, and then, lifting her face, she stood on tiptoes to kiss him. "How's my doll face?" she asked in a Cagney voice and kissed him again. "Keeping out of trouble?"

"If I kept out of trouble, I'd never make any friends," he answered and let his hands slide onto her rear. She did the same, and they pulled themselves together. "Ummph," they grunted, repeated it and laughed.

"You know," she said. "You're the best mechanic I've ever slept with."

"So, you've been sleeping around the shop again?" he asked in mock horror.

"Yes, but you're the only one courteous enough to wipe the grease off your hands before getting into bed." She slipped from his grip, and he scratched his head.

"So chivalry isn't dead."

"Merely underemployed."

It was a standard routine for them. Whenever she returned from a long trip their professional facade would crumble under their longing. This had been a two-day trip.

She walked away from him toward the shack. The door was unlocked, because there was nothing to steal. She went inside. Daryl stood for a moment watching her. Even in baggy trousers, leather jacket and boots she moved with an ease that fit her small frame. He plunged his hands deep inside his pockets and followed her. He loved Katharine Marie Strauss, and he had even tried to tell her so once.

"I thought we paid this," she said and waved a yellow property tax notice invoice toward him. Daryl was barely through the door. Kate draped her jacket over an old wing chair where the cat slept.

"What's that?"

"You know what it is." Her voice turned sharp. "I thought we paid this."

Daryl reached to scratch the cat, and it rolled in a half-turn onto its side exposing a white belly. He rubbed her, and she grabbed his hands in threatening grip—claws barely out. "You been a good girl, Eleanor, eating all those mouses?" he said in a high voice. "Let's see, you ate Mickey yesterday, and Minnie, and—"

"Daryl," Kate interrupted. He turned. His hand still rubbed the cat's belly. "This hasn't been paid. I thought this was paid. You said—"

"I said I took care of it," he countered, and the cat bit his hand. He pulled it away, and her claws took a strip of skin away from a knuckle.

"How does one '*take care*' of a bill without paying it?"

"I talked to someone at the courthouse—"

"One of your jailhouse friends? One of your saloon buddies?"

"No."

"Then, who?"

"Look, Katie—"

"*Who*, Daryl?" She held the yellow invoice toward him like a damning piece of evidence in a courtroom, proof that he'd evolved from a Scopes monkey. He said nothing. Blood bubbled where the cat had scratched him, and he wiped it against his pants. Silence filled the small room they called their office—the headquarters for *TRANS MIDWEST AIR TAXI SERVICE* of Chariton, Iowa.

Kate folded the bill and slipped it back inside the envelope.

"Gasoline we can do without," she said in a low voice. "Although, God only knows how I'll fly without it."

"We'll get some."

"But taxes, Daryl." She waved the envelope. "You can put off the wholesalers, but when it comes to taxes—" She dropped the envelope onto the desk and turned to the window. "It's hot in here," she said and undid the latch. She tried to open it, but it stuck.

"Here, let me help," Daryl said and moved toward her.

"I can get it, thank-you," she said. The chill in her voice stopped him.

"Of course you can," he mumbled.

"What's that mean?"

"Nothing." Hands up.

"I can open the window myself." She yanked on the brass handles, and the window budged a crack. "Who painted these damn things shut?" she demanded.

"You did."

"Well—doesn't that make me a big lug?" She yanked again, and the window gave with a shriek.

"Your sister called."

"What's she want?"

"I didn't talk long," he said. "She probably wants you to visit your mother."

"I saw her last week."

"That was last month."

"So, last month," Kate said and turned away from the window. She looked at Daryl, who sat on the edge of the desk, one foot on the floor and the other dangling, the heel tapping against the desk with a steady, thump—thump—thump.

"You'll scratch the furniture," she said and tried not to grin.

He kept tapping his heel against the desk, harder as though setting a beat on a bass drum. He grinned back.

"Quit it," she said and sat. He kept up the drumming and slowly leaned toward her, his white even teeth in the Irish grin she loved, the one that always softened her tough pilot demeanor. "What?" And she cocked her head to one side, a gesture she knew that he liked, especially when the light struck the side of her face the way she knew it did now.

He rolled completely over on the desk, stretching across it in a wiggling Jean Harlow slither.

"What?" she asked, again, smiled and looked over both shoulders.

"Expecting company?" he asked and reached a hand to unbutton her blouse.

8

"You're incorrigible," she said and instead of swatting his hand away, she caressed it, pushing his sleeve almost to the elbow. His arms were strong, lean, and the left forearm bore a tattoo of a snake winding around a blue date, *1918*, the head poking through the 8 with its mouth open, and fangs dripping red venom. He slid the hand with the snake tattoo under her bra and rubbed her breast. She reached over and kissed him hard on the mouth and for the next twenty minutes neither one thought about the Great Depression.

\*\*\*

"If I get pregnant," she said pushing from the floor, "I'll make you raise the thing." She kissed his nose and reached across the rug for her panties.

Daryl rolled onto his stomach, a sated grin on his face, his eyes half closed. He touched her bare thigh as she took her bra from the desk and worked her way into it. "Bye-bye, girls," he said and waved at her breasts. "Maybe Mommy will let you out later, and we can—"

Kate was beginning to laugh, and she rushed to fasten the bra clasp when the building shook with a flashing roar.

"Jeeesus, Mary and Charlie!" Daryl shouted and turned toward the window. Kate grabbed the window sill in time to see a Travel Air 4000 biplane shoot down the runway, wings rocking before it dropped below the river bank, disappeared, and then pulled up in a climbing, show-off turn.

"It's Joe," Daryl said and stood. "The man certainly knows how to make an entrance." He looked around the room for his hat and put it on.

Kate slipped into her pants, and with her bra still dangling she grabbed her leather jacket and pulled it on. "You might want to wear something else," she said.

Daryl, dressed only in a hat, grin and the flaccid remains of desire, looked down at himself and shrugged. Then he sucked in his gut and puffed his chest. "How's that?"

The Travel Air returned for a slow pass, wings rocking, the pilot waving. Then they heard him pass overhead, and he throttled the engine back. Kate slipped her bare feet into her boots, and with a quick look in the small mirror on the wall she brushed her hair and ran out the door.

"Zip up your jacket," Daryl said, standing beside her as they watched the biplane descend to land. Kate fiddled with her bra until getting every thing in place, and she zipped the jacket almost to her chin. Daryl, wearing only his brown fedora and a pair of gray boxer shorts that had once been white, waved at the landing pilot.

"He'll suspect we've been mating again," Kate said.

"No chance," Daryl replied. "He knows you went to a Catholic school."

"You told?"

"He forced it out of me."

"How?"

"After he first met you, he said, '*Nice kid; who is she?*' And I said, '*She's a pilot, and she comes from a huge Catholic family...*'"

"But only on my father's side."

"And he said, '*Catholic? Then she must be good in bed.*' And I said you were."

She hit his arm and ran toward the taxiing airplane.

Daryl held his hat against the prop blast, and Kate leaped onto the wing root before the propeller quit turning. She threw her arms around the pilot's neck and kissed him twice.

"Joe," Daryl heard her call. He walked toward them.

Joe was half out of the cockpit, his brown leather helmet still on, his goggles above his eyes. He was handsome, the kind of handsome that belonged on a movie screen, grinning while shooting down Germans with bad teeth. Daryl pushed his fedora low over his eyes and approached the fuselage. Kate took her hands off Joe so he could stand.

"Hello, Daryl," he called. "I hope you didn't wear that on my account."

"No," Daryl answered. "I always wear my good shorts when I meet real pilots."

"Ignore him," Kate said. "He's growing old—almost forty, you know."

"What's wrong with forty?" Joe asked. "Did I come at a bad time?"

"No," Kate said.

"Yes," Daryl interrupted. "We were in the middle of—"

"Daryl!"

"Katie!"

"I came at a bad time," Joe said. "I'll leave."

"You stay," Kate ordered. "And, Daryl, you behave." The laugh was tight, more warning than fun.

"Yes, Ma'am," he said and touched his hat in salute. "Sir, may I carry your bags?" He looked over the rim of the cockpit. "Bring your golf clubs this time?"

"Won't be staying long," Joe said and pulled off his helmet. His hair was almost black and slicked back with Brilliantine made his head seem lacquered. "Can you look the engine over for me, Daryl? Feels like a valve's sticking again, and I may be crazy, but—"

11

"We give discounts to the deranged," Daryl piped. "They're a great untapped resource, I keep telling Katie."

"He does," she said.

"Why keep the insane locked up in asylums when we can put them into airplanes and make money off them?"

"And at the same time keep them off the streets," she added.

"Makes good economic sense," he continued.

"When you think about it," she said.

"Which we don't," Daryl said. "So you needn't apologize for being crazy."

"Just give us your business."

"Or your money—you can keep the business. We're not proud."

Joe's head snapped from one to the other. He wrinkled his face and asked, "Did I just fly into a Marx Brothers movie?"

By then Daryl was studying the engine. "I'll want to run it again, so don't touch anything." He turned and walked away with all the dignity a man could muster wearing only shorts and a fedora, while his mate played coquette with a man who had fallen from the sky.

*** 

The steady growl of the Travel Air's Wright J5 engine vibrated the windowpanes, but Kate and Joe were used to airport sounds. She fanned the unpaid bills on the desk before him like a bad poker hand.

"He doesn't take it seriously," she complained. "He keeps saying everything will somehow work out. Things will *miraculously* improve despite all evidence to the contrary."

"'*Nothing to fear but fear itself*,' eh?" Joe said.

"Don't get him started," she blurted. "He considers that idiot in the White House to be mankind's savior."

"Still starry-eyed with the New Deal, is he?"

"Insists the NRA will come running to our rescue," she said.

"Sounds hopeless. Doesn't he know the courts are tossing out most of that Bolshevik horse manure? Roosevelt's a flash in the pan. Hoover'll be back and put everything right again."

"He lives in a dream world." She scooped all the bills into one stack and held them silently in both hands as she looked out the open window toward Daryl. Joe followed her gaze. He saw Daryl in the Travel Air's rear cockpit running the engine, his head over the rim, face in the slipstream, eyes closed and ears listening to every change in the motor's rhythm.

"He does know airplanes," Joe said and moved toward the window. Kate didn't move. "There's no one in Iowa can make an airplane sing the way he can."

"Iowa," she sniffed and turned to stare at Joe; her face was set in an appraising stare, her jaw firm. "And, airplanes don't sing," she said.

"Says who?"

"Now you sound like him." She jerked her thumb toward the open window. The Wright engine still howled, and then, with a backfire, it quit. "Airplanes fly because people make them fly."

"How cold."

"They fly because someone borrows money from a bank and promises to pay it back. They fly because steel and brass and rubber and cotton are all combined in the proper ratios, and mixed with gasoline and oil and a good spark from a hot magneto—"

"Is this lesson for my benefit?"

"And that spark only happens if the pilot in the cockpit has the dough in his pocket from paying customers who want the gas put in the tank to be burnt by the spark inside the steel components turning the propeller to lift the whole wing-ding pile of debt into the sky long enough to keep the money flowing in, thus—"

She took a breath and pointed a finger skyward, and continued: "Thus, keeping the banker from sending the sheriff, who's probably already out here serving notice that taxes haven't been paid, and if they aren't paid, then he's going to draw his gun and take the airplane with its cotton, rubber, steel and gasoline in payment, because sheriffs don't like folks not paying taxes, because if no one paid his taxes, then sheriffs couldn't afford to buy the bullets to put inside the guns that get waved at delinquent taxpayers as their airplanes, and other personal belongings, are being auctioned off."

"*Sold* to the feisty woman with the cute face and cynical eye!"

"Not cynical, just realistic."

"Is that it?"

"No that *isn't* it," she snapped. "But it's all you need to know." Her voice trailed off, and he moved toward her.

"Things that bad?"

"No," she said. "We still have our health."

"FDR will want to take that away, too."

"He can have it." She looked at him. "Is there a reason you're here?"

"Just stopped in to chat?"

She shook her head. "You never just chat."

"Right—a heartless observation, not in keeping with a trusting friendship—but correct nonetheless."

"Got a job for us?"

He nodded.

"A good one? We need the cash. God, how we need the cash."

The door swung open, and Daryl walked inside wiping his hands on a rag. He wore trousers and a shirt now, sleeves rolled above his elbows, shoes, no socks, and the same fedora was pushed back on his head. A grease smudge ran across his nose. His face was straight.

"Well, Doc?" Joe asked.

"You got a burnt valve," Daryl said.

"Serious?"

"Won't know 'til I pull the cylinder. Swapping jugs is easy enough."

"Can you do it? I mean, today?"

"Don't know if I've got a spare—wasn't expecting company." He flashed his Irish grin. "But I'll have a look."

"Is there anything this man doesn't know about airplanes?" Joe asked Kate.

"Just how to get money out of them."

"I'm working on that," Daryl said. "The way I figure it there's money waiting to be had out there."

"Got a plan, huh?" Joe asked.

"Not just a plan, but a whole strategy—a way of life almost. The Chinese call it the *Tao*—The *Way*."

Kate sighed. "It's called going broke in a *big* way."

"Somewhere," Daryl mused, ignoring her, "—is a whole lot of dough just waiting for a sharp cookie, like me—"

"Like you?"

"Like me to come along and match desire—" He held up the left hand. "With opportunity—" And held up the other. "To start the old money machine just spitting out hundred-dollar bills like they was autumn leaves flyin' off the trees."

"He reads too much," Kate said.

"Chinese philosophy?"

"That was last week. It's French books now." She closed her eyes.

"Can you read French?" Joe asked Daryl.

"I learned a few words over there, mostly I look at the pictures."

"Do your lips move?"

"Can't tell since I read in the dark—I don't wake Katie that way."

"You're a clever man, Mr. Fitzpatrick. No wonder you've won this young girl's heart." He winked. "Katie, let's say you dump this character and run off with me."

"You wouldn't like her," Daryl said and sat in the wing chair. The cat was elsewhere, probably hunting the fencerow. "She has cold feet, snores and expects us to make money at everything we do."

"Making money at *any*thing would do nicely right now," she said.

"A completely unreasonable sort," Daryl said. "Plus she doesn't like reading Antoine Exupery."

"That's the French stuff?" Joe asked.

"Mmmm," Daryl mumbled and leaned his chin against his chest. He looked as though he were about to drop into sleep. "It's all about aviators—the kind who fly, because—well, I guess because they love to fly. I wouldn't know."

"No one pays you to love flying," Joe said.

"No one pays us for anything," Kate added.

Joe rapped the desk with his fist. "Reminds me—I have an announcement."

Kate: "An announcement?"

Joe: "An announcement."

Daryl: "I do love announcements. Is it about Lindbergh? Think he'll ever fly the Atlantic?"

"It's been done," Kate said.

16

"What a shame. He'll be disappointed when he finds out."

"My friends," Joe began. "And I do consider most of you my friends."

"Oh, that is a good announcement," Daryl said. "Is there more?"

"There is."

"Will there be an intermission?"

"Daryl?" Kate said.

"Yes, dear?"

"Let the man speak. He may have something important on his mind, although that would be unusual."

"Thank-you," Joe said. "You're too kind." He leaned toward Kate. "You need money, right?"

"The county assessor would agree with that." She waved the tax bill.

"I may have a solution."

"To what?" Daryl asked.

"To our lack of money," Kate said too quickly.

"Oh, that. I thought you took care of that."

Joe held up a hand. "How would you like a steady customer?"

"Does he have money?" she asked.

"They do."

"Will they part with it?"

"They will." Joe sat on the desk so his right foot smacked the side.

"Careful doing that," Daryl warned. "You could end up naked on the floor."

Joe frowned—confused but pressed on. "I'd keep this job myself, but I'm heading out for Spain—"

"Spain?" Daryl asked. "You mean where they speak Spanish and torment bulls?"

"The same."

"What's the deal? Why Spain?" Kate asked.

"Can't tell you much; all very top secret, diplomatic stuff, clandestine operations and what-not. Suffice to say they've some kind of revolution going on—"

"Civil war," Daryl corrected.

"Whatever. Anyhow, they need airplanes, and I know this guy who tells me I can make a bundle flying airplanes into Spain from France."

"Which side?"

"Which side what?"

"Never mind," Daryl waved. "Go ahead with your revolution."

Somewhat put off, Joe continued. "Well, it all sounded very, ah, idealistic—"

"And coincidentally profitable?"

"Nothing wrong with making a few bucks off someone else's struggle against...whatever it is they're struggling against."

"Capitalism?"

"Hope not."

"Fascism?"

"Not sure, might be."

"Daryl!"

"Anyhow," Joe continued. "It sounds too good to pass up. Plus, I've never been to Spain. Might be fun, I figure."

"Don't drink the water," Daryl muttered and was ignored.

Kate leaned back in her chair. Her brown eyes were hard—the eyes of someone ready to do business. Daryl kept his closed.

"Where do we come in?" Kate asked.

"How far is Ottumwa from here?" Joe asked.

Kate frowned and said, "About 30 miles, you know that."

"And from there to Chicago?"

"Oh, another two, maybe, two hundred and fifty."

Joe pointed outside. "Can your bird out there fly a daily run from Ottumwa to Chicago, make a pick-up and beat it back to Ottumwa?"

"Yeah," she said. "Easy. With fuel stops."

"Seven days a week?"

She nodded.

"Rain or shine?  Hot or cold?"

Daryl added without opening his eyes, "Through gloom of night nor eye of newt?"

"Is this a mail route?" Kate asked.  "We don't qualify for mail contracts.  That's strictly big league—United Airlines or Braniff.  One of those guys."

Joe's voice hushed slightly.  "It's not the mail.  It's more of a *private* courier service."

"And—?" Kate suspicious.

"And—every morning you'd pick up a package, oh, about so big."  Joe indicated with his hands.  Daryl watched from under the rim of his hat.  "It goes to a coal mining outfit in Ottumwa."

"You want her to deliver coal by air?" Daryl asked. "That *is* clever.  I feel I must warn you in advance, however, it will be very expensive.  I suggest they stick with trains and barges."

Joe gave Daryl a wry frown before he continued. "You fly the package down to Ottumwa and deliver it to a driver who will meet you at the strip every afternoon."

"Strip?  I don't land at the airport?"

"No—" Joe said and was interrupted.

"Wouldn't want all that coal dust getting on municipal runways."

"Daryl, please," she said.  "Where do I land?"

"Oh, nice place," Joe said.  "It's a little grass strip along a small river west of town, ah, between Ottumwa and a little town called, Blakesburg."

"I know it," she said. "Not the specific strip, but I know the area, mostly trees and hills, some farms."

"And lots of coal."

"What does she take up to Chicago?" Daryl asked.

"Nothing, usually."

"How much are they paying to haul *nothing*?"

"How much do you want?"

Kate and Daryl both sat up. They looked at each other. Kate spoke. "Twenty cents a mile, plus two dollars per hour if I have to wait on the ground." Daryl shook his head. She's thinking big, he thought. Then she added, "Plus, weight charges, of course."

"Make it thirty-five a mile and four dollars an hour on the ground," Joe said. "Plus, weight charges." He leaned back for the reaction and pulled a cigarette case from his jacket pocket. Opening it with a flip, he offered it toward Kate. She took one, and Joe offered toward Daryl, who shook his head. He hated to see Kate smoke; hated the way it soured her breath, made her hair stink.

"What gives?" she asked, accepting a light. Smoke rose past her face and climbed in a lazy ghost toward the ceiling. A weak breeze through the window swirled it away like a stray thought.

Joe lit his cigarette and picked a speck of tobacco from his tongue. "You'll be carrying payroll."

Kate winced. Daryl squinted and leaned against the chair's wing. "Payroll?"

"Is that safe?" Kate asked.

"Is flying safe?" Joe countered. "Is anything safe? What difference does it make what you carry? Payroll's no different than any other cargo—just stuff in the front hole. Someone figured it would save them a lot of dough having an airplane haul it rather than some armored car. You can't stick up an airplane once it's off the ground."

He smiled and his even teeth gave him a dangerous look. "And I guarantee you, security's good at either end."

"Payroll, huh?" Daryl mused.

"Yeah. Swell angle, isn't it?"

Daryl thought for a moment. He looked to Kate and could tell she wanted the job, wanted it desperately. Even though they'd shared the same bed for the last few years, there were many chapters inside Kate's life he couldn't read. What he read now was a pilot anxious—not merely eager—to fly, listening to a sales pitch that sounded too smooth from an old friend he didn't trust.

"What kind of company runs a payroll seven days a week?"

Joe seemed caught off guard by the question, yet was ready with an answer. "A successful company."

"Bullcrap," Daryl said. His voice was flat. He stood up and stretched. "No one runs a payroll seven days a week." He waved smoke from his face and walked to the window. "Anyhow, Iowa is closed on Sundays. Didn't you see the sign coming in?"

Joe took a drag on his cigarette and looked around for an ashtray. Kate took one made from a burnt piston off a stack of books and slid it toward him. "Thanks."

"What else will she be running?" Daryl asked without turning.

"*Running*?" Joe shot back. "You make it sound so illegal, like we're bootleggers."

"Well?"

"Prohibition's over, Daryl; that ship sailed, although I must admit I do miss it. Made some good dough back then—"

"What else?"

"Oh, papers, books. You know, ledgers, that sort of thing."

"Important papers."

"Yes, very important." He joined Daryl at the window. "Is there a problem here?"

Daryl turned. "Could you point that in another direction?" He waved at the smoke and stepped back.

"Sorry." Joe held the cigarette at arm's length, which didn't do anything to lessen the smoke but made him look silly and Daryl liked that.

Joe continued: "It's a great job. A flying job. A paying—*cash* paying—flying job. Steady work." Receiving no answer from Daryl, he turned to Kate. "Why do I feel like I just handed him a dead skunk?"

She stood and crushed her cigarette in the ashtray. "I'll take it," she said. "It's wonderful, really. I just think the shock of a real job, well, you know. Just a half-hour ago we were about to lose the whole deal to the taxman, and now—"

"Don't thank me," Joe said.

"Okay," Daryl said. "I won't."

Smacking his forehead, Joe said, "Whoa, you know what? I just realized—I landed at the wrong airport."

Kate started to speak, "No, Joe, he didn't mean anything."

"Yes, I did."

Joe turned for the door. "Foolish me, I meant to land at the *other* impoverished airport where the only pilot and the only mechanic without any prospects between them would look forward to the chance to make a few bucks—"

"Honest bucks?"

"Bucks."

Kate hadn't been born female for nothing. "Is anyone hungry?"

"I'd say 'starving' but Joe might get the impression he's expected to feed us."

"No I wouldn't."

Kate took Daryl by one arm, Joe by the other and in a voice her mother taught her, said: "There, it's settled. We'll have lunch and talk this out."

Daryl wiggled free and walked out the door saying, "I've got a cylinder to replace." Before closing the door, he added, "See, Joe, we do have a paying customer." And: "You do have money don't you?"

"I do, but it's dirty."

"I'll wash my hands first."

The door closed.

***

# Chapter 2

"Certain you won't join us?" Joe called from the car.

Daryl shook his head. "If you want that jug replaced I'd better get on it."

Kate spoke. "Can we bring you anything back?"

"Maybe a loose-meat and a beer."

"Maybe and a malt," she said, correcting him. "Vanilla?"

"Yeah, what I meant," Daryl said and turned with a wave. Kate started the Nash. She slipped it into gear with a brief mashing sound and let out the clutch. Once out of earshot, Joe said, "If the man wants a beer, why not—"

"Mind your own business, Joe," she said calmly and turned onto the gravel.

After a quiet minute: "What's a loose-meat…?"

"It's like a hamburger that doesn't hold together."

"People eat that?"

"Times are tough."

"Not *that* tough."

Behind the shack, that *TRANS MIDWEST AIR TAXI SERVICE* called an office, was the hangar. Made of rusted sheet metal wrapped around old telephone poles and salvaged 2x4's, it rattled when the wind blew and leaked when it rained. A barrel stove gave the only heat in winter, and under the summer sun it baked inside. Birds lived in the rafters, and as Daryl slipped under the canvas door they took to flight.

"Out with you," he called in an Errol Flynn voice. He undid the cord that raised the canvas door like a rollup theater curtain.

"Be gone, or I'll turn the rabid cat loose to cull your inbred numbers." More W.C. Fields than Flynn. He pulled the cord, and the birds flew around the hangar annoyed rather than frightened. With one hand still holding the cord, he picked a stone from the gravel floor and loosed it at a pair directly above him. It ricocheted off the beam and flew back, striking him on the shoulder.

"Hah—Let that be a warning, ye sons of she-dogs!" The two birds took off. Once the door was raised, he coiled the rope around a hook and faced inside the hangar.

A small building, it was cluttered with airplane parts. Wings, some covered and some skeletons marked with bird crap, hung from the walls. Between the rafters were spars and struts and even a Curtiss JN-4 "Jenny" fuselage, although it was twisted and the front portion charred.

The hangar floor was limestone gravel, and along one wall were stacks of wooden propellers he had purchased in a government auction. Mostly intact, a few were shattered, having apparently been stopped abruptly in unfortunate miscalculations of exactly where the earth was in relation to landing gear. Those he split for kindling.

Against the opposite wall were the engines, again, most from auctions or salvaged from wrecks. One was held in a stand. Rags poked out of holes where cylinders should have been, and some kind of animal claimed one hole as a nest.

Daryl walked inside the hangar. He stepped over an upturned box and stopped to look at the one, almost complete, airplane in the hangar.

Once a biplane, it now had no wings. Where the cabane struts would have been above the fuselage, Daryl had welded a structure resembling a small Eiffel Tower. He took hold of the piece and shook it as though unconvinced it could serve any purpose, at least not the purpose he had in mind, which was to anchor flying wires to the single low-wing he planned to install some day.

He'd just looked inside the cockpit when: "Hi, Mr. Fitzpatrick."

The voice was unsteady, a boy's voice, and it came from behind.

"Jesus and Mary McGuire, Brian," Daryl said and clasped one hand to his chest. "You shouldn't sneak up on us old farts like that."

"Sorry," Brian said. He leaned a bicycle against the wall and walked inside. Tall for 14, Brian was as thin as any kid would want to be and still throw a shadow. His hair was a sandy brown and uncombed. He kept his hands inside his pockets, and when he smiled it was tight, shy.

"No school today?"

"No," he said, and Daryl knew not to ask any further. "You gonna work on the racer?"

Daryl looked at the fuselage. For the last year Brian had been hanging around the airfield, helping with the mowing, painting or whatever he could just to be near the airplanes. Whenever Kate flew he would stand and watch, eyes wide, taking in the whole process. Kate ignored him, although she would give him a friendly 'Hello' in passing, and once she even took him for a quick ride over town, letting him briefly handle the controls before they landed. Brian, in return had spent the rest of the afternoon waxing the biplane, leaving only when it was dark.

"Not today," Daryl said. "Did you see that Travel Air out there?"

"Whose is it?"

"Oh, a friend of ours from Chicago. He stops in now and again." Daryl walked around the fuselage toward the spare engines. "We were in the Army together—long time ago, before you were born—before anyone was born, except the Kaiser."

"Rich guy?" Brian asked.

"No, not really. He's just a pilot like Kate."

"Is Kate rich?"

"Yeah, but she buried all her money one day, and then fell under the spell of an evil witch causing her to forgot where she'd buried it."

"Did she make a map?"

"A map?"

"Yeah, a treasure map," Brian said. "You know, where she buried the dough. Did she make a map?"

"Oh, yeah, a map. But the witch made her forget where she put that, too."

"Some witch," Brian said.

"Republican witch," Daryl said absently and reached over to inspect an engine. "Help me look around for a J-5 cylinder, will you?"

Brian moved quickly toward the engines. Not certain what a J-5 cylinder looked like, he nonetheless began searching. Daryl smiled, pleased with the kid's enthusiasm.

"What's wrong with the Travel Air?" Brian asked.

"Burnt valve be my guess," Daryl answered and overturned a crankcase. Three mice stood for a moment in surprise as though G-men had just kicked open their hideout. And then they ran like mice.

"Oh," Brian muttered. "That's bad—isn't it?"

"Uh-huh."

They searched for several minutes in silence, carefully sorting through mounds of grimy parts. Brian offered a filthy cylinder for Daryl's inspection. Daryl knew it was cracked and useless. Inspecting it in the light shaft from a window he showed Brian the crack and handed it back. "Check what's under that tarp." He pointed.

Brian climbed over a sawhorse and began sifting through the lot. After several minutes he called, "How's this one?"

Daryl had been rubbing the inside of a rusted cylinder barrel, trying to decide if it would be worth saving. "What'd you find?"

"I think it's a J-5," Brian said pointing to a damaged radial engine on a pallet that had been covered by the tarp. Daryl looked and agreed.

"Fetch me a scalpel."

Brian ran to the workbench and was back with a handful of wrenches before Daryl had the engine dragged clear of the pile.

"Thanks."

"Don't you know what you've got in here?"

"Sure," Daryl answered. "I have it all catalogued, only I can't remember quite where I put the catalogue." He pressed the wrench onto the base nut and tugged.

"Witches buried that, too, huh?"

"Yep."

"Republican witches?"

"Non-union to boot." Daryl applied more pressure to the nut.

"Want a hammer?"

"Not unless I'm planning to break something." He pressed the wrench. "Uhh. There she goes." He slipped the wrench off, then on again and twisted the nut clear. "*Proper tool for a proper job*," he said in a cartoon Irish brogue. "My da used to say that. '*Daryl, me boyo, always use the proper tool for a proper job even if ya haf ta steal it and, then, preferably from a Brit.*' He'd say that—" He looked to Brian who nodded the way kids nod when they've heard something a hundred times.

"So's the guy I saw Kate driving off with, the one with the Travel Air?"

Daryl said nothing, and then, "His name's Joe. A pretty fair pilot, I guess." Daryl struggled with the rest of the base nuts, working them free. "Here, let's take this thing outside into the light."

"What's he doing here?"

"You ask a lot of questions, Brian."

"Is he Kate's boyfriend?"

"Not that I know of," Daryl said. Brian followed him outside. "Barrel's not bad." He ran his hand inside. "If the head's not cracked, I think we got us a good cylinder here." He looked at Brian with a quick grin, then at the empty road and frowned. "Of course I could use the car right about now."

"When're they coming back?"

"Hard to tell. Could be a while. Could be hours. Could be that he's really an enchanted fairy prince." Daryl twirled in a half-circle with a quick two-step at the end. "He's kissed her, so her memory suddenly returned, and she's spilled her guts about the map."

"The one that shows where the treasure's buried?"

"Yeah, that's the one," Daryl said absently. "Then once he's gotten her treasure, he may take her away, in *my* car, mind you, to a foreign land where only pilots dwell—"

"Like Chicago?"

"Oh, nothing that drastic. Although, one can never tell with evil prince types; might fly her there and then plow up the runway so she can never leave." Daryl stared at the empty road and then down at the cylinder. He tapped it with his fingers.

"Is he a Republican, too?" Brian asked.

"Hmm? Oh, ah, no." He stood silent for a moment, then, looking at Brian, said, "Worse. He's an independent." He rubbed a chunk of grime from a cooling fin. His tone changed. "Look, Brian, could you do me a favor?"

"Sure."

"You know Todd's Machine Shop, don't you?  The one on Euclid?"

"Yeah," Brian said.  "You took me there when you had that crankshaft turned down."

"Uh-huh.  Listen, if I give them a call—you see the car might not be back for a while—if I gave them a call, could you run this jug over there?"

"Sure," Brian answered, thrilled to be asked to help.

"I'll tell them over the phone what I want done.  I haven't got the equipment to bore it out."  He looked Brian in the face.  "You've got to promise me you won't drop it."

"I won't.  I can put it in the basket, maybe tie it."

"These are delicate, you know, like fancy clocks."

"I won't drop it."

Daryl turned.  He looked back at the road, thinking, 'they may be a while.'  "Here, let me give them a call." Brian followed him into the office.

Inside, Daryl set the cylinder on the pile of unpaid bills and reached for the phone on the wall.  Brian moved slowly around the small room looking at the photographs of airplanes and pilots with leather helmets and goggles pushed onto their foreheads.  Although he had seen them all before, he never tired.  He stopped at one group portrait.  It had been taken in southern California, and showed a younger Kate, her hair bobbed, her face bright. She and another woman, slightly older with light hair and taller than Kate, held a large trophy between them.  An arrangement of men in mechanic's overalls, three-piece suits, sports jackets and one in shirt sleeves stood behind them. All smiled. *WOMEN'S ALTITUDE RECORD* was printed at the bottom.  *CLOVER FIELD, SANTA MONICA 1929* was below that.

Daryl pressed his forehead against the wall and held the telephone earpiece loose against his ear.  "They must have gone to lunch," he said to Brian. "You hungry?" Before Brian could answer, Daryl spoke into the mouthpiece on the wall, "Bill? Yeah, Daryl here. Listen, did I catch you at a bad time?" He listened, smiling. "Yeah, times is bad all over." He laughed. "Hey, I'm sending a kid over—" Brian cringed—'*a kid.*' "He's got a cylinder I need bored out—uh-huh—yeah, I'll write all the numbers down for you. Just clean it up for me, and if you could lap those valves in for me, I'd appreciate it—uh-huh—yeah, you might want to gas check it when you're done—what?" He listened. "Yeah, I got the dough. This is a paying customer, for Christ's sake." He laughed and winked at Brian. "Look, Bill, I appreciate it. You do good work. Huh? Yeah, she's in town—what do you mean with her boyfriend? That's just some customer. He's buying her lunch." He listened. "No, he's an old friend—yeah, an old army friend," Daryl said the last in a flat voice. "Yeah, thanks, Bill. So long." He replaced the earpiece on the hook and stared the way people do when they hang up phones and wonder if they'd said anything important.

"Want me to run it in for you?" Brian asked.

Daryl turned slowly, his gaze distant. "Yeah." He put a hand on the cylinder and twisted it first one way and then the next. He took a manual from a shelf and sat in the chair. "Hand me that pencil, will you, Bri? Thanks." He opened the book. Black smudges marked the more popular sections. Running the pencil along a chart of numbers, he copied several onto a scrap of paper, closed the book and handed the paper to Brian. "Give this to Mr. Todd when you give him the cylinder. He knows what to do."

"How long will it take?" Brian asked.

"Oh, you don't have to wait for it. Kate'll be back by then, I'll fetch it myself."

"I can wait for it. Honest."

Daryl shrugged. "Well, if you don't mind. Shouldn't take too long." Brian smiled, barely showing a row of even small teeth. He wasn't a kid who smiled too often.

\*\*\*

Daryl Fitzpatrick tugged the cord tight against the cylinder to the basket. He tucked in a corner of the rag protecting the fins and said to Brian, "Now, I want you to remember something. Mexico is about 900 miles thataway." He pointed southwest. "And if you drop this thing," he tapped the cylinder. "That's about where you'll have to hide where I don't find you and put a knot on your head." He smiled.

"I won't drop it," Brian protested and pushing his bike to speed, leaped on, wobbled and pedaled away. "I won't," he called over his shoulder.

Daryl: "Watch the fence post!"

Brian: "I am—*whoa*—I am!" He missed and pedaled faster. Daryl shook his head and watched him disappear down the road through the dust billowing behind a truck that passed in the opposite direction. The driver waved as he passed, and Daryl waved back, uncertain who it was. Iowa—everyone waves; there's little else to do. He walked back to the hangar.

\*\*\*

"Who had the roast beef?" the waitress asked. She balanced an oblong platter on a wide forearm while looking from Kate to Joe.

"He's the beef," Kate said.

"Here you go, sweetie."

"Thanks," Joe said and snuffed a cigarette in an ashtray.

"More coffee?"

"Please," Kate said and held her cigarette over her shoulder while the waitress poured. "Thanks, Irma."

"Where's Daryl?" Irma asked.

"Had to work. Someone has to watch the shop." Kate tried to laugh.

Irma leaned forward. "*God*, don't tell me about work. I've been at this since five, and I don't get off for another three hours."

"Oh," Kate said, voice flat wishing she would leave.

"Breakfast weren't so bad, ya know, but the lunch crowd. *God*. Some of them just wouldn't leave. You know the type, sit and drink coffee for about a million hours, then don't leave nearly a decent a tip, five percent, maybe, at that. *God*." Each time she said, '*God*,' the coffeepot swung past Joe's head.

"Could you hold that clear?" he said and ducked.

"What? This? I ain't gonna hit you, sweetie." Hand on his shoulder, a little squeeze. "*God*. You'd think I'd never done this before." She screwed her face into what resembled a rotting grapefruit and turned away. Someone called her from the lunch counter, and she hurled back, "You keep your shirt on, Wayne! *God*, place'd fall 'part without me—" She left.

Kate sipped her coffee. "*God*," she mimicked. "You're so mean to the old gal, Joe."

"Old? She looks about your age."

"Careful—"

"I should buy this place just so I could fire her," he said.

"You'd lose all your business."

"Over that one?"

"Irma? They adore her. She's been insulting customers here for years. You should see her when the mayor comes in."

"Can't he have her shot or something?"

"Our dear mayor couldn't get Irma's car towed away if it was parked on his foot. He's somewhat of an idiot himself."

"Then how does he get elected?"

"I think this town has a sense of humor, and they like to vote for whoever looks the least likely to display any competence. Mayor Hadley's their man. City council's even worse."

Joe scraped mashed potatoes into his peas, and then pressed it all onto his fork with a strip of dripping beef. Kate only drank coffee and lit a second cigarette off the first. "Take the whole pack," he said.

"I'm sorry," she said. "I'm out. It feels good to smoke as much as I like."

"Doesn't Papa Daryl let you smoke at home?"

"I have to go outside to."

"Interesting man. Only one I know who doesn't smoke. Can't be healthy."

Kate blew smoke from the corner of her mouth. She watched Joe eat. The door opened to the street, and a short man in a white suit entered. He looked around, nodded to Kate before sitting at the counter. Irma was there with a cup and the coffee pot.

"*God*," she hollered. "I thought maybe you'd died and the hogs ate ya. Where have you been all week?" The man in the white suit wheezed something neither Kate nor Joe could hear as he picked up his cup with both hands and drank. The cup shook and was slow reaching his lips. Irma wiped a spill without drawing attention.

"You know him?" Joe asked.

Kate shook her head. "Not really. I recognize him. See him around town a lot, but—no, not really."

Joe set his fork on the plate, the food barely touched. He lifted his water glass, and before it reached his lips he said, "Katie, tell me something."

34

Her eyebrows rose.

"What the hell are you doing here?" He drank.

Kate stuck the cigarette into her mouth and drew in the smoke to buy time. Her brown eyes stared unblinking at him.

"I live here," she said. "I was born here in Chariton, although, we moved to Des Moines when I was eight." Smoke puffed out with each statement. "And I fly here."

"Ever been to Times Square in New York?" Joe asked.

She shook here head. "No." The smoke puffed again.

"Times Square is something else," he said leaning back. "It's like nowhere you've ever been."

"Not even Hollywood?" she asked.

"Close, but no," he said. "Times Square is this canyon of tall buildings with all these signs flashing and winking like crazy eyeballs, all trying to catch your attention. And most of them are just that—trying to catch you."

"What does this have to do with anything?" she asked and blew smoke.

"Well, Katie dear, I'm getting to that. You see, there's this one sign in among all the others."

"Signs?"

"Yeah, it's a cigarette sign. I forget the brand—*Camel, Lucky Strike* or something. Anyhow, it's big, sits over the street where it blows out smoke." He puckered his lips and blew.

"You look like a fish," she said.

"And they paint these different faces on the sign, you know, with the mouth always the same. And whatever face they got up there keeps pumping this smoke out— Poof, Poof." He demonstrated. "All day, all night it blows this smoke."

"This is fascinating," she said but not fascinated.

"Anyhow," Joe said, "I thought maybe your face would look good up there. The way you're putting out the smoke it reminded me of that sign." His voice trailed away. Kate held her cigarette to one side and said nothing. If that was his idea of a compliment to a girl—

Joe ate.

"Tell me about Spain," she said after a while.

"There's nothing much to tell. They've got a war started, and that means airplanes. They need 'em, lots of 'em."

"So?"

"So, someone I know is in the airplane brokering business, and I get to deliver a few."

"To Spain?"

"Among other places."

She stared, waiting for more, but with Joe there often wasn't more. His plans were often anything but. Still, he always managed to score big or at least big enough to keep going.

He spread his hands apart. "That's all. I'll now take questions." He pointed at her. "You, the pretty girl with the wrinkled brow, what's your question?"

She thought for a moment and flicked the end of her cigarette with her thumbnail. "Could I get in on that?"

"Nope," he said without hesitation.

"No women allowed?"

"Something like that."

"Is that your rule?"

"Hey, Katie. It's Spain. You think those bull-stabbers want a bunch of women—American women—flying their airplanes? It's bad enough they have to use us to get the damn things in there in the first place."

"What do you know about combat flying?" she asked.

"Combat? Oh, no, I just ferry the beasts in there; after that it's someone else's game. I don't take to getting shot

36

at. They don't pay nearly enough for that kind of nonsense."

"How much will you be making?"

"Can't say."

"Can't or won't?"

"Take your pick."

"It's good, though, isn't it?"

Joe glanced over both shoulders and leaned toward Kate. "Damn good."

"Then I want in," she said and thumped the table. "I can fly the pants off of any of you show-offs any day of the week."

Joe leaned back. "Katie, if it was left to me, you could fly my pants off any time—"

"Oh, Joe."

"—anytime you want."

She threw a napkin at him and covered her face but not too embarrassed.

"I'm serious," he said. "I agree with you one-hundred percent. I think all you lady pilots should have the chance to fly my pants off."

Kate stood. "It's obvious you've never met Pancho Barnes."

Joe followed. Reaching into his pocket he took out a dollar and dropped it on the table. Irma noted the silver ring. "Keep the change," Joe called following Kate through the door. Irma calculated the tip—big tip—and blew him a kiss.

"Come back again, sweetie," she hollered.

\*\*\*

Joe caught up to Kate on the sidewalk. The afternoon was warm, and a slight breeze rustled the elm trees around the square. Joe reached for her arm and turned her toward him. She shook her arm, but he kept his grip. "Car's over there," he said, pointing.

"What's the hurry?" she asked.

"You're in a pissy mood."

She turned on him. "You want smiles?"

"Maybe," he said. "Or, at least, civility."

"Oh, thank-you, Joseph, for the wonderful cup of coffee." She curtsied.

"You're most welcome, m'Lady," he said and bowed. "Now, will you explain what's got you all fired up? And don't lay any banana oil on me about not going to Spain. Until I told you about it, you probably didn't care where Spain was."

"I didn't," she said. "But now I do." She stepped off the curb, and he followed.

They passed Piper's grocery store. The screen door swung open. A delivery boy raced past them, a bag of groceries under each arm. Joe leaned close to Kate, and she slipped her hand through his arm. "I'm sorry," she said. "But I don't like being excluded."

He kissed her lightly on the top of her head and asked: "Does anyone here know who you are?"

"You mean, *who I was*," she corrected.

"Still are," he said. They stopped under a large foot. *M*. PENNEGRESSO, PODIATRIST, the sign read. From a distance it looked as though they were in danger of being squashed. "Kate, why didn't you stay in California?"

She sighed—half sigh, half laugh. "I guess it was time to come home from the circus."

"From what I hear, they loved you out there."

"They love *everyone* out there. Pretty soon love gets old, though, and it's time to find real life again."

"Tired of being loved?"

"Tired of being pandered to. Is that right? Does that sound right? Pandered to? When everyone's pandering to you because you're a celebrity?"

"They liked you," he said. "You were front page: *AVIATRIX SETS NEW RECORD*. I remember seeing you in newsreels, your face in the magazines. I'll bet these people remember." He indicated the store windows on the square. "Should we ask them?"

"No."

"You were hot stuff."

"A million years ago."

"Not so long ago."

"You know something? The same reason you won't let me fly with you in Spain is the same reason I made such a big splash flying in California—"

"Because you're a dame?"

"Because I'm female."

"So?" he asked. "What's wrong with that?"

"Nothing, damn it, but why should that matter?"

"Because—it does. In California it did."

"Exactly."

"Exactly what?" he exclaimed. "If you can't fly in Spain why not take advantage of California? You don't have to hide in Iowa."

"Where do you fly?" she asked.

"Where?"

"Yes, where? Where do you fly?"

"Hell, I don't know, wherever I want, I guess."

"See?"

"See what?" he asked. "If you're trying to convince me that I get all the breaks because I'm a guy and you aren't, well I don't buy it."

"No one asked you to *buy it*."

"No one made me a big star in California for breaking altitude records or whatever it was you girls were breaking."

"Did you ever try?"

"Why should I bother? If I'd have flown the exact same day as you and broke the exact same altitude record under the same conditions, do you think anyone would have paid me a flying fig about it?"

"No," she said.

"Right," he answered.

"And do you know why?"

"Yes. Because I ain't a dame, and it's big news if a dame manages to take off and land without busting a nail, but who cares if some guy's been doing the same thing for the last ten years."

"Exactly," she growled.

"What?"

By now a few passersby turned, wondering what the argument under the giant foot was about. "It's okay," Kate said to them. "He lost his hearing in the war. A bomb went off next to him. I have to shout." They immediately looked the other way.

She spoke before he could: "Why the hell should I get some kind of advantage just because my voice is an octave higher than yours? It isn't fair. It's degrading. Why should there be one standard for women and a higher, a somehow more important standard, for men?" Her voice croaked and she turned away.

Joe looked around the square wondering what to say. He felt insignificant beneath the foot and wanted to touch the woman beside him. She turned before he could. "You know what?" she asked.

"No."

"When I was a kid, I always wanted to go in there." She indicated the podiatrist's office with a nod. "I never had any reason to, and my mother never would explain what went on inside." She looked up at the foot. "Wouldn't you love to have a sign like that, I mean with your own name on it? People could walk past your house, and you could sit in the attic, staring at them from a tiny window, and you'd see their faces screw up wondering why you had this huge foot hanging over your front door."

Joe stepped back to look at the sign, and then, pointing toward the office door, said, "Why don't we go in?"

She stared at the door. "No, because then there'd be nothing left; no wonderment. Is that a word, *wonderment?*"

"Should be."

"Come on. Daryl will be wondering what happened to us."

"In wonderment."

She took his arm.

"You could run away with me, Kate."

"In the Nash?"

"So, it'd be a slow run away."

"Who'd fly the payroll for those poor coal miners?"

"Oh, that's not really payroll," Joe said.

"I didn't think so."

"Daryl was right. You'll really be smuggling coal into Chicago for the mob."

"You are devious."

"Handsome, too."

"And modest."

***

They could hear the radial engine before they reached the airport.

"Sounds like he's got it running for you," Kate said. They rode over a slight rise and followed the highway around the cornfield beside the airport. The new corn was short and leaned in the wind. Overhead, white clouds grew, throwing quick shadows on the ground.

"Doesn't sound like mine," Joe said, and he leaned around the windshield to hear. "That's a bigger engine." He listened. "Damn big."

The Nash took another rise. Southern Iowa, unlike much of the Midwest, is hilly with small farms cut out of the forests and rolling prairie. Despite the growing lack of demand for it, corn had taken over. Kate often noticed the change when flying. Up there it was easy to see the ravages of erosion brought on by farmers forced into tearing out more woods to plant more corn to make up for falling prices. Each spring the rivers ran thick with the vanishing topsoil, and come summer when the land dried, it turned to dust and swirled away leaving the ruts of dead earth. She turned off the road and onto the airport.

"What's he got there?" Joe asked. He stood holding onto the windshield. His hair streamlined in the breeze, and before they reached the shack, his right leg was over the door. He skipped off the running board and ran toward Daryl.

The gut-churning roar came from a radial engine on a wingless fuselage. Chocked at the wheels and tied at the tail, it strained under the power. Daryl failed to notice them drive up. His head was deep inside the cockpit, only the tip of leather helmet showed above the rim. The fuselage trembled. Joe was certain the wheels would jump the chocks and Daryl, inside the bellowing monster, would shoot into the corn to explode in a cloud of flame and debris.

"It's the racer!" Kate hollered.

"Huh?" Joe shouted back.

Kate tugged his shoulder, bringing his ear close to her mouth. She yelled, "He calls it *the racer*. It's his racing ship—his dream."

"The one that's going to make you rich?"

She pursed her lips.

Joe turned, catching her gaze. She held his arm slightly too long, and he kept his face too close to hers.

"Does it fly?" he finally asked. His voice was weak against the motor.

She shook her head, "Can't hear."

"Does it fly?" he shouted.

"Not yet."

Joe nodded and thought, 'Not ever.' He looked back at the airplane. Wingless, it looked more like a long engine stand on wheels. The fuselage was covered in cotton and painted in silver dope in need of sanding. A temporary fuel tank was lashed above the boot cowl with a tube leading to the carburetor. Joe guessed the tower-like structure behind the tank would eventually—in Daryl's imagination, anyhow—hold flying wires to a lower wing. He'd need to streamline that, he thought.

Daryl's face peered over the rim. He appeared to be listening. His eyes were closed, his face bathed in the slipstream, and he was smelling the wind. He used every sense to understand an engine. *'If God, or President Roosevelt, saw fit to give us noses,'* he'd say to anyone who'd listen, *'Then* we *should use the silly things. Otherwise, there's no reason to have the fool contraptions sticking out of your face.'* So, Daryl Fitzpatrick, mechanic, smelled the wind.

He saw Joe and Kate. A quick wave, and his head went into the cockpit again. *Pop!* The engine backfired, and then ran smoothly. Pop! Pop! It went again in pistol shots, and Joe could see Daryl shaking his head.

"He's been having trouble with one magneto." Kate shouted. "He's been trying a variety of different timing schemes."

"What does the manufacturer call for?"

Kate felt pride answering, "He *is* the manufacturer. Applied for a patent and everything."

Joe pulled the corners of his mouth down in an appraising look. Unfortunately, it just made him appear to be imitating Mussolini.

The engine backfired again and died. The long propeller swung several times, the motor clacking with each revolution before it stopped. When they reached Daryl, he was staring at the instrument panel, his brow furrowed, his right hand toyed with the joystick and his left still clasped the throttle. Lost in thought, he ignored them.

"Sounds like a real brute," Joe called. He clapped the fuselage behind the cockpit.

Daryl turned slightly. "That was only half-throttle."

"When do I get to fly it?"

Daryl ignored the question and looked back at the instrument panel. He scratched his cheek and looked toward the western sky where clouds thickened.

"What's the matter, Daryl?" Kate asked. "Still having that problem with the mag?" She tended to ignore the mechanical aspects of flight, preferring, instead, to leave that to Daryl. She would fly; he would wrench. Daryl unclasped his hand from the throttle.

"You know," he said, and then thought for a moment. Kate and Joe stood quietly, waiting for him to continue. "Hmm."

"What?" Kate asked.

"What, hmm?" Joe asked. They watched him stand inside the cockpit, rub his chin, then throw a leg over the rim.

"Hmm, I was just trying to remember—"

Kate stood back, letting him drop to the ground. "What?" she asked. Joe stood beside her, slightly shorter than Daryl but a head taller than Kate. His eyes stared at

Daryl who suddenly looked at them as though they had just appeared. "Oh sorry," he said. "I was just trying to remember if I'd closed that upstairs window at home."

"Oh," Kate blurted.

"Well, I can't remember."

"What window?" Joe asked, confused.

"I opened a window last night, at home, and when I came to the airport, I knew it was going to rain, and, now, well, I just can't seem to remember. Funny."

Kate clasped her face in her hand and slowly shook her head.

"Funny," Daryl repeated. "Did you bring me that loose meat sandwich, lots of onions?"

Kate sighed. "Oh, I forgot, Daryl."

He shrugged.

"I'm sorry, we got to talking..." and her voice weakened.

"Hmm. Pity. I am hungry—oh well." He pulled off his helmet and walked toward the hangar in martyred silence.

\*\*\*

The first thunder rumble barely dissipated when Daryl slipped the reworked cylinder over the piston.

"Squeeze those rings in, Brian," he said gently. Brian ran his fingers along the ring compressor, adjusting it where it had come off. "That's it."

"Can I help?" Joe asked.

"Nope."

"You going get it done before dark?"

"Dunno."

The sky drummed again. "Before it rains?"

Daryl and Brian stood on overturned crates. Tools lie scattered at their feet, on the boot cowl and wedged around the engine itself. A greasy rag hung from Daryl's back pocket, and Brian, hoping for the same effect, kept one in his pocket.

"Squirt some oil on there," Daryl mumbled. He sounded like a surgeon instructing a nurse.

Brian dribbled a few drops from the oilcan onto the piston while Daryl wiggled the cylinder back and forth. "Squeeze the rings," he said calmly and pressed the jug home in a satisfying hollow *thunk*. A side wink at Brian showed his pleasure. "'*Skilled hands with skilled tools.* That's what my da always said. "'*Skilled hands—*"

"I thought he said, '*Proper tool for a proper job*'?"

"Ah, he did," Daryl admitted. "He said that, too. In fact, he said many things. He was a talkative old sort. Doesn't your old man say things like that?" Instantly he flushed.

"No." Brian said.

"Sorry," Daryl muttered and pressed the cylinder base over the studs. "Let me have the nuts." His voice was soft.

Brian reached inside a tobacco can and fished out one of the nuts. He dropped it in Daryl's hand.

"It's okay," Brian said.

"Sorry. I forgot."

Brian shrugged. His first visit to the airport had been the previous autumn, the day his father had been buried. Kate was away on a trip, and the hangar was shut, which made the runway look more like a pasture. It had been on a Saturday, and Daryl grew curious about the tall kid dressed in Sunday clothes pushing a bicycle across the runway. He saw him sit along the drainage ditch and not move for over an hour. A kid hanging around airports was a natural sight, to be encouraged. Often one would wait all morning hoping to see someone fly—just one landing, one take-off. Airplanes were common enough.

Des Moines had the commercial flights; Ottumwa had a few parked around plus the ones that belonged to the meat packers, and this strip outside Chariton had a hangar and at least one airplane in mostly airworthy condition. The problem was money. Few had the money to buy the fuel that made them fly. Ten years earlier it seemed as though airplanes were everywhere. Every little village had a strip, but, now, the money was gone and few flew.

Out of some feeling of duty to kids around airports, Daryl had called an invitation. "No one's flying today. You're welcome to look around the hangar." To his surprise the kid just pushed his bicycle across the runway and disappeared down the road. A week later as Daryl was draining fuel from a carburetor bowl he looked up to see the tall kid with the bicycle, again. This time he wore work jeans and a faded jacket. "Could I look at the airplane?" he asked.

Now, Daryl applied the torque wrench to the base nut and asked, "What's it call for?" He already knew the answer but wanted to see Brian look it up.

Joe lit a cigarette and paced around the airplane. He flicked a dead bug from the wing's leading edge and looked toward the west. "I wonder if they have thunderstorms in Spain," he said.

"You mean, you haven't heard?" Daryl asked with mock surprise.

"Heard what?"

Daryl leaned around the engine and pointing the wrench at Joe said, "The rain in Spain stays mainly in your aeroplane."

"Go to hell."

Brian looked up from the manual and snickered.

"It's true," Daryl called. "The rain in Spain—stays mainly—"

"Oh, go blow." Joe threw his cigarette on the ground.

"He didn't know that," Daryl said, leaning over Brian. "Look, it even says so in the book. See?" He pointed to the numbers Brian was trying to find. "The rain in Spain—unlike the ants in France—settles mainly on the brain."

"Just fix the motor."

"Everyone's a critic."

\*\*\*

Rain streaked down the window, and, when the thunder struck the office shook. Water dripped into a pan on the desk with a metronome beat.

"You could stay with me in New York," Joe said. He sat in the wing chair, the cat on his lap, his legs crossed at the ankles. "Before you say no—"

"No," Kate said.

"Before you say no, again, just give it a thought. You'd still get to fly. We could rent a room out on the Island. Maybe you could fly out of Roosevelt Field."

"Is that still there?"

"I think so," Joe said. "It was last time I was out there."

"You're going to be in Spain. What would I want to do in New York?"

"I'll pick up the tab."

"Oh, make me a kept woman, huh? Mother would like that."

"You worry too much about your mother's opinion. You'd still be in California, if it wasn't for your mother."

"Not true," Kate said without conviction. "I was done with California. It was time to come home."

"To *Ioway*?"

"To Iowa. We've had this conversation, and I'm no longer interested."

Joe pulled his feet toward him and reached for Kate's hand. She stood beside the window staring into the rain. A flash lit her face, and she let her hand slip into his. The cat jumped from Joe's lap. "It's not Daryl that keeps you here, is it?"

She moved her head in a gesture that lacked conviction, and then: "I can't leave him—or this." She looked around the room. "Who'd do the dusting?"

Joe stood beside her and with his free hand ran a finger along a tabletop. "Who does it now?"

"The cat."

He kissed the top of her head, and she hesitated before moving away. The office was slipping into the weak darkness that preceded night. Lightning froze motion, and Joe caught her glancing at him before she switched on a light.

The door opened.

"I'm done," Daryl announced walking through the door. Rain followed him in, and he slapped his hat against his leg before tossing it on the desk. It landed in the pan of water. "Bull's-eye."

"Yes, but can you do it five times out of six?" Joe asked through a forced laugh.

Kate took a soiled towel from atop a cabinet. "Here, you fool. Let me dry your head." Daryl leaned over, and Kate rubbed his hair and down his neck.

"Don't forget to make a wish," he said. "My ears. Do my ears."

She pulled his face toward her and kissed him hard on the lips. "All better?"

He looked toward Joe. "See what you get if you're willing to stand around in a thunderstorm fixing motors? Pilots fall all over you."

"Nice work, but I'm not going to kiss you." Joe nervously looked at his watch and then out the window. "Is this squall line about through?"

Daryl ran his fingers through his hair and said, "Should be. Not spending the night? There's room in the hangar."

"No," Joe answered. "Think you can get that kid to fuel me up?"

"Kid's already gone home."

"Plus, there's no gas," Kate said. "Are you out?"

"No, just wanted to top off, you know. Might as well toss some business your way." His laugh was flat.

Daryl pulled an invoice from his back pocket. "Don't mind the water stains," he said handing it to Joe. "We take cash, trinkets or unskilled virgins in trade."

"Don't know any virgins," Joe said and reached for his wallet. Kate spotted the green leaf bulge as he opened it. She wondered if that was for her benefit, a sort of inducement. He set a twenty-dollar bill on the desk with the bill.

"We may not have change. Kate, have you got change of one of those things?"

"I'll catch it next time I'm in," Joe said while pulling his jacket over his arms. He picked his helmet from the table and looked through the window again. "I think this storm has pretty much gone through." A deep rumble answered from outside. "Give me a spin?"

Daryl took his hat and was first through the door. Joe looked back at Kate. "I'll call you later in the week about that job," he said. She nodded. "Good-bye, Kate." He was through the door.

***

The rain had almost stopped. The thunder was east of them. In the failing light she watched the two men shake hands before Joe climbed into the cockpit, and Daryl took hold of the propeller. On a signal from Joe, Daryl swung the blade through. It took three tries, but the engine fired, and after a brief warm-up Joe was gone, his two wings a silhouette against the orange bursts of the retreating storm.

\*\*\*

# Chapter 3

Daryl rode in the front cockpit; Kate flew from the rear. The biplane lifted from the runway with a bounce as it hit a gopher mound that launched it into an easy climb toward the north. Daryl gazed back at the runway. The grass was light green with the even texture of a long pool table. Where the mower had broken down the grass turned to a more ragged swath, the wind pressing it in waves that continued into the neighboring corn. The biplane leveled, and Daryl looked back at Kate.

"You got it!" she mouthed into the wind and pointed toward him. He waved and pressed both feet on the rudder pedals and took the stick in one hand, the throttle in the other.

Immediately the right wings dipped. He felt pressure on the stick from her correction. He glanced over his shoulder, Kate was shaking her head and mouthing, *straight and level!* He turned back, and the opposite wings dipped. Again, she corrected for him.

"Okay, okay," he called into the wind. "I can fly this silly thing." He stared at the cylinder heads peeking over the nose. The propeller was a blurred arc. He tried a turn. "Rudder, c'mon more rudder, dammit, boyo," he swore to himself. "Damn idiot, why can't you get that rudder in there?" The uncoordinated turns blew warm air against his face so his eyes watered. He pulled his goggles down and instantly went cross-eyed from the lenses. He hated wearing them and pushed them back onto his forehead. It wouldn't be the first time he'd arrived with dry eyeballs.

After 20 minutes of badgering the airplane around the sky, Daryl felt the throttle retard from Kate cutting the engine. A few gentle backfires, and the wind hissed through the wires and struts. Daryl turned. Kate shouted: "Do you know where you are?"

"Huh?" He put a hand to his ear.

She waved her hand at the landscape. "Where are we?" Big question mark with her hand. "Which way is Des Moines?"

His blank face told her he was lost. Slowly, he looked around at the countryside. Nothing was more beautiful, though, than Iowa in the springtime. As far as he could see were green and brown fields with small woodlots and lazy creeks and rivers cutting through it all. To the north the farms were laid out in even sections, bordered by gravel or dirt roads as straight as chalk lines. Cattle stood in dots along hillsides and river bottoms. A car raised a cloud of gray dust miles away; even in rainy season it didn't take long for gravel roads to dry out. This year might prove to be as dry as last.

Daryl, though, sure was lost, but Iowa sure was pretty. And that was Daryl's view of life—lost but appreciative of the beauty.

"Well?" she called and held both hands up. Kate was more concerned with results, actually getting somewhere.

He shook his head and let the left wings drop. While searching for clues to their location, he let them drop further, and the nose fell with it. Kate settled back in her seat with arms crossed. She gently shook her head and watched the countryside begin its gradual spiral. First they were headed north, but as Daryl continued to search the horizon, their bank angle and airspeed increased. Soon they passed west, south, and then as they approached east, Kate asked herself, "How long do I let this continue?"

Whether it was the shrill wind through the wires or the fact that the sun had shifted positions, again, or the cattle below grew larger—the engine was still retarded—Daryl panicked.

Barely 300 feet above the ground, he pulled back—sharply.

"Shiii..." Kate hissed. "I got it, I got it!" She fought against his grip and hit the throttle. The engine coughed and roared to life. The sudden torque exacerbated the situation. "I said, I got it!" she shouted, and he let go.

The stall was imminent. The increasing bank and the backpressure on the stick combined with Daryl's propensity to fly cross-controlled—rudder one way, ailerons the other—put them in danger of snap rolling inverted and slamming into the ground. Kate had seen the exact same maneuver performed in California. A low-time pilot, trying to impress those on the ground, tried to skid his way out of a turn on a low pass. When they pulled him from the wreckage, a dead, pulpy bag of human stuff, what remained of his face wore the expression of one totally bewildered: *What happened?*

With Daryl finally off the controls, she leveled the wings and swooped low over what had been an idle herd of cattle. Over her shoulder, she saw them scatter toward the trees, one calf running straight into a wire fence, like a boxer against the ropes.

"Sorry about that," she mumbled.

At full power she climbed back up. Daryl's head was motionless before her. She leveled off and turned toward Des Moines. The warm air would dry the icy sweat running down her back.

As though to underscore Daryl's terrible performance at the controls, Kate made a flawless landing in Des Moines. Against a slight crosswind, she touched one wheel down, rolled a bit and touched the other one. When the tail settled she was almost stopped. It was a short taxi to the ramp, and she was out of the biplane before he could dismount.

"Does this mean I don't solo today, Ma'am?" he asked, still seated in the airplane.

"Solo? The Bureau of Air Commerce might consider revoking your passenger privileges."

"Then you're saying I'm improving?"

"Don't fall on your head getting out."

"You wouldn't catch me?"

"Sorry, only one lifesaving per flight."

He worked his way up the seatback and dropped a leg over the cockpit rim. "You realize what this is doing to my masculine self-esteem, don't you?"

"You have some?"

"As bread-winner, master-of-the-hunt and all that, I feel a little insignificant right about now."

"You haven't won much bread lately, and you despise hunting, but if it'll make you feel any better, I'll let you tip the cab driver."

"Can we afford a cab?"

"No, but if we could, you'd be in command."

"Hardly compensation, but I accept your apology." He jumped down. "Honestly, you think I'll ever learn?"

"Maybe," she said. "You're still the best mechanic I've ever met."

"One step above janitor."

"Oh, no. A janitor makes lots more money."

"Good point. Will you marry me?"

"No."

"Can't hurt to ask," he said. "Oh, look. That man approaching thinks we have money. Won't he be disappointed when he finds out just who we are?"

"It's getting so I can't land anywhere without someone claiming I owe them money."

"Do you?"

"Probably."

"Maybe it's time to move."

"Change our names."

"Good idea. I'll be Herbert Hoover."

"I thought you didn't like Republicans."

"That doesn't mean I wouldn't make a good one, besides Hoover's from Iowa and it's easy to spell, probably why they put it on vacuum cleaners."

A gray-haired lanky man rubbed his hands on stained overalls as he ambled toward them. His mouth held a short cigarette and smiled through the smoke. "Is that who I think it is?"

"Hello, Stanley," Kate managed.

"I do believe that's a different kind of accent for these here parts. Maybe a—could it be?"

"Go to hell, Stanley," Kate drawled.

"It is. It must be. Where else do women talk like that?"

"Crawl back under your rock, Stanley. Just give us the key to your car before you do." She spoke without looking directly at him, as though to do so would somehow encourage him.

"*Just give us the car key.*' Lordy, this is one tough dolly." He turned. "Hello, Daryl." Daryl waved and removed his helmet, setting it inside the cockpit. "So, what brings the Hollywood girl to Des Moines?"

"Could we *please* borrow your car?" Kate asked.

"Of course. Anything for the Hollywood girl."

"Knock it off," she said and tossed her own helmet inside the cockpit. She walked past him toward the office, a wooden structure attached to the hangar. LICENSED FLIGHT INSTRUCTION, the sign read. Smaller lettering read, TRANSPORT PILOT ON DUTY. Parked around were the idle flying machines—an

Alexander Eaglerock, a Waco 9, its radiator removed, the hoses dangling, a Waco 10 that looked as though it might fly, and even a Kari-Keen monoplane, the windshield so grimy no one could have flown it in weeks. At the far end of the field a United Airlines Boeing 247 ran its engines, the only airplane sound on the field from the only airplane operator making money.

"I'm surprised at you, Stanley," she said.

"Why's that?" He followed at her elbow. Daryl followed them both.

"I've been on the ground over three minutes, and so far you haven't told me how much I owe you. I'm disappointed, Stanley. You must be slipping. Is it part of the aging process?" She opened the door to the office. Like any other airport line office, it had a counter with a glass case displaying helmets, maps and books for sale, and a handful of pilots lounged around the room— waiting. She nodded her hello, and Daryl snapped a British palm-out salute.

"Gentlemen, please remain seated," he said. They did. One pilot put the final crease in a paper airplane and let it fly. A brief climb, a half-roll and it dove into the floor. There it stayed with a dozen other wrecks. "Maybe a slightly longer fuselage," he said and tore another page from *G-8 And His Battle Aces*.

"Needs a bigger power plant," another pilot, who'd been ripping out pages from a *Jake Hollow, Air Mail Pilot* comic book, said without opening his eyes. "A guy could, maybe, launch it from the roof."

"Maybe Stanley would let us take the Waco up, launch it from up there. Hey, Stan, we need the Waco to test a theory, highly scientific stuff."

They were ignored.

Daryl stared at a framed autographed portrait on the opposite wall, impossible to miss.

TO MY FRIEND, STANLEY (signed) CHARLES
'LUCKY' LINDBERGH

"Is it true you kidnapped the Lindbergh baby?" Daryl
asked.

Stanley hesitated before a slow grin spread across his
mouth exposing yellow teeth behind the cigarette that was
so short it seemed about to burn his lip.

"You're looking very French, today, Stanley," Daryl
commented.

Stan snuffed the cigarette in a cluttered ashtray made
from an upturned valve cover. "May I have everybody's
attention, please?"

He rapped his knuckles against the counter.

"Stanley," Kate said through gritted teeth.

"Everyone—."

"Stanley, don't do this."

"Gentlemen, (pause) and ladies," he persisted. "Let us
discuss debt. You all know debt, of course. Our New
Deal lives are teetering on a mountain of debt."

"Just give us the god damn car key," she said.

Stanley would hear nothing of it. He despised the
woman pilot and longed to humiliate her. While his
business floundered, and his pilots sat idle, she seemed to
have customers. True, the customers she flew might not
have been the real moneymakers they all sought—a flight
over town in exchange for some welding or a trip to
Moline for a week's groceries or just for gasoline—but
she did fly. More than once she had used his ramp to
pick-up charters that his pilots could have flown. At least
she bought gas from him now and then, even if it was on
credit. He hated to admit that he'd made some money off
her, unlike his own stable of flyers.

A paper airplane looped past and crashed into the wall. Daryl walked toward him and whispered, "Stanley, do us both a favor, knock this crap off." Stanley faced him and saw a quiet violence somewhere behind the pale blue eyes. The Irish chin was set, that sharp nose now a hawk's beak.

Stan hesitated. The pilots slowly leaned forward waiting for the announcement. They should have been flying, but without customers, without gasoline, without money, few flew. Stanley blinked; Daryl winked.

Silence filled the room, interrupted by a warm breeze hissing through the screens. "Ah, piss on it," Stan muttered and turned away. "Just wanted some fun around here—liven this morgue up." He snatched a stack of green receipts from a clipboard on the wall. "Here," he said to Kate.

"What's this?" she asked.

"It's your account," he said, and before she could say anything, he added, "It's been settled. Paid-in-full."

Her mouth opened. Daryl leaned over the counter to see. "I don't get it," she said. "What gives?"

Stanley relished saying, "Your *boyfriend* paid you off."

Kate looked at Daryl.

Daryl shrugged a *not me.*

Snickers cackled through the pilots. Stanley said, "Mr. Joseph Big New Deal, wiped your slate clean, sister."

Kate started to ask, stopped and said only, "Uh-huh." She scooped all the receipts into a pile and folded them over. "He's not my boyfriend," she added quietly, but the snickers came again. It reminded her of a hen house, a place where pampered, clip-winged birds did nothing. "We need the car (pause) please."

Stanley waited a second to answer. "Lock's busted; you don't need a key."

"C'mon, Daryl," she said and left. Daryl nodded to Stanley, walked a few gunfighter steps backward and followed Kate outside. Before they reached the door Stanley called, "Be sure and fill the tank when you bring it back. This ain't Hollywood, you know. Everything ain't free here, just 'cause you got a pretty face." The screen door slammed, but the snickers followed.

"Does he really think I've got a pretty face?" Daryl asked Kate once outside. "I always considered myself rather ordinary. Funny what people think of you, and you don't even—

"Knock it off."

The airport car, a 1927 Hudson, resembled an armored car painted barn red, the same color used to checker the water tower beside the runway. All over town it was known as "the airport car." It was unlikely anyone would steal it.

"Why'd he do it?" Kate asked.

"Stanley's a jackass, you know that."

"Not him." She waved the paid bills. "Joe. Why'd he go and pay this off?"

Daryl shrugged. "Don't look a gift jackass in the mouth."

"Very clever. Did you just make that up?"

Daryl stepped in front of her and planted a foot on the running board as she reached for the door handle on the driver's side. "You, Miss Strauss, are in one prickly mood again, and I have no intention of taking any grief from you the rest of the day." He opened the door. "Now, we're going to visit your mother, and you will behave. Understood?" Kate rolled her eyes and crossed her arms. "Good. I'll drive, as you seem to be a bit overwrought."

He slid around the door and onto the driver's seat. Kate stood for a second as she considered going back to the airplane and flying home—or anywhere else. New York popped into her head. Finally, because life doesn't work that way, she walked around to the passenger's side.

"When's he going to call us?" she asked and opened the door. "It's been over a week."

She climbed onto the seat and closed the door—twice because it didn't hang straight anymore.

"Who, Joe? Oh, I suppose he'll call whenever he's ready but no sooner. This—" He indicated the bills still in Kate's hand, "—is probably just a payment in advance."

"Well, I don't need his help."

"Funny, I thought we did." He started the motor. "To Mother's."

\*\*\*

"Katie's here," her sister called up the front hall stairs while holding the screen door open. "Hello, Daryl."

Daryl followed Kate through the door and stood behind her in the entranceway. "Miss Anna," he said, but she didn't catch that he'd changed to southern gentleman's accent.

Anna quickly studied her sister. "Katie, you look absolutely ridiculous in those clothes."

"Thank you," Kate said. "And you're in full bloom today," indicating her sister's frilly spring dress. "Mary Pickford must be jealous."

But Anna ignored her sister, the way only sisters can, and pressed the velvet attack. "One shouldn't wear riding boots unless actually, well, riding."

"She removes them before bed," Daryl noted.

Anna smiled as though Daryl spoke Dutch. She was five years older than Kate and three inches taller. Her gray hair was pulled into a bun on the back of her head. Daryl imagined a lag bolt screwing it to her skull. She wore oval glasses and smelled of Ivory soap.

Anna had been briefly married to a Des Moines boy, but he'd died in France after the Armistice. His name was Merle and his oval-framed picture hung above the mantle piece with two unlit candles on either side.

"I don't mind being a war widow," Anna informed Daryl while ignoring her sister, and, "Did you know that the first American soldier to be killed in combat in France was from Iowa? And his name, too, was Merle. Merle Hay. But he wasn't an officer like my Merle."

"Her Merle died from influenza," Kate whispered when Anna left the room. Daryl's eye had gone to the portrait of the boy in a soldier's uniform as soon as they stepped into the front room. "He was a supply officer," she added.

"Mmm," he answered.

"I think he really died of clap."

"Mmmm, that could be, too," he said and turned away.

"She's never re-married."

"Mmm."

"Is that all you're going to say today, 'Mmm'?"

"Nope."

"Katharine, dearest." It was her mother entering in tiny quick steps, arms slightly wide to indicate the need to nearly embrace but, please, let's not. She and Kate shared the same build, although, the mother was noticeably plumper. The faces were the same as were the eyes. The mother, however, lacked the angry mask Kate displayed, warning anyone getting too close that she could sting. Maybe her mother had it once but no more, the venom somehow used up.

Her mother's hair was completely gray and cut shorter than Kate's. "You've brought Daryl," she said the way you might say, "You've brought your dog, how (pause for the exact word) nice."

"I can't be trusted all alone at the airport."

"Has she agreed to marry you, yet?"

"No, but I think she's softening," he said and stooped to accept a peck on the cheek.

"Katharine, this is a good man. Perhaps, you shouldn't lose this one."

"What makes you think I will?" But her mother wasn't listening.

They walked through the house. It smelled of toasted bread and camphor that blended with freshly cut grass when they stepped onto the back porch. From there a short flight of stairs led to a rock garden overlooking a wide lawn bordered by tall fence thick with ivy. Shade from two oak trees kept the backyard cool and almost dark. A small dog named Chrissy slept on a lounge chair in the sun. Kate's mother shooed it away. "You give them half a chance, and they'll take over the whole house."

"What? Republicans?" Daryl asked.

"Now, don't start on that," she snapped, her voice full of something approaching fun. "It's going to take some good Republicans to unsnarl this mess your Mr. Roosevelt has gotten us into." She pronounced it, "Rooo-sefeld," like a sour note on a flute.

"I'm changing my name to Hoover, did you know that?"

"He is," Kate said. She looked around the yard.

"Are you?" her mother asked without interest.

"I thought of changing it to 'Franco,' but people might think I'm Italian."

"Wouldn't want that," she said.

"Did you know Franco is Jewish?" He'd leaned forward to ask her in confidence. "It's true. I read it somewhere." He scratched his chin.

"I'll bet he doesn't mention that to his friend Mr. Hitler," Kate said. Her sister appeared at the top of the stairway with a tray of glasses and a pitcher of lemonade. "Do you need any help?" Kate called.

"Well, I think—that is, the first step is always the hardest—maybe—"

Kate tapped Daryl's knee, giving it a little squeeze. "Here's a chance to display some that manhood for us. Give her a hand, will you. She's the helpless type."

Daryl stood.

"I am not, Katie Marie." Anna continued feeling with her toe for the first step. Daryl took them two at a time to meet her.

"Here," he said and took the tray.

"How nice of you," she cooed. "Katie's so lucky, but then she's always been lucky with the men."

Kate asked, "Anna, are you still seeing Mr. Crisfield?"

"No," she answered. "He always smelled of formaldehyde." She wrinkled her nose.

"A mortician?" Daryl asked. He set the tray on a wrought iron table.

"A biology teacher at the high school," Kate said. "Very prominent man. I had him for a teacher, and you're right, Anna, he did smell like formaldehyde. What is he now, sixty, sixty-five?"

"He has a steady income," the mother said. Embarrassed, she looked to Daryl. "That can be important."

"So I've heard."

"Has your work been (pause for the correct word in her quiver) steady?"

"Not in the least. Leaves plenty of time for loafing. I'm all in favor of loafing. I think it should be a national goal—more than a pastime. *Idle minds for the devil's workshop,* and what with so many out of work these days—"

"Spoken like a true Democrat," the mother said. "Katie," she changed subjects. "Do you remember when I caught you out here one night with, oh, what was that boy's name?"

"Marty Thorndale," Anna piped in.

"Anna!" Kate exclaimed. "Mother—"

"Oh, Katharine. He practically had your bloomers around your ankles. Was his name Thorndale?" She thought. "Not the same Thorndales in Windsor Heights? Is that the family?" She patted Daryl's arm. "You should have been around then. What a little tramp our Katie was."

Kate slumped in her seat.

"Daryl," the mother said. "Would you like a little something for that lemonade? It is so boring that way." Daryl let a smirk appear while Anna disappeared inside and returned with a bottle of Templeton Rye. "Iowa's finest," she said. "Hard to find now that Prohibition's over, but Katie gets home so infrequently."

Sound of a cork pulled from a bottle.

\*\*\*

Two photo albums spread across the table. The lemonade was gone, and Daryl, Anna and Mother passed the almost finished rye whiskey bottle.

"Here she is in California with Bobby Trout and Eleanor Smith," Kate's mother said. "They set some women's altitude record that day." She flipped a page and took a pull at the bottle. For all she drank it hardly showed.

"There." She thumped a picture. "That's Harold Hughes." She spun the book for Kate, the only sober one, to see. "Harold Hughes, dear."

"*Howard*, Mother. Daryl, you've had enough." She kept a hand over her eyes, protecting against the lowering sun. "We should go."

Her mother made a sound like water spitting out of a teapot. "Phht. Sit still; you're always in such a hurry. Now, Daryl."

"Yes, Ma'am?"

"Did you know that Katie was in the movies?"

"I wasn't in the movies," Kate sighed.

"Well, in Hollywood, same thing, and she was friends with Mr. Hughes. Oh, and who was that woman?"

"What woman?"

"That actress with Hughes."

Kate frowned, thinking, and then: "Oh, Jean Harlow. She was in one of his movies."

Daryl's face wrinkled in surprise. "You knew Jean Harlow? That's hard to say, *Yooo knuuu Joon Hooloo…*"

"Here they are at the premier." She pointed to another photograph showing a younger Kate in a long gown with bare shoulders. She was posed beneath a biplane suspended in the lobby at Grauman's Chinese Theater. Daryl thought her beautiful, although, she did look uncomfortably out of place.

Daryl looked at Kate. "You didn't tell me you were in *Hell's Angels*."

"I don't tell you everything." Kate stood to leave. "Thank-you for a wonderful afternoon, Mother. Can't think when I enjoyed myself less."

"What part did you have?" Daryl asked.

"I was a Gotha bomber. Not many lines but plenty of exposure. Now, let's go." She kissed her mother's cheek and said "good-bye" to her sister. Pulling Daryl's hand, she led him up the stairs and through the house. "I didn't need you getting drunk," she said so the others could not hear.

"Who's drunk?" he asked. "Where's my hat?"

"You didn't bring one. Get in the car, I'll drive."

"Have to pee."

Kate pointed down the hallway, "On the right and watch your aim."

He staggered off.

Six minutes later, Daryl walked unsteadily down the front stairs. Before he climbed inside the Hudson he turned and with a wave to Mrs. Strauss called, "Thank-you for a most enjoyable afternoon, dear lady." He tried to bow and smacked his head against the car door. "Oh, Jesus," he muttered and slumped inside.

"Goodbye, Mother," Kate said, and her mother stopped her.

"He's nice."

"Lots of people are nice, Howard Hughes was nice—odd but nice. That doesn't mean you marry them."

"I hear you're going to work for some coal company in Ottumwa."

"Daryl tell you that?"

"You never would," she said. "What do they want with a woman-pilot?"

"I'm not a *woman*-pilot; I'm a pilot—period. And they want a pilot, someone who flies—to deliver bookkeeping material." Her voice trailed away on the last realizing how ridiculous it sounded. "Goodbye, Mother."

"Goodbye, Katharine, and be careful." It was a mother's admonishment and made Kate uneasy. "Promise me?"

Kate smelled the liquor on her breath and nodded. "I'm careful, Mom. Bye."

***

It was sunset. Stan and the pilots had left the airport. Daryl followed Kate from the parking lot to the airplane. "You get in first," she said evenly. "I'll prop us."

"I can do it," he answered.

"No. Hold the brakes, set the throttle." She expected no argument; none came. Instead, he walked to the fuselage, undid the baggage door and removed an oilcan wrapped in a rag. "Gotta oil the rockers 'fore the flight." His words slurred in the way a drunk trying not to sound drunk slurs, and Kate said nothing as she climbed into the rear cockpit and watched him too methodically oil each of the nine cylinders. And dribble even more down his arms.

When they landed in Chariton it was nearly dark. The sun shone on another part of the world, she thought while rolling the biplane onto a long final approach. "Sunset in California," she said to herself and pulled the power all the way back. By the scarlet glow of the high clouds, she rolled the biplane onto the sod, the wheels tapping gently against the ruts. The smell of a cooling planet filled the air. She turned around at the end of the runway and taxied back.

"Wake up," she said and nudged his shoulder.

"Huh? We here?" Daryl asked.

"We're here." She jumped from the wing. "I'll tie it down."

68

"No," he said. He stood inside the cockpit and rubbed his face. "I'll get it."

"Fine." She walked away. Daryl stepped off the wing, the dull ache of dying alcohol pressed through blood vessels around his brain. He felt bad and wanted another drink. "But none of that Contemplative Rye." He looped a rope around a strut and pulled it tight. "No, sir. Can't take that strong stuff." He knotted the rope and, hunched over, walked to the other wing. "Or, maybe, it was the damn lemonade."

Watching him from the darkened office, Kate felt an emptiness strangely akin to affection. Against the night his silhouette was bent and old, his movements painful to watch. She shook her head and pulled her arms tighter against herself. She wanted a cigarette and wondered why Joe had not called.

***

Joe glanced at the airspeed. Rule number one for buzzing, he thought: *Watch your airspeed.*

He dropped over the trees and banked to follow the Des Moines River. Ottumwa was to his right. If he looked he'd see the airport, a wide patch of aviation respectability. Nordello Meat Packing had even offered him a job there once. If he'd wanted, he could have donned a double-breasted navy blue blazer, complete with epaulets, brass buttons and gold piping around the sleeve.

"Is that so I don't wipe my nose on it?" he had asked the interviewer, the company's chief pilot, a mousy character who seemed afraid of flying. "That's the way Mr. Nordello wants it, so that's what we wear," had been the answer. It took Joe thirty seconds to decide he had no interest in becoming a chauffeur in a cabin class Stinson Reliant to a bunch of three-piece-suited butchers.

They didn't want him, either.

The river turned. He banked—steep. Rudder came in to keep him from floating over the trees. The river turned again, the other way, and Joe rolled into that turn, almost putting the wing tip into the water.

Rule number two for buzzing: *Make one pass.* Don't give them time to react. Don't let them get your number. Buzz and go. No encores.

The river straightened for about a thousand feet, and Joe was practically skimming his wheels. He didn't have to look. He could feel every inch of that airplane, inside. He knew how far the wings reached. He knew how much room was under the landing gear. If the engine had quit, he knew just how high he could get before speed bled off too far to fly. He was good, and he knew that.

The bridge. A quick look at the water, and, even with the drought, it was running too high to go under. Late summer or early fall was the time for going under bridges. He slid over and dropped down the other side. He doubted if the driver in the truck below even saw him. Probably wondering what that racket was. He was around the next bend and banking for the final run toward the mine.

Rule number three for buzzing: *Never, never look back.* Pick your run, your path. Make certain it's clear before you take it. Don't get so proud of yourself that you end up looking all around to see who's below. That's when things go wrong.

There was a break in the woods along the bank where a farmer had cut too many trees and planted too much corn. A sudden rain the year before had washed the whole bank into the river, a few more acres of Iowa flushed into the Gulf of Mexico. For Joe it was a natural door.

Throttle wide open, wings level. The morning sun low and to his right, he had a clear shot at the mine. The wind screamed through the wires and struts. The air was still, the heat of the day yet to come, so it felt like flying on nothing at all.

He glanced at the airspeed—lots and lots. The Wright J-5 clacked. He crossed the riverbank. He thought someone was below him on a tractor, but this was no time to look back. He pushed the nose over further, and his wheels skimmed the young corn. His fingers flexed on the joystick and throttle, and he moved his eyes in quick glances at the approaching hillside a mile a head.

Thick with trees, he knew that just over the ridge was the open-pit coalmine of Southern Iowa Minerals, Inc. It was dawn. They would be drinking coffee and scanning the skies, listening and wondering from which direction he would strike this morning.

Past the cornfield.

Over the ridge, and he pushed the nose down and banked slightly left. Engine's howl obliterating the morning air. The orange sun at his back, he flashed across the engineer's shack and pulled up in a banking, climbing wingover.

Rule number four for buzzing: *Savor the hell out of a good buzz-job!*

*** 

"You know, you're friggin' nuts, donchya?" Angelo looked and sounded like Eugene Pallette, the squat actor with the gravel-in-a-coffee-can voice who played tough rich guys or softie movie gangsters. Angelo's flat Chicago accent was brutal. "You damn near took the roof off."

"You mean I didn't?" Joe pushed his goggles onto his forehead. "Hello, Angelo, whaddya know?"

"Hello, your ass. Give me the package." He wiggled his stubby fingers.

Joe climbed from the rear cockpit and up the wing to the front, unstrapped a small box from the seat and handed it down. "Still sealed."

"Better be," Angelo said and tossed it inside his Ford V-8 roadster. It bounced off the seat and onto the floor. "You know, you're gonna kill yourself one of these days."

"Your concern touches me, Ang. But, hey, don't worry." He dropped to the ground and held two fingers out. "Cigarette me."

"You're a bum, too, you know that, don't you?" Angelo dug inside his suit jacket and pulled out a pack of *Lucky Strikes*. Shaking it, he slipped one in his own mouth and then offered to Joe.

"Thanks." He accepted a light, exhaled a blue cloud and stretched. "Man, what a gorgeous morning. Hey, why don't you let me take you up, Ang? You'd love it."

"Kiss my ass and make it last. You ain't never gettin' me in one of them things, and that goes double if *you*'re flying the damn thing."

"I think you're weakening, Angelo. You can't fool me. C'mon, hop in, I'll give you a spin over the pits; show you the operation from the air."

"What the hell do I care about the pits?"

"You're safety engineer. Wouldn't you like to see the operation from above? Give you a whole new outlook on your job; see how you can get the coal out better."

"Fuck coal."

"You're missing a golden opportunity."

"I'll miss it, then."

Joe looked up the hill, where the tip of a steam shovel barely showed above the rim of the first pit. For over a year he had been flying into the ragged strip below the pits and had never seen the machine operate. Come to think of it, he rarely saw anyone do much of anything around the old pit. Most of the other mining companies in the area had gone bust even before hard times had set in. No one wanted bituminous Iowa coal anymore, or at least that's what the mining companies in Wyoming had made the world believe. Southern Iowa Minerals, Inc. had come out of nowhere and reopened this bankrupt pit. To the bankers in Ottumwa, it was now a successful mining operation with a healthy payroll. To Joe it was a laundry and he a delivery boy.

"When you goin' to Spain?" Angelo asked.

"Soon," Joe said. "I got a call last night from New York. Guy named Frank Deagan's running the deal; you know him?"

"Nah."

"Deagan says he's backed by a guy named Zwillman—"

Angelo's eyebrows went up. "'Longy' Zwillman?"

"He just said, 'Zwillman;' made like he shouldn't've said that, like it slipped—"

"He should watch that."

"You know him—Zwillman?"

"Heard the name," Angelo said. "He's connected to us somehow. There's a lot a guys connected; it's all gettin' connected anymore, coast to coast like Ma Bell."

"Well, I guess they got the first shipment ready."

"You gonna fly them crates across the ocean?"

"No," Joe said through a laugh. He drew on his cigarette. "They box them up in New York, put 'em on boats and then unload them in France. From there they've got a crew that puts them together, and I come along and fly them into Spain. 'Here's your aeroplane, *Senor*; give me *el dinero, por favor,* and have a swell war.'"

"How come them Spicks don't do it themselves?"

"Too busy fighting each other, hell, I don't know. Has something to do with neutrality and France and who's supplying the airplanes—it's all complicated. Nobody fills me in on the details."

"How you gonna fly in a country you've never been in before? You speak the language?"

"Flying's flying," Joe said. "Doesn't matter where it is. I expect it'll be about like flying here, maybe more like California with mountains and all. So long as they pay me, I don't care."

"Pay good?" Angelo dropped his cigarette to the ground and crushed it with his toe.

"Five-hundred bucks a ride," Joe said. "I take one in, it's five-hundred bucks. I take in another, that's a grand; take in another, and I'm on my way to a bundle. All cash, too, no taxes, no questions. I talked to a guy that just came back, and he told me the Spaniards treated him like he was a hero. Of course, they think he's a goddam Bolshevik to boot."

"Are you a Red?" A menacing trace in Angelo's voice, his tiny black eyes stared hard at Joe who laughed and clapped him on the shoulder.

"Red? Me? Hell, I charge too much to be a Red."

"That's good," Angelo said. "'Cause I don't like Reds." He opened the door to the Ford and put a foot on the running board.

"That car's awfully red," Joe noted.

"I like the *color* red, but I don't like Reds—if you know what I mean."

"Couldn't agree more," Joe said.

Angelo dropped onto the seat, and Joe closed the door for him. For a brief moment he considered asking Angelo if he realized the loose connection between Southern Iowa Minerals, Inc. and the airplanes being smuggled to the Reds in Spain. He thought better of it.

"See you tomorrow, Ang."

"Going back to Chicago now?"

"Yeah, I got a room in town, catch some sleep before the turn-around."

Angelo nodded and started the engine. "Hey, when's that broad start?"

"What do you want to know for?"

"Dames get all funny around me. I just wanna be ready for her. Maybe take a bath."

"You'll scare her off."

Angelo put the car in gear and drove off. Joe watched him top the hill near the pit. He knew he was headed straight for the Ottumwa banks with, what he guessed, was over 10,000 dollars in cash, enough money to buy a couple of houses in town—or one in California or New York if Kate would come along.

\*\*\*

The clock above the coffee urn ticked ten minutes to nine. Most of the breakfast crowd had gone, and the cook sat out front smoking a cigarette and listening to Angelo comment on the morning's news.

"Newton, where's Newton?"

"Up north about thirty, forty mile."

"Says they make washing machines there."

"Yeah, Maytag—big place."

"Says here there's a gonna be a strike, maybe."

"Everybody's on strike these days. Whole country's overrun with Communists, if you ask me. 'Sides, there ain't gonna be no strike."

"No?"

"No, sir. Maytag owns that town, and everyone loves it that way."

"Maybe, they close the factory if there's a strike, just move out. Fug 'em all."

"Maytag? No, they'll never leave."

"They oughta' shoot 'em," Angelo said.

"Who, Maytag?"

"Nah, them strikers." And turned the page. "Cubs dropped another one."

"Maybe they ought to shoot them, too." The cook snuffed his cigarette in the ashtray. "Almost time for you to go."

Angelo looked at the clock. "Mmm," he mumbled and opened to the funnies. "Gotta see what Dick Tracy's doin'." He read silently, his lips moving carefully with each word. "Yeah," he said finally. "Dick Tracy'd shoot 'em all."

"Who? The Cubs?"

"The Reds," Angelo said and stood. He dropped a silver dollar on the table. The cook made his usual effort to refuse it, but Angelo's wave cut him off, and he slid it into his apron pocket.

"Thanks, Ang," he said. He lit another cigarette. Angelo carefully set his hat on his head, drawing his fingers along the brim. "See you for dinner. Beef 'n noodles."

Angelo nodded and picked his package from the seat. Walking past the cash register, he dropped another silver dollar in front of Ethyl, the waitress.

"Thanks, Ang," she said. Her smile was bright, her face open and friendly. She liked Angelo, but then, everyone in Ottumwa seemed to like him. Quiet, large but unassuming, he paid his bills, drove a smart car and tipped big. "See you later." Angelo nodded in reply and left.

He cut across the square with the package under his arm, his step unhurried. The morning air felt warm and was rich with the new growth on the trees around the courthouse. Had he looked up, he could have seen a face peer through the parted blinds in Sheriff Rosenow's office, but he had no reason to look up. He knew the sheriff had better things to do, like think about his new Pontiac Deluxe Six, a nice car on a sheriff's salary, especially when you don't have to make payments by not noticing who's in town.

"Good morning, sir," the bank officer said while holding the door open for Angelo. He locked it after Angelo entered. Their footsteps echoed off the marble floor past the shut teller windows toward the windowless back room. When the door clicked behind them with the sound of a Springfield '03 rifle bolt, Angelo set the box on the polished oak table and took a penknife from his pocket. He slit the tape. The blade cut like a new scalpel.

The clerk, already seated with an adding machine and deposit slips, watched Angelo scoop two handsful of loose bills from the box and shut the top. The rest would be for another bank. He said nothing and sorted the bills into piles—10s, 20s, and 100s. In his mind he repeated, *"Handsful...handsful..."* thinking how he might scoop one for himself. A quick glance at the customer reaffirmed that he'd have no hands if caught, so he sorted, counted and mused: *"Handsful..."*

Angelo sat and lit a cigarette. He dropped the smoldering match into an amber glass ashtray. A slight breeze puffed through the crack beneath the door, indicating a change in air pressure outside, explained when Angelo heard the front doors open for business a second after a regulator clock chimed ten. Muffled voices and an occasional cough were about the only noises. A telephone rang—two rings, "Good morning, *Ottumwa Trust...*" Money flowed on bells and soft, polite words.

Someone dropped a heavy book—*Fwamp!* Angelo flinched at what sounded like a distant trench mortar round, and he hoped no one had seen.

The clerk finished counting and handed a slip to the bank officer who passed it to Angelo. Angelo nodded and pushed it back. The money was gathered into a single pile, and the clerk carried it outside to the vault. The bank officer scribbled his name across the receipt and handed it to Angelo. The wash cycle was complete. *Who needs Maytag?* Angelo thought.

\*\*\*

# Chapter 4

## Ottumwa, Iowa

Angelo left the third bank with an empty cardboard box under his arm. "Hey, kid," he called to a lanky boy who was trying to fish a dime through a storm grate.

"Me?"

"Yeah, throw this away for me, will ya?" Angelo said, and then became curious. "Whachya doin', fishin' pennies?"

"Got a whole dime on the line."

"Usin' bubblegum?"

The kid nodded and pointed through the grate where at the end of his string a thick wad of gum bobbed over a dime. "It's stuck on the side."

"Here lemme try," Angelo said and knelt beside him. "Did you get the gum good and wet? It don't work good 'les you got the gum good and wet."

He took the string in his thick fingers and hauled the gum wad up. "Looks good," he said and lowered it again toward the dime. "I ain't done this in a while. I find it's best on a leaner like this one, leanin' itself up against the wall, to come up at it from below, tap it a bit, you know, sorta test it to see if it's gonna fall. Like tappin' a drunk before ya roll him to see if he's really out."

"Jeez, Mister, don't let it fall in. That's a whole dime."

"Don't sweat it, kid," Angelo said and tugged at the string, the gum wad gently tapping the dime. "It's wedged in there pretty good, probably been there a while." He exhaled and looked around. Several pedestrians stared at the pair, but he ignored them. "Did you try a stick?"

"Can't get one long enough, besides, I think that'll knock it in."

Angelo nodded again and pushed his hat back on his head. It was a classic dilemma—fortune within grasp, but try too hard and it'll drop down the sewer on you. "I'm goin' for the hard drop."

"I tried that—kept hitting the side."

"You ain't aimin' right, kid," Angelo said, his voice a little boastful. He drew the string up the hole. "You gotta pick the right height—there's a science to this, I learned all about it in Chicago."

"You're from Chicago?"

"I just told you that, kid, pay attention," he said. And then: "What's your name?" He dangled the gum wad, sighting on the dime.

"Rob, Robert Taylor."

"Well, Bobbie—"

"Rob."

"Whatever. You gotta take real careful aim, get all the swing outa the gum 'til the string is real steady, maybe rest your finger against the grate, sorta like aimin' a gun."

"You got a gun?"

"Yeah, sometimes."

"You shoot?"

"I did. (pause) Long time ago."

"In the Army?"

"Yeah," Angelo replied vaguely.

"No kidding?" Rob asked. "Are you getting the bonus? The Veterans Bonus?"

"Sure...Hey, what is this a goddamn interrogation, given me the third-degree? We fishin' here or what?"

"Sorry."

"Now, pay attention." Rob moved closer and stared into the storm sewer. A woman stopped long enough to warn, "You'll catch your death of cold doing that."

Angelo flipped her the bird without looking up and she hurried off in a goose waddle.

"Now watch how my hand gets real steady. See the string? It's against the grate—that's steady, and the grate acts like a pulley. Now I slide the gum slowly over the target, 'bout ten inches, then we wait for it to stop swaying—"

"You got it high enough?"

"I got it just at the right height—trust me. I was doin' this before your mother was born." They watched the gum swing. "What you gonna do with ten cents, anyhow?"

Rob looked up, his eyes bright. "Buy a model—an airplane."

"What kind?"

"Spad."

"You ever seen a real airplane fly?"

"I ride my bike out to the airport all the time. Sometimes I get to see one land. The other day I seen three of 'em take off."

"Anyone who flies is a nut," Angelo declared. "Here, now, watch the gum. See, it's almost stopped and right over target. Now, I hold my breath, take one more sighting—"

"You almost got it—"

Angelo's voice was steady, "Yeah, right on the money, then—and here's the tricky part. You can't just jerk your hand away, 'cause that string's probably stuck to your skin right about now, and if you just yank it'll tug the string and screw-up the whole shot." He winked. "This is where we separate the pros from the wieners."

"Wieners?"

"Watch. I slide my finger off the string, while pressing my other finger from my other hand onto it, but just for a half-second. Then—" He pulled his hand away.

Rob leaned closer. The gum dropped, and the string trailed through the grate.

"Hey!" the kid shouted. "You let go of the end."

He grabbed but too late. The gum smacked the dime and stuck. The string coiled around it, dangling out of reach into the sewer pipe. "Ah, beans, mister, ya lost it." Long face staring into the sewer at a Spad down the drain.

"Ah, Christ, I'm sorry, kid," Angelo said and stood. He looked around and brushed gravel from his knees. Rob stared at the dime still in the sewer and Angelo said, "Life's a kick in the ass sometimes, ain't it?" He turned to walk away. Then: "Hey, don't forget to toss that box out for me." Rob started to look up when he heard something hit the box. It bounced, and he had to scramble to catch the silver dollar before it bounced out and joined the dime. "Keep your nose outa the sewer, kid. You'll catch a cold doin' that."

Angelo walked on.

A flight of carpeted stairs led to a hallway and three rooms at the top, two on each side one at the end. The carpet was burgundy with gold trim, clean but worn in the center and held down by dull carpet rails. The stairs creaked. The hallway smelled of ammonia and boiled cabbage. Angelo turned the skeleton key, pushed the door at the end of the hall open and entered. The room was stark. A Montgomery Wards catalogue bed against the far wall, a chair, a nightstand and a small dresser were the only other pieces. All from Wards and all in close proximity.

He removed his coat and carefully hung it on the chair back, set his hat on the dresser and undid his tie. Sitting on the edge of the bed, he strained to untie his shoes. Once the shoetrees were inserted, he placed the shoes into the closet and closed the door, twice because the latch didn't catch on the first try. Opening a small drawer in the dresser, he dropped in two gold cufflinks and his gold tie clasp with the diamond point beside a lump wrapped in a blue rag. He slipped his suspenders off his shoulders and draped his trousers over the back of the chair atop the jacket. A button popped off his shirt and he had to search under the bed until he found it. Removing the shirt, he placed it over the trousers and sat on the bed again. He was about to lie back when he noticed the curtains.

Angelo was a heavy man, and standing required effort. He moaned and pulled the curtains shut. Returning to the bed, he caught a glimpse of himself in the dresser mirror. He made no effort to suck in his gut. His body was beer-barrel round, his arms thick and powerful. Black hair, almost like fur, poked from under his undershirt strap, shaved where his bull neck started. A breeze pushed the curtains letting in enough light for him to see the tattoo on his shoulder: *1918*, and a snake curling through the 8.

Angelo sat on the bed, and in the weak light filtering around the curtains he read a chapter of cheap novel about gambling ships off the California coast. He lit a cigarette, stared at the book and then at the ceiling. He snuffed the cigarette in the ashtray and let the book fall from his fingers. He listened to the sounds from the street below and fell asleep. "Something has to change," he said to himself before his eyes closed.

\*\*\*

At first she thought it was thunder, but as it persisted Kate realized someone was pounding on the door.

"All right," she said and pulled the sheet over her bare shoulders. The pounding continued. The room was dark. Far to the east lightning flashed in diffused blurs. The curtains flipped in a cool breeze. She tried to take the sheet with her, but Daryl had it anchored down with his body. He slept without stirring. He always slept that way. She often wondered if he had slept that way in the war.

Abandoning the sheet, she walked naked across the room, feeling for the bedroom door. She stubbed her toe against the dresser. "God—blessed," she hissed and leaned against the wall on one foot and gently feeling the toe. "Why do we even have toes? *Sunuva*...stupid design..."

*BAM, BAM!* The knocking turned vicious.

She opened the bedroom door and slipped through, closing it behind her. The latch clicked and Daryl's left eyelid opened.

"Who is it?" Kate asked without opening the front door.

"You have a phone call," came the landlady's voice. An older woman, she lived alone in the huge house, renting out the upstairs rooms, '*but only to Christian folks.*' Or in lieu that, to anyone with cash in advance.

Kate opened the door a crack. Mrs. Denest stood with her nightgown wrapped tight around her small frame. She wore something over her head. In the weak light of the hallway, it looked to Kate like a dishtowel. "It's five a.m. in the morning," the woman said.

"That's redundant," Kate mumbled.

"Five in the morning is no time to be getting telephone calls from strange men, if you ask me."

"Who is it?"

"I didn't ask."

Kate rolled her head against the door, while rubbing her face with one hand and holding her other arm across her breasts. She looked through the crack and with a forced smile said, "Thank-you, Mrs. Denest, I'll be right down." She tried to close the door, but it was blocked.

"What I don't understand, is why strange men are calling in the middle of the night asking for you." Her face pressed through the crack forcing it wider. Kate tried to keep the door from opening any further, but the old woman was strong. "Why isn't your husband getting these calls? Now, I don't mind taking your calls for you—"

"I appreciate that, Mrs. Denest. Now, if you'll—"

The door pressed further, and the woman's face was in far enough for Kate to see her dark eyes straining to take in the room. Kate pulled the door open. Mrs. Denest lost her balance and fell through, almost colliding with Kate, who stood, arms akimbo, before her naked as a ten-dollar whore.

"Mrs. Denest," Kate snapped. "I must insist." She pointed away from the apartment. The woman stumbled back, mouth agape. Clutching her flannel gown as tight as she could get it, she retreated toward the stairwell. Kate stood unflinching. "Please tell the caller to wait." She then closed the door and listened to Mrs. Denest's padded feet retreat down the stairs.

"Who was it?" Daryl asked. He barely stirred.

"Mrs. Denest. There's a call."

"For me?"

"No," Kate said and took a pair of slacks from the closet and slipped into them.

"No undies?"

"I'm only going to the phone." She pulled Daryl's shirt over her shoulders.

"You never can tell who you'll meet on the way." He rolled over. The thin sheet outlined his body. It was apparent he wanted her to return to bed.

She tapped his knee. "This is a Christian house, Mr. Husband-of-Mine."

"Did we get married, or did I just dream that?"

"Go back to sleep."

"I guess I dreamt it." He started to roll back on his stomach, when he turned. "Sure you won't reconsider?"

"What?"

"If you have to ask, you wouldn't understand," he said and rolled over, burying his face in the pillow.

Kate stared at his back for a moment admiring the deep curve of his spine before it flared at his buttocks. She ran her hand over the sheet covering him. "I'll be right back," she said.

His voice was muffled by the pillow, "Marry me, and we'll make Mrs. Denest a respectable landlady. She'll be able to hold her head up at choir practice."

"Mrs. Denest thinks we're already married." Kate slipped her feet into shoes.

"She only pretends."

"So do we."

Mrs. Denest stood holding the telephone, the mouthpiece pressed against her stomach. "I do not appreciate my guests prancing about my house in a state of undress," she said, handing Kate the phone.

Kate smiled, "You came at a bad time. May I?" She took the phone, smiled again and waited for Mrs. Denest to go into the kitchen. She could hear her banging pans as though to emphasize her position as mistress of the house. "Hello?"

"Katie!"

"Joe?"

"Who else? Say, what the hell was I listening to for ten minutes? Sounded like glue being churned."

"Oh, that was Mrs. Denest's stomach. Do you know what time it is?"

"No, should I?"

"It's early."

"Best time of day if you ask me—the air's still, and all the honest cops are in bed."

"Why should you care about police?"

"Hey, I didn't catch you and Daryl in the middle of something, did I, doing the naughty deed?" He laughed. Kate had to smile and felt her face blush, less from thinking of Daryl, than from the warmth she felt hearing Joe's voice.

"Did you want something or just calling to interfere with the possibility of sexual activity?" She heard a pan slam the stove in the kitchen, followed by a gasp from Mrs. Denest. "I think I just killed the landlady."

"Great, you probably owed her back rent, anyhow," Joe said. "Say, listen, doll—"

"Don't call me that—"

"Get your panties on and meet me at the airport as quick as you can."

"What gives?" she asked. "And what makes you think I'm not wearing panties?"

"Just wishful thinking," Joe said.

"Where are you calling from?"

"Your office," he said.

"At our airport? Here in Chariton?"

"You really should invest in better locks."

"Why didn't you let us know you were coming?"

"I like surprises." And trying to end the call: "Nuf talk, just get out here. I want you to make the run with me to Chicago today."

"Short notice. I mean, I don't hear from you all week, and then…"

"I gotta scram outa town, Kate, and I want you all squared away on this deal. So, meet me out here in, say, half-hour?"

Kate felt a dull annoyance with Joe. "Couldn't you have called me yesterday?"

"Hey, sister, you gotta be ready when the ringmaster blows the whistle. You don't want the circus pulling up stakes without you, and that don't always mean a fancy invitation all signed and formal." The intentional misuse of "don't" emphasized the edge in his laughing voice. "You want the job or not?"

Kate answered quickly, "I want it." Too quickly.

"Then be out at the field in thirty minutes. Get that lazy, no-good Irish dreamboat of yours out of the sack and get him out there, too. We got some flying to do."

"I'll—I'll be there, Joe," she said. She heard Mrs. Denest breathing close to the other side of the kitchen door.

"Great, doll face, now wear something cute for me," he said and hung up.

Kate lowered the phone and set it back on the table. "That son-of-a-bitch," she murmured but felt a strong thrill, knowing she would see him. "I'm all done, Mrs. Denest," she called and rapped her knuckles against the door. "You can stop listening." There was another gasp from behind the door, and Kate went back to their apartment.

Daryl walked toward the bathroom at the end of the hallway, trousers on, fly open, no shirt and his hair disheveled. "Joe?"

Kate ignored him, and then, "Yes. I have to fly with him in a half-hour."

Daryl nodded his head. "I thought so. I'll get ready. I need a shave. Do you want to use the bathroom first?"

Kate looked up at him. She was still off balance from talking to Joe and now looking at Daryl—as steady and warm as anyone could want—she grew angry, then depressed. "No," she said. "I'll—" And she entered the bedroom. She was finding it harder to finish sentences with him. The words just didn't—

\*\*\*

Dawn colored the world purple and gold. Daryl turned the Nash off the gravel and onto the dirt road that ran beside the runway. They splashed through a puddle. Kate brushed her hair off her face and tried to act casual when she saw Joe leaning on his biplane, the sunlight bright on his face, a cigarette dangling from his lower lip. He waved, dropped the cigarette to the grass and crushed it with his toe. Daryl parked the Nash beside the shack and set the brake. He noticed how quickly Kate was out of the car, and the feeling that left behind twisted in his guts.

"Well good morning, sleepyheads," Joe called. He caught Kate in a bear hug, lifting her off her feet. She squealed a quick laugh and pushed herself free—a trace of pelvic motion? "Thought I'd forgotten all about my two friends, didn't you?"

"Let's say I've had my doubts," Kate said.

"Not me," Daryl said. "I recognize a man of his word." He approached Joe, paused and threw wide his arms. "No kiss and hug for me?"

"No chance. You'd probably like it, then I'd never be rid of you." Joe laughed.

"See," Daryl said to Kate. "I told you he was trying to get rid of me. I know these pilot types." He clutched his chest as though reciting Shakespeare: *"Deceivers ever, they fly in, let you fix their airplanes, molest the maidens…"*

"Maidens?"

"…And *be they blithe and bonny*, take off again without so much as a *hey nonny, nonny*."

"Nice work, if you can get it," Joe said. "Whaddya say? We're burning daylight. Your ship all gassed up, Katie? I topped mine waiting for you—I owe you for ten gallons; what's that, three bucks?"

"Two-fifty," Daryl said, but Joe wasn't listening. When Joe asked a question, he already had the answer he wanted, and facts never interfered.

*"What time is it?"*

*"What time do you want it to be, Joe?"*

Kate looked to Daryl, who nodded and turned for the biplane tied down beside the hangar. "We should be ready in a few minutes," she said. "Have you had breakfast? I can heat some water inside, make some coffee. Frankly, I'm famished."

"No time, sweet cakes—"

"Joe, do me a favor."

"Name it."

"Don't call me, 'sweet cakes' or 'doll face' or 'lamby pie'—"

"How 'bout, 'Tootsie'?"

"Or any other of your two-bit monikers—"

"Monikers? Big word—"

"The name is Kate," she said.

"Katharine, actually," Daryl called without looking. He untied a wing and let the rope drop into the damp grass. "She's named after Catherine of Aragon, or was that Arrogant?" He mumbled the last. "Oh, and she spells it with a K, not a C...or a D, as some people might."

"Please just call me Kate, and we'll get along fine. Can you do that for me, *Joey boy*?"

Joe's smile was fixed and slowly expanded, until she thought his teeth would fall from his trim back mustache. "You are a dear, ah, Kate."

She turned because she didn't want him to see her smile.

Daryl saw. He undid the straps holding the tarpaulin over the cockpit. As he rolled it back, water ran across the fuselage and dripped to the ground.

"You had some rain last night," Joe said.

"Not much," Kate said. "I think we're in for another dry summer." She climbed onto the landing gear to remove the oil cap.

"I topped it last night," Daryl said. "When you get back I want to pull those plugs. They need cleaning. Need replacing, actually, but…" and his voice trailed off.

Kate climbed off the landing gear. Daryl cleaned the windscreen and reaching into his pocket he took out a dry rag and carefully polished the glass. With the same rag, he moved along the fuselage, wiping the dew away and privately admiring the beauty of the machine. Not a pilot himself, yet he always felt that an airplane at dawn was the second most beautiful thing in life. He looked over his shoulder to where his first love entered the shack with Joe and that sight enlarged the hole in his guts.

Once the door closed behind them, Joe took her arm turning her toward him. He glanced toward the window, making certain Daryl couldn't see them. "I'm sorry," he said.

"For what?" she asked, her eyes darting to his face, then quickly away and toward the window.

"The names."

"That?" she asked with a grin. "Hey, sometimes you're just a jerk, that's all. Doesn't mean you have to apologize." She tried to pull away, but his grip kept her.

"Still love me?"

She kissed his mouth, lightly, almost without touching, as though to imply, *That was for your benefit, not mine.* But it wasn't. "Let go of my arm."

He did.

She took her helmet and leather jacket from the hook on the wall and set them on the desk. She opened a window. "Sure you don't want any coffee?"

"Thanks, no," he said and sat on the desk's edge. "I ate before I called. Besides, we've got a long flight to Chicago; I'd have to pee before we'd gone ten miles."

Kate pulled a map from a shelf. "Want to go over the route?" She started to unfold the map on the desk.

"Why?" he asked. "You've been there before, haven't you?"

"It's been a while," she said. "It can't hurt to plan a little."

"That's the problem with you, Katie—" Hands up. "Ah, it is okay to call you, Katie, isn't it?"

She nodded and grinned. "Yes."

"Good. Can't be too careful, anymore." He moved around the desk to stand beside her. He brushed against her arm and pointed at the map. It was an old *area chart*, printed on one side, creased in the middle and marked with numerous pencil lines. "You'd think a fancy airline like this could afford a new map."

"This one's still good," she defended herself. "Besides, these things cost a nickel apiece."

"How do you know they haven't moved Illinois?"

"If they had, the Mississippi River would've run all over the place, and I would have heard about that."

"Been known to happen." His words were slow.

She felt his closeness and her mouth went dry. "So, where are we landing?"

She could smell the oiled leather in his jacket as he leaned over the map.

"We'll stop in Davenport for fuel." He tapped the chart. "And from there..." His finger traced across western Illinois, stopping at: "Here, west of Chicago Heights."

"There's no airport."

"Don't need one. It's more convenient than going to Chicago Municipal."

She looked into his profile. "Who are we trying to avoid? The airport manager, that Durden guy?"

"Avoid?"

"Obviously, Joe, you haven't quite related all the details about this enterprise." She looked through the window to where Daryl was walking toward them. Unthinking, she moved her arm away from Joe's. "What's the scoop?"

Joe straightened and took a cigarette case from his jacket. It opened with a faint click, and he slipped one between his lips before he offered to Kate.

"Thanks," she said and accepted a light. "What am I hauling?" Smoke obscured their faces, and Daryl entered.

"So what is she smuggling for you, Joe? Dope? Diamonds? Democrats? I hear they've got too many in Chicago."

Joe moved around the desk and leaned against the windowsill. "You'd think two kids, flat busted on their flying asses, would know how to take a job without asking a lot of questions."

"Tell the lady what she's flying." Daryl's voice was cool. He stood in the doorway, sunrise outlining him. One hand rested against the doorframe, the other was hooked in his belt. "She's got the right to know."

Kate said nothing.

Joe inhaled on the cigarette and flicked the ash on the floor. "Numbers," he said and exhaled smoke. "Numbers and numbers and numbers." He waved the cigarette as though chalking numbers on a blackboard.

Kate looked to Daryl who frowned.

"Proceeds from the numbers rackets," Joe continued in a matter-of-fact tone. "Time was, Chicago was run by a

man named Al Capone. You remember him? Fat, ugly—
"

"Third baseman for the '19 White Sox?" Daryl asked.

"No, you're thinking of his cousin, Larry, a common mistake. No, Mr. *Alfonso* Capone once ran the whole show up there, until the feds stuck him in the pokey—"

"Ow, that's gotta hurt."

"—where still he sits, shamefaced, no doubt. His empire has since passed to less competent hands, and with the demise of Prohibition—"

Daryl quickly crossed himself. "May it rest in hell."

As Joe continued: "—all the little hoods in the windy city had to look for alternate employment."

"Most went into radio ministries, I understand," Daryl said.

"Only the dangerous ones. The rest moved into gambling, pimping, loan-sharking, meatpacking, flooring, just a host of lucrative enterprises. One game, however, has proven very interesting and profitable."

"Numbers?"

"Numbers."

"Sounds to me like you've been working with Angelo, again," Daryl ventured.

Kate looked confused. "What's numbers? Who's Angelo?"

Daryl pushed away from the door and walked toward them.

"Angelo's a thug," he said and picked the coffee pot from a shelf, shook it and set it on a hot plate. He plugged a cord in the wall. "We were in the Army with him—"

"He's not important," Joe said. "But he has connections."

"In Spain, too, I'd imagine," Daryl said.

"Yes, in Spain; well, in New York, anyhow."

"This Angelo is Spanish?" Kate asked.

"Italian," Daryl said. "That's like Irish, only they eat better."

"So what's *numbers*?"

Daryl sighed. "It's pronounced 'numbahs.' People bet on things with numbers—any kind of numbers, ah, horse track tallies, U.S. Treasury numbers, ah—"

"Newspaper circulations," Joe added. "Just about any kind of number that comes up on a daily or routine basis, a number that's easily verifiable and can't be fixed, like the number of spectators through the gate for Army-Navy game at Soldier Field."

"How do they bet on these?"

"Easy," Daryl said. "They walk down to the grocery store, pharmacy, or gas station, barber shop, just about anywhere.  Then, pick a number and plunk down whatever they want, nickels, dimes—"

"Pennies," Joe said. "The poor dump a load of copper into the game."

"You've played it?" Kate asked Daryl.

He shrugged. "A few times.  Down at the tavern.  You can order up a beer and toss another nickel out for a number.  It's all on the up and up—no fix, no cheats. Someone collects the take, figures the odds and makes the payoff."

"It's a straight game," Joe said. "People win all the time, the secret of smart gambling: let the suckers win."

"A few of them."

"Those running the numbers are real careful about paying off on time.  No one ever gets stiffed, and to these folks, plunking down their pennies, it's a—, a hope, a chance to win just once in their lives."

"Cheap hope."

"And someone keeps track of all those pennies and dimes? Hardly seems worth it."

Joe grinned. "Katie, we're talking about a multi-million-dollar operation in nickels and dimes—bigger than Coca-Cola or MGM."

"Who also make fortunes through nickels and dimes," Daryl noted.

"But with a lot more overhead."

It was apparent Kate still had little idea what she or Joe had to do with the operation. "Where do you come in?"

"I'm overhead. A courier, a sort of special delivery system. All that money's got to go somewhere."

"You pick up all those coins?" she asked. "Must weigh a ton."

"No," he said. "The coins, well, I really don't know what they do with them. Process them through the Chicago banks, I guess; I hear they run a lot through arcades and city parking meter, street cars or church bingo collections. Then they mix it all up and swap it for greenbacks. That's someone else's problem. Where I come in, and now you, Kate, is somehow, all that fresh dough has to make it's way into legitimate banks and preferably outside the Chicago area."

"So I'm going to smuggle dirty money?"

"Like it so far?" Daryl asked.

"It's a job," Joe defended.

"Can't they just," I don't know, drive the money in a car? Seems cheaper."

"It is, but too many miles with too many tolls—county, state and local officials to pay off for clear passage. Flying tops it all. Plus, cops can't trace an airplane once it's off the ground."

"Cops," she worried.

"Look, Joe said. "If you're not interested, I'll leave right now. I've got other pilots I can use. I just thought, what with old friends in need—" He made to leave, but

Kate reached to stop him. He grinned and looked to Daryl. "She knows a good chance."

"And you've got a million of them."

"Ah, c'mon, Daryl, we've made money before—"

"*You've* made money before," Daryl said to Joe. "Somehow, I've always ended up on the short end of the stick." He scooped coffee from a can and sprinkled it into the pot's basket. The hot plate glowed red, the water starting to boil.

Joe dropped his cigarette on the floor and crushed it.

"Don't worry about that," Daryl said, pointing. "The maid'll get it, or did we fire her, Katharine?"

"She left on her own," Kate absently said.

"That's right, the poor girl was pregnant. I warned her about scrubbing floors with her skirts up. Silly wench."

"Joe," Kate said. "No baloney. Just how illegal is this?"

"Just how pregnant was that scullery maid?" Daryl quipped.

"Please, Daryl," she snapped. "Joe, what are we getting into?"

Joe looked her in the face. "A flying job, Kate. A flying job that pays cash and promises to be there tomorrow and tomorrow and the week after that."

"What a wonderful life," Daryl mumbled.

Joe ignored him and continued: "You want to fly? This is it. No uniforms, no punch clocks, no cranky passengers barfing over the cockpit and streaming back on your windshield. This is one hundred percent flying—for cash. Literally. You make the pick-up; you make the drop. You don't see the dough, you don't ask questions, and you get paid. Now, are you in or out?"

Kate swept her helmet from the desk. "Let's go." She brushed past Daryl, giving him a quick look. He was busy with the coffee.

"It's almost done," he said, but the two pilots were out the door. "Thank-you, Daryl," he said to himself. "We'd love to sit and chat, but we pilots have miles to cover and piles of money to launder. See you in bed tonight, unless of course Joe beats you to it." He closed his eyes and wanted a drink.

***

"Switch on?" Daryl called.

"Switch *on*," Kate answered. She buckled her helmet strap and looked around the struts.

"Throttle cracked, brakes on," Daryl called. He held the propeller blade in one hand.

"Cracked and brakes," she answered. Joe's motor ticked over in an uneven beat across the runway. Daryl took the propeller in both hands, shifted his weight slightly and pulled it through in an easy heave. It clanked through once and stopped.

"Leave it hot," he shouted and took the propeller again.

"It's hot," she answered.

He grabbed the blade and heaved again. Again, the propeller clanked through turning the engine but lighting no fires. He tried again, and again, and was about to accuse her of having the switch off, when he threw his weight into pulling it through, and it kicked off with a roar.

"Moody piece of..." he muttered walking clear. He turned, waved and snapped a quick salute. Kate smiled and saluted back. She looked good in there with the goggles pushed above her dark eyes set off by the white leather helmet. A bit of hair slapped free and she tucked it away and fastened the chinstrap. Daryl then turned to Joe and clicking his heels together rendered a more formal salute toward him. He could only see the wide bright smile beneath the goggles and the leather gauntlet wave back from this black knight of his soul.

It was almost seven o'clock when the two biplanes lifted from the runway. The air was still, the sky clear of clouds, except for a few strips of scud, remnants of the previous night's thunderstorms. Daryl inhaled the cool morning air and stretched his arms over his head.

Kate's biplane lifted first and rose over the river and banked away in a climbing turn. Joe was half-a-runway length behind her. Almost as soon as he broke ground, he dipped the wings in a steep turn brushing the corn to head her off. They joined in a loose formation, pointed northeast. Daryl watched. They continued to climb, their wings growing thinner, until they looked like flimsy models. Joe's airplane moved in closer to Kate's the farther they flew from Daryl. Or at least that's what Daryl saw. He watched until they merged into one dot and then into none.

He turned for the hangar and saw Brian pedaling his bicycle along the highway. He waved, and Daryl waved back. There was work to do, and Brian's help would be welcome.

\*\*\*

# Chapter 5

Kate held a steady course, while Joe nudged his left wings toward her. Closer and closer he slid. The air was dead still and the sky empty except for the two biplanes on an immense dance floor all to themselves. She watched his upper wing tip slide gently under her lower, first directly beneath, before rising slightly, almost caressing, and he pulled back and tucked in behind her wing and a little below.

She could see his face, intense, smiling, the two glass eyes of his goggles flashed at her when he moved. She watched his wings suddenly rise, brushing past hers. He corrected and slid back in tight formation. She wanted to peel away, to run for fear of striking him, but she also wanted to trust his skill, his flying. She wanted to trust Joe.

Once they found the formation that worked, they flew. Kate held the map in her lap, half tucked under her thigh to keep it from blowing away. Iowa's landscape slid beneath them, the colors muting from crisp morning to warmer tones. Joe never left her side. Each time she looked over her shoulder his biplane was there, backed off slightly from the original tight slot but there, always there.

Davenport came into view as a distant cluster of smokestacks and square buildings spilling down the Biederbeck hills toward the Mississippi River. The wind carried the waste from one stack eastward into the soft green Illinois plains. She motioned to Joe with a quick wave and pointed down to show she was ready to descend. He nodded, and she expected him to move away, giving her room, but he slid in closer, his face now expressionless. They were joined in flight, and he wasn't going anywhere.

Kate pushed the stick forward and trimmed the biplane for a slow descent. She brought the throttle back and watched the airspeed increase and altitude fall.

When they crossed the dirt runway at Davenport, she felt the warmer air. The wind now blew from the southwest. The surface of the river was, as yet, calm, except where a barge left a lazy V in its wake.

Kate looked toward Joe—he was there. She banked toward the downwind leg, pulling the throttle further back. Turning 90 degrees to intercept the base leg she retarded the power all the way, and, slightly cross-controlled, let the biplane sink toward the ground. Wind curled around the windscreen, lapping her face, catching a strand of hair that had slipped from beneath her helmet. She thought, maybe, she should have it all cut short—like a boy's, like California in her 1920s. She glanced over her shoulder—quickly—Joe's biplane hovered above her, looking as though at any moment he would drop into her lap, and she'd catch him and hold him as they crashed entangled into the earth. She continued the turn onto final and caught a wayward draft. It lifted her wing abruptly, and she waited for the impact.

He was there, but he saw her rise and lifted away and then back. They kept the formation all the way through the approach.

Both leveled off and crossed the runway threshold. Kate's head moved from side to side to see past the airplane's nose and pick her spot on the runway. It was wide, and the wind blew slightly from the left. She held aileron into the wind, and with opposite rudder lined up along the left edge of the strip. As much as she wanted to look she knew not to. Joe was there, she felt his presence, and it was a strange comfort—a thrill. She couldn't think about it as the left wheel touched and she pressed forward on the stick.

The wind was light. She dropped the other main and held the tail off to kill lift. Finally, the tail lowered itself gently to the dirt. The deep rumble of the tail wheel against the ruts dispelled the magic of the approach. She slowed. She tapped the rudders and held a straight course. Off to her right, Joe's biplane rolled past, and she turned inside him, taking position on the far side of the runway, pointed the other way. He turned in an opposite arc. The biplane's tail swung kicking up gravel and dried mud. He tapped the throttle to catch up to her. Once again in formation, with him slightly behind, they taxied toward the hangars, S-turning and glancing at each other.

It was a dance.

She said nothing after shutting down the engine. She usually flew alone with no other airplanes near and no other pilots to challenge her. There had been California, but that was long ago and had all been staged. Thinking back, she admitted how little flying she actually did there. Always there was Bobby Trout, Theresa Byers or Eleanor Smith sharing the controls of whatever airplane they were setting whatever record. That was California. That was unreal.

She undid her belt and stood in the seat. Joe was already talking to the fuel truck driver when he pointed at Kate and flashed his Hollywood grin, also unreal. She slid from the cockpit and dropped to the ground. He approached.

"Don't skid around those base turns. You get slow doing that, and you're going to find yourself flat on your back, real low and real dead. And I don't want you taking me with you, either."

She nodded and felt the something that had, moments before, made her want to slip her arms around him, fade away. "I wasn't sure where you were," she defended.

"Don't worry about me. When you're in the lead, you fly the approach, and I'll do what I have to keep out of your way." She nodded again—chastised. He ruffled her hair like he would have done to a little sister. "You're a pretty good airplane driver, you know that?" Again, she nodded and knew she was blushing. Christ, she hated blushing.

"I got them to sell us some fuel," Joe said. "Are you still hungry?" Kate nodded her head, her voice momentarily lost. "There's a cafe around back of the hangar. Get yourself something quick. I got a tab running with Louie. You tell him to fix you up something, put it on the tab."

"All right," Kate forced herself to say.

"Meetchya back here," he called and started for the hangar at a trot. Kate turned and heard him call, "Have him just make up a couple of sandwiches, something we can take. I don't want to waste much time here." He entered the hangar.

"All right," Kate said without turning. "All, right, all right, all…"

She opened a small gate in the fence. Four cars: a Ford Model T, a Dodge and two Model A's were parked outside the diner. The aroma of onions and grilled meat caught her stomach before she opened the café door.

"What'll it be, sister?" the cook called. He was the only one behind the counter, so it must have been the cook. "Hungry or just wanted to see me?" His laugh was wheezing and unpleasant. He sounded as though he wanted to spit—or drop dead on the floor. She hoped he didn't spit.

"Are you Louie?"

"At your service," he answered with a bow. One of the coffee drinkers at the counter looked up, his old face a blank. A younger man, dressed like a pilot, or at least what he thought a pilot should be dressed like, also looked up. "If you've come for breakfast," Louie said, "I'm your man. Now, should you be looking for a trip in the clouds, see our resident aviator, Maxwell, here." The pilot brought his fingers to his brow in a quick salute.

"Got any money?" he asked.

"None," Kate said.

"Then you'll probably make a swell flyer."

"I just landed," Kate said and pointed toward the ramp and the two airplanes.

"Seen ya come in," Louie said. "Who was flying?"

"I was."

"*You* was the pilot?"

"Only of one machine," Kate said and heard Maxwell grunt. It was an approving response. She glanced at him, nice profile, although somewhat young. He kept his eyes focused on the coffee urn against the wall, maybe, looking at his own reflection. "We're on our way to...we just stopped for gas...that's Joe—"

"Hold the phone, sister," Louie said. "Everyone here knows old Joe."

"And how," Maxwell muttered.

"He's been in and out of here so many times, you'd swear he liked the place." Louie turned his back on Kate and without asking what she wanted he slapped a spoonful of butter on the grill and reached for the eggs above the stove. "Have a seat. The egg sandwiches will be ready in a minute."

Kate sat. The butter hissed and bubbled on the grill, and Louie, holding four eggs in his thick hands, cracked them one at a time against the griddle and dropped them into the hot butter.

The edges turned crisp and brown. He slit the whites with his spatula to spread them out. Without asking, he placed a cup of coffee in front of Kate and slid a metal creamer beside the cup. He flipped the first egg and tapped the yolk to break it.

Kate looked around for a spoon.

"Looking for the sugar?" Maxwell asked.

"No, spoon."

Barely lifting himself from the stool, he reached behind the counter and fished out a spoon. "Here," he said, and Kate had to stretch toward him to take it. "It's probably clean. Louie has a woman come in once a week to do the dishes. Isn't that right, Louie?"

"Yeah, but she don't come in 'til Tuesday." He took a loaf of bread from a box and cut eight thick slices. Like a card dealer, he fanned the pieces onto the griddle then scooped the eggs over. His hands moving with practiced speed, he removed the bread from the stove, placed them on the cutting board and slipped an egg onto each. "Ketchup?" he asked.

Kate had been watching him work and was unprepared for the question. "Ah, I don't know," she stammered.

"You don't know if you like ketchup?"

"I like it, but I don't know if Joe does."

"Joe likes everything, except ketchup," Louie said. Waiting for her answer, he sprinkled pepper on two of the sandwiches, covered them, placed each on a piece of waxed paper and cut them in half. He turned. "Have you decided whether you like ketchup yet or not?" His sweaty face was friendly, the eyes wide and amusing, his chin fat, layered to his neck. He took Kate's cup and refilled it. "Ketchup?"

"Please," she answered and sipped at her coffee. Maxwell caught her looking toward him from the corner of her eye. She made no effort to turn away. "You're a pilot here?" she asked him.

He found this quietly amusing. "That I am; chief pilot *Illinois-Iowa Airways and School of Aeronautics*—"

"*Chief* pilot—impressive."

"Except one thing."

"And that is?"

"No customers."

"Not an uncommon malady these days," she said.

"Is that your ship?" he asked looking through the window. "The one beside Joe's, looks like a taxicab?"

"Yes, I'm out of Chariton."

"First time in here?"

"No, but I've never stayed long—no reason to."

"Got that right," Maxwell said.

"Sorry, I didn't mean to—"

"Don't apologize. No reason in the world why anyone'd want to stay put in Davenport, *Ioway*. Except Louie here, but he's nuts."

"You should be so crazy," Louie said. He set two paper bags in front of Kate, then before closing them, dropped an apple into each. "Tell Joe to eat the fruit I put in and not pitch it overboard as soon as he crosses the river." He rolled the tops closed and took a pencil from behind his ear. Wiping his hands on his apron, he scratched a few numbers, ripped the ticket from the pad and holding it to Kate said, "Four egg sandwiches, two apples, one coffee—refills free—comes to fifty-five cents. No charge for the floor show."

Kate looked at the bill and started to speak. Louie interrupted, "I know, put it on his tab." He dropped the ticket into a cigar box under the counter.

"I can pay," Kate said.

"No, he's good for it—eventually." He reached for Maxwell's coffee cup but was waved away. The coffee drinker beyond Maxwell—another out of work pilot named Elliott—pushed his cup forward, but Louie ignored it. Joe pushed through the door.

"Chef Louie, good morning! Chief Pilot, Maxwell, how are you?" He slipped onto the stool beside Kate before either Louie or Maxwell could answer and looked her in the eyes. "Had your breakfast?" Kate indicated the sandwiches. "Oh, Louie wouldn't let you eat with the riff-raff, huh?"

"Egg sandwiches," Louie said. He leaned close to Joe, his face almost touching. "She takes ketchup on hers." They both turned and stared.

"A very unusual woman, indeed," Joe said and clapped Louie's arm. "Has she introduced herself, yet?"

"No."

"She's terribly shy," Joe said and stood. "Her mother was frightened by a short-order cook."

"You're getting it all wrong," Kate said. "She *married* a short-order cook, then he ran off with a tattooed lady contortionist at the state fair." She extended her hand to Louie. "I'm Kate, and we have to go." She took a bag. "Don't forget yours," she said passing Joe. "And pay the man, will you? He has a business to run."

"Oh, I like her," Louie said and held out his hand palm up. Joe grabbed the other bag and waved him off. Kate was almost to the door but stopped behind Maxwell.

"Good luck," she said, but he barely turned.

"Yeah," he said and returned to his coffee. Kate opened the door and left. Joe followed.

"You've made quite the impression," he said. "Free meal and a new boyfriend. Not bad for a pit stop."

"Go to hell, Joe," she said sweetly and kept ahead of him. "Where's the bathroom?" He pointed. "Don't leave without me," she said walking toward the hangar. "And don't throw that apple away."

\*\*\*

The fuel truck was pulling away when Kate walked back to the airplanes. The wind was stronger now, warm and gusting from the southwest. She glanced at the sky knowing the calm morning air would be gone and the easy part of the flight over. The fuel truck stopped; the driver climbed out and walked toward them. "Put the fuel on your tab, Joe?" His young voice was loaded with respect for the aviator.

"Yeah, Brent," Joe answered and pulled his leather helmet over his head. He left the earflaps up. "You haven't met Katie, yet." He pointed toward Kate who was buttoning her jacket. "Kate, this here's Brent. No one knows his last name, but he's relatively honest. Says he wants to meet you."

Brent walked awkwardly toward Kate and took his cap from his head. Tall, thin, with straight red hair and almost scarlet freckles, this Penrod half bowed and grinned taking Kate's hand. "Pleased to meet you, Ma'am."

"And you," Kate answered. She was about to make some polite comment about weather, when Joe blurted, "Brent's never been laid, and he's got a silver dollar burning a hole in his pocket—"

"Oh...oh," Brent stammered, his freckles glowing to the point of popping off his face. Kate's eyes flashed anger at Joe. Her hand still held Brent's and she turned to him mustering all the charm her mother had ever tried to impart. "Well, Brent, there's a time for everything, and don't you let any insecure lugs pressure you into anything." She retrieved her hand, sweaty from his. "Could you give us a spin, please?"

Brent shifted from foot to foot, his eyes downcast, then he caught Kate's firm stare and nodded. "Sure, Ma'am," he said. "Hop in."

"Hey, it was a joke," Joe pleaded; arms up. "Doesn't anyone have a sense of humor around here?" His grin faded. "What a collection of stuffed shirts."

"Switch is off," Kate called to Brent, who took the propeller. "Pull it through a couple of times, please." She settled into the cockpit and buckled her belt.

"It's getting gas," Brent called. "Make it hot, er, the switch, I mean—"

"It was just a joke," Joe still pleaded.

"Switch is on. Throttle cracked, brakes on." Kate replied. Brent took the propeller in both hands.

"A joke," Joe said getting into his airplane. "Granted, a stupid joke, but, hell, those are the best kind—" His voice was lost to the crackling roar of Kate's engine. She adjusted the throttle, checked oil pressure while tapping the gauge and looked to Brent. "Thank-you," she called and waved. He waved back. Kate looked to Joe, waved and opened the throttle blasting him with her prop-wash as she swung the tail. She really didn't need to swing it that way. But did.

"Brother," he mumbled. "Some people are too damn sensitive." He looked around the airplane's nose for Brent to spin the prop, but the boy had gone. He saw him slip into the fuel truck and drive away leaving Joe to start the engine alone.

"It was just a joke!"

\*\*\*

Kate's biplane climbed in a lazy circle, riding the thermals. She glanced over her shoulder. Below, she saw Joe struggling with the airplane trying to start it then run around to the cockpit before the engine quit. Twice he did this, and apparently tiring, he must have set the throttle open wider, because as Kate saw it from 500 feet above, Joe, one moment, was grabbing the propeller to spin it, and when she looked again, he was chasing the biplane across the grass.

'Now *that,*' she thought, 'is funny.'

\*\*\*

Kate chewed the sandwich and ignored Joe climbing at full throttle to catch her. The air was smooth 2,000 feet above the ground and just atop the haze layer. The Illinois landscape stretched into the hazy distance, a patchwork of farms and woods with the occasional glint from ponds and creeks. The Green River was off to her right, and she looked for the Illinois River.

Sandwich finished, she took a bite from the apple and retarded the throttle to give Joe a chance. When he finally joined her she was nibbling the apple as though on a break. As he pulled alongside, his wing tip almost touching hers, she looked up with pretended silent-movie surprise. *Oh, look who's here!*

Joe's eyes were two flashing shields of glass. His mouth was set in a grimace, his face unmoving and locked to hers. She held the apple out as though offering him a piece and then threw it. It instantly vanished in the slipstream and, without warning, she pushed the biplane's nose over, chopped the throttle and, in a banking dive, pulled away from him.

Joe was caught off guard but only for the second it took him to kick rudder, drop a wing and dive after her.

Down she went while glancing over her shoulder to see how close behind he would keep it. Her first advantage shrank as he gained on her, his propeller a flat disk almost

110

chewing at her tail. His face was visible through the blur, a determined mask much like the movie posters at the Ritz Theater. Kate stomped hard right rudder and, leaning into the stick, she banked hard on the right wing, giving little concern for Joe's position. *'You fly lead,'* he had told her. *'And I'll do whatever I have to keep out of your way.'*

His voice was fresh in her mind. "Well," she shouted at the wind, screaming around the struts and wires, "You just stay-the-hell out of *my* way." Airspeed near red line, and she eased back on the stick, pulling the nose into a climb. The G-force pressed her into the seat.

Before the speed could bleed off, she advanced the throttle wide open, the radial engine shook the airplane and pulled her in an ever-tightening turn. She continued adding right rudder, countering torque and squeezing in the upward spiral.

A glance over the cockpit rim showed Joe fast on her tail but skidding slightly out of the turn. *'Sloppy, Joey, sloppy—'* Kate stomped the other rudder and simultaneously reversed the ailerons. She moved with the engine's torque now, and it pulled her in so tight she thought the airplane would stall and flip onto its back— she thought, but she *knew* there was more room to play.

Up and up they spiraled, Kate leading the chase and Joe pressing. Each time he maneuvered onto her tail, she would shake him, until he was anticipating her moves and was about to close where she wouldn't lose him.

"Heads up," Kate shouted, and chopping the throttle on the verge of a stall, she let the biplane slide.

Joe was hanging on the prop, his airspeed bled almost to nothing, the wings barely flying, and Kate's biplane still above and slightly to his left.

"Jesus." He swallowed the words before they left his mouth. "What the hell is she...?"

He was hard on the rudder and tried to hammerhead away from her sliding airplane when he lost her. What took barely three seconds, seemed to Joe an endless moment. One instant he had her, unable to shake him—easy prey—and suddenly her airplane was dropping backwards out of the sky, ready to slam into his airplane's nose and tear him apart.

In the agonizingly long moment it took to get away, Joe had no control over his fate; Kate—a woman—had taken it away. His airplane was almost stalled, sluggish, compromised. Kate was somewhere falling through him, backwards, obviously unconcerned about smashing into her pursuer.

The dance had turned to a *Tango*—deadly.

Joe forced the nose over, picking up airspeed. Feeling the wings come alive again, he swooped away. Pulling out of the bottom of his dive, he opened the throttle and climbed, his head snapped from side to side, eyes checking above him, searching for Kate.

"Where is she?"

He leveled.

"Where in hell did she go?"

Cool air slipped past an open collar and chilled his sweaty body. He scanned the sky above and, almost as an afterthought, looked over the rim and beneath him.

There, slightly behind and below, her left wing tip nearly touching his right wheel, was Kate. Her face looked up at him, the two glass eyes seemed to mock, but the bright smile beneath told him he'd been had, and that was that.

Joe raised both hands. "You win," he mouthed the words. "This time."

Kate nodded, pulled back, up and abeam until their wings were in line and cockpits even. She stared at the man across the short distance of sky. He stared back. Only minutes before he was an annoying clod, fast becoming a burden. Now, straight and level, after giving her a chance to show her worth in a machine, he was an equal, something she had never considered Joe. He had always been Joe, the better pilot, the moneymaker working the angles—the man. Effusive and charming, he had taken her heart many times. Boorish and rude, he had sent it back just as often. For now they flew as equals, and that needling desire smoldered inside both of them.

Two miles south of Hooppole, Illinois, a girl named, Emily sat under a tree with her dog. Together they'd been watching an unusual aerial joust overhead. There was no one to run tell, and no one would believe her later, so she only watched. When finally the two airplanes quit their duel and flew level, she and the dog set off across a pasture toward the creek.

It was the change in pitch that made her look up again. Before they vanished, the two airplanes dropped their noses in unison, and as though performing for her alone, they executed three perfect loops, one after the other.

"No sense telling anyone about that," Emily said to her dog, and the airplane motors faded.

*** 

The ten-mile drive from Cicero to the airfield west of Chicago Heights went quickly for Lenny. The Buick roadster easily topped 70 on the long stretch of the newly paved Lincoln Highway but he slowed as he approached a curve where an *Old Style Beer* billboard stood. Chances were there was a motorcycle cop waiting.

Lenny took the turn and was disappointed when there was no one there. "Hmm," he sniffed and pressed the accelerator to the floor. The long 'eight' under the hood rumbled. It was Lenny's first car, and he had bought it new, straight off the showroom floor. He loved to reminisce about the salesman's expression when Lenny had walked into the dealership and had to wait for a salesman to even ask him what he wanted.

"I wanna buy a car," Lenny had said. "That *is* what you guys sell here, ain't it?"

The salesman then ran his pinkie along his trim mustache, giving Lenny the once over. Riff-raff in workingman's clothing and wearing cloth caps usually didn't walk into Buick dealerships. "Used cars are out back," the salesman had said and turned, his eyebrows arched.

"I don't want no used car," Lenny called after him. "You got new ones or what?" He thumped the curvy fender of a bright yellow Buick, the chrome as shiny as he suspected silver in a vault would be, had he ever been inside a vault, legally. It wasn't that he'd never tried. In fact, *trying* was the reason he was now only six months out of Joliet penitentiary. He had *tried*—unsuccessfully—to enter a vault at two in the morning.

"That, sir," the salesman said. "Sells for one thousand, eight hundred and thirty-five dollars." He moved to wipe the palm print Lenny had made in the shiny lacquer finish.

"Goes pretty quick, does it?"

"Yes, 'pretty quick.'"

"Them good tires?" He kicked one.

"*Those* are Firestones, the best. Now, if you would care to see the cars out back…"

"How much did you say?" Lenny reached inside his pocket.

"For this?" the salesman asked, openly amused.

"Yeah, eighteen, what?" Lenny was peeling hundred-dollar bills onto the car's hood.

"Ah, eighteen, ah, hundred and, ah, thirty-five dollars."

"Got change of a c-note?" Lenny asked, holding up a hundred-dollar bill. "There's eighteen bills and, if you got change of the last one here, I'll take it." He waved the nineteenth hundred-dollar bill over the stack of eighteen. The salesman advanced slowly, gazing at the money.

"There's a dealer's prep charge," he stammered.

"Dealer's prep? What's that? Sounds like something for hemorrhoids."

The salesman stared incredulously at Lenny, his thoughts obvious—*how did this greasy little shit get all that money*? The wad of bills in his hand seemed to remain constant even after Lenny took almost $2,000 away. He had to be a thief, a gangster, bootlegger—no wait, there were no bootleggers, anymore—but a criminal, no doubt. "Dealer's prep, *sir*, is the fee for getting the automobile ready for sale. Final *prep*aration."

"You mean the damn thing ain't done being built?" Lenny asked and stuck his head inside the window. He tried the horn. It sounded like a ship had pulled through the showroom door. "Looks okay to me, Pop. You get me the change and keep the prep-shit." He grabbed all the bills into one cluster and thrust it in the salesman's hand. "Now, go get the keys or I go buy a Studebaker."

It was a sweet memory.

Lenny now looked at his gold watch and at the sleeve of his new suit coat. Tailor-made, it fit him like a glove. That's what the tailor kept saying, "Fits you like a glove, Mr. Lenny."

Lenny eased off the accelerator while approaching another car. When almost on the bumper, he sounded the horn and passed. He waved as he flew by and sounded the horn again for kicks.

It felt good to drive fast. He loved the time alone on the road, the wind through the windows, the tires whining on the pavement and the looks he received from those wondering who this kid in the shiny roadster could be.

"Jeez, if the guys in the joint could see me," he said and felt that fear massage his spine with the cold fingers. It happened every time he remembered prison. He shifted gears at a GO SLOW sign. Letting a truck through the Y-intersection, he squeezed on the power, shifted and settled into high gear. His pleasure in the drive, the car, the new suit vanished remembering Joliet.

He had entered prison a brash kid, all piss and vinegar as his old man used to say—back when he had an old man. Twenty minutes into the system, head shaved, lip bloodied and shaking like a skinny weed in scarecrow clothes, he learned things he'd never imagined, things one human—or in his case, five humans the size of gorillas—could do to another, especially one skinny-assed 18-year old.

Lenny took a cigar from his coat pocket. He bit the end and spit the tip through the window. Inside a side pocket he found his lighter and, in a practiced move, flipped it open, flame lit. Forget Joliet. This was his new life—flame lit.

He blew smoke at the windshield and turned off the pavement onto a gravel road. A small farm, where nothing seemed to grow anymore, took up one corner, the farmhouse old and leaning; a fat dog slept near the road. Further along was a junkyard with acres of rusted cars, trucks, buses, old signs, lampposts and another dog. This one was shorthaired, dirty gray and chained to a telephone pole it walked in a circle at the end of its lead. For the radius of the chain the ground was smooth and dusty, littered with crap and bones. Lenny slowed the car and turned onto the shoulder.

He set the cigar in the ashtray and, leaving the motor running, walked through the weeds to the wire fence, behind which stood the dog. He stopped a short distance away and waited. At first, the dog just watched from the corner of its eye, then as Lenny crossed some unseen, but definite, line it exploded in snapping rage.

Lenny stopped. He wondered if the chain would hold, if, indeed, the telephone pole would remain standing. The dog, both front paws off the ground, strained to lace into him. From the house inside the junkyard a woman called, "Don' be teasin' that poh an'mal, now." Her voice was tired, almost bored. The slow drawl of a Kentucky accent was foreign to what he heard in Chicago ten miles away. Lenny ignored her and reached inside his pocket.

He took out a large knucklebone wrapped in butcher paper. Removing it, he let the paper float to the weeds then inched toward the dog.

"You leave him be, or I'll call the law." Again, lazy, like she didn't have the strength to swat a fly, let alone call anyone, especially since there weren't any wires leading to the house.

Lenny stopped a few feet from the fence and squatted. The dog, a square thing with long ears and a mangy coat half chewed away, changed its attack. No longer content to strain at the chain, it hopped from side to side as though trying to rid itself of the collar that dug into its neck. Lenny could see the red tissue where the greasy fur had been chaffed away. The dog's eyes were beady orbs of brown and green, reflecting the oily puddles in the junkyard. The dog was the living extension of automotive waste.

"Here," Lenny said and threw the bone. It landed inside the dog's circle of dust and crap. The dog ignored it, still trying to tear at Lenny.

"Ain't you gone?" the voice came again from the house. "Thought I said..."

Lenny stood and carefully backed away. He glanced at the house, but there was only the vague outline of a figure in the window beyond the porch. He saw a cat slip off the railing and disappear under the porch. A car passed on the gravel road. Lenny turned. Once he crossed the unseen line, again, the dog fell silent—switch on, switch off. He opened the car door and before getting in looked at the dog now quietly gnawing the bone.

Lenny depressed the clutch and pulled the lever into gear. He glanced at his watch and continued down the road. He sniffed the fingers of his right hand, still smelling of the fresh bone.

\*\*\*

# Chapter 6

# Chicago Heights

Lenny, his foot on the running board, hat low across his eyes, finished the cigar and flicked the butt into a stand of dried weeds. Smoke rose in a lazy curl and was whisked off by the wind. He waited for the smoldering butt to catch the weeds on fire, but after several minutes the smoke disappeared, and he turned away bored.

"Where the hell are they?" he asked himself because there was no one else on the airfield. He leaned against the Buick's fender and wiped at the bugs smashed to the chrome grill with his handkerchief.

A tractor worked a small plot between the warehouses across the runway, its low speed engine sounded like an approaching airplane, and Lenny had to keep himself from looking up each time it passed. He took another cigar from his jacket, placed it in his mouth then changed his mind and put it back. He took a leak in the weeds where the cigar had died.

The day was warm, and he waited. He hated to wait for anything.

\*\*\*

Kate signaled Joe to move ahead. "You lead; I'll follow." Her call was swallowed by the wind. By tapping the top of her head and then pointing at him the message was delivered—you lead. Joe pressed the throttle forward, and she slipped in trail, slightly to his right and above.

They approached Chicago from the southwest. The day had grown hazy, especially nearing the lake. She could see the vast expanse of suburbs around the city. Lake Michigan was a gray forbidding emptiness in the distance. A mist hung above it, duller than she remembered near the ocean in California.

Chicago.

The premier city in the Midwest, it was an easy rival to New York and a world tougher than Los Angeles. Carl Sandburg, she thought, was right. It looked like the *hog butcher to the world.* Hell, it looked as though, unchecked, it'd butcher anyone for fun. She rarely flew this far to the East. Most of her flying was around Iowa, and, of that, most was in the center of the state—hopping rides at county fairs or airport dedications, flight instruction that barely paid for the gas the students burned and never paid for the wear they inflicted on her airplane. Kate flew professionally but at amateur rates and never to a destination she chose.

She watched Joe begin a long descent. The tall buildings of downtown were far off. The rich suburbs gave way to wood-frame two stories, then one-story clapboards, where English, when spoken, was done so with thick accents, and the people resembled their homes—square and plain, mortgaged and rundown. She squeezed the power back and looked for a field.

Joe continued the descent across a marshy area where a couple of kids threw stones at old cars in the muck. They crossed several railroad tracks. On one a line of cattle cars hauled wide-eyed livestock to the slaughterhouse, too stupid to know they were about to die, too frightened to do anything except stand, nose to tail, waiting for the *hog butcher to the world* to club them over the head, slit their throats and call, "Who wants bacon?"

Kate saw none of this detail, but had she looked it would have been there. She followed Joe.

He banked and dropped to just above the trees and the few houses along the slough that ran behind the houses. Kate saw their shadows flash over a woman hanging out laundry. She never looked up.

They banked again; dropping even lower now into the slough itself, wheels barely above the water. Kate kept her eye on Joe's airplane and on the pilot himself, trying to match his moves without being lost.

They flashed across a road. Two kids fished from the levee. One waved, one thumbed his nose. Both should've been in school. Kate saw neither. A telephone pole appeared ahead on the right. She caught the faint image of the thin wires stretching across their flight path and waited for Joe to pull up. He continued.

Kate flexed her fingers on the stick and pressed the throttle almost to its stop trying to keep up. Joe was snaking his way along the slough and was headed straight for the wires. While her mind considered the options— add power and go over, break right while he broke left, crash, burn, die—Joe's biplane shot underneath. Kate never flinched and flew right behind him, rocking in his wake, the wires passing overhead like a 90-mile-per-hour cheese slicer.

\*\*\*

Lenny looked up again at the sound of the tractor motor, but this time the tractor was in a different place from the sound. On his feet, hat back, hands blocking the sun from his eyes, he heard the racket grow. The field was in a hollow surrounded on three sides by warehouses and a long wooden fence. A railroad track bordered the far end of the field, and the levee road was where he stood. Around it all was marshy grassland—mosquitoes, a few ducks, muskrats and a lot of old tires and rusted cars. A short distance from where he stood, someone had dumped several barrels that leaked noxious brown ooze, and even the local kids gave them wide berth.

*BLAAHH!*

*"Mama putah!"* Lenny shouted and ducked.

*BLAAHH!* The roar of a second airplane motor blew across his head, and he spun around to watch the two biplanes skim across the slough and pull up just short of the warehouses. The lead airplane banked left, the wingman broke right. Lenny pushed to his feet wiping dust from his trouser legs and, despite himself, admired the beauty of the maneuver.

The lead airplane continued its bank and slowing as it turned into the wind to line up with the narrow dirt runway beyond where Lenny stood.

Joe stared over the side of the cockpit, the biplane in a left slip—wing low, the earth growing toward him. Over a strand of wires, and he glanced at the makeshift windsock that hung on the dead tree beside the runway. Not even a real runway, the 1500-foot strip of bare ground belonged to the warehouses on the far side of the slough, and they, in turn, belonged to Lenny's employers in Chicago, who in their turn, paid tribute to higher forces on the East Coast, who had friends all over the world.

Joe kept a hand loose on the throttle pulled all the way back. Wind buffeted his face and the engine gently *pok-pokked* in tiny backfires. Lenny's Buick was in its usual place, right below his wheels on short final. A shallow ditch separated the car from the runway. Joe rode a brief gust that tumbled over the fence, and with rudder to point the airplane straight down the narrow runway, he kept aileron in against the wind and rolled the left wheel onto the dirt. A brief roll, and he eased the right down. A few more seconds, and the tail dropped in its familiar rumble.

Kate studied the runway. Joe seemed to use no more than a third of the length getting stopped and turned around, but then, Joe had been in there many times before. She banked into a turn the other way and decided on her approach. Her first thought was to make it a little wider than she might at home—not much, just a little to give her that extra room to familiarize herself with the obstacles and winds and grade of the runway. But, too much and she'd look scared. Like a girl.

***

"Think she'll make it this time?" Lenny asked.

Joe leaned on his airplane, helmet off, jacket unbuttoned. The breeze helped against the growing heat, but he knew it was making Kate's successive landing attempts all the more difficult. The crosswind didn't help.

"Dollar says she don't make it this time," Lenny said and held a silver coin in his open palm.

"Third times a charmer," Joe said without conviction. "She'll make it. Give her a chance."

Lenny watched the biplane turn onto final, its wings kicked by the rough air blowing across the warehouses, tumbling in her path like invisible ocean breakers.

"Lemme see your money," he said.

Joe fished a dollar and set it on his airplane's tail. Lenny set his there, too. Kate pulled the power all the way back. They heard her engine backfire and saw her drop.

"Too damn low, Katie," Joe snapped. "She's going to be riding over that levee, carrying power again, and she's going to hit just like she did last time and bounce that piece of—"

123

"Care to make it two dollars?" Lenny asked. "Give you odds."

Joe saw Kate add power, and the biplane rose slightly. Something inside told him the approach was salvageable. She was just slow enough, and low enough that if she dragged it in without stalling and rolling the whole thing up in a ball, she might just drop it in this time.

"What kind of odds?" Joe asked.

"Two to one."

"Make it five to one," he countered, and the biplane drew closer.

Lenny studied the approach. He knew he was at a technical disadvantage. "Four to one, and a five-dollar bet."

Joe hesitated. "Done." They shook hands.

"C'mon, Katie. Drag it. Drag your ass, woman. Hang on to that power—"

"She's dropping. She's dropping. She'd better give it up, or she's in the swamp," Lenny said gleefully. "It don't count if she crashes."

"Hey, a landing's a landing."

They watched. Kate bounced in the rough air. She fought against the currents and jockeyed the throttle to keep the biplane hovering above a stall and floating toward the runway. Suddenly, the wind quit where the buildings had blocked it. She dropped, but ready for it, she was on the throttle.

"*Off* the power, Kate!" Joe shouted, and almost the instant he said it, she killed the engine and dropped like a fat cow over the Buick and three-pointed onto the runway.

"Oh, Jesus," Lenny said and cringed. "That's gotta smart."

"Style don't matter," Joe said. "You owe me a double-sawbuck, my friend." His grin spread from ear to ear, and

Lenny slapped a $20 bill into his palm. "Thank-you, and never bet unless you personally know the horse."

"She was lucky," he drawled.

"All her life," Joe added.

*** 

"You're a lucky woman, Katie Strauss," Joe called.

The propeller swung to a stop, and Kate pulled the helmet from her ears. "You'll have to speak up," she said. "I thought I heard you complimenting my landing." She stood.

"No chance. Kate, meet Lenny. Lenny, that's Kate. She's a damn good pilot, and tells me she's seen all your movies."

"Hello, Larry," Kate said.

"Lenny."

"Sorry." She climbed down from the cockpit and extended her hand. "I assume you have the dirty money with you?"

Lenny hesitantly took her hand and looked to Joe. It was difficult to tell whether he was smiling or scowling. "Ain't you kinda small for a pilot?" he asked.

"Yes, but not for a dame," Kate said, imitating his Chicago accent—flat, the vowels squashed like crickets under a bald tire. "How big should pilots be? Maybe Joe-size?"

"I didn't mean nuthin' by it, just—"

"Women grow bigger in your neighborhood?"

"Hey, don't get me wrong or nuthin'. I just ain't never seen no girl flying no airplane. In fact, before I seen Joe, I ain't never seen nobody flyin' no airplane. Christ, you don't gotta bite my head off."

"It's her way sometimes, Lenny," Joe said. "Don't let it bother you. She's almost pleasant when you get to know her."

Kate dropped her eyes and kicked at the dust. "Sorry," she said to Lenny. "It's been a long flight."

"And you're only halfway there," Joe said. "We've still got to go back." He walked toward the car. "Where's the package, Lenny?"

"On the back seat." He stayed with Kate, trying to look her over without being noticed. Kate felt his eyes studying her and kept her eyes lowered a moment, and then looking him in the face said, "Do I meet you here every day?"

"Yeah, sure," Lenny said. "I bring the package," he added, because he had to have something else to say. He knew he was staring too long at her.

She smiled and her eyes grew friendly. Her dark hair blew in wild curls around her face, and she tried ineffectively to keep it from her eyes. "Maybe you should get it cut," he said before he realized what he was saying.

"I've considered it," she said and laughed.

"Hey, Jeez, I didn't mean nuthin' by it. I was just, you know, it looked like your hair was gettin' in the way, and...Hey, I think your hair's just swell, don't get me wrong or nuthin'."

"It's okay, Lenny," she said.

"Jeez, I tend to fuck-up a lot around women, you know," he said. "Ah, shit, sorry, I shouldn't a said that..."

"It's all right." She reached to pat his arm but reconsidered. The aborted gesture only added to his discomfort, and she plunged both hands into her pockets.

"Hey, Lenny," Joe called. "Where's the dough? There isn't anything here but some bones." He held up a small packet of bones wrapped in butcher paper. He sniffed at them. "What'd you do murder a cow? Or is this cow?"

Lenny ran toward him and Joe added: "We don't ferry stiffs for you, now, Lenny."

"Gimme those," Lenny said and swiped the bones away. He rewrapped and tossed them onto the front seat. "I said, *back* seat. Here." He handed Joe a large package tied with string and taped at the seams.

"I think your brother, Angelo, would wonder if we showed up with your lunch."

"That ain't my lunch," Lenny said defensively.

"So you did chop someone up, huh?"

"It's for a dog." He waved vacantly toward the road. He never told anyone about the junkyard dog chained to the pole. There were things no one had a need to know about him. "You got the dough," he said. "You'd better blow."

"Hey, Katie," Joe called. "You're taking over this route, come get your luggage." She approached at a quick walk, hips swinging, her hair blowing back over her shoulders. "Ain't she sweet?" Joe whispered to Lenny.

Lenny looked toward her and felt his chest pulse with something he tried to ignore. She was pretty, he thought, pretty like none of the girls he had known before prison, and like none he knew now.

The image of the bright face and tight figure dressed in men's clothes and black riding boots excited and confused him. He stared at her until she took the package from Joe, and he watched her all the way back to her airplane. Her face was close to him for an instant when she passed. Her skin was freckled and tan. Her nose, although slightly large, gave her whole face character. This was a distinct person, more than "...some dame," which was how he thought of women. They were the pancake faces above tight dresses in smoky lounges or heavy, motherly things in diners. He knew whores in Cicero; he knew show girls on the Lakefront. Lenny knew women—dames, dolls, chippies, snatch, molls—but, seeing Kate, he saw personality in the form of a woman. He saw something new and wanted to keep looking. He wanted something but turned away.

"Is she gonna be here on time?" he snapped at Joe. "I mean like every day we got a run?"

"Sure, Lenny."

"I don't want no damn broad screwin' this whole thing up, now." He kicked at the dirt and looked away. He knew he sounded false, but Joe seemed to buy it.

"She's good, Lenny," Joe said and clasped his shoulder.

"Don't touch me."

"Sorry." Joe took his hand away, and for an instant looked as though he didn't know what to do with it. "I can vouch for her. Nobody's got to worry. She'll...she's a good pilot. She's reliable, Lenny." They both looked toward Kate, standing on the wing. She leaned over the cockpit rim to strap the package to the front seat. "She's a hell of a good pilot."

"So long as she don't do nuthin' dumb," Lenny said and knew *that* sounded dumb. He turned for the car. He opened the door and was about to step in. "How old is she, anyhow?"

Joe looked at him with a spreading grin. "Too old for you, my friend." The grin widened, and Lenny waved his hand and slipped behind the wheel. He started the motor.

"So long as she don't do nuthin' dumb." It didn't sound any better the second time.

Joe stood aside to let him back down the levee and turn on a wide spot. He thought he saw Lenny hesitate and glance at Kate, before putting the car in gear. Then, gravel kicking the wheel wells, Lenny pulled away.

"He didn't stick around long," Kate said as she jumped off the wing.

"I think he's in love."

She looked where the car had been. "Oh? Couldn't wait to get back to her?" She looked to Joe. "Classy bunch you deal with." Then, imitating Lenny, she added, *"Youse knows?"* And hitched her shoulders Cagney-style.

Joe merely smiled and thought, *Lenny, you poor, dumb bastard.*

\*\*\*

They flew high to avoid rough air, but even so, they bounced like little sailboats far above the earth. After landing at Davenport for fuel Kate crawled from the airplane, wishing the day was through. She was exhausted.

"You've still got a hundred miles to go," Joe reminded her. "Bladder holding up?"

"Mind your own bladder, and let's get going," she said.

Refueled, rockers oiled, bladders drained, and Maxwell, the under-employed pilot, was there to help start the engines, after which he waved and walked back to the coffee shop. Kate watched him for a moment, and then turned to Joe who was already taking the runway. They abandoned their formation on the last leg, flying, instead, with Kate far behind and to the right.

Cumulus clouds grew in shaving-cream mountains along the route. At first they were only puffs of white, casting shadows on the fields below. As they approached Ottumwa, the clouds thickened into giant towers. As yet, no anvil tops, but Kate knew from the rough treatment the air was giving them, the clouds could become thunderstorms by dusk. She adjusted herself again and leaned to one side. Her bottom was numb. Her legs were stiff, and she felt her eyes grow heavy from the bright glare of the blue sky and brilliantly white clouds. The howl of the radial engine massaged her whole body into a heavy dullness. She wanted to sleep. She thought about Lindbergh flying a day-and-a-half without sleep, alone, over water behind the same model engine. She imagined Paris crowds cheering her arrival, she pictured herself waving from a hotel balcony to the crowds, the reporters and newsreel cameras...

"Wake up, girl!" she yelled and stuck her hand into the slipstream to redirect a blast of air at her face. Gripping the joystick between her knees, she lifted her goggles, closed her eyes and let the warm air press against her skin. She felt a bug sting against her fingertips and was surprised it had been up so high.

"Probably thought you were safe, didn't you?" she said to the gooey smear on her hand. Working her fingers in the wind, she rubbed its existence away. She looked for Joe. He was off to her right now, having adjusted his course. Or, she thought, had she simply wandered away from him? She looked at the compass now 20 degrees off her original heading.

"Fool," she muttered and banked to follow him. She shook her head. "Get your head out of the clouds, little girl."

More power moved her closer to him. Scanning the air before him, his head rolled back and forth in an even motion, almost as though he had set his mind on a tempo matching some distant rhythm only he could hear. Kate pulled in behind and to his left. His biplane hung as though from a string before her. His propeller seemed unable to move him along; all sensation of speed was lost.

She studied his airplane, admiring the sunlight reflecting off the taut fabric. She let her airplane drop, until she could look into the belly where the exhaust and oil had painted a black streak that tapered under the tail. She rose up again and pulled alongside him.

It took a minute before he noticed, and she felt she had stirred him from a dream. He looked. His goggles were off his eyes, pressed to his forehead, and across the empty sky she could see his eyes blankly gaze at her. She wanted to wave, but refrained. His head rolled to one side, then in a slight circle back toward the clouds and then again to her. When, at last his eyes met hers, she saw him smile and nod. His hand rose in a wave, and she waved back. They were approaching a skinny tower of cloud, so Joe banked slightly to his right. Kate approached the tower and banked left, her wing tips slicing into the cloud as she passed.

Around the other side, and there he was, banking toward her, eyes on her. They joined in formation, wings even.

Approaching a round puff of cloud, they held their positions, as though holding hands, and flew into it. To Kate it was like deliberately flying into a snow-capped mountain. Her senses rose to a false peak of fear, her logical mind overrode the fear as they bored into the cloud.

As quickly as they were swallowed in cool whiteness, they popped out the other side. Their wings bounced in the turbulence, and she looked at him. He looked back. She decided at that moment, she never wanted to fly in the same airplane with him, but she would always fly by his side—abeam—together but separated by a piece of sky.

\*\*\*

Joe never simply arrived at an airfield. Joe always made an entrance.

Kate fell in trail, her biplane slightly above to stay out of his wake. Joe led her down the river and across the trees and cornfields leading to the pits. Before they reached them, however, she saw him wave her away. His arm pumped in short, choppy strokes. Uncertain what he meant by it, Kate banked away, letting him buzz the pits from the river, his biplane barely clearing the trees and the steam shovel in the center of the crater.

She saw a car, bright red, and beside it a squat figure waving an angry fist and watching Joe peel away in a taunting chandelle. Kate saw all this while skimming across the trees from the opposite direction, sun at her back, throttle wide open, the red roadster bore-sighted on her nose.

Angelo flipped Joe a finger, indicating what he thought of his attack. "You're slipping, Joey-boy. Saw you comin' a mile off."

Had Angelo been listening instead of shouting; had he been looking over his shoulder instead of making rude gestures at Joe; had he been paying attention, he might have noticed that Joe's was not the only airplane noise reverberating off the pit walls. But Angelo was watching Joe when Kate flashed over his hat in a deafening, heart-slamming roar of wind and insult, before she dropped below the distant trees and retraced the route where Joe had entered. She stayed low, tires skimming corn. Angelo stayed low, now, too. Face in the dirt, hat off to his side and his hand groping for his pistol, or was it his heart to make certain it still worked?

Joe rolled out of the climbing, turning chandelle and waited for Kate to form up beside him. Letting her slide in tight beside him, her upper wing tucked beneath his lower, he looked her in the eyes and brought his hand to his forehead in a quick salute. Kate nodded, returned the salute, and motioned him to lead her in.

*** 

The approach was uneven. Kate had to back away from Joe's wing to keep from hitting. Turning base leg, she widened out, letting him land first. His airplane bounced from side to side on the rough updrafts short of the touchdown spot. When she saw him drop a wing into the slight crosswind she turned onto final. He was already rolling toward the car at the end when Kate slipped her biplane to lose altitude.

The runway was short, but no shorter than dozens of others she'd been into. Low at the approach end near the gully, it rose quickly to a peak where it leveled for a few hundred feet and then dipped into a hollow before rising again toward the car—an easy landing.

Until she touched.

An adult badger (*Taxidea taxus*) weighs about twenty pounds, has poor eyesight, moves slowly but can dig. Sharp teeth and long claws attached to short but powerful legs make it a formidable threat to mice, ground squirrels or just about anything. Hiding beneath the earth provides little protection against the badger, and during the previous night the badger that lived in the trees east of the runway had found its meal eight inches below the surface on the exact spot Kate's left wheel now touched.

Kate knew she tended to land slightly sideways when touching on grass. It was a lazy habit, one she warned herself to avoid. The same technique on pavement would result in a nasty squeal of rubber, but a tire touching crooked on lush grass merely slides.

When she hit the badger hole her speed was too high. She felt the jolt, corrected with rudder, but that brought a wing up and slammed the opposite wheel onto the ground.

It was that wheel, suffering an excessive side load that buckled.

"Some replacement you brought there," Angelo drawled and nodded toward Kate. Joe had turned his head before she settled to the runway and spun around in time to see her ground loop to the right, her wing tip dragging in the weeds, her gear leg crumbling under the stress.

"Ahh, Shiieet," he sighed and was already running toward her.

"You gonna hire blind pilots next?" Angelo shouted. "Maybe cripples and retards? Or you could import a slug of them Chinee coolies—get a whole slug o' them Chinkees flying for you, huh?" Joe ran as fast as he could down the runway. The remainder of Angelo's asocial comment was lost to him. "And now they let goddamn women fly airplanes. Ah, balls," Angelo said to himself and climbed into the Ford.

Kate held the stick tight to keep her hand from shaking. Her legs moved slowly off the rudder pedals and she sat for a moment before killing the engine. It made its usual few turns then stopped. Looking past the cylinder heads she saw the prop tips were untouched and she felt the blood drain from her face.

"Oh, God," she mumbled and looked at the rest of the biplane. "Oh, God in heaven…"

She heard Joe's voice calling her name and felt the fuselage shift under his weight as he jumped on the wing.

"Kate, you all right?" He shook her. "Kate?"

She looked at him, her eyes frozen holding back tears. "Fine," she choked.

"What happened?"

Her head turned from one side to the other, surveying the damage. "Looks like I ground looped." She undid her belt, but her legs refused to do more than shiver.

"How?"

"How?" she repeated. "I suspect," and her voice cracked. She pushed the tears back with anger. "I suspect, first one wing went up, and then—" The tears flooded her eyes and she wiped with her sleeve. The red Ford pulled slowly toward the wreck, and a squat ugly man, chewing a fresh cigar studied her, his face a blank. "Then the other wing must have hit the grass, and maybe a wheel popped, I mean a tire, because the wheels don't really pop, do they? And then the whole thing started to...to spin. I can only guess that was from the uneven lift caused by the one wing, now, being buried in the dirt, while the other was increasing its airspeed so could fly..." She blubbered the last and wiped her nose. Closing her eyes as tight as she could, she turned her face toward the instrument panel, sobbed, and said, "I crashed, Joseph. I simply crashed my airplane." And her shoulders heaved uncontrollably.

Joe's arm was around her, an awkward hug in the cockpit, smothering more than comforting. She heard the car move closer, and a voice asked: "Is it that time of the month for her?"

Joe spun. He glared at Angelo's blank face, the cigar working around the thick lips like some kind of probe. He reached inside the forward cockpit and unlashed the package of money. Tossing it at Angelo, it bounced off his shoulder and landed on the seat.

"She delivered. That's all you need. Take it and get the hell outa here!"

Angelo pushed the package onto the floor without looking at it and glancing at Joe he said, "So long as she delivers." And he pulled away, his expression never changing, only the cigar working faster in his mouth.

"He's a jerk," Joe said to Kate. "He's always been a jerk; just ask Daryl. He always expects too much—"

Kate dried her eyes, undid her belt and pushed herself onto the seat to stand. "So what?"

She stepped over the rim. Joe dropped to the ground and helped her down. She surveyed the damage and said, "He wasn't the one who ground looped. I was." And she walked away.

Tears of rage, tears of embarrassment—just damn, stupid, pointless, girly tears! And that just made more tears, dammit!

\*\*\*

# Chapter 7

They sat on a dump truck's running board outside the office above the coal pits. A lone employee, named Benjamin, kept watch over the dormant operation. It was Benjamin's job to go into the pit once a week, scoop a wheelbarrow full of coal and bring it to the top of the mine. By doing this, the mine was still technically "active" in the view of the state inspector of mines, who drove a late model Oldsmobile, which like Sheriff Rosenow's Pontiac, was fairly impressive given a state employee's salary. Benjamin, age 64, had earned his $35 for that week and was a little put off that Kate and Joe now kept him from his nap. Still, he had let them use the telephone, and then, seeing that they wouldn't leave, he picked up his *Stevens Crackshot* .22 rifle to go shoot rats in the pits. The carcasses he sold to the county health officer for a nickel apiece, claiming he'd shot them by the sewage lagoon outside the packing plants. The health officer, in turn, sold them to the plant manager for a buck a piece, claiming he'd found them in the ground-round vat.

"I knew Angelo in the Army," Joe said. "He was a pain in the ass back then, and he still is, but he's connected."

"To what?" Kate asked.

"Just about anything; numbers, for instance."

"And Spain?"

"And Spain, yes. Not him directly, but the people he knows know the people that I need to know, if you know what I mean."

Kate didn't but wasn't really listening. She stood and ran her fingers through her hair; it was knotted and unruly.

Frustrated, she pulled it back with both hands as though into a ponytail but kept tugging to rip it off her skull.

She relaxed. The shaking was gone as was the initial rage from the crash. She knew it would be weeks—or months, even—before the guilty feeling left. She hoped it wouldn't take that long for Daryl to fix the airplane.

She stretched. Warm air dried the sweat on her back and scalp. She rolled her sleeves above the elbow and wanted to open her blouse. "I can't imagine Daryl being involved with someone like Angelo. Too much authority there."

"Ang really wasn't with our outfit all that long."

Kate looked at him. *'Ang' huh?*

"He joined us just after we arrived in France; he was a sergeant. Daryl and I were privates, bottom of the barrel, down there with the plowboys and slum kids."

"You don't fit into either category, though," Kate said. "You're from somewhere outside Chicago, aren't you?"

"Oak Park. Very respectable neighborhood; very safe; very dull."

"You were drafted?"

"Nope; I volunteered; didn't want to miss the show, so I lied about my age."

"Daryl was drafted."

"I know," Joe said. "Angelo joined to avoid a prison term; there was a lot of that going on. It was Woodrow Wilson's unsung social reform program—join the Army, get out of jail. Sort of a cleansing process, a way to reenter society with a clean record or die trying and get a nice funeral to go with your clean record."

"So how'd you meet Daryl? You two never talk about that."

"You've never asked."

She shrugged and grinned. It was true, she rarely asked Daryl about his military time, assuming he'd forgotten it as easily as someone forgets high school.

Joe looked past her and absently picked a pebble off the ground. "I met him on guard duty." He threw it.

"What were you guarding?"

"Prisoners."

"German?"

"Daryl."

"Daryl—? Against what?"

"Not *against* what, but *for* what," he said. "He was being court-martialed."

"I guess I'm not really surprised. What was he being court-martialed for?" she asked. "He never said anything about—"

"Oh, I forget the exact charges, but it came down to—" Joe thought. "He wasn't any different than the rest of us. We were all always drinking and carrying on like there was no tomorrow, which for some there wasn't, of course."

"Was he court-martialed for being drunk?"

Joe hesitated; a lot of thoughts flashed through his eyes, then, "Yeah, it wasn't anything big...I think Ang was in charge of our platoon, and, well, hell, Ang doesn't drink much, and I think he just had it in for all the Micks in the unit, was all—" His voice trailed off. "It wasn't anything important. Daryl got off okay, and by then the war ended before we ever went back on line. Fact is we only saw action a couple of times; once that was really anything that mattered." He fell silent and stared at his feet. "Angelo, I guess saw a lot of combat before he joined our outfit; been wounded, too."

"Did you all form some kind of fraternity over there? Sign some secret pact?" She looked him in the face. Her tone, Joe thought, was unfair.

"We knew each other," he said. "Is there a problem with that?"

"No. I've just always wondered about those silly tattoos—"

"It didn't seem silly at the time. We all got tattooed before we ever saw combat, copied one Angelo already had, him being the 'old man', the veteran. I guess it was like, oh, like voodoo, painting some magic..." He hesitated, voice suddenly tight. He coughed and, "It didn't seem so important later on, though. I don't think you'd understand."

"It's just funny you all kept in touch," she said and started down the hill toward the strip. "It's funny, that's all."

"Funny?" Joe asked. He followed her.

"Maybe not funny—just, I don't know, strange. I mean, why do men keep in touch with people from the past like that? It's...funny."

"There are, believe it or not, quite a few we didn't keep in touch with." He caught up with her. "And quite a few more we left behind. They're easy to find, though. Planted in neat rows with little white crosses overhead. Oh, there's the odd star, indicating those who didn't die for Jesus; instead, had a different dumb-ass reason for getting killed. I guess that's funny."

She started to speak, but he cut her off. "Someone was even *funny* enough to write a poem about it. Ah, lessee: 'In Flanders Fields the poppies grow...' Or is that 'blow'? I never can remember—"

"I'm sorry," Kate said.

"For what? For the war? You didn't start it."

"Not that."

"Sorry for me? For Daryl? Angelo? The poppies blowing? That's it; *the poppies blow*—"

"No, I..."

"'Between the crosses, row on row'..."

"I apologize for mentioning any of it," Kate said.

Joe looked at Kate. "Personally, I believe there is entirely too much apologizing in our lives." And he continued reciting: "'That mark our place, and in the sky, the lark—still bravely singing, flies.'" He stopped and repeated, "Flies." And then he rubbed a hand across his sleeve and said, "Everybody is sorry, and as far as I'm concerned everybody's apology is accepted. War's over."

He was silent again. Then: "Yes, Daryl knew Angelo, and so did I, and that's how I'm here, and you're here, and Daryl's wherever he is, doing whatever it is he does, when he could be in on this." He indicated the coal pits and the rusted steam shovel. "Some of us kept in touch after the war, that's all."

Kate slowed her pace and looked up at him. She reached a hand and rubbed his arm. "I didn't mean anything," she said. "You say more than Daryl. I wish he would tell me these things or *any*thing."

They walked together down the long dirt road leading to the runway. The leaves in the trees below fluttered in the wind like small applause.

"Think it'll rain?" Joe asked and didn't care.

Kate glanced at the sky. "Could," she answered and didn't know. "It really hasn't been a wet spring."

"Think the drought will continue?"

"It could."

"Mmmm," he said. They both privately wondered why they'd brought up the weather, but both knew it was because that's what you talked about in Iowa when you didn't want to discuss the dead monkey floating in the soup tureen.

The wind blew a flock of birds from the trees. Kate and Joe walked across the runway toward his airplane.

Sunlight poked through the clouds, and she dropped to the grass and slipped beneath the wing into the shade.

"Cooler under here," he said, joining her.

"Why'd I go and ground loop, Joe? I should have seen that hole."

"*I* didn't see it," he said. "Could have been me just as easily."

"But it wasn't."

"If a badger digs a hole on a runway, and no one lands in it, does it really exist?"

She turned, her face screwed into a frown. "What?"

"It's philosophy—how to turn any disaster into a profound-sounding thought. I learned it in college."

"Where'd you ever go to college?"

"Right here in Iowa after the war. I wanted to be a lawyer, but they kicked me out."

"Sleeping with the dean's wife?"

"Daughter, actually, but that wasn't the reason. No, they said I didn't have what it took to be a lawyer."

"How could that be? You're as crooked as the next guy."

"Thank-you."

"You're welcome," she said and patted his knee.

He leaned on an elbow and plucked a blade of grass. He chewed it while staring toward the trees. A bug landed on the wing above his head, and he flicked it away without crushing it.

"I had no money," he said. "My family pulled the plug—something about excessive drinking, failing grades, I never did understand what they were talking about."

"Families *are* a burden."

"Plus, they had this dumb rule at the university: No money; no degree. And they stood by it, the swine."

"So you were forced to go straight?"

"And leave the dean's daughter, although it was a good thing, because I think she was pregnant. Can't imagine how a girl could be so careless."

Kate leaned back, her hair fanned behind her in the grass. Joe looked down at her and rubbed his hand across her shoulder. He picked a strand of grass off her right breast. Gently.

"Daryl wanted to go to college," she said and knew she wasn't thinking of Daryl.

"He should have," Joe said. "He's a sight brighter than I am."

"Maybe, but less ambitious."

It was then they stared at each other. Kate slipped a hand behind her head and felt herself smile inside. Joe leaned closer. The wind swirled under the wing, lifting the hair across her face, and he wiped it back. In a soft voice, "Maybe you should—"

"I've been told. Nobody likes my hair anymore."

"I like it."

He ran his fingers through the long curls and let his fingertips caress her face. She kissed his hand as he held it over her lips. They were cool. He leaned closer. She reached her arm around him, her fingers working under his jacket. It came off easily, as did her blouse. She ran a hand across the 1918 tattoo on his arm and was surprised how light Joe was—almost hovering like a snake from a tree above her as she closed her eyes.

Beyond the pits, Benjamin's .22 punctured a rat, although, the sound was lost to Kate and Joe.

* * *

"That was Kate," Daryl said, returning to the shop.

"Where is she?" Brian asked.

143

"She ground looped near Blakesburg." He looked at the racer. Brian was seated in the pilot's seat. Together they'd been running new wires through the firewall when the phone rang, and he'd left to answer it.

"Is she okay?" Brian asked.

"She sounded a little shook-up, but I think she's fine." He paused to think, and then, "Look, we're going to have to leave off here, and I'm going to run over there and fix whatever she's busted."

He took a rag from atop the toolbox and wiped a screwdriver clean and put it away. "We'll toss your bike in the car, and I'll drop you off home. I appreciate the help today."

"Could I come with you?" Brian asked. "You might need the help. My mom won't mind. Fact is she won't give much of a hoot." He started to laugh, but Daryl suddenly kicked the stand with the toolbox as hard as he could.

An explosion of wrenches, screws and wire sprayed across the fuselage, bouncing onto the gravel floor. Brian winced, enclosed inside the cockpit, unable to move. Eyes wide, he stared at Daryl, who picked a long wrench from the engine and threw it with vicious power at the hangar wall.

"GOD DAMN BITCH!" he bellowed and kicked over a sawhorse. Actually, he kicked at it. His judgment, clouded by the sudden rage, caused him to miss, lose his balance and spin around in a pirouette. He toppled into the dirt, but not without upsetting a pan of used motor oil.

Still muttering about women and airplanes, Joe and the "fucking oil" all over his clothes, Daryl pushed himself to his knees, his face scarlet.

"Please!"

He looked up.

"Don't!"

It was Brian. Petrified and confused, still seated in the cockpit, the boy looked like an animal in a trap about to be clubbed. "She didn't mean nothin'," he stammered. "She couldn't help it."

Daryl felt the anger dissolve away, leaving shame for himself and pity for the boy. Quickly, he got to his feet and approached the racer. "No," he managed.

"She's okay, Daryl," the boy said, hands up. "You said she's okay; she ain't dead."

Daryl realized Brian had no idea what had caused the outburst, and he knew he could never tell him. How could he? How could he tell a 14-year-old about love and jealousy and fear and emptiness? These were things he would find on his own someday. There was no way he could explain how much he hated Kate being gone, and how much he hated Joe and his flying ability and his airplane and his money. But there was no way he could tell Brian—or anyone. It was over now—the rage. It had come on like a summer squall, dropped its fury and, now, dissipated it passed. "I'll clean this up," he said and tried to smile. "Sorry. I just got worried, that's all." He leaned to pick a screwdriver from the gravel and dirt. There was no way he could tell anyone, no way.

Climbing silently from the cockpit, Brian glanced once at Daryl, and then began picking up tools and replacing them in the box. It was Daryl who broke the silence. "I could use some help, if you still want to come along."

He thought Brian would say no, and that might've been better. "Sure," Brian said. "It don't matter."

"Thanks," Daryl said. "I'll bring the car around. We can load it up." He walked out. Brian watched him leave, and then looked at the fuselage cockpit where he had frozen in terror against the rage. He felt confused and, for some reason, guilty. A day that had begun so comfortably, working with his friend inside an airplane—

an airplane they were building together—was now changed. Something cold and vague had destroyed the peace inside the hangar, inside Brian's refuge. The guilt almost overwhelmed him, and he wanted to leave.

Daryl backed the Nash inside the hangar and switched off the engine.

"If you're hungry we can stop for a couple of hamburgers at Aunt Elzine's along the way," Daryl said. "She's got a pretty fair menu, if you can get past the grease." He laughed and tossed a length of steel tubing behind the seat. It tore a hole in the upholstery, and he laughed again. "So, you hungry?"

"Sure," Brian said. He grasped for the change in mood, hoping to wipe away the unpleasantness, but somehow it continued to gnaw at him.

"Think your mother will mind you running all over the countryside, chasing down beautiful pilots in distress?"

"She don't mind none," he said and knew she might not even be home. Usually she stayed out until after he had already gone to sleep. She would, however, leave him dinner in the icebox, although she never asked whether he ate.

"Good," Daryl said. "Give me a hand with the sawhorses, and we'll blow this popcorn stand."

They both laughed a little too long and loaded the rest of the tools, parts and bicycle into the Nash, mostly jammed behind the seat, some hanging from the trunk or strapped to the running boards.

"Folks'll think we're Oakies moving to California."

Rolling down the canvas hangar door, Daryl said, "I don't think we'll ever really finish the racer." He set the bricks on the canvas to keep it from flapping.

"Sure we will."

"Think so?" He climbed inside the car, started the motor, and then slid across to the passenger's side. "You drive. I'm tired of doing all the work."

Brian grinned, and before the offer could be revoked, he ran around the car, jumped over the door, and while Daryl leaned against the opposite door, Brian depressed the clutch. After a few jarring bucks, they were off.

"You drive divinely," Daryl said, once on the highway.

"Thank-you, suh."

"Do you think you might try doing just as divinely on your own side of the road, though?"

"Certainly," Brian answered, and they crossed the road and into a ditch.

Bouncing out again onto the road Daryl commented, "Much better. You should take up flying. I just happen to know an instructor."

It was better between them, but not the same.

*       *       *

Kate walked the runway toward her wrecked biplane. The sun was almost below the trees, and the air had calmed from the afternoon's threat of a storm. A lone redwing blackbird shot across the runway and landed on a tall stalk of weed. It bobbed under the weight, and the bird balanced itself and gave a sweet call as though drawing her attention to how good she now felt.

"Did you ever notice how useless an airplane looks when it can't fly?"

Joe held her hand in his, their fingers entwined. He studied the biplane with its broken gear leg and wing tip in the grass. "Ungainly things, aren't they? Sort of like ballet dancers with broken toes."

"I've never seen a ballet dance with broken toes."

"It's an evil sight. They usually turn to drink and become trollops in Mexico."

"Trollops?"

"Or librarians."

"Have you ever slept with a prostitute?" She stopped. "That's none of my business. Pretend I didn't ask."

He laughed. "I don't mind."

"I do," she protested. "Don't answer it." They walked toward the airplane.

Joe surveyed the wreckage. "You won't be able to fly it for a while, at least not by tomorrow."

"Daryl will get it back in the air. It doesn't look too bad."

"But not by tomorrow. We need someone to fly tomorrow." His voice was firm without being cruel.

"Do you have to leave tomorrow?"

"I should."

Kate thought for a minute. "You can't imagine how stupid this makes me feel."

"Yes, I can."

"Oh," she laughed in protest and slapped his arm. "At least give me the chance to play out my misery. I'm groping for sympathy."

"I know, and you won't get any from me. I don't care how good you've been in the grass."

She looked at him, still holding his hand. The sun's orange glare made her squint. "Why did we do it?"

"You mean...?" He made a gesture clearly illustrating their recent coupling.

She rolled her eyes. "Yes, although I think you shouldn't be ashamed to say it." She hesitated, not wanting to say it. "Why'd we do it?"

Joe shrugged.

He was handsome, she thought.

"Why not?" he said and squeezed her hand. Looking at her he asked, "Is it Daryl?"

"Of course it's Daryl," she answered. "Lately, everything's Daryl."

"Then it's time you married him." He let go of her hand to fish the cigarette pack from his shirt pocket. "Want one?"

She shook her head and crossed her arms beneath her breasts. They pushed up like two bunnies snuggling. "You sound like my mother."

"I've never been accused of that one before." He flipped open his lighter—click, scratch, flame, inhale, exhale—and picked a speck of tobacco from his tongue. "Maybe your mother is right. What's wrong with Daryl?"

"Whose side are you on here?"

"Mine."

"As always, Joe looks out for Joe."

"No one else will."

"Have you ever tried to find someone..." She knew where that led and stopped.

"How many times have you turned me down? I asked you to come with me to New York."

"To Spain?"

"You know you can't go, but that doesn't mean I wouldn't want you along."

"No, thank-you."

"You're a lovely woman, Katie Strauss. I mean it."

She looked toward the setting sun, aflame, stalled above the trees. Birds flew across the brilliant light and disappeared in the woods. "A lovely woman, huh?" she asked.

"I suppose you have trouble with that?"

She shrugged. "It doesn't sound quite right, 'a lovely woman.' Sounds like something from one of those magazines my sister reads." She turned on Joe, taking his hand. "Maybe you should hook up with my sister. I don't know if she's still a virgin, but she definitely falls for lines such as, 'a lovely woman.'"

"Why do you find it so hard being what you are?" he asked.

"I don't," she said. "I find it hard being what everyone says I should be: a *woman*-pilot, an avia*trix*. Do you know how much that word irks me? *Aviatrix*. 'Oh, isn't she cute. Not a real aviator, but an 'AV-I-A-*TRIX*'. Sounds like a circus act. Maybe I should be wearing sequins—"

"Have you ever been in love?"

"No," she answered too quickly.

"I see," Joe said. He looked toward the hill where he hoped to see Daryl's Nash, but there was only the steam shovel and the road to the pits, both glowing in the fading sunlight. "Think you can fly my airplane?"

"Yes," she answered. Confident. Of course I can.

"Then you take it back to your place and make the run tomorrow with it." He started away from the wreck. Kate stayed at his side. "Tell Daryl to take as long as he needs fixing yours, and when he's done you can leave mine in Ottumwa. I'll telephone the folks over there to stick it inside a hangar, until I can get back. C'mon, I'll give you a quick check-out in it."

"But how will you get to New York?"

"Train, chug-chug-chug. I wasn't planning on flying. I'll just take a train from here."

"Where are your things?"

"I'll get them okay. That's my problem."

\*\*\*

150

"You want another beer, there, Daryl?" Mike called from the kitchen of *Aunt Elzine's Roadhouse*. Customers were beginning to come in, taking tables around the narrow dining room.

"Yeah, Mike," Daryl answered and downed the remainder of the one he had. "Lemmee have one for the road." He clapped the bottle on the table and grinned at Brian. "Want another Coca Cola, Ace?" His words slurred to, *wan'nother Coh-Cola?*

Brian shook his head and glanced at the beer bottle. Mike approached with a full one. "Want a beer, Brian?" Daryl asked and picking the empty from the table, blew across the top. It gave a flat *'twoot'*.

Brian shook his head, no.

"What else can I get you two?" Mike asked. He was a friendly man. Fat, as a man named 'Mike,' running a cafe should be. His Aunt Elzine owned the place, but at 300 plus pounds and with only one leg, she didn't get around much anymore, so Mike ran the front while Elzine supervised the blanket-roller crap games in the back room. That's where the money was, anyhow. Mike wore a stained apron over a white shirt and loose gray trousers. The shirt was open at the top with a red bow tie over the opening like a little propeller. His throat jiggled when he spoke.

"Bring a beer for my partner, here," Daryl said and took a swallow of the new beer. Brian grinned and looked down.

"How old's this kid?" Mike asked good-naturedly.

Daryl leaned toward him, hand at his mouth as though sharing a secret. "He only looks twelve…"

"Fourteen," Brian protested.

"I meant fourteen," Daryl corrected. "He looks young, but he's really thirty-two." He winked at Brian.

Mike scratched his jowls and squinted one eye, studying Brian. "Thirty-two, huh? Well, I dunno."

"Ah, c'mon, Mike. Bring my associate a beer. I'll even let him buy the next round."

Mike put a hand on the table. It sagged under the weight. He spoke to Brian. "Aren't you Sarah's kid? Sarah Winston, works over to the laundry in Chariton on Elm?"

Brian nodded.

"Okay," Daryl interrupted. "So he's only twenty-nine. Bring him a brew, willya, Mikey?"

Mike still spoke to Brian. "I ain't seen her in here for a while. She doing okay?"

"She's fine," Brian managed. Daryl took another pull on the beer. He seemed to lose interest in the conversation.

"You want another Coca Cola?" Mike asked.

"No, thanks," Brian answered and looked away. "We got to get going." He looked to Daryl who raised his eyebrows.

"Oh, yes," he said over the bottle. "We've a beautiful young pilot to rescue from the clutches of one of my best and soon-to-be ex-friends."

"Kate broken down somewhere?" Mike asked.

"Oh, she's beginning to sag a bit in the seat, I suppose, but that's common with most women her age," Daryl answered. He drank off the entire beer in several gulping swallows and carefully set the bottle on the table. "She's never been married, you know, so she'll probably hold up better than most women." He turned to Brian. "Women tend to go all to hell after they get wedded, you understand. Something in the hormones. Remind me to tell your mother to tell you all about hormones." He stood. "Where's my hat?"

"You didn't bring one," Brian said, standing.

152

"Good," Daryl said. "Less to lose. You have the keys?"

"The car doesn't have keys, just that switch."

"Excellent. Mike, give this lad the bill; he deserves something for being such a perspicacious asshole." He saw Brian wince. "Oh, I'm sorry. I didn't mean to call you an asshole. It's just an expression, learned it in the Army—foul place the Army, everyone running around dressed like tents, and using the most god awful language. Someone really should clean it up, teach old soldiers how to talk like civilized assholes before they get mustered out. Did I say 'asshole,' again?"

Brian nodded and half-smiled.

"Don't let your mother know I said that."

"I won't," Brian said. Being young he tried to be amused with Daryl's beery charm.

"Bet you don't know what 'perspicacious' means."

Brian shook his head.

"It means you're too smart to get involved with dames who run around with old Army buddies." He turned for the door.

"Daryl?" Mike called. Daryl turned back. "The bill?" Mike waved a check.

"Oh," Daryl said and fumbled in his pocket. "How much?"

"With the beers, two hamburgers, one without onions, one pop, comes to seventy cents."

"Jumpin' Jehasaphat," Daryl shouted, imitating W.C. Fields. "Brian, we've stumbled into a den of thieving Yoo-bangies." He set three quarters on the counter. "Count the change, lad. I don't trust this lot."

Brian took the change and thanked Mike who asked, "Can you drive all right, Daryl?"

"Me?" Daryl asked. Although having only had three beers, it seemed to affect him more than most. "Shouldn't pose any trouble at all," he said and then pointed at Brian. "My valet does all the driving. I'm merely along for conversation. Come, driver." He turned and walked out. Once outside, he waved Brian toward the driver's seat. "Start her up. I've got to see a man about a rare Arabian." And he wandered into some bushes beside the road.

***

The low sun cut scarlet and gold shafts through the trees in the surrounding hills. Daryl pointed toward a dirt road leading off the highway. "There," he said. "She said it's over the hill."

Brian turned the Nash onto the dirt road. Rutted and thick with weeds, it led to a gate over which hung a sign: SOUTHERN IOWA MINERALS and another: NO WORK—KEEP OUT. They drove in.

The steam shovel was visible from the curve in the road before they saw the pits. Brian downshifted and held fast to the steering wheel bucking in his hands against the ruts. Daryl, the beer wearing off, sat quietly by his door. His head bounced loosely on his neck, and he looked in need of sleep. He belched and spit over the door.

"She said it's past the engineer's shack—there—and down the hill. Jeez, that sun's blinding." He reached for a visor, but it had been removed long ago, and he swore to himself.

They bounced down the short road toward the runway. "Keep it in low," Daryl said.

"I am," Brian answered.

"Don't ride the brakes. Everyone wants to ride the brakes all the time. Not good. One more thing for me to fix." He spoke to himself, although Brian felt the comments were for him.

"There's Kate," Brian said. "Walking toward us."

Daryl looked to his left. The sunlight smeared the dirty windshield, making it difficult to see. She appeared as a silhouette. Her full hair made her head look unusually large above her slight shoulders. He thought how cute she looked in the California photographs with it bobbed. She waved.

"Where's Joe?" Daryl asked. Brian stopped the car.

Kate put her foot on the running board on Brian's side. "Hello, Brian."

"Hi."

"Joe had to leave. I flew him to Ottumwa. Catching a train to New York. He's gone." If she'd added "Stop" between sentences she'd have sounded like a telegram.

Daryl nodded, the gesture noncommittal.

"Brian, did he make you drive in here?"

"I drove all the way from *Aunt Elzine's*," Brian answered. "I don't mind."

"I'll bet you don't," she said through a smile and tapped his shoulder. It was one of the rare times she showed anything approaching affection for him. Mostly, she ignored him—a cordial ignoring. "Elzine's, huh? Shooting dice?"

Daryl moaned, "No. You know her games are fixed."

"You never seemed to catch on."

"We just had a bite." He showed teeth. "A bite."

She inhaled, smelled beer and looked at him a long moment before asking, "Do you want to take a look at the airplane?"

"That's what I'm here for," Daryl drawled.

Tightlipped, she paused and said, "Fine."

"Fine."

"Fine." She walked away. "I'll meet you there."

Brian watched her retreat, backside swaying and hair bouncing. He wasn't sure what to make of the feeling it gave him, but he sure liked to watch her. He turned to

Daryl whose eyes were shaded against the low sun and his face a blank. Brian slipped the Nash into gear and followed Kate. Before they stopped, Daryl rolled over the door and out. Brian knew enough to wait.

"You're drunk," she said. Not yelling, just saying.

"One beer does not 'drunk' make," Daryl argued back. He walked around the biplane, tugging roughly at struts and making a show of sighing over the bent gear leg. "Really bunged this up, didn't you?"

"Hit a hole."

"Mmmm." He looked around as though inspecting the runway.

"It's back there," she said. "The hole—gopher or something. Joe thinks it was badger."

"Does he?"

"Yes."

"Mmm."

There was a long pause. The sun disappeared. In the twilight she watched him cut away a strip of fabric on the damaged wing tip. "Bad?" she ventured.

"Breaking airplanes is rarely ever good."

She inhaled deeply, feeling the ice grow thicker in the conversation. "Can you fix it?"

"I can fix it," he answered. "I can fix anything." He climbed onto the wing root and looked inside the cockpit. "Yes, friends," he announced putting a little Ireland into his voice. "Daryl Francis Raymond Fitzpatrick—knows all, sees all, fixes all."

"I don't think there's anything broken in there," she said.

"Mmmm, a mechanic, now, are ya? Never can tell." He jumped down. "Did you hit the prop?"

"No."

"Sure?"

"Yes," she said. "I am sure." She walked toward him. "Do you want to say it now, or shall we wait until you've sobered and Brian's gone home?"

He turned on her, eyes slits, jaw tight. "I've got nothing to say."

"Fine."

"Mmmm."

\*\*\*

It was dark when Kate strapped herself inside the cockpit. Brian sat quietly in the front seat, eyes staring at the instrument panel. "All buckled in?" Kate asked him cheerfully.

"Yes," he answered and glanced back at her. She grinned and looked around the airplane's nose at Daryl who waited with one hand on the propeller. "Joe says not to pull it through. I'll just make it hot, and you give it a spin."

Daryl answered, "If that's what Joe says."

Kate clenched her fists and called, "Contact!"

Daryl nodded and swung the propeller. The engine caught. He turned away and walked toward the wrecked biplane. Taking a flashlight from the Nash, he flicked it on and waved them off.

She let the engine warm for several minutes, and then with a wave, she taxied to the far end of the field where she turned and taking advantage of the downhill slope, took off. Daryl barely looked up when the dark roar passed overhead. The exhaust stacks throwing red flame like rockets.

By lantern light, he took a jack from the Nash and placed it under the broken wing. He looked up at the dark sky full of depressing stars and listened to the fading hum of Kate and Brian in Joe's airplane.

And Daryl felt the loneliest feeling in the world, but knew it was a constant part of his life. In a way, that was comforting.

\*\*\*

# Chapter 8

Aloft, Kate and Brian had a second sunset. To her it was the norm seeing beyond the earth's curve and stretching a day beyond its scheduled close. To Brian it was magic. "Two for the price of one," he said to himself.

Wind rushed across the windscreen, and he stuck his head over the cockpit's rim. Battered by the air he turned his face into the blast and inhaled the coolness tinged with the faint aroma of burnt oil from the round engine five feet in front of his face.

"You'll get bugs up your nose doing that," Kate shouted, but her words were lost. Brian turned his head in the wind. She could see him crouch on the seat, his belt apparently loose, trying to get more of the sky through his senses. He looked ready to jump and fly on his own.

The air was still and the sky deep purple, almost black, when they crossed Chariton. Lights flickered like so many campfires below. Brian strained to find his house.

"There!" He pointed, and Kate banked the Travel Air into a shallow turn. "My house." She saw his lips form the words, and she throttled back. "My house. There, off the square," he shouted. His voice was thin and excited against the idling motor and the cello hum of night sky through the wires and struts.

Kate looked where he pointed. The square was marked by yellow streetlamps and busy with pedestrians moving like bugs from a dead stump. The courthouse was dark, except for a faint glow over the main entrance. She thought of the money she owed, the back taxes, and she was grateful Joe had found her this job. She thought of Joe.

She opened the throttle, and had she looked down she might have seen a half-dozen faces turn up wondering why an airplane had flown so low across their town, or she may have seen the other faces, the majority, with eyes cast to the sidewalk, disinterested, wrapped in thoughts of their own with no need of wings. Pity. She flew away from town and strained to pick out the grass runway against the river.

It was dark when she turned onto final. The runway was hidden in shadow with the only light from a single bulb on the operations shack. Daryl always left that one lit.

"I'll leave the light on for you," he would say if she had an overnight flight. But he was always there for her with more than a light.

Now Kate felt empty groping for the runway in the darkness, plotting her arrival course from familiar angles off known objects—the barn silhouette 500 feet north, the barely discernable highway curve and the single light on the shack. Daryl was miles behind her, and perhaps more importantly, Joe was farther yet.

The road slipped beneath them. She squeezed back on the stick, and closed the throttle. The corn was a dark blur on either side, and the trees at the end were vague giants dusted in moonlight waiting to crush her should she misjudge.

She didn't misjudge.

She was stopped and turned around before half the runway was spent. Taxiing back, she saw Brian turn, his face hidden in shadow until they pulled beside the hangar, where the weak light from the lone bulb showed his cautious smile. She smiled back and realized how little thought she gave to her passenger, to this boy who loved what she did and adored who she was, or at least who he thought she was. He stood in the front cockpit waiting for her to climb out. When he scrambled off the wing, Kate saw for the first time how tall he was. Standing beside

Daryl he was a boy, an apprentice always looking up—watching, learning. But as Kate climbed from the cockpit and stood beside him she was astonished to find herself looking him square in the eyes.

"I didn't realize how tall you were," she said and thought it might sound stupid.

To Brian it was music. Kate had noticed him. He said nothing, and she said, "We need to tie it down. I think I've taxied close enough—"

Brian moved past her and had the first rope looped around a strut, cinching it the way Daryl had taught him. "Can you get that?" Kate asked.

"Yes," and he wanted to add something else but felt stupid, again, as though the only thing he knew about airplanes was how to tie one down, and if he said any more she would discover his ignorance and make fun of him. At school they'd labeled him 'shy,' and he thought, maybe, it was true.

"If you can manage by yourself," she said, "I'll slip inside and see if I can get us a ride into town." Brian said nothing and nodded. "Can you manage?"

She heard his mumbled, "Uh-huh", and she turned.

\*\*\*

Kate sat at the desk inside the office, the phone at her ear, her hand shading her eyes from the glare of the overhead bulb. Getting no answer, she hung up and scanned the list of names on her pad. "Not home; not home," she said moving down the list. "Died last spring." She scratched over a name—Herman Lyons. "Didn't like him anyway."

Brian entered quietly.

"I covered the airplane."

Kate jumped. "Oh," she gasped. "I—I forgot you were out there. You scared the, ah, I wasn't expecting you." She looked back at the list knowing there were few names she could call for a favor. Sure, there were some who would rush out to give her a lift, but the needling she would receive made it unthinkable. *'Our little flyer's gone and lost her chauffeur, eh?'* Or, *'Can't just drive that aeroplane into town, now, can you? Not like an auto. 'Course, can't say I'd like women aeroplane drivers on the road. Heh, heh.'*

She pushed the phone away to rub her head and felt exhausted. "I'll just spend the night here," she said to herself. "Can you find your way home alone?" she asked Brian.

He shifted his weight and glanced through the window at the darkness. "I left my bicycle in the Nash," he apologized.

"Oh," she noted and wished he were gone, although she tried not to show it. "Well, then, up for a walk?"

"Sure."

"Your mother doesn't have a car does she?"

He shook his head. "Don't even have a telephone."

She stood. "So we couldn't call her even if she drove a Dussenburg." She gave a quick laugh to ease the tension. Brian smiled back, and she walked toward him. "Hope your shoes don't have too many holes in them."

"It's not far," he said. "I'll bet it's only three mile."

"That's awfully far for us old ladies."

Brian cringed hearing her refer to herself as 'old.' He knew some 'old ladies,' but none of them flew biplanes or wore leather jackets. Kate was pretty, he'd decided, not pretty like girls in school or the women in the Sears catalogue lingerie ads he studied in the bathroom. Kate was more of a functional beauty without need of ribbons and sweet perfumes. He followed her outside and closed the door.

"Nice night," Kate said. "For a walk."

"Yeah," Brian answered. "Warm."

Their feet crunched in cadence on the gravel. They walked in almost complete darkness toward the glow of town beyond the trees. Brian felt himself pulling toward Kate to the point they bumped shoulders. "Oh, excuse me," he stammered.

"I'm being clumsy," she countered. "We may need the flashlight. You were smart to bring it."

Brian flicked on the beam. It cut before them in a yellow cone. He swiveled it from side to side defining the edges of the road, and then flashed it through the trees along a small creek. Two eyes, yellow and narrow, were caught in the beam.

"What's that?" Kate asked. "Fox?"

"Probably a skunk," he said. "Maybe a raccoon, although most of them have been killed off by trappers. Probably skunk." The two eyes blinked, and Brian turned the light away. "Trappers kill off everything."

"Furs have to come from somewhere," Kate said absently.

"They don't have to kill everything off to do it."

She recognized the firm tone in Brian's voice and dropped the subject. He flicked off the light, and they walked in silence.

\*\*\*

They climbed a slight grade, the road winding through a glade of oaks and then across a pasture.

"You know," Kate said. "I've never paid much attention when driving along this road; didn't realized this hill was here." She looked up. "Or these trees. I guess you don't notice how steep something is until you have to walk it."

Brian was close beside her but almost a ghost. "You can see the runway from the top of the hill here." He pointed toward the airport. "I used to go into the woods and climb a tree and wait for you to come in and land."

That worried her a little.

"Sometimes I'd wait up there all day just hoping you'd come in. Sometimes there'd never be an airplane in all week. But I'd wait all the same."

Kate looked at him, an outline the size of a man. She noted how easily he spoke to her in the darkness. The worry faded. "What made you come to the airport?"

It was a moment before he answered, and when he did his voice was soft. "I love airplanes. There's just something about them, I dunno. Something about the way they can just..." He paused. "Just go wherever they want, like when we flew over town. Do you know there probably aren't two other people in that whole town who ever flew over it?"

"I've given rides over town before," Kate said. "I've taken quite a few up, actually. People who live right in town, your neighbors, maybe."

They walked in silence, only the crunch of their feet on the gravel and the rustling of something in the brush. At the edge of town they passed a gas station, the garage door shut for the night, the pumps like idle sentries. Brian could barely make out the round CLARK'S SUPER GAS sign atop a pole. A dog barked.

"Who ever came back for another flight?" he asked.

"Who? What do you mean?"

"Who came back for a second ride? Did anyone you ever took up from here ever come back for another ride?"

"Well..."

"Or'd anyone just come out to the airport to watch?"

Kate's smile was hidden. "No one," she admitted.

"Except me," Brian said. The dog stopped barking after they passed the station. "I'm the only one comes out to the airport, regular, that is."

"Daryl's there. I'm there. Joe's there," and she stopped herself.

"He don't come in but once and a while, and he don't stay."

"I've noticed."

"You like him?"

"Yes."

"You in love with him?"

Kate felt the question, so innocently asked, slap her like a dead tuna. "Yes," she said and had no idea why she answered him. Maybe it was the safety of the darkness or the perceived innocence of the boy. Either way, it felt good answering. "He's a good friend...of ours," she added.

"Daryl don't like him, does he?"

Again, a slam deep inside her chest. Her throat constricted, and she wanted to stop, to stare at this young boy and ask how he learned to be so hurtful. "They were in the Army together," was what she said. "They're friends."

They entered town, and passing through the faint glow of a porch lamp, she glanced at Brian. A boy's face was all that was there, slightly long with a plain nose and vague eyes. He didn't look capable of asking the questions that pierced her.

"Will Daryl get the bonus?"

"What bonus?" she asked, caught off balance by the shift in topics.

"Veteran's Bonus. I read about it in the paper. All the war vets get their bonus this summer. They got to go down to the Legion Hall next week and sign-up. It's a couple hundred bucks."

Kate answered blankly, "I guess he knows." And she wondered why Daryl had said nothing, and at the same time, she felt ashamed for not reading the papers.

When they reached the square it was vacant, the courthouse dark like an empty medieval castle. A single light guarded the front doors and another the back. They stopped. Kate pointed toward the roof.

"Did you know that if you pour a glass of water on the courthouse roof..."

"Do what?"

"Pour water on the roof..."

"Why would I do that?" Brian asked.

"Let me finish. It's a science thing. Geology or something. Anyhow, if you—or anyone—were to pour water on the roof peak, the half that runs down the east side will flow into the Mississippi River."

"Mississippi? That's a hundred mile from here."

"I'm talking about eventually," she said and tapped his nose with her index finger. "Listen. I learned this from my father when I was a little girl."

"What's he like?"

"Who?"

"Your father, what's he like?"

Kate hesitated, and then: "He's dead. Long time ago, ah, 1920, the flu." After a pause, she shook her hand as though brushing something away, pointed at the courthouse and continued: "Anyhow, half the water running down the roof *eventually* goes to the Mississippi, and the west half eventually makes its way to the Missouri River."

"Why?"

Kate stared at the courthouse and remembered standing there when she was a little girl, with her father, listening to him explain this courthouse anomaly. She missed him in that distant way you can yearn for someone long gone and never returning.

"It's the only courthouse in Iowa," she said, feeling her throat constrict, "maybe the world, where this happens. I guess it sits on some divide."

"Like the Continental Divide?"

"So you *do* pay attention in school."

"Sometimes."

There followed a long pause while they both stared at the courthouse.

"Which way would you go?" he asked.

She knew what he meant but answered with a question, "If I were water?"

"If you could chose," he said. "East or west?"

"Been west," she said. "Can't go too far east, it seems."

At that point it would've been so appropriate for the sky to flash lightning, rumble and spit fat drops so they could end all thought and watch the water divide. But it didn't.

"Can you find your own way?" she asked and added, "Home."

"Oh, yeah," he answered and looked her in the eyes. "Thanks."

"Well, thank-you for walking me home," she said. "A girl hates to walk home alone."

He blushed. "S'long," he said and started to turn. "Thanks for the airplane ride."

"Sure," she said. "Anytime." And, "I mean it."

He nodded, half-waved and started across the square. She watched him disappear around the courthouse and reappear on the lawn beyond. He crossed another street, ran beneath the giant foot and slipped down the alleyway behind the laundry.  She stood on the corner for a minute thinking about his questions asked in darkness and answered, so truthfully and safely, in that darkness to a boy who could never comprehend what he had asked.

She glanced briefly at the courthouse roofline, smiled at her father's memory and walked home.

\*\*\*

A quarter-moon rose late to barely smudge the night. Kate stared through the open bedroom window.  A slight breeze brushed past the curtains and ruffled her hair.  She tried to sleep but thought about too many things—a man who shared her bed and was gone that night, a lover on his way to Spain, and a fourteen-year-old boy who saw through her facade without knowing it.

She turned.

"Have to get up in a few hours," she said aloud.  She heard a dog bark, a steady *oof, oof, oof,* a pause, and then repeating the sequence again—bored barking. Downstairs, Mrs. Denest flushed the toilet, and Kate listened for the sound of her bedroom door closing again. Kate tucked a hand under her head and thought about her flight tomorrow to keep from thinking about today.

Chicago was a long ride in an open cockpit.  Mentally, she ran through the headings to Davenport and the time it should take.  "Depart before dawn; should be a good tail wind," she said.  "Usually is."  She calculated the fuel needed, and then figured how far she could go beyond Chicago.

"Cleveland?" she asked the night.  "Nah, too far; maybe somewhere in Indiana, South Bend or Elkhart."  She adjusted herself, and her mind wandered across the route. She pictured the Mississippi River and the flat Illinois landscape. Then she pictured the billowing clouds and Joe's biplane flying beside her. She tried to picture his face, but her mind wandered again, this time westward toward California. Kate was unaware, but she was sinking into sleep. Awake enough to still feel the cool breeze through the window, she felt herself slide backwards in time.

It was 1929, and she was in Santa Monica—a cool breeze—she stood near the ocean. She walked with someone, and their arms were wrapped around each other.

Kate tried to wake up.

The beach was empty, the surf near and pounding. Mist hovered above the sand, and she could see the pier further down the beach. Someone squeezed her, and she responded squeezing back.

Kate fought to stay focused.

The other person, a man, stepped to block her. His hands took both her shoulders, and his face...

"No," Kate struggled to say.

His face was only inches from hers, and she wanted to reach him, to let him...

"Go away," Kate said and rolled on the bed.

The beach wavered. Airplanes flew across her vision— several airplanes, all in different directions. She tried to stare at the man holding her arms. She wanted to see him, but he looked to the sky, his handsome profile silhouetted by the glare of a setting sun. His hands slipped from her arms.

"Come back," Kate screamed and woke herself.

The room was quiet. She sat up in the bed. Sweat tacked her skin to the sheets, and she kicked them away. Wearing only one of Daryl's sleeveless undershirts, she dropped her feet to the floor and walked to the window. The dog barked again. *Oof, oof, oof*—pause, repeat.

"Cold," she said feeling the breeze dry her skin. She stared through the window at the quarter moon in a cloudless sky occasionally lit by faraway heat lightning and felt the tears in her eyes. "Damn you," she said. "Damn you for coming back." She closed the window and returned to bed, afraid to dream.

\*\*\*

The small room held three men and two women. They sat at tables counting rolls of coins and making notations in ledger books. They worked quickly and only looked up when the boy who operated the counting machine dumped another bag of rolled coins on their desks.

"Hello, Lenny," the man at the door said letting him in. The doorman wore a vest and an elaborate shoulder holster containing a small automatic. He smoked a pipe and held a copy of *Popular Mechanics* in his hand.

"Hello, Paulie," Lenny said. He set his hat on a peg and took off his jacket. "Hot in here."

"Yeah," Paulie said and latched the door. It was heavy oak reinforced with steel rod welded together like a cage. "We had a fan, but it busted on us."

"Hotter 'n hell," one of the women counting money said without looking up.

"Did you call the office?" Lenny asked. He picked a clipboard from the wall and flipped over a page.

"Yeah," Paulie said. "They said they'd get us a new one by morning." He took his jacket from the same rack where Lenny had set his. "That one we had was a piece of crap. I think someone in the front office is buying wholesale and charging the company retail, and at that, they're buying second-rate junk."

"Third-rate," the woman said, again, without looking up.

Lenny shook his head, more of a way to end the conversation than to take sides. Paulie found his hat, checked himself in the mirror and adjusted the brim pulling it slightly over one eye. "Makes me look like a silly outlaw," he said and set the hat straight. "Oh, Lenny, I nearly forgot. Did you want me to take your shift tomorrow for meeting the airplane? I can make the switch, no problem. I just need to tell the missus if I'm going to be home for breakfast. She gets real upset with me when I don't show up when I say I'm going to show up."

Lenny lowered the clipboard. "Ah, no. No need."

"It's no problem, now."

"No, thanks, Paulie. I had a change of plans...I can keep my own shifts."

"Sure?"

"Yeah, thanks."

"Well, if you change your mind," Paulie said and buttoned his jacket hiding the pistol. He looked more like an office worker—slightly chubby and red-faced—than a mid-level manager in a Chicago money-laundering operation.

"Sure," Lenny said and read the figures on the clipboard. The two men were silent while Lenny reviewed the day's receipts. It was the on-coming shift supervisor's responsibility to review the logs before the previous shift could leave. Lenny always checked in early enough to let Paulie get home on time. "Good day?" he asked. Flipped a page.

"Fair," Paulie said and tapped his pipe on an ashtray. The boy at the coin counter poured another bagful of nickels into the counter and cranked the handle. With the free hand, he adjusted the paper wraps, and the loose coins dropped out the other end in neat tubes like shotgun shells.

Lenny flipped another page after first initialing the entries in column 7 on the previous page. Paulie packed his pipe from a leather pouch.

"Smells good," Lenny commented.

"It is," Paulie said. He held the pouch for Lenny to sniff. "It's got a little cocoa blended in. I have the tobacconist mix it up for me special. The missus doesn't care for it too much."

Lenny sniffed the pouch.

"Smells like candy," he said and returned to the logs.

"Actually," Paulie said and put the pouch into his jacket pocket, before he took a match and struck it against the wall, pausing the sentence the way only pipe smokers can. "I think the missus is right." He touched the bowl with the flame and puffed—*Pause, pause, pause*. Blue clouds rose in smoke signals at the ceiling, and he sucked on the stem puffing little tufts out his mouth. It reminded Lenny of the Broadway Limited's locomotive pulling away from Union Station. The aroma became too much in the hot room.

"What's she right about?" Lenny asked, disinterested, although he'd noticed how pipe smokers took for fucking ever to make a simple statement.

Paulie took the pipe from his mouth and stared at it. "This really tastes awful," he said. He stuck it back in his mouth. "But I hate for her to think she made me change." He puffed away.

"Well, everything looks okay here," Lenny said and signed the top sheet on line 42a using his alias, 'D. Martino'. He handed the clipboard to Paulie who signed on 42b with a flourish, 'W. Wilson' and handed it back.

"Heard from your brother?"

"Naw," Lenny answered. "We don't talk much. I guess he likes it okay down there in Iowa. Beats the shit outa me why."

Paulie smiled and gave a puff on the pipe and reached for the door latch, a solid affair resembling the breech lock on a cannon. "I hear they've got some woman flying the run down there," he said opening the door.

Lenny avoided looking him in the eye. "Yeah, I guess," he mumbled.

"Have you met her?"

"Huh? Ah, yeah, I guess."

"And?" Drawn out, teasing.

Lenny looked up quickly then away. "Ah, she's just a dumb broad; you know."

"Uh-huh," Paulie said and slipped through the door. Before Lenny could close it behind him, Paulie stuck his face around the corner. "Certain you don't want me to meet the airplane tomorrow?" He grinned, his teeth clamped to the pipe stem.

"Get outa here," Lenny said and pressed the door shut. He shot the bolt closed on the latch and turned to the room with the moneychangers grinding nickels and dimes into ledger numbers. He watched for a few minutes without speaking. Someone lit a cigarette, and someone coughed. They seemed able to do this without interrupting the flow. The boy at the machine—Willard, he called himself—whistled while running the coins through. He was full of energy and danced a few steps each time he set fresh rolls on the tables. No one paid him any mind.

Lenny walked to his own desk and picked up the phone. After dialing a number he waited while it rang.

"Need more over here," someone said, and Willard danced over with a new pile.

Someone sneezed.

"When we gettin' that fan?"

"That's what I'm checkin' on right now," Lenny said. A woman answered the phone at the other end. Lenny turned and spoke, "Rose Marie. Lenny, here. Hey listen, Doll, I got bad news."

He listened to her figure it out.

"Yeah, I gotta beg outa takin' you to the lake tomorrow…"

She asked if the car was busted—dumb broad.

"No, it ain't the car. I gotta work, that's all."

He listened for a moment with his hand over the mouthpiece while she went on about what she'd been planning to wear and how he was a heel….

"What'd they say about the fan?" someone asked, annoyed.

"I'm waiting," Lenny said over his shoulder, and then into the phone: "Listen, Rose Marie, just forget it, huh. I gotta work and that's that and speaking of which, tell June Bug to send us a couple of fans down here—it's swelterin' ….yeah, fans, you know—round and round blow the air—fans! Whaddya think I mean, Cubs fans?"

He set the receiver down on the desk and stared at the wall. Rose Marie's squeaky voice crackled through the earpiece. Still pissed about the lake.

"Well?" someone shouted. "We gettin' a fan or what?"

"Yeah," Lenny said. "Or what." He glanced at his watch. His crew would be arriving in 20 minutes, and he wanted the fan for them. Lenny prided himself in his relationship with his employees. Paulie was a good company man, pleasant enough to deal with, but gave little thought for his crew. Never unfair or cruel, he simply neglected them and himself in the process. Lenny strove to do better, and it paid off in higher productivity. The receipts proved him out. He picked up the receiver and spoke into it: "Well, do me a favor, Babe. Put it in a cab and get it down here right away."

*Are you payin' the cab fare?*

"Yeah, I'll pay the fare." He sighed and listened while rubbing his eyes. He listened to Rose Marie's voice. A pretty girl—full name Annabella Rose Marie Ricolli— Lenny had known her since grammar school at St. Anthony's and had been her occasional bed partner since they had initially figured out how most of the routine worked. Now, with his eyes closed listening to her flat whining voice, he pictured Kate. She was nothing like anything from St. Anthony's.

"I gotta go," he said cutting her off. "Just put the fan in a cab, willya? Yeah, see ya."

He hung up. Click.

"Say, why don't you folks wrap it up here," he called and was rewarded with dull grunts. "It's hotter'n hell in here, so take off; I'll watch the store."

"We get paid a full day?"

"Yeah, sure," Lenny said. "I'll square everything."

Chairs scraped, and they left. No one thanked him, but the last one out reminded him to get a new fan. Lenny closed the door and sat on the edge of a desk. He looked at his watch again and calculated the number of hours until he saw Kate and tried to think of an excuse to delay her if only for a few minutes. He had never felt like this before, and it bothered him.

\*\*\*

Dawn didn't come up like thunder but, instead, hid behind dark stained glass, revealing itself in whispers. Kate wiped the dew from the Travel Air biplane. She removed the cockpit cover and shook the dew off before hanging the cover on the ladder near the fuel barrel. She wiped the rear windshield clean and took the grease gun to grease the rockers. She was uneasy pre-flighting someone else's airplane, even someone as familiar as Joe. Of course, that might have been part of the problem. She wanted to be close to him at times. She wanted to know more of him, but inspecting his airplane she found too much of him. It was like going through his closet and finding traces of him without him. Where the joystick was worn smooth was where he had held it. The seat cushion was formed to his body. He was neat, the cockpit clean except for the odd scrap of dried grass; the instrument faces polished bright. Kate both admired and felt overwhelmed by the traces of his strong personality still lingering in the airplane. It all made her miss him. That hurt.

Enough light filtered through the far trees to cast a violet glow across the field. There was no wind and a flock of birds dipped low across the runway before heading toward the open fields. She saw Brian's thin silhouette on the highway walking toward the airport. She untied the wings.

"You're up early," Kate called to him. He walked across the runway, water droplets kicking around his feet, the light catching them in tiny sparkles.

"I knew you'd need help," he said. "Daryl isn't back yet is he?"

"No. I don't expect him for a while, maybe tonight."

"How will you get the airplane back here?"

She thought for a second. "Fly, I guess. Daryl will have to drive back out here and pick us up first."

Brian caught the 'us.' "You'll need help?"

"I should think so." She took her helmet from the lower wing and pulled it over her head. "Did you ever learn how to start one of these?"

"Sure," Brian answered, although it was less than truthful. Daryl had demonstrated how to hand-prop, but Brian had never actually done it himself.

"Great," Kate said. "While I'm getting all strapped inside, you pull the prop through to prime it." She glanced at the magneto switch. "It's cold."

Brian walked directly to the propeller and, without hesitation, took the blade. It pulled harder than he expected, but he put his weight into it and after two pulls felt he could teach a class in it.

"Getting any gas?" Kate asked over the cockpit's rim.

Brian looked under the engine. He saw something drip, although what it was and where it came from he could only guess. Smelled like fuel. "Yeah," he answered.

"Okay, Contact, " she called and gave a thumbs-up.

He'd seen it done many times—the downward swing and quick bark of the engine coming to life. To actually '*prop*' an airplane, however, made Brian feel a little intimidated; no, a lot intimidated. But there it was—the gauntlet thrown down by this lady fair and he, Squire Brian, the only potential knight in sight. Time to pull the sword from the stone or go home to mamma.

He grabbed the propeller blade in a good place—not too far from the hub and not too close to the tip. He swung his leg—maybe unnecessary, definitely a little too high and he decided that probably wasn't safe. But he swung the prop and stepped back gracefully as the trailing blade snapped around trying to bite off his arm.

It fired.

It scared him. The way a shotgun scares you the first time you pull the trigger. But it made something sparkle inside him, knowing he'd done it—started an airplane.

Wasn't any other kid in town ever done that. Hell, there was no longer a *kid* on the airfield.

Kate waved and pulled on her goggles. Brian waved back and saluted the way he'd seen Daryl do it. Kate's warm smile beneath the goggles told him he'd done well, and as she taxied away with the first spears of sunlight cutting through the wings, struts and wires making the whole ship look aflame, Brian flexed his fingers. He had started it. Without knowing it, he was one step deeper inside a circle he couldn't yet see.

***

Lenny had been up all night working a long shift in the counting house. A surprise audit from the downtown headquarters had caught him off-guard, but he ran a tight operation and except for a few bookkeeping errors from the previous shift—Paulie's shift—all was in order as indicated by a noncommittal grunt from Dennis the headquarters' accountant.

"Tougher than any tax agent," he was told after the accountant left. "Meaner than Ness. Don't wanna screw with that one."

Now, Lenny drove his Buick into the alleyway behind his apartment. Parking outside the garage, he waved to his neighbor, Mrs. DiGatto. She leaned out her window still dressed in a low nightgown and curlers. She smoked a cigarette and looked drunk.

"You're in late," she noted and waved.

"You've started early," Lenny thought and simply nodded to avoid further conversation. He opened the door and took the steps two at a time to his second-floor apartment.

His clothes stayed on the bed where he tossed them. He wanted to sleep, but something was driving him, an excited energy. Yeah, sex.

He wanted to get to the airstrip and see Kate. He ran water in the wide sink and soaked his head under the cold flow. Barely 9 o'clock, and the morning was already warm—Chicago sticky warm. He ran the washcloth under his arms, sniffed at them and ran the cloth again. He slapped cologne across his neck, and then splashed a bit on his chest and stared at himself in the small mirror over the sink.

Olive skin pale from too many daylight hours indoors; his eyes were redlined, and the skin sagged beneath from lack of sleep. He slapped the skin bringing life to the surface. His reflection looked as though it wanted to slap him back. He flexed his muscles and was pleased with the powerful young body, pleased that he looked nothing like his older brother. He slipped a clean white shirt over his torso. Picturing himself as Clark Gable in *It Happened One Night*—no undershirt—he convinced himself he could stop the woman who flew the airplane. *There wasn't nuthin he couldn't do...yeah!*

\*\*\*

Sunlight warmed the earth, and Kate bounced in the thermals over the checkered farmland. Below was a neatly laid map of little Iowa towns: *Eddyville, Sigourney, Lone Tree*—surrounded by countless fields, some a flat green but many brown from lack of rain. Snake-dancing dust devils stretched from the dry land into the sky above her, unusual so early in the day.

Despite recent thunderstorms the land was dry, the rivers low. Newspapers were full of pictures of the

179

parched land to the south, Missouri, Kansas and Oklahoma. The phrase, *Dust Bowl,* slipped into the vocabulary. She wondered if by late summer, Iowa, too, would dry up and blow away. Then, she wondered who would care.

Visibility was reduced to five section lines or five miles. Kate tried climbing for smoother air. This worked for the first hour, but as the sun burnt the earth and sky, smooth air vanished. She rode a constantly bucking machine toward the Mississippi.

She found Davenport airport. Pilots know that turbulence increases in direct proportion to the nearness of the runway. "The closer you are to landing," she'd said to Daryl on several occasions, "The rougher it gets; like the gods don't want you to make a good landing." But Daryl wasn't a pilot. He didn't believe in the gods of flight. Frankly, she didn't know what he believed in.

The Travel Air sank descending over Division Street. Kate was ready for anything. Her own airplane she could talk to the ground, "C'mon, that's it. Almost there. Watch the cross wind." But Joe's airplane, while obeying her well enough, spoke a different language—at least an unfamiliar dialect.

Wheels touched, and she bounced.

And she landed.

"Thank-you," she muttered to the machine and taxied toward the hangars and the smell of bacon from the cafe.

She glanced at the eight-day clock on the instrument panel—a square piece originally from a Packard and mounted, by Joe, in a walnut frame. She was ahead of schedule.

\*\*\*

"Hello," Brent, the line boy, called. His ruddy complexion seemed ready to burst. His eyes avoided Kate's direct gaze.

"Hello," she said and climbed over the cockpit rim. She draped her helmet over the joystick after first tying it back with the seat belt. She dropped to the ground and almost fell on the line boy. "Oh, excuse…"

"Sorry!"

"Warm," she said and pulled open her jacket. She shook her hair out and stretched to touch her toes. When she looked, again, Brent was staring at her as though he expected her to break into song or give birth or to do anything women should do except be around airplanes. "Selling gas today?" she asked.

"Yes," he said and didn't move. She waved a hand before him. "Oh, ah…I'll get the truck." He pointed and sidestepped away. "It's over there."

"Good," she said. "Maybe, bring it," and she pointed at the biplane, "over here?"

He turned and broke into a run glancing once over his shoulder at her. She scratched her scalp and headed for the cafe. "Nice kid; needs to get out more, though," she said to herself and grabbed the screen door handle.

The door squeaked against the strain of the spring and returned with a sharp clap. Kate caught the dozen eyeballs appraising her entrance. Blank faces all, they, too, waited for her to do something, so she reached inside her jacket for a cigarette and slipped one from the pack and asked, "Anyone got a light?"

Most turned back to their eggs and coffee. She noticed the pilot, Maxwell, seated exactly where he had been the day before leaning over his cup. She wondered if he had moved or had spent the night on the stool. "Mind if I sit?" she asked and started for the vacant stool beside him.

Louie, the cook, slid a pack of matches toward her with, "Egg sandwich, hold the ketchup?"

"Just coffee," she said, and then added, "and whatever it is you're baking there."

"Biscuits for 'biscuits 'n gravy'. Interested?"

She nodded and took the matches. "Thanks, sounds great." She pulled a match and was about to strike when a flame appeared before her face. She recoiled slightly and focused on the gold lighter held by Maxwell. She pointed the cigarette into the flame and inhaled, and then with a nod exhaled a blue cloud across his hand. In an easy move, he snapped the lighter shut snuffing the flame.

"Thanks," she said. She inhaled another lungful of smoke, held it and asked, "Not flying today?" And all that smoke rolled from her head as though her brain smoldered, about to combust.

Maxwell's expression hovered between side-glance amused and downright annoyed. "You making this a regular stop on your runs?" he asked. His voice was as easy as his posture, lazy almost.

Kate shifted her weight and turned to look at him. "Two days makes a run?"

"Being associated with Joe makes a run," he answered and sipped his coffee.

Kate stared, her cigarette burning at the end of two fingers like a fuse. Smoke rolled toward her eyes stinging them. She brushed the smoke away. Louie placed a cup of coffee in front of her.

"Don't mind him," he said leaning close to her ear. "He gets moody when someone's flying, and he ain't." He retreated.

"Just asked a question," Maxwell said.

"A loaded question," Kate said. "Is there a problem?"

"No problem," he answered. "These days, it's good news if anyone gets a flying job."

"Thank-you," she said. "Although, I get the impression you're not entirely sincere in your congratulations."

"Who you fly for is your business, sister." He stared straight ahead stirring his coffee.

Kate's mouth flapped trying to form a retort but Maxwell turned on her, a thin smile on his lips, his gray eyes playful. She was struck with his soft good looks. "What really disturbs me," he said. He nodded his thanks as Louie refilled his cup and slid Kate's biscuits and gravy in front of her.

"Ketchup?" Louie asked.

"Huh?" she said.

"Let's not go through this again."

"Ah, no ketchup." She turned back to Maxwell. "What really disturbs you?"

"The fact that he didn't ask me." He glanced down Kate's figure and shrugged. "Then, again, I guess I never stood a chance."

Kate speared a biscuit. "Joe asked me because he knows I can fly."

Maxwell just grinned.

\*\*\*

# Chapter 9

Throughout the night Daryl listened to the thunderstorms roving far to the southeast like distant artillery. He had stretched a tarp from the corner of the rear cockpit—a length of twine fastened between an eyelet in the tarp and looped around the throttle, from there to a wing strut and then to a stake he'd whittled from a hickory stick and driven into the ground. Beneath the tent, he worked on the biplane's landing gear and waited for the rain.

Mostly, the damage was limited to a bent wheel and popped tire. The gear legs themselves were intact although twisted back where a bolt had sheared away.

The air beneath the shelter was stuffy with that mildew smell of old army tents. He waited for the cooling breezes that were sure to come with the rain. Sweating in the confined area, he swore to himself—severely at first, cursing Kate's name, her mother's name, and finally the names of everyone remotely associated with Kate. After an hour, however, his face running with sweat, his eyes sagging from the heat and stifling air, he swore in vague grumbles, and then only at himself and once at Gavrilo Princip—the Bosnian kid who'd shot the Archduke Ferdinand in 1914, which in a roundabout way led to Daryl spending the night in smelly makeshift tent beside a bent airplane. He'd run out of people to be mad at.

To Daryl, the effort outweighed the results, and he sank into a mood between melancholy and desperation. The sadness he could feel; the unknown fear of being caught by something he could not define gradually squeezed his emotions until, by dawn, he was lost to himself. And the rain never came.

\*\*\*

Dew rolled off the upper wing and struck the tarp with a flat rap, and in Daryl's breaking sleep it was the sound of distant rifle fire—less the volleys of a trench under attack, but more the sporadic crack of a sniper's rifle—desultory and almost insignificant. His eyes remained closed even as his mind tried to waken.

*Rap—Rap—Rap...* The drops struck the tent. He stirred, and the musty smell triggered memories before his logical mind had time to sort half-dreams from damp earth and canvas.

No one knows a soldier's mind, not even the soldier. He keeps the line between past and present well guarded. Daryl had only worn a uniform for 18 months and that so long ago. He wore a physical reminder—the 1918 snake tattoo—but belittled it as a silly reminder of teenage romanticism.

*Rap—Rap—Rap....*

He rolled to one side, his body awake, mind aware but refusing to react. He smelled the canvas and shivered. He drew his legs closer to his torso, his head curling toward his chest. He wanted to pull inside himself and hide.

Daryl hated to wake. It was a time when his brain played games refusing to let him forget or ignore what he no longer needed. In the handful of timeless seconds between complete sleep and the conscious safety of a new day, he sometimes encountered old terrors from long ago in France when he'd been so young.

*Rap—*

He sat upright, his head poking into the canvas, his hair stuck to the dampness and his mind suffocating from a long ago gas attack. He kicked his way through the small opening near the ground and scrambled into the open air, into the cool morning, into consciousness where he could laugh at the receding fears of the vanished night.

"Ha," he stammered, coughed and breathed deep. Fresh air swept his brain. He ran a hand through his matted hair pressing it against his damp scalp to shove his mind back inside its shell. He inhaled and surveyed the runway and the trees and the steam shovel's rusted crane hovering above the knoll between him and the pits.

The air barely stirred, and he began to walk, slowly at first, and then briskly moving clean air across his stiff and wet body. He unbuttoned his shirt. He bent to touch his toes feeling the familiar crack of his back objecting to the strain.

"Good morning," he muttered and heard the tremor in his voice. He felt the groggy leftovers of metabolized alcohol weaken his frame and tap his eyeballs. He wiped a hand across his face in a gesture Kate said reminded her of Wallace Beery, and that was something they could laugh about. He turned to face the airplane.

Sunlight through the trees lit the machine in clear brilliance so he could almost see through it. The night, despite its continuing rumbles of thunder, had been dry. With dawn, the moisture in the air had formed thick dew, which Daryl watched roll from the upper wing and strike his canvas tarp. Moving closer, he chuckled and listened to the flat rap of the drops. He leaned toward it. The sound fascinated him, mimicking rifle shots. He stuck his hand out and caught a drop—cold and silvery, it rolled quicksilver in his palm, and as he tilted his arm it mingled with his sweat.

His mind was clear and, alone on the grass strip, he allowed a memory to peek into his vision: water running down another arm, a tattooed arm that that didn't live beyond 1918. He remembered water running into blood near a muddy sleeve, and he turned away, wiping his hand on his pant leg and switching his thoughts to this 1937 dawn and the runway and the airplane with the repaired gear leg and patched tire.

"Lot of work to do," he said in a voice as weak as an old man's.

He reached inside the cockpit and untied the twine that held the tarp in place. He dropped a corner, and the moisture flowed into a stream and onto the ground. He untied the cord from the strut and pulled the stake holding the other corner. Draping the tarp across the tail, he left it there to dry while he went to the car for a roll of tape. It took a second for him to remember why Brian's bicycle was wedged behind the front seat, handlebars poking into the upholstery.

"Hell of a swap. I send the boy off with my gal, and all he leaves me is his bicycle. Probably doesn't even have a bell."

He looked. It didn't.

\*\*\*

The wing tip Kate had dragged across the ground was chewed and packed with dirt and grass. Daryl picked at the shattered mess with his fingers. He took a knife from his toolbox and carefully sliced away the ragged ends of yellow fabric. He worked like a battlefield surgeon debriding a wound and preparing the patient for transport. The analogy played on his mind and seemed to guide his fingers.

He stretched a strip of tape to the leading edge as though binding the wound. He wrapped it round and round, occasionally tucking in a piece of shattered airplane bone, until the entire tip was neatly swathed and resembled a wing again.

"Good enough to get you home," he said and tossed the empty spool into the weeds.

The sun, by now, was well above the trees and steaming the air. The sky turned battleship gray. Daryl worked until the airplane was patched and ready to fly.

He stood back. The biplane listed to one side on its slightly bent wheel. He had a spare back in the hangar and would swap it later. Walking around the nose, he ran his hand along the black-checkered boot cowl and then over the propeller feeling for damage. Except for a layer of smashed bugs, there was none. He looked through the cylinders for debris and walked around the wing inspecting the leading edge and stopping now and then to scrutinize the odd tear or scratch.

"All in all, a fine piece of flying machine, I'd say," and he did. He stood behind the cockpit and stared at the instrument panel. His gaze wandered across the joystick and throttle and settled on the windshield above the rim. "Now," he said, his voice becoming soft and distant with a twinge of Irish, "If you'd only promise not to kill my Katie." He clasped a hand to the leather trim around the rim and slowly shook his head.

***

Angelo redid the knot in his tie, took his Palm Beach jacket from the chair back and slid, first one arm, and then the other into the sleeves. He studied himself in the mirror, his image deep with shadows from the weak light inside his boarding house room. The blinds were pulled tight against the morning sunlight. He lifted his Panama hat from the dresser, took a few seconds to admire the fresh block and, carrying it in his right hand, left the room.

Along the hallway and down the carpeted stairs to the front room he listened to the old wooden building creak

188

beneath his weight. The only sound came from the landlord absently pushing a carpet sweeper back and forth in the front room.

On the front porch the morning was gray and sticky, the air hot. Perspiration already soaked into Angelo's shirt, and he knew by the time he reached the cafe his jacket would be stained. He'd slept well and enjoyed the part of the day when he could stroll around the square killing time until he met the airplane. Thinking of himself as an independent businessman, he imagined being a part of the Midwestern culture, a leading citizen, or if not, at least a respectable one and, if not that, at least respected.

He loved walking around the town square and wished that something, some feeling of belonging would soon take hold. He carefully placed his hat on his head, adjusted it and set off down the front porch steps.

\*\*\*

Lenny stopped the Buick in front of the butcher shop.

"Good morning, Lenny," the owner called after looking up when he heard the bell over the door. He opened a wooden freezer door behind him and entered through ground fog. "You're a little early," he called from inside the locker, his voice muffled by the thick walls and animal carcasses suspended from hooks. Lenny saw him push aside a string of sausage as though fighting his way through jungle vines. "But I got everything all made up for you," he said and reappeared holding a bag. He closed the door. The handle snapped heavy and cold. "How's business?" he asked and dropped the bag on the counter top. He was a large man, thick in the neck and breathed evenly through his mouth.

"Not bad," Lenny answered and reached for his wallet.

"Hey, no," the butcher complained waving Lenny to put his wallet away. Both he and Lenny knew it was a practiced routine, Lenny offering to pay for the soup bones, the butcher, in debt up to his eyeballs to Lenny's employer, magnanimously refusing payment. Lenny was too young to remember, but in a time before the war when Chicago was a city of wide-open entrepreneurial spirit, the butcher had lost both small fingers to a local 'Black Hand' gang after refusing to pay protection.

A successful businessman, his scales were only slightly tilted in his favor, but his customers never complained. He carried accounts when times were tough and always gave generously when the Church held its hand out. His store prospered, and even if he wasn't loved, he was well liked and more importantly, he was respected.

The 'Black Hand' scares from the turn of the century had all but vanished, so it was with skepticism that he had viewed the crudely-scrawled threats demanding tribute, '...OR ELSE!!!' and the black hand logo.

The threats tapered off, until he completely forgot them. And then, one morning, about four, he opened the shop and, as he entered the locker, heard the door click shut behind him.

Sound.

"What...?"

A flash of lights inside his head.

Darkness.

Upon waking, his legs were trussed in heavy cord, his mouth gagged, his neck tied to his ankles making it impossible to move, and worst of all, both hands were strapped to separate butcher blocks, fingers splayed.

The light was dim, the air cold—perfect for dead meat. His head throbbed, but he could plainly hear the twanging voice that spoke to him from the shadows. Appalled at the audacity, he writhed to free himself. He tried to see

190

over his shoulder, to confront his captors, because, despite his tender position he recognized their voices.

How could they be so stupid? Didn't they know he could identify their voices? He knew everyone in the neighborhood—everyone. He recognized the leader's voice as belonging to a seventeen-year-old who lived above the hardware store a block from his own shop. The boy, and several of his friends, had been developing a reputation for petty thieving, a not uncommon practice often viewed with amusement. Apparently, tiring of small change, they were attempting to revive old fears of the Black Hand.

"Take this stupid gag out," he wanted to shout. "Get home before you find yourselves in some kind of trouble." But he could not shout, and he could only listen to the boy explain the terms of the deal: One hundred dollars per month, protection money, an insurance policy. Simple.

His body shook with rage. No way would he pay the punks. First, he would slap them over his knee and...

He only saw the flash of his own cleaver slicing out of the shadows. In the split second it took to comprehend, he took pride in the fact his cutlery was always sharp, and he saw a fingertip fly across the room before he felt the slam of pain a second later.

The boy's voice was in his ear: "One hundred dollars per month—due on the first." And the cleaver struck again, but his eyes were clouded with tears of rage and pain and so never saw the second finger hop to the sawdust on the floor.

Then he was alone and heard the door click again.

It was Lenny's big brother, Angelo, who found him when he came in to pick up the sausage his mother had ordered. Finding the front door still locked, he had walked around back, then becoming scared ran for Desmond the cop, who, with pistol drawn, crept through the unlocked back door and, with Angelo in trail, found the butcher passed out in his locker; blood in coagulated puddles under each swollen hand.

The 'Black Hand' never made a collection and the cops never an arrest. The butcher turned to his meat suppliers, who seemed to know who should be notified. Within one week, the imitation Black Hand gang members were found in conspicuous parts of Chicago, throats slit, and fingers missing. Somehow, coroners have a way of deciding these things, and it was made known the fingers had been slowly removed hours prior to the throats being sliced—also slowly.

The butcher, minus two fingers, found himself still paying for insurance, but on terms he could appreciate to people he respected.

"So, Lenny, how's your brother?"

"Good, good," Lenny answered and slipped the bag of bones under his arm. "I'll tell him you asked."

"You know, that dog you're feeding gets better meat than some of my customers," the butcher said and laughed. It, too, was part of the routine, part of life in the neighborhood, part of the familial atmosphere where problems were settled reasonably, and friends were made for life. "How's Rose Marie?"

Lenny looked out the window, pictured Kate and answered, "She's fine. Look, I gotta run. Thanks for the—" and he tapped the bag. The butcher smiled and waved him away.

"It's nothin'," he said. And they said their goodbyes. The butcher watched Lenny depart and get into his Buick roadster. He was a good kid. He liked Lenny. He liked the whole family. The Buick, too.

\*\*\*

The dog growled while chewing on the bone. Lenny walked away and wadded the butcher paper before dropping it to the ground. He looked over his shoulder as he climbed into the car and pushed the bag with the remaining knuckle bones aside, an excuse to stop on the way back.

He lit a cigarette and saw the faint outline through the screen door of the woman who lived inside the house. He started the car and gunned the engine before slipping it into gear. He wondered if, after he drove off, she sneaked down to steal the bones from the dog.

"Just like to catch her trying," he said and pressed the gas pedal to the floor. Thoughts of the old woman in the house and the dog, faded as he drove toward the airfield.

The air had a sulfurous stink rising from the marshes and the occasional factory that still had a working smoke stack. Lenny actually liked the smell. It was familiar—definitely Chicago Heights. He always thought if he ever married, and that probably meant Rose Marie, then they'd live in the Heights in a big house. Maybe he'd build one. The company had plenty of contractors on the payroll; he'd get it for cost—one of the benefits of working for these people. He pictured the house with a big lawn and kids playing around a blue Virgin Mary statue, maybe, have lights around her for Christmas.

He glanced in the rearview mirror, stretching to catch his own reflection. He liked what he saw and wiped his hand along his plastered hair, pressing a renegade strand back in place. He wondered if Kate would like him better with a mustache, one of those thin kinds like Ronald Colman's. And he pictured flying with her like Colman in *Lost Horizon*, and crashing in the Himalayas, surviving, and he'd be the hero, because, maybe, she'd have a minor injury and she'd be afraid and reach for him, and he'd have to...

It happened fast. His right front tire strayed off the road onto the gravel, spitting a gray cloud into the air and spraying his fender wells with pebbles.

"Pay attention, meat-brain," he muttered using the nickname his brother had dubbed him.

Annoyed, maybe a little embarrassed, he swerved to recover and over-reacted. Four thousand pounds of bulbous Buick steel shot into the opposite lane. Luckily, vacant. Lenny turned the wheel hard to regain the road but only exacerbated the skid. The rear wheels hit gravel again and seemed to be trying to get ahead of the front end.

"Oh, BULLSHIT!" He spat and slammed the brakes. The Buick shuddered, fish-tailed—first left, then right, then, hitting the opposite shoulder, lost all sense of directional control and spun, end for end, back across the two lanes. Tires screeching, soup bones flying.

\*\*\*

Jack Crowe, 18, stood over six-foot six and had a long skinny nose and a friendly smile, making him look like a scarecrow, which was why he was nicknamed that: 'Scarecrow.'

The Crowe family had come from western Kentucky three years prior looking for work. Since then, his father had passed on—meaning died—and his mother mostly sat on the porch of their rented house in the Heights, watching trains go by.

Scarecrow had found work only the week before, driving truck for a small outfit about a block from his home. The pay was average and the boss not too mean, so he was happy. Except the truck's windshield vent never stayed opened all the way unless you held it, and on hot days, like this one, he sure would've liked the breeze coming straight in. Still, Scarecrow didn't mind.

He rounded a long curve with one hand trying to wedge a stick into the vent to keep it open, the other hand steering the truck, when he saw the Buick spinning across the road like a giant epileptic banana. It suddenly regained control, unfortunately, though, in the wrong lane, nose to nose with the truck.

Scarecrow locked the brakes. The load of scrap iron shifted, over-riding his efforts. For a long second, he stared helplessly, foot smashed against the brake pedal, while the Buick—its driver apparently swearing, fighting the steering wheel, and for some dumb reason, sounding the horn—slammed into the truck head-on.

Lenny only saw the truck at the last instant of his life, and his reaction was mostly bewilderment: *'How-the-hell'd that get there?'* Nature's way of beating fear.

Through the Buick's windshield Lenny went and splattered against the truck.

Scarecrow did the same thing, only in reverse.

***

Kate looked at her watch. "Where is he?" she asked herself, again. She walked—again—to the levee road, looking in both directions trying to spot his car. She remembered he drove something flashy, maybe a Buick, maybe a Packard. Even his name escaped her—*Larry, Lee, Lefty*—? She wondered, with growing unease, if she'd come at the wrong time to the wrong place. She glanced back at the Travel Air. The warm gray sun bore down on her head. Had she missed some instructions to land somewhere else?

She kicked the gravel. It sprayed in a fan across the weeds below the levee and peppered the slime-green water. She looked along the road again. "Little girl," she said to herself, "you're not doing too well."

She walked back to the airplane and sank to the grass beneath the wing. At least she could wait in the shade. From beyond the runway and behind the warehouse past the fence, she saw two cars race from the parking lot. "Little early for lunch," she mused. A third car, long and black, soon followed. "Must be the boss," she added and leaned against the tire. "God, it's hot out here." Then, louder, "Where the hell *is* he?"

\*\*\*

The Ridgemont Apartments, where Angelo kept a room at four dollars per week—towels and sheets included—were managed by Myron B. Enslow, Jr., son of Myron B., Sr., who owned the building. Myron Sr. was 94 and had lived in a 'home' in Des Moines since his 91st birthday when he was last able to use most of his body. Myron Jr., managed the apartments in Ottumwa and waited for news of his father's passing. When he heard the telephone ring at 10:35 that morning, he thought it might be such news.

"Hello," he said breathing heavily. Junior was at least 30 pounds too heavy for his five-foot two-inch frame. Why his father had installed the one telephone on the second floor landing he never understood. "Let the goddamn tenants get their own goddamn calls," he muttered under his heaving breath.

A deep and slow voice asked, "Angelo?" It sounded more like a demand—*Gimme Angelo.*

Myron Jr. was about to ask the caller to repeat himself, when he looked toward the top of the next flight where Angelo's room was. His best lodger, the man kept to himself except to occasionally join him on the porch on a warm evening to share a glass of iced tea. He paid his rent on time and kept his room clean.

"I don't believe he's in right now," Myron ventured. "He usually heads into town about this time—has breakfast at the cafe and then goes about his business. I don't ask him where he's—"

The voice at the other end silenced him with an iciness that disturbed him: "Listen," it commanded, followed by silence while Myron Jr. listened to the static indicating the call was long distance. His own heart pounded in his ears from the walk up the single flight. "Tell him to call in," the voice said. Junior giggled because the voice reminded him of Frank Readick, Jr., on the radio's *The Shadow.*

"In where?" Myron, Jr. asked.

*"The Shadow knows where...whah-ha-ha..."* But the caller really said: "Just deliver the message—please." The last word sounded more ominous than anything else the caller, who probably wasn't anyone's junior, had said. Myron Jr. recoiled slightly from the mouthpiece on the wall.

Finally, deciding the caller had nothing else to add, Myron Jr. said, "Yes, I'll tell him you called." There was a soft click, and the line was clear. Myron Jr. set the earpiece in its cradle and stared at the wall phone for a moment. He thought of ringing the operator to ask where the call had originated, thought better of it and walked down the flight of stairs to his own apartment just off the front room.

Returning three minutes later, "I don't like it," he mumbled and taped a note to Angelo's door. TELEPHONE CALL: 10:35 A.M.; YOU ARE TO "CALL IN." He stared at the yellow slip of paper, folded neatly so Angelo's neighbors couldn't see.

"No, I just don't like it," he said and quickly retreated with *The Shadow's* evil laugh rolling inside his head.

\*\*\*

Angelo slipped into his booth at the *Pale Moon Cafe*. The waitress brought his coffee and unfolded a fresh newspaper before him. "Same as usual?" she asked; her voice rich with experience.

He nodded, tried to smile and spread the paper before him covering the cup.

"Too warm for a kind word?" she asked. He looked up, saw her face—angular with deep lines and straight teeth stained from cigarettes—smiling at him. He folded the paper over his hand keeping his finger on the article he wanted to read first.

"I'm sorry, Ethyl," he said. "I guess it's the heat. It's got me a little slow this morning. You know how it is."

"Nothing like the heat to get a person feeling lowly," she said. "Last I looked at the thermometer it was reading almost ninety, and that at before ten o'clock in the morning." They both nodded their heads wondering at the heat. She was slow to leave, and Angelo made no indication he was in a hurry, although he was hungry.

"You suppose it's gonna rain?" he asked. The words were awkward, his thick city accent labored to form the easy homilies of rural conversation.

"Wouldn't s'prise me," she said and scratched her ear. "You probably want this," she said and waved the ticket.

"No hurry."

"I'll get on it." And she turned for the kitchen, Angelo watching her calves beneath the loose hem of her plain white skirt. Thicker than the magazines seemed to indicate was fashionable he nonetheless enjoyed the view. She made the cafe a place where he could linger.

Turning back to his newspaper, he started to read the article under his finger. VETERANS BONUS. He read without noticing Ethyl staring at him from behind the coffee urn, where she pretended to stack saucers and ignored another customer who waved his cup like a blind man begging.

The cafe rattled softly from the late morning business, mostly coffee-drinkers and the occasional breakfast platter being slid across the counter top. Ethyl went about her work. Hers was a position requiring great vision. It was her presence the regulars wanted, even though they might never say so with actual words—folks from southern Iowa said little with actual words. A tip nudging over ten percent might communicate a secret desire from the man who always smoked two cigarettes after having his poached egg and toast. A knowing shake of the head from Ethyl to a young man who came by at nine o'clock complaining about the lack of work in town was enough to send him back onto the street looking for what he would never find.

Ethyl was a whore—the kind allowed, and men with nowhere to go and no one who could listen to them grumble, needed. The cafe was a man's haven, a place of tobacco smoke and lazy solitude, overseen by waitress Ethyl.

Ethyl was as deeply in love with Angelo as any whore could be.

"Here you go," she said and placed the oval plate, loaded with potatoes, ham and eggs, under Angelo's newspaper. He lifted his arms and pushed the ashtray aside to make room. "Watch your sleeve, there, Ang."

*Ang.* She liked saying his name. He glanced at her. His dark eyes caught hers for the briefest instant before he looked back at the table and carefully folded the paper leaving the article about the veteran's bonus on top. He had circled something in pencil about halfway through the last paragraph.

"Thanks," he said. Again, he glanced at her. Again, she looked into his eyes.

He ain't the best looking guy in town, she thought but said, "I see you're reading about the bonus money." He looked at the paper pretending to see the article for the first time. He chewed silently on his toast and stirred his coffee.

"Yeah," he said and nodded.

"You a veteran?"

"Yeah," he said and thought there should be something else, but the question was far too complicated to answer so quickly. There was so much more to being a veteran than he could tell a waitress between bites. "I was. I mean, I am a vet, yeah. I was in France," and he waved his fork, "a long time ago. You know."

She did not know but said, "Lot of fellas come in here was in the Army, in the war and all." There was a pause while she watched him stick his fork into a neat cube of ham and smear it through the egg yolk. A drop fell to his tie as he lifted the fork to his mouth. She reached to wipe at the spot but caught herself. Angelo was not the type to be told he'd spilled food on his clothes. "I think you fellas deserved that money long ago."

"I don't need it," he said and pushed the fork into his mouth, his thick lips closing around the ham. His eyes looked down at the newspaper.

"I can tell you don't *need* it," she said and tried a laugh. It came out weak. "I seen that Ford you're drivin', and I figure you don't need the dough." She waited for him to say something, but when nothing came she added, "Do you want me to warm that up for you?" She indicated his coffee cup, barely touched.

"No," he answered and looked away from the paper. His face was pulling into a frown. It looked menacing until he said, "I don't need the dough, that's true, but," and he took a swallow of coffee and ran his finger tips over the article about the bonus and said, more to himself than to her, "I still *earned* it."

\*\*\*

The Cook County sheriff deputy waved a car past the wreck. The occupants twisted their necks to catch a peek of gore. Two lanes of pavement stretched across the flat marshlands, past wood-framed houses and the numerous rail crossings and factories—most idle. An ambulance was parked on the gravel shoulder, a tow truck 'wrecker' behind it. The two drivers smoked cigarettes and stood in the shade of a wide tree. A long sedan approached and pulled off the road.

"Where is he?" the driver called barely out the door, which he didn't close. He walked past the deputy almost ignoring him. He was a tall man, middle 20s, with neatly trimmed black hair and a thin bandleader's mustache. He smoked a short cigarette and wore sunglasses.

"In the meat wagon…"

A look.

"Ah, the ambulance," the deputy corrected and followed. "I called as soon as I seen who it was. There weren't nothin' much anyone coulda done, Mr. Trucci."

"Was there a package? Where's the package?" Trucci asked.

"I got that in the car," he answered and pointed toward the patrol car.

"Get it," Trucci said and slowed as he passed the Buick. Seeing the amber smear of drying blood on yellow paint, intermingled with the glass shards staggered him. His legs were suddenly weak, shaking as they had the night when he and Lenny had been caught breaking into a jewelry store vault—actually when Lenny had been caught, while Trucci cowered in the shadows. It was Lenny who took the fall. It was Lenny who had served the time. It had been Trucci who met Lenny the day he left Joliet. It was now Trucci who felt the blood drain from his face as he leaned on the Buick with his hand on the leather seat back, his vision blurring from tears.

"Mr. Trucci, would you like us to take the bodies away?" the deputy asked. Trucci looked up and said nothing. "It's kind of hot, and you know how bodies get—"

"I wanna see him."

"Yes, sir; over this way." The deputy pointed.

Trucci pushed himself away from the car, snagging his suit jacket on a burr of jagged metal. The fabric ripped in a long strip dangling a button. He fumbled at it with his hand and walked toward the ambulance. The deputy knew to stay back.

"In here?" Trucci asked the driver in white.

A door opened, and he looked inside the dark truck, the two bodies laid out still and lumpy under sheets on opposite sides of the truck like they were asleep, camping. He grabbed the side of the door and hoisted himself up and inside. "Which one?" he asked and removed his sunglasses placing them carefully into his jacket pocket. His eyes were slow adjusting to the darkness.

"Which one what?" the driver asked.

"Which one is my fuckin'—which one was in the Buick?" Trucci roared losing control for the first time since he had received the call. "Which one is Lenny, you dickhead?"

The driver, his head snapping from one corpse to the other, shrugged and looked to the deputy. Trucci waved his hand, dismissing the driver, who stood there uncomprehending and unmoved. Trucci kicked him on the shoulder. "Get outa' my sight," he growled. Before the driver could react, the deputy led him away.

"Hey," the driver started. "Don't go kickin' people!" he shouted, but the deputy, who earned an extra twenty dollars per week patrolling the organization's airfield keeping out the curious, pushed the ambulance driver away.

"Just let it drop," he warned.

"I don't let nobody go pushing me around—"

The deputy shoved the driver hard into the road and made a fist as though ready to pop him. "Let it drop, I tell ya!" he hissed, and the driver began to comprehend. He turned away, kicked the road and ran his fingers through his hair. Certain things didn't need pursuing in the Heights.

Trucci lifted the sheet from the body to his right. At first, he was uncertain what he saw. Finally, in the dim light, he saw a face, or what was left, mainly lower jaw and a few teeth, the top portion of the head being reduced to a pulpy mess held together by dark gauze. Only by lifting the covers further, and viewing the clothes—union suit and soft plaid shirt, the collar frayed after too many washings—could he tell it was the dead truck driver. He dropped the sheet.

The long sigh was his own. Trucci looked to the form that had been Lenny. Under the sheet, his powerful, but lean, body looked weak and insignificant. He stared at the mound where Lenny's chest should have been rising and falling, but it was still. He reached to take the sheet where the head was covered, outlining the skull. The shape somewhat different from the friend Trucci knew. He looked to the feet poking from the sheet. Two highly polished shoes, the waxed laces neatly tied. And the cologne, yeah that was Lenny.

"Lenny, you dumb fuckin' dago," he muttered into a sob and left the truck.

"Gimme the package," Trucci said and opened the door to his car, a black Packard, and climbed in without making eye contact. The deputy handed him the package and Trucci started the car. "Get this cleaned up," he said, then before putting the car in gear, reached inside his pocket, pulled out two twenties and pressed them into the deputy's hand.

"That's not necessary," the deputy protested, but the Packard was backing away, almost running over his foot. Necessary or not, he kept it.

***

Kate, her head cradled in her arm, plucked a blade of grass and stared at the road. "Well, Katie-girl," she said, "you haven't even seen your first paycheck out of these people, and already you've screwed-up somehow." She chewed the grass and moved herself to remain in the shade of the wing.

"That's okay," she answered aloud. "You haven't held onto a customer for much longer than two days, anyhow." She rolled onto her back. "I've got to start charging in advance—maybe sell tickets like United Airlines, or maybe, just go to work for United Airlines." This made her laugh. "Imagine that, would you. *'Ladies and Gentleman, I'm you're new captain—EEK! EEGAD! A dame at the controls!'*"

She ran her finger along the underside of the Travel Air's wing, inscribing a line in the thin layer of dust. "Leave it to Joe to keep the underside of his airplane clean," she said through a sigh. "That name again—Joe,

Joe, Joe—" She rolled onto her other side. "Daryl, Daryl—" She sang the names like notes on a scale—Joe up one side; Daryl down the other. A car approached along the levee.

"What have we here?" Kate sat up, her head touching the bottom of the wing. The long black sedan pulled off the road and stopped at the end of the runway. A door opened. Didn't close. Kate crawled from beneath the wing and started toward the man in the light blue suit. He wore no hat—unusual for a day with so much sun, even hazy sun.

"Hello," she called.

He took a few more steps without answering. His eyes sized her from head to toe and looked around as though disbelieving what he saw. "Who the hell are you?"

"Kate," she answered and felt her pulse quicken. "Who the hell are *you*?"

Trucci shifted a package from one hand to the other. He looked to Kate like he might be freeing a hand for a fight. "Where's the pilot of this thing?"

Kate stopped and looked back to the airplane. "He went into labor pains and had to get to a hospital. Luckily, I was available to step in." Trucci started to speak, but she continued, "Don't tell me I have to take a load of crap from every messenger boy in this organization every day I show up."

"How the hell did you get to be a pilot?" Trucci asked. He stood within a foot of her, peering down, squinting his eyes the way he did at anyone he tried to intimidate.

"I saved enough *WHEATIES* box tops and sent in my thirty-five cents," she snapped. "Took about six weeks, but they even included a decoder ring and secret membership card. I'd show it to you, but I've been sworn to secrecy, and you don't look like one of us."

Trucci barely moved his head, his eyes squinting into even tighter slits. "I ain't never hit no broad before, but..."

Kate took a step closer. "Afraid one might hit back?" She stared at his burning eyes for an instant, certain his free hand would suddenly crash into her face making her truly sorry the world was as it was. "Might that package be for me?" she asked.

"They didn't tell me you was a dame," Trucci said, his voice softening a trace. "I don't get it."

"Neither do I," Kate said and held her hand out for the package. Trucci started to hand it to her, hesitated and walked past her looking toward the Travel Air while ignoring her.

"I don't know about this," he said. "Lenny made no mention there was a dame flying this thing."

"Look, would it help if I lowered my voice a couple of octaves? Or, maybe, we could talk baseball and spit on the ground a few times? Would that make you believe I can fly an airplane?"

"This is a lot of dough in here," he said and tapped the package. "You gonna be able to handle that?"

"Well, gosh," Kate answered sarcastically and fluttered her eyelids. "Maybe I jus' might forget my silly self and fly on over to Marshall Fields department store and buy up ten thousand dollars worth of lipstick and cold cream."

Her voice took a deeper growl, "I don't know what your role in this comedy is, but I'm here to do a job, and you're standing in the way, and if I have to go through this nonsense every day, I don't think this is going to work out. Now, you either want me to make the runs or you don't. You say the word; I'll hop into that airplane and get the hell out of here. Then it'll be up to you to explain to *your* boss just why today's take didn't make it to the bank. You want that? You decide. Me? I've got better things to do. You are certainly not my only customer, although you're quickly becoming the biggest pain-in-the-butt customer I've had in some time."

She stared at Trucci, who stood near the biplane's tail, the package secure under his arm, his eyes in the narrowest of slits, his mouth set in a grimace. Kate felt panic wondering if she had just lost her only paying customer. Shit, she hoped she didn't cry.

He was slow. "I don't like it, that's all," he said and set the package on the tail.

"No one asked you to," she said and reached to take it, when he leaned toward her, his face inches from hers. Up close, she could see the smoothness to his young skin with only the faintest of laugh lines creeping away from his eyes.

"What I don't like, I put a stop to," he said.

"Great," she replied.

"You make the run, but don't expect to keep on. You understand me?"

She turned away and reached inside the cockpit for her helmet. Her jacket was draped around a wing strut, and she slipped that on, too. "I shouldn't have to apologize every time I step into an airplane," she said.

"I just don't like it."

"You've said that," she answered and stared at him. Holding her gaze for a few seconds, he finally blinked and turned for the car. She heard his voice in a stage whisper as he retreated, "Don't like some dame mixin' in business."

Kate pulled her helmet tight over her head and tucked the loose hair under the flaps. Her movements were quick, venting rage. She wanted so much to run after him, spin him around and thrust the package into his face with a *Do it yourself!* And then she'd fly away.

Instead, she stuck out her tongue. It'd have to do, since reality held unpaid bills and a flying business teetering on collapse.

She reached inside the cockpit and snapped on the switch. She heard the Packard's door slam and the engine start. Tires on gravel told her he was gone. "A thoroughly less than pleasant individual," she muttered and heard her voice shake, whether from frustrated rage or fear, she couldn't tell. She leaned on the fuselage and wished things were different—somehow different.

\*\*\*

Aloft, Kate's mind raced between navigating toward Ottumwa and wishing she could have told…

*"OH, GOD!"* she screamed and smashed the joystick into the left quadrant while punching the left rudder as hard as she had ever muscled an airplane to turn.

\*\*\*

# Chapter 10

Barely ten minutes out of Chicago Heights, the Travel Air reversed course in a lumbering wingover.

"Crap-Damn-*Shit!*" Kate bellowed—madder with every curse. She wrenched the biplane around, her eyes clouding with tears of utter despondency. "Oh, Christ-Dumb-Dumb-Dumb…" Pointed again at the airfield, she pushed the nose over, throttle wide open, the round engine shaking the airframe, making it feel as though it would hammer itself apart. And she hoped it would—ripped to pieces—*Damn! Shit! How Stupid!*

She glanced around the windshield past the struts and wires, past the spinning propeller disc and the protruding black cylinders. She inhaled the hot blast of burnt oil that wafted back from the straining motor. In short, she was beating hell out of the machine to return to the airfield.

Banking over the factory and rail lines, she pulled the power back to idle, the exhaust popped from unburned gas on hot stacks. Kicking rudder, holding opposite aileron, she slipped over the power lines and low across the levee road, where two kids on bicycles stopped to point and wave. She hoped they had the good sense to stay out of her way, because she wasn't about to go around for anyone's safety.

*Blunk!* The mains hit. *Ba-blunk!* The tail hit the ground, and she fishtailed to slow the biplane's roll.

The tail swung around with Kate jockeying the throttle and riding brakes. She headed back along the grass runway, straining to see past the nose, straining to…

"Where the hell is it?" she begged as she searched the runway. She looked where the car had been, where the airplane had been parked when the package had been delivered—the package with all the money, maybe,

$10,000—where it had been set on the tail and left, and was now nowhere in sight.

She spotted the two kids on bikes and pressed the throttle further, the radial engine barking and clacking, the two kids staring in bewilderment at the deranged pilot heading their way, arm waving frantically above the cockpit's rim. The biplane's tail swung around in a swirl of noise and dust. Kate was climbing out of the cockpit before the propeller had stopped. She jumped—fell—to the ground.

"Hey!" she called and pulled off her helmet, her curly dark hair tumbling over her collar and a wild strand slapped against her face. She asked, "Have you kids seen a package around here?"

The two kids, faces long and disbelieving, stared. One shook his head. "We didn' do nuthin'." He straddled his bike, both feet on the ground. The other kept one foot on the pedal, one on the ground ready to push off. "We was just ridin' across here; honest, (pause) *Lady*?"

Kate approached them running. "Listen—" she caught her breath, suddenly feeling the cumulative effects of 15 years of cigarettes wrenching her lungs. "I lost a package. (*Gasp*) Fell off the airplane. (*Pant*) It's, ah, (*Inhale, wheeze*) about so big; full of...of...laundry." She indicated with her hands. "And is all taped up." (*Exhale*)

Their blank expressions told her they'd not seen it, or if they had, they were playing dumb, having squirreled away ten grand for their college educations—hell, enough money to start a college in Chicago Heights. She sighed, swallowed and caught her breath.

"Christ it's hot," she muttered feeling her heartbeat pump through her temples and seeming to pulse through every strand of her hair. "Look, you want to make some money? Say, a dollar apiece?"

The two boys stared at her, and then at each other. "What do we gotta do?"

Her hand spun in a circular motion. "Look around here for the package." She mimed the size and shape and looked toward the warehouse on the hill, where she was certain her return was causing alarm. "First one who finds it gets two dollars."

"Each?"

"You can't both be first." Her eyes narrowed to slits but knew she was skunked. "Yes. Now, spread out here and help me find the package."

They looked over their shoulders without moving, as though the package would be in plain sight and they could simply point to it and collect the reward—four dollars, enough to see fifty episodes of *"The Midnight Ace,"* or fill their bellies until they exploded on jawbreakers and *Moxie*.

"Could you, maybe, take your bikes and ride up and down the runway looking," Kate said, her voice tinged with impatience. Her hands changed from a circular *go look* to an up-and-down-the-runway *go look*. "One of you could take the left side and one the right. Check the ditches, the weeds and someone's going to have to check-out the swamp."

"I ain't goin' in no swamp, Lady. They got snakes in there."

"There ain't neither," the other boy injected. "There ain't nothin' livin' in that muck but 'skitoes."

"Water spiders, too."

"Look," Kate interrupted. "I'll check the swamp. Okay? You just start riding around and see what you can find." She waved her hands as though shooing them off.

"Which side you want, Les?"

"I dunno, maybe the left. Which side you want, Barry?"

"I dunno, maybe I could take the right—"

"Terrific," Kate said and pushed the one called, Les, along by the shoulder. "Let's get moving—first one in with the package gets the money. Let's go, hop-hop—" Her smile was tight and verging on a growl.

The two boys pushed off on their bikes, heading down the runway at a pace Kate considered slower than she could walk it.

"Uhhh," she grumbled and removed her leather jacket and tossed it on the tail—right where the money had been left. Anger boiled inside her and she wanted, desperately, to hit something—*any*thing.

She headed for the levee road at a trot, again, glancing toward the warehouse on the hill. She imagined the creep who had delivered the money, staring through an office window at her, chuckling at her misfortune while holding the money at his side, having seen it fall off the airplane and retrieved it. Him, she wanted to hit.

Her face recoiled at the watery fart stink from the green marsh. Still on the levee, the gnats were thick around her legs and soon found her face, damp with sweat. She swatted and dropped down the embankment, her right foot slipped on a loose rock, and she fell to her hands and backside, riding an avalanche of dirt and gravel into the sludge.

"Crap," she mumbled and pulled her foot from the slime, kicking at a rusted oil drum, peppered with tiny bullet holes. It lethargically rolled in the goo and rolled back. Mosquitoes attacked her face and arms. Gnats infiltrated her curly hair, and she swung her fist hoping to hit and kill just one.

"This isn't working out," she finally admitted and stared at the vast expanse of putrefying industrial waste. "This aviation business is just not panning out."

\*\*\*

"Hey, Lady!"

Kate turned. The voice came from the levee above and behind her. Les leaned on his bicycle, face beaming, short-cropped hair damp. Kate was poking through some weeds with a stick. It was a pointless gesture, but she had to try something. She had given up trying to keep the gnats from her hair and concentrated on swatting only those mosquitoes actually drinking her blood. She was crying.

"What?" Vicious.

Les recoiled. "Ah, we found your package," he said. "It was..."

Kate missed the rest as she clawed her way up the embankment. "Where?" she gasped, and again felt her lungs burn. She reached for a cigarette but didn't have any—damn.

"Ah, we found it over to the side of the grass by the place where the rain pipe comes outa the ditch where they got that long..."

"No," Kate snapped. Her head throbbed from the sun, and she felt weak from the swamp gasses and heat. She forced a smile and tilted her head the way her mother did when dealing with inferiors. Slowly: "Where is the package?" Smile.

"It's over there." He pointed toward his companion, leaning on the wing of the Travel Air, the package under the wing in the shade. Kate ran.

"Oh," she gasped, reaching for the package. Still sealed. "Good, good, good."

The two boys stared at her, keeping a safe distance away from the crazy lady in the swampy trousers, mucky boots, sweat-drenched blouse and Medusa curly hair pointing in all directions.

"God, am I glad you found this," she said and stared at the package.

"Ah, can we get our dough, now?"

"Huh?" Kate looked at them, bewildered that they should still be there. "Money. Yes, ah…"

She rummaged through her pockets finding only 27 cents, mostly in pennies. The boys flinched when she pulled a knife, flipped open the blade and slit the tape on the box. Cash—bundles of green money tightly packed inside made them gasp. Fumbling through several stacks, she finally found a bundle of tens, smallest thing in there. Peeling one off, she said, "I don't suppose you've got change?"

Blank stares.

"Never mind," she said and pressed the ten on Les, who stared at it, showed it to his friend, Barry, who pocketed it quickly lest it vanish. "You can owe me the difference," she said and knew she'd never see them again.

With that, she folded the box closed and worked the tape as best she could to hold it shut. She stepped onto the wing, and set the box on the front seat, strapping it down with the belt. She gave it a tug. Her brain pounded. She glanced at her watch—Jeez, was she late.

"Either one of you know how to prop a Wright J-5?"

\*\*\*

Minutes later, Les and his friend stared in amazement at the biplane lifting from the runway and watched it climb into the haze over an approaching freight train. They looked, again, at the ten-dollar bill, and then, without a word, hopped on their bikes and pedaled like hell toward town. They had to spend this money fast, before some adult found out they had it.

\*\*\*

Angelo stepped outside the shack at the top of the hill. To his right was the short road leading to the airfield. To his left stood the rusted steam shovel and the superstructure of conveyor belts and loaders rising from the idle mine shaft. He looked to the sky, empty, except for the gray summer afternoon haze and a lone turkey vulture circling in the thermals, waiting for something to die.

A rifle shot snapped from the pits as Benjamin dispatched another rat. The vulture looked, saw no opportunity unless Benjamin accidentally shot himself—a possibility—and flew to the next thermal to wait dinner. Angelo, not thinking of dinner, walked toward his car, gripped the chrome handle and placed one foot on the running board. Deep inside him a swirling anger threatened to rise to the surface. His hand tightened on the door handle, wanting to rip it clean from the car, something he just might have the strength to do.

"Worthless," he muttered. "Every broad is a hundred percent worthless." His voice rolled from his thick lips into the warm air. In fairness he added, "Everyone is worthless." He opened the door and glanced first at his watch, and then at the sky.

"No sign of her?"

Angelo turned. It was Daryl. Unnoticed, he'd walked up the hill from where he'd been working on the wrecked airplane and approached Angelo from behind.

"No," Angelo said. He slid onto the car seat and wiped a hand across his scalp after lifting his hat. "Is this how you run your business?"

Daryl glanced over his shoulder to avoid eye contact. "Sometimes she forgets to come home at all. Then I have to send the cat out looking for her. Very clever cat we have for that. Once, she traced Kate all the way to Cleveland, where Kate was having her nails done—you know how women can get. Anyhow, Kate was supposed to be hauling a load of Norwegian diplomats across country for a League of Nations basketball game, when she read this article about a sale on curling irons—her hair's not naturally curly, you know—and she up and changes course, leaving these Norwegians…"

"Haven't changed much, have you, Fitzpatrick?" Angelo asked. A grin pushed the smooth flesh around on his cheeks.

"I've put on some weight, if that's what you mean," Daryl said. "It's the lack of Army food. Although, you seemed to have slimmed down a trace."

"Someone should have shot you long ago," Angelo said.

"Someone tried," Daryl said. "A whole bunch of nasty fellows in funny metal hats tried. Maybe you've seen them—periodically overrun France, have terrible German accents and a penchant for sticking bayonets into anyone making fun of that Kaiser fellow they all liked; you know who I mean—withered arm, pointy mustache and had a spike sticking out of his head?"

"You're a worthless turd, Fitzpatrick." Angelo's voice was tired.

Daryl looked at his feet. "Maybe you're right, Ang. Maybe you're right."

"I know I'm right."

"That's what I've always admired most about you, Angie. You're unsupportable sense of self-worth."

"Not interested in your opinions."

"And that's another thing I've always liked in you—"

"Get lost, Fitzpatrick."

"Your genuine interest in others."

"Look, if I want any more crap outa you—"

Daryl finished, "Then I'll squeeze your head." He mock laughed, hands on belly—*Ho, ho...* "It's just great to see you can still remember all the clever ditties, Sarg. Did the Army teach you all those cute little phrases in Sarg-school? Maybe they gave you a book, a collection of truly vapid phrases for all occasions like, 'Don't call me *Sir*; I work for a living!'" He forced another laugh. "Or that clever way all you Army-types had to remember left from right by singing such happy songs about screwing and dying with '*gimme your left, your right, now step on your dick, your left your right, your le-e-efft.* '"

Daryl marched around the Ford, singing a cadence and saluting with his left hand. "Kind of makes you want to go back and re-enlist, don't it, Sarg?"

Angelo slid off the seat, his hand on the door, his foot reaching for the ground. Daryl was too busy breaking into a goosestep to notice the huge man's frame suddenly lunge at him, and he barely saw the soup bone fist that slammed into his nose.

It made a sound inside his head like a baseball bat striking a watermelon. Had about the same effect, too.

Daryl fell backward, his hands groping for his shattered nose. Blood gushed between his fingers, and his vision blackened before it returned—blurred. Angelo's voice was clear through the fog of pain that quickly crossed Daryl's face.

"Get up," he snapped, his voice clipped. "Get up!" He slammed a foot into Daryl's side, the blow exploding the wind from his lungs.

Daryl rolled over, gulping for breath, his head swimming in dull pain, blood all over his face and shirt. He tried to press himself onto one arm but collapsed.

"Still a useless coward," Angelo growled. He leaned closer to Daryl. "Someone should have put a .45 to your head nineteen years ago." He squatted and pressed Daryl's shoulder, rolling him until he looked directly into his eyes. Daryl stared, his breath in sobs. "You were a useless coward then, and someone should have blown your useless brains into the mud. And you know something?" He smiled. "It should have been me."

He stood. "Somehow, I figured the war would take care of that for me. What a shame the goddamn Armistice came along too soon."

Daryl rolled to one side and pressed himself into a sitting position. He stared at the ground and took a deep rattling breath. "You're a prick," he muttered.

"At least you still got a way with words," Angelo replied.

They stared at each other for a few seconds, each analyzing the other, deciding what the other was. The anger that had sparked the clash lifted. It was a long wait, and the words sounded strange when Daryl asked, "How old were you then?"

Angelo was slow to answer; to do so admitted he couldn't stay mad. "In '18, you mean?"

Daryl nodded.

Angelo rubbed his chin. "Oh, about twenty, I guess. Damn lot older than you. Hell, you couldn't have been more than sixteen. Probably lied about your age to get in. Tall skinny Mick in a uniform, your Springfield rifle had more meat on it than you did."

"I made less of a target that way." Daryl slowly rose to his feet. His fingers gently probed his face. "I think it's busted. Ow..."

"No 'thinking' about it."

Daryl pressed the tip of his nose. "Jesu-ba-damn!" he shouted over an unpleasant crunching sound. "Yeah, busted."

"Congratulations. About time someone busted your pretty face."

"Thank-you."

"Think nothing of it."

"I don't," Daryl said and leaned against the car.

"You're getting blood and snot on the paint."

"It's all red; should match."

"Good point."

They stood side by side, staring absently toward the shack while neither spoke. Finally, Angelo reached inside the glove box.

"Bourbon," he said. "I don't drink much. I keep it for guests." He extended the pint bottle toward Daryl who hesitated, then took it. Unscrewing the cap, he nodded and took a long swallow.

"Decidedly crappy bourbon," he said and took another.

"Leave it to an Irishman to know."

"Leave it to a dago sergeant to buy cheap bourbon."

"Next time I beat the shit outa you I'll have champagne."

"Too many bubbles," Daryl said and took a swallow. "Tickles the nose."

Angelo's voice softened, "Hey, sorry about the—" He pointed toward his own nose, which now that Daryl looked at it, appeared to have been busted more than once itself.

Daryl grinned, the cracks between his white teeth red from blood. It mixed with the bourbon in a pink mouthwash. "I probably had it coming."

"You did."

"Thanks."

"Don't mention it."

"I won't."

"You got a handkerchief or something?"

"No."

"You should always carry a hankie," Angelo said and reached inside his jacket. "Here."

"No, I couldn't."

"Oh, go ahead. I got plenty more."

Daryl wiped his face and sniffed the handkerchief. "Is that lilac?"

"Yeah." Angelo smiled. "Lady does my laundry sprinkles it on when she irons 'em."

"Nice," Daryl admitted.

"Least your smeller ain't busted."

Daryl drank a long swallow of bourbon. His face grew numb. He felt self-conscious knowing his nose was swelling into something resembling a red potato. "Bet I look like W.C. Fields," he said and leaned to inspect himself in the car's side mirror. *"Ahh, yes,"* he imitated the comedian's voice. *"It would seem the proboscis has taken a bit of a thrashing. Chances are it will have to be surgically removed after an application of sufficient anesthesia,"* and he drew on the bourbon bottle.

Angelo looked into the mirror with him. He cringed as Daryl pressed delicately at the bloody sides of his nose. "You always were a good-looking devil," Angelo said.

"I'll bet you say that to all the pretty faces you smash."

"Well, yes."

"Maybe Kate won't notice," Daryl said and stood. "Lately, she hasn't noticed much of anything away from her airplane."

"Typical dame."

"They've only one thing on their minds: Profit per passenger mile ratios." He looked to Angelo, who wore the expression he'd come to see on many faces. "Don't try to understand. The universe is just too complicated for old dog soldiers like us to handle. It's best to leave everything to the fates."

"Don't believe in fate."

"President Roosevelt, then."

"He's a Bolshevik—"

"Aren't we all, comrade?" He had to touch the nose again. "Ow, this hurts—"

"Fitz," Angelo said. "I never liked you—not then—not now."

"That certainly explains the lack of Christmas cards."

"I may not have liked you, but I want you to know it wasn't personal."

"That's what the Germans said, but they still kept throwing all that explosive nonsense at me—some people have strange ways of saying they care."

"At first—back then, in '18, that is—at first, I couldn't stand you just 'cause you was another Mick screw-up the Army dumped on me; some kid waitin' to get his ass blowed off and make a pile of paperwork for me. I didn't like that."

"Speaking for the platoon, we all sensed the concern."

"Then, after a few weeks, I figured you different. It was after we'd been on the line for about two days. I knew then you wasn't no ordinary screw-up."

"One likes to excel at one's specialty, doesn't one?"

"Now, don't get me wrong here, Fitz. What's done is done. What's past is history."

Daryl frowned. "That's from *Tacitus*, isn't it?"

"A screw-up I could handle. Hell, the whole outfit was made up of nothin' but screw-ups—self included."

"And I thought you were officer material."

"No, Fitz, the eight-balls and fuck-ups are just a part of Army life—something that's always been there, but when I seen you under fire, I knew you was more than that."

Daryl walked two steps from the car and turned. He stared at Angelo, their eyes meeting, and their thoughts on the exact same word: *Coward.* Daryl spoke first, "Can't all be heroes."

"Never asked for that. Just wanted everyone to get in line with the program."

"Never liked lines."

"Army's full of lines, Fitz. Chow line, pay line, front line—"

"Lines of crosses row on row?"

"Life's a line."

"Definitely *Tacitus*," Daryl said and turned to walk down the hill. "I'd love to linger and compare thoughts on Roman historians, Sarg, but I've an airline to run, and airlines do not thrive on memories alone." He walked a few steps and called over his shoulder, "That's *Shakespeare.* But, then, you probably caught that."

Angelo slid across the front seat and started the motor. Easing into first gear he followed Daryl a short distance and pulled alongside him. "No sense walking." The car stopped.

Daryl stopped.

The dull glare of the sun made him squint, and he wiped at the gnats buzzing around his face, drawn to the blood. "When Joe mentioned you were out here, I felt something kick at my insides." He turned on Angelo. "Something I hadn't felt in over ten years, something evil." He moved closer. "I'd thought it was all gone—all the hate, the memories, the fear—"

"The fear."

"The shame," Daryl added and put his hands on the door. "I thought I could put all that behind, put it away somewhere, you know?" Angelo only stared. "Maybe I did put it away, but not far enough away, because when

Joe said you were in the neighborhood... Oh, it was like 1918 all over again.

"I felt the same sweat creep across my back; the same dry throat that came whenever I'd hear your voice giving orders." He pointed an accusing finger and grinned. "You know, you had the same tone no matter what the orders were: *'Pick-up that cigarette butt; get those hands out of those pockets; you, you and you, make yourself into targets for the gentlemen with the machineguns.'*

"Whatever, it was, Ang, you spoke like we were all puppets—yourself included." He shook his head. "You're a strange man, Angelo, a very strange man, indeed."

Angelo said nothing for a full minute, and then reached across the seat and opened the door. "Lemme give you a ride."

Daryl hesitated before he moved around the door, took the seat beside him and closed the door. Angelo slowly let out the clutch, and the car rolled down the winding grade to the runway. They were almost to the biplane when Daryl asked, "Did you like the war?"

Angelo shrugged.

Daryl wagged a finger toward him. "You know a lot of people in funny hats went through a great deal of trouble to avenge the archduke's assassination—"

"Who?"

"Franz Ferdinand, the archduke we all went over there to avenge," Daryl paused. "Wait, maybe he was on the other side...I guess he wasn't important. Still, he did give us a splendid war. Sure you don't miss it, just a little?"

Angelo pulled the Ford beside Kate's biplane, switched off the motor and set the emergency brake. He looked straight ahead through the windshield. His face oily with sweat, his white suit stained gray in large ovals under his arms. He flexed both hands around the steering wheel.

"Like it, the war?" he asked and thought. Then slowly shook his head. "No, but I do miss it."

***

Kate slammed the Travel Air onto the runway at Davenport and was frantically waving the line boy over before the biplane rolled to a stop.

"Get the fuel truck, Brent," she called. "Quickly, please," she added when he slowly turned away.

She was climbing onto the wing, making her way to the fuel tank when she saw Maxwell walking toward her, shoulders drooped, hands deep inside his pockets. He moved effortlessly, as though he had all time on his side—nowhere to go, no reason to hurry. He seemed to glide more than actually step. "Running late?" he asked.

"Slightly," Kate said. Seeing him she felt a trace of a thrill nip at her. "If things can get fouled-up today, they will."

"Bad philosophy." He walked into the shade of the upper wing. He wore his leather jacket, and even though the day was warm, he looked cool. "At least you've been working."

"Huh," she said and ran a hand across her forehead, where curly strands of hair poked from her helmet. "Yes, busy day."

"Busy's good. Busy means customers; customers mean money; money means flying, but then flying means debt and debt means bankruptcy, and that means failure, so I guess busy might not be so good at that." He leaned against the lower wing and chewed a toothpick. "You're not married, are you?"

Kate shook her head and smiled. She waved Brent to back the fuel truck in closer and held her hand for the hose even though it had yet to be unreeled. "No," she said.

"Good," Maxwell said. "Marriage does funny things to pilots."

"You know?" she asked and took the hose.

"Yeah, I do."

The fuel pump engaged and Kate opened the nozzle. Fumes rose around her head, and she stared at the filler neck listening to the swoosh of the gasoline rushing into the tank. "Are you married?"

"Not now," he answered.

"Get your windshield?" Brent asked.

"Please," Kate said and turned back to Maxwell. "What's 'not now' mean?"

"Been married. Just not now, you know—divorced." He said the last in a hushed voice and looked around. Brent snickered.

"How long?" Kate asked. She adjusted her foot against the strut and pulled the nozzle slightly from the filler neck to check the level.

"How long is what?" Maxwell asked, eyebrows up.

"How long have you been divorced?"

"Oh. Lessee, what's today?"

She thought. "I've lost track. Ah, Tuesday?"

"Two years, then," he said. "Three, if you count from when she actually left me—that was a Sunday. I remember, because I had a hangover."

"Do all pilots drink to excess?"

"Don't you?"

"Sometimes," she admitted almost under her breath.

"Then, yes, all pilots are drunks."

"Why'd she leave?"

"Who?"

"Your wife—"

"Oh, God. I didn't know she was here," he said with mock horror and looked around.

"No," Kate laughed.

"Did she see me? I hope not. I had Louie tell her I'd died in a horrible crash while trying to fly round-the-world."

"That's been done already."

"What, crashing into the ocean?"

"'Fraid so. Amelia Earhart's attempt seems to have fizzled."

"She'll turn up."

"Where, New Jersey?" Kate asked.

"My theory is she landed in Wales where she married King Edward…"

"So that's why he abdicated."

"And that whole getting lost over the Pacific nonsense was just a ruse to throw off the press so they could honeymoon in peace."

"It'll be tough to top that."

"No wonder I can't seem to get any backing."

"'Cause you're not a dame?" Kate asked.

"That, and all the really good aviation stunts have been taken."

"Except earning a living at it."

"Oh, now, that *would* be a stunt," he said. "No, I don't think I'm crazy enough to try that one."

They were silent while Kate pulled the nozzle from the filler neck again to recheck the level. Maxwell stepped around the nose of the airplane and ran a hand across the propeller blade.

"I met Lindbergh once," he said. "Well, not exactly met as in, 'Pleased to meet you,' but I saw him once—out here. He came to the airport dedication, parked right where you are and came right into the cafe."

Brent stuck his head around the corner of the truck. "He autographed a picture for me."

Maxwell continued around the airplane and looked up at Kate who was watching him. Her face, covered with mosquito bites, was bright, chicken pox bright. "That's my brush with fame, I guess," he said.

Kate knew she should've kept silent but, maybe it was the sun or the gas fumes, or maybe because she was perched above Maxwell, and she had a flying job and he didn't; either way she said, "I've met him—several times, actually."

She saw the line boy's jaw lower; his eyes stared at her.

"I was at a dinner party in Santa Monica. It was for Bobby Trout and me. We were going to set a new altitude record, and Lindbergh was there. I remember he looked tired. Roscoe Turner was there, too, for a little bit, and then, as soon as the pictures were taken, he left. Roscoe never lingered where there wasn't a news camera."

Suddenly, fuel gushed over the neck, and she jumped, "Nuts," she growled. "Toss me a rag—a couple of rags." She was inching away from the spill when she felt Maxwell at her side mopping at the fuel with a rag. "Thanks," she said.

"No problem," he said.

"Guess I deserved it; dropping names when I should have been paying attention."

"Maybe, but, then, what's the use of having names if they can't be dropped?"

She caught his wry smile and wanted to touch her hand to his sleeve. She replaced the fuel cap and handed the hose back to Brent, the line boy. Maxwell was off the landing gear before she dropped to the ramp beside him. "I'm sorry," she said.

"For what?"

"For sounding like an ass, pretending I'm a big shot."

"We're all family here and not in the least impressed by that sort of thing. Jealous, maybe, especially if large sums of money are involved, but never impressed."

They both smiled, the quiet way people do when they want to say something else but won't or can't because the chances of being rejected or embarrassed appear overwhelming. It was easier for her to say, "I'm in a hurry, could you give me a spin?"

"Sure." Easy answer. "Let's get you turned around." He walked to the opposite wing. "Ready?" She nodded and, with him pulling on a strut and her pushing on the opposite leading edge, they swiveled the Travel Air until it faced toward the runway.

She was climbing into the cockpit when Brent returned with the fuel bill. "Run a tab for me, will you, please?" she called.

It stopped him, and he nodded. "Sure." Then, mumbled, "No different than anyone else around here— *run a tab; pay you Tuesday, catch you next time—*"

Kate settled into the cockpit, pulled her helmet off, and then on, again, to move fresh air against her damp matted scalp. She looked around the nose at Maxwell who leaned casually against the prop. "Switch on," she called.

"Did you really meet Lindbergh?"

She smiled, embarrassed and dropped her head. "Yes," she said, then looked at him again. "Are you really divorced?"

He nodded. "Yep."

"Not just separated or thinking about separating?"

"Nope. All legal—split sheets. She got the car; I got the clothes I have on."

"Any children?"

"None that I recall."

She studied him. "Brakes on, throttle's back, switch on!" she called.

He leaned into the prop and swung the propeller through.

Standing to the side, he watched her buckle herself in and then, she waved him over. Holding his hat against the prop blast with one hand, he leaned toward the cockpit. Kate asked through cupped hand, "Are you sure you're divorced?"

"Cross my heart and hope she dies," he said and held a three-fingered Boy Scout salute.

\*\*\*

Maxwell stood in the shade of *Louie's Airporter Cafe* awning and watched Kate depart. The Travel Air lifted slowly and banked away leaving him feeling empty and incredibly small.

\*\*\*

"You sure you can fly this piece of trash?" Angelo asked for the third time.

Daryl dropped himself heavily into the rear cockpit, his feet banged against the joystick and floorboards. "No problem." His voice was thick from the swollen nose and half-pint of bourbon he'd consumed. "Done it a million times." He slipped the bourbon bottle into the map case. "Just like falling off a wagon."

"Your funeral," Angelo said and cautiously approached the propeller as though reaching for a frozen rattlesnake, one that might just thaw out at any time.

"Now, just wait for my commands," Daryl said. He fumbled under the seat for the belt, couldn't find it so gave up. "Ah, switch is, lessee, it's hot. Throttle's cracked. It's already primed from you practicing, so it should turn right over."

"I ain't so certain I like this," Angelo said, his voice even and betrayed a little stress. "You really sure you can fly?"

"Positive."

"Fly drunk?"

"Safer than driving, no road signs to hit. Now, take hold of the propeller...no, right where I told you and..."

*BRUMPH!*

The engine barked to life before Daryl could finish his sentence.

"Shit—"

He set the engine to idling and then looked around the nose expecting to see Angelo knocked to the ground, his head split open by the propeller. Instead, Angelo stood to one side with a nervous grin of self-accomplishment on his face. He wiped his hands on his trousers and nodded when Daryl caught his eye.

"NEXT TIME WAIT FOR MY COMMANDS!" Daryl shouted above the clack of the radial, but his voice was lost in the slipstream. Angelo waved and smiled, proud that he'd done something new, something with an element of danger, but, more importantly, something that might bring him back to life.

\*\*\*

# Chapter 11

Heat rose from the fields and kicked the Travel Air biplane as though it had no business flying. Kate glanced again between the growing cumulus clouds at the higher cirrus. She knew that the ride would be smoother above the heat, but she also knew, by looking at the higher mare's tales, that what she lost in comfort she now made up for in speed by staying low in the weaker headwinds. She checked her watch for the fifth time in as many minutes and wondered if as airplanes became faster would pilots still be late, and if so, would they be more late or less late or just the same amount of late only more often since they could cover more ground over which to be late. She checked her watch: Still late. She was done swearing; all of her heat gone, and she said nothing, even if it was only to herself, because who the hell else was listening anymore? Oh sorry, maybe a little swearing left in her.

\*\*\*

Daryl climbed to the smooth sky above the scattered cumulus clouds. The cool air rushed against his face and stung his swollen nose when he poked it around the windscreen into the slipstream. His hair whipped against his face, and he closed his eyes. The combination of fresh bourbon in his blood and the satisfaction of making his first solo flight made him grin and then laugh. He could never have imagined how delightful being aloft without Kate could be. Something opened inside him the moment he left the runway; his senses, somehow, became more aware, or, at least, he tried to believe they'd done so.

*But, God, this was dumb…*

Off both sides, the massive layers of wings seemed to be extensions of him. He leaned the joystick to the left, and felt the exhilaration that came with controlling a flying machine all on his own—that pure feeling that can only happen once in a lifetime on the first solo, detached from the planet. Lazy on the rudders, he felt his body press against the side of the cockpit. The biplane slipped in the half-assed turn. He rolled level, and then, leaning to his right, he rolled his way into a bank in that direction. Mostly, he fell out of the turns and slopped around the sky.

"Giving a thoroughly amateurish performance," he shouted. "Kate's mentioned something about this sort of pilot technique. Oh, yes, I remember, now. She said it was less than adequate."

He mushed into another mess of a turn, the wind curling around the windscreen to pummel his face. "She may have been right."

Fear reached an icy finger under his shirt.

He reached inside the map case and pulled out the half-empty bottle. Offering a toast to the gods, "Here's the reason there are no reasons," he raised the bottle to his lips. Taking a swallow, he saw his hand shaking and quickly took another. "And with reason for all, and to all a good night." He drank the rest and tossed the empty overboard. "Oh." He looked over the side. "I hope there wasn't a deposit on that."

***

Her landing was good. Even Angelo had to admit that, and he did, which was what surprised the hell out of Kate.

"How would you know a good landing?" she asked, her voice not so much unfriendly as it was cautious.

"Can't a girl take a compliment?" Angelo asked.

"All depends on what's behind it," Kate said. She climbed from the rear cockpit onto the wing, reached inside the front hole and unstrapped the box. "Sorry I'm late," she said and handed it down.

"No one said you were." He took the box and his fingers instantly found where the tape had been cut and patched together. His eyes caught her.

"I had expenses," she said. "You'll have to deduct ten dollars from my pay. You can count it."

"Never open the box," he said evenly and walked to the car. He tossed it onto the seat so casually that it made her whole trip seem insignificant. "Payday's on Friday. Don't ever open the box again."

Kate almost protested, but saw the even stare, the cold determination in his eyes, a look she herself could give and reduce Daryl to pulp when needed, a look she knew to use sparingly. Confronted by it now, she knew to acquiesce. "Right," she said.

Angelo opened the car door and placed a foot on the running board. "Daryl finished your airplane."

Kate looked up. "I'd forgotten," she said and glanced down the runway where the Nash was still parked. "Where is it?"

"He left," he said and dropped heavily onto the driver's seat and closed the door. "Said he'd gotten tired of waiting for you." He reached for the starter and called as he pointed to the Travel Air, "You need help propping that thing?"

Kate looked at him, confused. "No, ah, thanks. I can...who'd you say flew it out?"

"I didn't." Angelo hit the starter. "But it was Daryl." He backed around her wing, pulled forward and stopped. "Did a damn pretty takeoff, if you wanna know." He slipped the car into first and said, "See you tomorrow. And don't make me wait." He left.

She watched the Ford bounce along the runway, turn and climb the short grade up the hill and disappear around the trees. A gust of hot wind rustled the leaves behind her and carried the dank smell of the low river toward her. Kate looked up and down the runway. She looked at the hazy sky with its small clusters of boiling clouds. She ran her fingers through her hair and slowly dropped to the ground where she laid in the shade of the wing, her thoughts a jumble of images and half sentences. She felt the day slip around her, passing her as though whatever she did, nothing mattered. Something else was dictating the outcome; someone else was making all the decisions while she simply passed through without control.

And there, outlined in sunset, Kate saw Benjamin with his .22 rifle tucked under his arm, a string of dead rats—like catfish—dangling against his legs as he walked out of sight.

\*\*\*

"Piddle on me, that's a short bastard," Daryl swore and mashed the throttle against the stop trying to out climb the row of trees at the end of the runway.

The biplane wallowed through the hot air, the wings shuddering above stall, and the engine coughing from the sudden flood of gas dumped into the carburetor by Daryl's panicked go-around.

"Seventh time's a charmer, they always say," he said and banked toward the downwind for another try at landing. "I will admit," he said to himself, "Landings are not my strongest talent."

Below, outside the hangar Brian stood with hands shading his eyes against the sun as he watched Kate's biplane circle the field for another try. On the second pass, he'd noticed Daryl at the controls.

"That ain't right," he mumbled.

Each time the biplane glided across the road and settled toward the runway, he could feel himself trying to will it to land, to make Daryl get that joystick back in his lap.

"Too high, too high," he muttered. The biplane banked from downwind. Brian heard the engine bark, Daryl unsure where the power should be. "Cut the power," Brian snapped. "Cut it."

For a brief moment he thought the approach would work. Daryl seemed to drop smoothly into the slot on final with the wings rolling level as it crossed the road. But, slightly high, the nose suddenly rose.

"Too high!" Brian shouted and waved his arms. The biplane slowed. The wings shuddered like arms that held a laundry basket too long and just wanted to let go. He waited for the gust of power that would take it around again.

Daryl worked his shoulders like a prizefighter too punch drunk to know he's been defeated.

"Watch the airspeed, watch the airspeed," he repeated and ignored the airspeed indicator. Eye on the runway, he cut the power and banked toward final, his natural tendency to dive in a turn the only thing saving him from breaking into a spin. He leveled onto a good final—good alignment, good luck. He glanced at the airspeed and hoped that was good too. Things were a little vague in his brain as to what a good speed would have been. "Something in the 70's, maybe," he said, or thought. It was hard to tell which. He kicked rudder to see past the nose and felt the airplane settle. He straightened and, again, the nose dropped. Airspeed shot up. He saw the road slide beneath and pulled back on the stick. "Too high," he thought.

"Screw it," he said and sucked the joystick full back into his lap.

A ballooning pause before: *WHA-WHUMP!*

The gear impacted the ground, and for the second time that day Daryl had the wind punched from his lungs. Up the biplane bounced like a winged buffalo reaching for the sky.

"Ahhh," he stammered when the wings quit flying, again, and the whole structure of tubes, spars, cloth, dope, rubber, metal, gas and oil and half-drunk, busted-nose Daryl Fitzpatrick gave one death-heaving shudder 30 feet above the grass—slightly above the level of the hangar— and then almost with a shrug, as though saying, *'I can't take any more of this abuse,'* it broke into a stall.

Had there been a thousand feet of empty sky below, would have done a nice spin to the left. Instead, it smacked the earth.

Brian was running toward the wreckage even before all the sound had reached him. It reminded him of the time he had stacked packing crates on the Burlington Northern tracks and hid in the bushes waiting for the 6:14 to roar through. When the train hit—the engineer decided it wasn't worth stopping for—the instant violence of machinery splattering crates into a spray of kindling impressed the hell out of him. The impression stuck, and Brian, now running toward the biplane with its nose in the turf, felt the same thrill he'd experienced before.

"Daryl!" he called. His voice cracked. "Daryl!"

He clawed his way onto the mangled wing and reached for the cockpit rim where he could see Daryl's head bob from side to side. Alive! Getting a grip on the fuselage, his sneaker punching through fabric, he reached for Daryl.

Eyes half-shut, face bloodied, Daryl mouthed the same unintelligible words over and over. It was only as Brian anxiously pushed his head to one side that he could hear them: "Hell of a way to run an airline—"

"Drunk," Brian said and pulled his hand away. "Piss drunk and flying."

"Now wait a damn minute, there, Skippy—"

"You're drunk! You can't do that."

"I would have to agree with you—I can*not* land an aeroplane—"

"I mean, you can't do this to, to her, to the airplane— Kate's airplane."

"It's not all hers," Daryl tried to defend himself. "Although, I must admit most of this does belong to her." He spit blood at the instrument panel and tried to wipe it away with his sleeve. "She isn't around is she?"

"What difference does it make?" Brian's voice peaked beyond puberty and into adult rage.

"We mustn't let her find out," Daryl said in an Oliver Hardy whisper as though confiding with Stan Laurel. "Help me out. I seem to be stuck."

"Help yourself out." Brian jumped down. "You're drunk!" He punched the fuselage, and then kicked a hole in the wing.

"There now," Daryl called. "You'll wrinkle the fabric." He pushed himself halfway from the cockpit and stopped, head dangling. "I really should have been wearing my safety belt. This could have been a fairly serious predicament I'll dare say."

Letting his arms drop, he hung over the side like a dead man, the blood running from his mouth onto the fuselage, eyes bulging under the pressure, his fingers dangling toward the ground. "Quick," he called. "Someone call the squadron commander. Captain Fitzpatrick has been shot through and through by the unholy Hun."

*"Drunk!"* Brian shrieked and kicked the wing again, punching another hole.

"Blast you, Lieutenant, those Germans are shooting again—nasty habit they have of that—return fire, avenge the archduke's sacred memory! Avast, ye pimpled blackguards—" He spat blood again. "Quick, now before they shoot us down for I doth feel my senses flagging." He looked up. "Where is that bourbon bottle? You there, boy, fetch me the bourbon, if you'd be so kind."

*"Drunk!"* And the wing took another hit.

"Have you perchance seen where I dropped the bourbon?"

Brian kicked holes until the wing was peppered with a neat row and he ran out of wing. By then, he was crying. He sniffled and wiped at the tears with his sleeve. He turned, walked a few steps and sat, plucked a blade of grass, stripped it into two halves and dropped them both to the ground.

Daryl hung by his waist. His brain was numb. The enormity of his misdeeds prevented him from moving. He merely stirred his fingers watching them twitch beneath him. He walked one hand up the side of the fuselage until it was within inches of his face.

"Hello there," he said in a high voice. "Come to visit Uncle Daryl? He's been a big dumb Mick again. Broke Katie's airplane all to pieces, and now's he's likely to catch hell when she—" And he heard the familiar clacking of the Wright J-5 engine approaching from the east. "There she is now," he said and reached inside the cockpit to pull himself up. Brian watched from a short distance away. Still seated on the grass, his eyes red but quiet, he merely watched.

"It's okay," Daryl called. "I can get myself out. Thanks for offering." He pressed himself on one hand and reached for a strut with the other. "Almost there.

Won't be but a minute." He inched a leg out and pushed against the instrument panel with his knee. Glass crackled. "Don't worry. We can fix that; we can fix anything." Out his leg came—

*   *   *

"I've seen crap fall off a cow's ass better than that," Brian said looking down at Daryl, a heap at his feet, head on the ground, one leg caught on a jagged edge of the twisted wing.

"Do I sense disapproval?"

Brian ignored him and unhooked Daryl's pant leg from the wing. The leg fell as though dead.

"Much obliged," Daryl offered and rolled onto his back just as the Travel Air flashed overhead, banking into a climbing turn, Kate's face peering over the cockpit rim with the glare of a pissed-off nun. "Be sure to wave," Daryl said, and he did. "Oh, she's mad." He looked at Brian. "Do you think she's mad at us for smashing the hell out of her aeroplane? It'd be so like her to start making accusations before getting all the facts."

He pushed himself onto his knees and ran a finger through his mouth counting teeth. "She's so unfair at times." He spit blood. "Good thing the girl can't live without me—Oooh, that hurt—or I'd simply dump her. Be for her own good." He finished counting teeth. "All there."

"She's landing," Brian said.

"What? Here?" Daryl stood. "The woman's insane. Doesn't she realize this runway's completely unsafe? Should be declared a hazard, a nuisance to aerial navigation. I think I'll cable the Secretary of Commerce immediately." He turned to Brian. "Say, you wouldn't happen to have a spare Western Union form on you?"

Brian ignored him and watched Kate slipping the Travel Air across the road. One wing low, the fuselage cocked into the descent, she came down as though guided by a wire, and just before touching, eased rudder and aileron rounding out to a smooth touchdown.

Daryl arched his eyebrows, "Truly impressive landing. *Brava!* Do you know her? Does she have large breasts? It's important pilots have large breasts, you know."

The Travel Air rumbled past, the tail swinging and bouncing through the ruts. A burst of power, and she turned to taxi back. Stopping briefly at the wreckage, she took a quick inventory of the damage, including Daryl, now waving and smiling, blood clotting at his lips. She pointed at Brian and waved him forward.

"Can you drive the Nash?" she called against the engine noise.

"Yes."

"Get in."

He scrambled up the wing and opened the half-door to the front cockpit.

"Strapped in?" she called, and after a few seconds Brian waved back at her—yes.

Without a glance at Daryl she taxied back down the runway, turned and took off. Daryl stood waving. He waved until the biplane was a smudge against the afternoon sky, and he only dropped his arms when the sound blended with the hum and chatter of the insects in the corn.

Kate did look back at Daryl. She saw an airfield with two cheap buildings and a crumpled biplane two-thirds of the way down the runway. Standing beside the biplane, like some castaway awaiting rescue on a deserted island, was Daryl.

His long Irish face was discernible for some time, and his pathetic constant wave at her retreating airplane made her eyes swell with warm tears—tears that flowed across her cheekbones and collected in the rubber cups of her goggles until she was forced to push them back against her forehead. Only then would the tears dry. Only then, with the wind of flight howling around the cockpit, and the rage and pity gripping her throat until she had to cough with fury and heartbreak, only then did she decide.

$$***$$

# Chapter 12

## Late Summer
## Chicago Heights

"Say 'Hi' to Ang for me," Trucci said through a quick smile and closed the car door.

"I will," Kate answered and climbed onto the Travel Air's wing root and leaned into the forward cockpit to secure the package to the seat. She heard the car back across the gravel road, and she looked up from her work to watch him leave. She hated to admit it, but he was handsome.

Older than Lenny and more confident in his moves, Trucci exuded an air of controlled temper, a personality of violence held in check by a veneer of good looks, smart clothes and amused cynicism.

Slowly, over the summer, Kate had learned of his friendship with Lenny. Trucci gave her bits of insight into his life, but he did so in measured increments, carefully doling out the information, a brief lesson each day when he met her at the airfield. Each day lingering a bit longer than the day before. Altogether, he'd provided only a shallow image of himself. She knew he lived alone, in a better than average apartment. He rented; hated the thought of buying, thought prices were too high. He liked black cars; nothing smaller than a Packard, which was why he drove one, and she didn't even have to ask.

Trucci smoked Lucky Strike cigarettes but never offered her one; probably thought women shouldn't smoke. He never smelled of booze and, other than reminding her what he thought of women flying, "It's just wrong," he never commented on her sex or any sex or sex whatsoever. Probably why she found him so sexy.

242

Kate finished strapping the package to the seat when she noticed a small envelope taped to the package like a packing invoice.

*KATE*, her name printed in neat letters.

Her pocketknife slit the tape, and she slowly opened the envelope. Something slid out, and she grabbed it before it disappeared beneath the seat.

A medallion dangled from a fine silver chain. It turned at the end of the chain, and she raised it to her eyes. Sunlight flashed against the chain, but the medallion, itself, was a dull thick piece the color of lead, maybe, pewter. It looked old. It twirled before her eyes, and she hesitated before reaching with her other hand to stop it.

A man carrying a child through a river. They both wore robes, and the man leaned on a staff while the child held a chubby hand out as though blessing the holder. Their heads were ringed with haloes with the child's a double-halo as though of saintlier grade. The man's expression said, *"Jeez, you're heavy,"* in an Edgar Bergen voice.

Kate tapped the medal setting it to spin. The obverse child and man twirled round and round, their image in a ghostly ball blending with the smooth reverse where something was inscribed.

She took the medal in her hand and turned it over. At first she thought the three ornate words to be some Latin phrase, a secret code between Catholics, a trace of the arcane religion her Presbyterian mother viewed with scorn on the rare occasion she admitted the existence of Catholics at all, mostly when they delivered coal or cleaned out her gutters. "Those *macaronis*," she called them, lumping all papists together as Italians in her mind, despite having married one. And, then before she could remember the loss, she'd sniff the air and take another sip of Templeton Rye. "Daryl," she would say when pressed, "was fine," because he was "Orange Irish." He wasn't.

## KATHARINE MARIE STRAUSS

Her name, inscribed so deliberately on the medal made her stop. He knew her name—*all* of it and how to spell it with an "a" in the middle. He'd had it printed on this talisman, this mystic charm to St. Christopher. How long Trucci had carried her name with him she could only imagine. That he had found the courage to give it to her....

She was repulsed. She looked at the medal, and then away and quickly stuffed it back inside its envelope and held it for a moment.

"Oh," she breathed out in despair. "How dare him; how God Damn dare him?" She thought of throwing the envelope away but pushed it into her pocket and reached inside the cockpit and switched on the magneto.

"This, I don't need," she said and jumped from the wing. "Why the hell can't they just leave me the hell alone?"

She rounded the wing and reached for the prop. Throwing all her weight into it, she swung through, and the engine popped to life. It didn't dare not.

"I don't ask for their nonsense," she yelled at the spinning disk. "I really don't." The airplane agreed; again, daring not disagree.

She took a step and re-addressed the airplane as though confiding in a friend: "When have you heard me say to him, 'Hey, I think you're cute, please take me home to meet your Italian mamma, so we can get married and have bambinos.' Huh?"

The airplane, being polite, shrugged, a little embarrassed and unsure how to respond.

"When have you heard me say that? I'll tell you when: Never. That's when."

She kicked the ground and stomped around the wing. "Never!" she yelled at the airplane. "I didn't say it to Daryl; I didn't say it to Joe, or to, to—ahhh—to anyone." She climbed onto the wing and snatched her helmet off the stick. Pulling it over her head, she tucked her loose hair underneath and threw a leg over the cockpit rim.

"All right," she admitted. "Once. Just once I said it." She stared into nothing. "But that was years ago, and he's dead now. You're dead. You're dead. You're dead, and that was a long time ago."

She dropped onto the seat and felt her hands automatically go for the seatbelt, throttle and stick. "That was California, and that was a long time ago—" Her voice trailed away. There were no tears, no lump in the throat, just a blankness of feeling that came when she stumbled onto a memory. And the biplane understood this.

\*\*\*

Trucci stood where he did each day when Kate flew away, alone outside the warehouse beside a stack of barrels where no one could see him. He watched her start the engine and walk around doing what he assumed was her pre-flight, something she had explained to him the day he brought her lunch—*"Here, I thought you might be hungry. It's sausage and peppers. I hope you like iced coffee; that's what's in the thermos. You don't gotta drink it or nothin'."*

Now, he watched her biplane taxi, turn at the end of the field and fly out. He watched her bank away and disappear to the southwest. He walked inside feeling the same uplifting emptiness except, today, he felt an added burden—fear. Fear that he'd done something completely stupid.

\*\*\*

## Elizabeth, New Jersey

"You don't go to Spain, so quit asking."

Joe followed Frank Deagan around the huge hangar, their footsteps echoed against the concrete floor.

"Look, Frank, I signed up to fly in Spain—"

"You signed-up to fly," Frank replied. "You fly where and when we tell you."

"And you told me I'd fly in Spain—in fighters. You said you needed fighter pilots not cab drivers. I could go to New York, if I wanted to be a cab driver."

Frank turned. His head was beaded with sweat, his eyes tired. He was shorter than Joe and weighed at least 30 pounds more. He pointed. "New York's that way; be a cab driver."

"I don't want to be a cab driver."

"Good, 'cause you'd never get a hack license."

"I want to fly fighters."

"I never said you'd be a *fighter* pilot."

"All right, not you, but the guy that gave me the sales pitch. Zwillman—"

"It wasn't Zwillman."

"Okay, whoever it was—"

"No one talks to Zwillman."

"Fine." Hands up. "Whoever it was, said I—"

"I don't care what you claim anyone said; I never said you'd go to Spain. I don't say those kinds of things. I'm not that kind of person. *'Go to Long Island,'* maybe; *'Go to Scranton,'* possibly, but Spain? Never. I make it a rule never to send pilots to Spain." He threw his clipboard onto a toolbox beside a Lockheed Vega and opened its door.

"Frankie, I'm bored," Joe whined.

"Joey," Frank whined back, "I don't care. Now, go away. Go eat some lunch, take yourself a shave."

"I don't need a shave."

"Then eat some lunch."

"Not hungry."

"Then just go away. See a movie. Here." He tossed a quarter and climbed inside the Vega.

The coin bounced on the floor. "I want to go to Spain."

Frank's voice came back muffled by the airplane. "Then go. Go to Spain for all I care. But don't bother me about it. I can't shit you to Spain, all right already?"

Joe turned and picked a wrench from the toolbox. He tossed it lightly in the air and caught it behind his back. "I thought you were all fired-up to fight the fascists and wanted guys like me to shoot them out of the skies for you."

Frank's head poked through the cockpit window of the tall cabin monoplane. Given Frank's look, Joe knew he was about to get a speech.

"Fascism is on the run, Joseph. The workers' revolution will soon liberate the oppressed masses. The Messrs. Hitler, Mussolini and Franco are on the run; their days are numbered. Righteousness always conquers over might, and, and all that bullshit, I forget how the rest goes, something about evil...Point is, when the United States comes to its senses, when it finally sees what's going on in Spain—"

"Just what *is* going on in Spain?"

"When the American people—and I don't mean those politicians, including Mister *Rooooo*sevelt, but the good, hard-working, dues-paying masses see what a threat fascism is—"

Joe yawned.

"Well, something will just have to happen. It's just that simple."

"Do you believe all of that?"

Frank shifted. "No. Not the flowery parts, just, well, just some of the stuff about making fascists run. I just think fascists should run, that's all." He thought for a second, and then, "Now go away, I've work to do if the fascist are to be kept running."

"How many fascists are here in Jersey?"

"You'd be surprised. And don't call it Jersey, unless you grew up here. It's *New* Jersey to you. Now, beat it." Frank pulled his head inside the cockpit, like an eel done explaining sea life to a toad.

Joe set the wrench on the toolbox and looked around at the hangar. The Vega was being readied for shipment to France, where it would be off-loaded in Marseilles, stripped of all identification numbers, reassembled and flown into Spain for use by the Loyalist forces. Once in the hands of Spanish pilots, Joe thought, it wouldn't last a day against the fascists.

Men like Frank—a lackluster communist with organizational skills but too old, fat and worn out to fight—kept an eclectic supply of arms, money, airplanes and zealots flowing through underworld channels into Spain. It was an odd alliance between gangland mobsters—capitalists all—and Stalinists determined to bring down capitalism at any cost provided they could find the investment capital at good rates. Hence the mob.

Adventurers, such as Joe, motivated by everything from fanatical leftist passion to level society, to pure opportunism, made up the international force flooding in ahead of the supplies. Most of them wouldn't last a day against the fascists, either.

To Joe it was simple, although not exactly what he'd told Kate he'd be doing. If he got to Spain, he'd fly, shoot down fascists and collect a fat bounty for each confirmed kill. Not that he had anything against Franco, or was even sure who he was, but the Loyalists had made the best offer. Now, it seemed they were more eager to have him act as ferry pilot up and down the East Coast, bringing in the airplanes to be shipped.

"I'm going out," he said.

"Mmm."

"You want anything?"

"Ah, no," Frank answered. Joe started to leave, and Frank called after him, "Be back by one; we've got a line on a Stinson SR down in Virginia. May need to run after that one tonight."

"Yeah, sure," Joe said. He went to leave but turned to pick up the quarter before walking through the hangar into the milky New Jersey sunshine. "Oh, how I hate this place," he said looking around at the marshland and distant refineries. The air smelled of sulfur and unidentifiable smells from the smoke stacks upwind. He listened to an engine run up behind him and turned to watch a Fairchild 24, cabin monoplane with a long-nosed Ranger engine, rise from the heat and bank toward Staten Island. As large as the airport was, little actually flew. Few had money. And no one seemed to care.

Joe walked slowly along the ramp toward the asphalt road that led to the highway. He could've taken the car, but he had time to waste. Lots of it.

Entering the diner, he tossed his hat on the counter and grabbed the menu from behind the sugar. He knew it by heart and disliked everything on it. He glanced at a truck driver seated alone at the far end of the counter. He methodically scooped mashed potatoes into a wide face and alternately wiped sweat from his upper lip and gravy from his chin. He read the *NEW YORK DAILY NEWS*, folded in half, opened to the sports page. One corner kept dipping into the gravy.

Beverly, the waitress approached. "Hey, Joe, whaddya know?"

Joe's rehearsed reply: "Just got back from the girlie show."

She slid a coffee cup in front of him. It was the same greeting every time. He looked up at her. Somewhere in that vague feminine range between 30 and 50, her good looks were mostly the product of heavy make-up and big tits. She, too, sweated but didn't seem to mind. "Is it just me, Beverly?"

"Probably," she answered.

"Am I the only one who thinks Jersey smells like a cauliflower fart?"

"It's you," she said. "What'll it be?"

Joe shrugged and gave a quick look at the menu. "Ah, just bring me a sandwich, ah, ham salad, no, make it chicken; hell, it's probably the same thing."

She nodded—yes, no, who cares.

Joe looked at the truck driver now loading his fork with pale green peas. "No, bring me what he's having," he said and poured cream in his coffee.

"Whatever you say, Hon."

Beverly left, and Joe turned on the stool to look out the windows at the highway. Cars streamed past. One turned off the road—a 1935 Studebaker Dictator. He loved that name. "Marketing genius," he giggled, "Must sell out in Rome."

No one listened, but two men dressed in square suits walked inside and took a booth by the door. The diner was small, and their presence annoyed Joe, so he turned three-quarters away so he could watch them without seeming to do so. He heard the one say something about the New York Yankees. The other one belched and swatted at a fly. He missed—a Red Sox fan, no doubt.

"Be right with you boys," Beverly called to them, and they didn't answer.

Joe stirred his coffee and was disappointed when his meal arrived. "I bet if I was in a hurry it would've taken longer."

"So sue me," she said and walked around the counter toward the Studebaker men.

"Didn't mean nothing by it." He lifted a fork and speared the flat meat under the gravy. He tried several times to smile at Beverly, to let her know he'd just been in a mood, depressed by New Jersey and the pressing boredom of hanging around the airport waiting.

The truck driver finished his lunch and carefully folded his newspaper. He pushed away from the counter, the weight of the mashed potatoes holding him back. With the paper held under his arm, he approached the cash register beside Joe. Beverly returned and took the pad from her apron pocket. "Thirty-five cents," she said and punched the register. "Everything okay today?"

The driver grunted and counted out seven nickels and placed them in a neat pile on the counter before her. Joe watched. "Hey, with all those nickels, you should've gone to the Automat." He half-laughed—Ha, ha.

Big mistake.

The driver slowly moved his head. His tiny eyes stared at Joe and blinked. It reminded Joe of an old mud turtle. "What's wrong with this place?"

"Nothing," Joe was quick to answer. "I just saw you had all those nickels—" He pointed. "You know, like they use at the Automat?"

"You got a problem or somethin'?" The turtle's head turned further, and the huge body creaked around to face Joe.

Joe looked up. "No. Just saw you had a load of nickels, that's all...Ah, I see you're a Teamster." He pointed at the tiny lapel pin the driver wore on his jacket.

"Got a beef with that?" Meaner.

"No!"

Leaning closer, the truck driver's breath smelled of tobacco and gravy. "I don't like you," he said. "You're too damn nosy, you know that. You need a nickel?" He pressed one into Joe's lunch. It left a crater in the potatoes that slowly filled with gravy. "Don't never make fun of the Teamsters, you hear me—Rat?"

"I wasn't—I won't," Joe said. He smiled. "You got me all wrong, brother. I just was admiring the pin, that's all. I'm a union man myself, ah, I got a lot of sympathy for the labor movement. You got me all wrong when I mentioned the...Hey, do I look like some kind of company man or something?" He tried to laugh, again, but his voice came out thin.

The truck driver turned, and, shaking his head, left. Joe watched him climb into the Mack cab. It growled to life and with a puff of blue smoke pulled onto the road and was gone.

"Some days you can't make any friends," Joe said. He turned back to his plate and fished the nickel out with his fork. Wiping it clean on his napkin, he tossed it in the air and caught it again. Beverly walked past, and he grabbed her wrist. "For you," he said and pressed it into her hand. "For just being you, today."

"Joe, you're all laughs," she mumbled and walked away. "A regular Will Rogers."

"He's dead."

"You keep on like you did just then, and you'll be a regular Will Rogers."

\*\*\*

Few cars traveled the narrow road between the diner and the airport. Its name was even depressing—*Lower Road*. From the slight rise it offered Joe a panoramic view of the Rahway Penitentiary to the southwest, Staten Island to the southeast, and on a clear day he might see Newark to the north, on a clear day. From the hill, Joe looked down on the runway below—the Elizabeth airport almost dead. He started down the grade and, reaching the bottom, he slowed to pick a stone from the shoulder. In a side-arm pitch, he threw it into the marsh grass—a splash. He scooped another stone and rubbed the dirt clean with his fingers. The distant runway shimmered in heat waves.

Behind and above him, the highway whined from the endless stream of cars. He tossed the stone. A hollow report told him he'd hit one of the many steel barrels or car bodies hidden in the grass. It reminded him of Chicago and he briefly thought of Kate, a subject he avoided, but the more he tried not to think of her, well, he tried even harder. He continued walking.

It was hot, and he wished he hadn't worn the leather jacket. But he was pilot, and pilots wear leather jackets, even walking pilots. The road dipped around a curve, and the runway disappeared. The air was heavy with swamp gas mixed with yellow haze from the refineries. He removed his hat and wiped sweat from his forehead. A car approached from behind. He looked back.

"Now, who's that?" Then he recognized the Dictator he'd seen at the diner.

\*\*\*

"That him?"

"Yeah."

"Pull up in front of him."

"What if he runs?"

The one in the passenger seat gave a sidelong glance at the driver and pointed a thumb at the broad marshlands on either side of the road. "Where the hell's he gonna run?"

"I dunno."

"Wouldn't catch me wading out in that shit. Ruin a good pair of shoes."

"Meaning to ask, where'd you get those? What're they, Florsheims?"

"These?" He lifted a foot off the floorboards, turning his thick ankle to view the shoe.

"Yeah, I need a new pair, and those look comfortable."

"Wife bought 'em when she's visiting her sister in Westwood."

"You like 'em?"

"They're a little tight, not bad. Hey, watch it. Don't hit hem, just pull in front of him."

\*\*\*

Joe kept walking. The Dictator slowed and passed him. As it pulled in front of him, blocking his way, he thought, "Doesn't look good."

He stopped.

Two doors opened, and the engine stayed running. He saw a red-winged blackbird fly from one of the cattails in the water. "I think you're in a no-parking zone," Joe said and continued toward them. They walked to the end of the car and no further. One opened his suit jacket. Joe saw the leather strap of a shoulder holster. They stood like sentries.

"I can tell you're from out of town," Joe said. "No one comes down this road unless they're lost. You must be lost. Highway One's back that way." He jerked his thumb over his shoulder. He approached the car, and the one with the suit jacket open held out a hand indicating he should stop. It was a big hand, like a catcher's mitt.

"I really don't need a ride," Joe said. "But thanks for offering." He turned slightly to face the other man approaching from the side. "You with him?" No response. "Nice shoes. Florsheims?"

A hand shot out and grabbed his arm before he could get clear. Amazed at how quickly he'd been caught, Joe missed the fist that crashed into his stomach, exploding air from his lungs like someone had popped a balloon. *Whoof!*

\*\*\*

"Pick him up," the one who'd hit him said. The other one hauled Joe off the road and dumped him against the Studebaker's trunk. He slumped to the bumper. "Give him his hat; it's hot out here."

Joe felt his hat placed carefully on his head, then someone brushed gravel from his pant leg near the knee. "You listening okay, pal?" Almost tender.

He nodded. His breath came in painful gasps as though his lungs had collapsed and would never re-inflate. He tried to speak, but nothing came. A wave of nausea ran through him, and he leaned over.

"Leave him," the same voice said. "It's probably that diner food that's doin' him in."

"I kinda liked it—"

"That's 'cause you're a garbage gut, you know that donchya?"

"The banana cream pie was good."

"Too runny."

As they argued, Joe straightened and inched himself up the trunk until he almost stood. His body ached, his lungs burned. More amazed than scared, he couldn't believe how one blow could so completely weaken him. "Didn't I leave a big enough tip?" he gasped and leaned over.

"Hey, sorry about the introduction," the one who'd struck him said.

"Apology accepted."

"Sometimes you gotta get a guy's attention to make 'em listen; nothin' personal. We just need to talk a little business."

"Business? I was beginning to worry you might be Democrats out canvassing. I've heard about Jersey politics."

"Us? Hell no, we ain't Democrats. We look like Democrats?" The two men looked at each other over Joe's head. "I didn't think we looked like Democrats."

The driver tilted Joe's head back by his chin. Joe's breath came quicker now, although he still held his stomach. "Hey, Bud," the man said. "You really a communist?"

Joe shook his head and gave a short laugh through the nose, "No," he said and straightened. "Seventh Day Adventist." The driver frowned, still holding Joe's chin. "Don't worry," Joe added, "It's a common mistake." He felt his breath returning and with it an indignant, swelling anger. He shook his chin free from the meaty hand. He looked the driver in the face, a face as broad and ugly as any he'd seen. Worse than Angie's.

A finger poked into his shoulder. Fat lips spoke close to his face. "A communist *and* a comedian."

"Maybe he should be on Fred Allen?"

"Don't tell me," Joe said. "You're talent scouts. I knew this was my lucky day." He shifted his weight pressing it further up the trunk, positioning himself where he could ram a fist into the one's belly, turn before the other realized what had happened and kick him square in the nuts.

The one who had poked the finger into his shoulder spoke, "You work for Frank Deagan?"

"Name's vaguely familiar."

"Well, he's a communist."

"Funny, he's never mentioned that to me, not that I know him."

"Deagan's moving a shit-load of guns through this place to Spain." He nodded toward the airport. "We hear he's running airplanes through there, and he's recruiting turds like you to fly them out."

"Actually, I'm more of an errand boy; go for coffee, place bets with his bookie, sew red stars on his underwear, that sort of thing."

Joe now had one foot set on the ground and one behind him on the bumper, set like a coiled spring. His right hand slowly knotted into a tight fist, his left pressed against the Studebaker's trunk.

"He's got a pisspot full of cash comes through this place every week, cash from all the communists all over the country trying to buy airplanes, guns and whatever else he's got in there, all heading over to a bunch of foreign communists, and we don't like that." (Pause) "Unless we get a cut."

"Who's we?" Joe asked. He felt the driver standing behind him move back, dropping his guard. "How'd you fellas find out, anyhow?" They seemed flattered and smiled. "And why do you sound like you're in an Edward G. Robinson movie?"

The one in front of Joe shrugged. Just that slight carelessness, that brief instant of closing his eyes and spreading his hands, gave Joe his opportunity.

His breath had returned. His body, rigid with suppressed indignation, suddenly uncoiled. His right fist, propelled by the lunging force of his entire body bursting away from the Studebaker, shot out, aimed dead on the center of the man's gut.

An instant, a brief effervescent spit of time froze the look of total surprise on the man's face. Joe's momentum carried him through the attack, his fist now at the full thrust of its power.

He connected.

With the pavement.

One instant the man was there, and the next there was empty air and hard asphalt digging into his palms and chin. His knees ripped through his trouser legs, skin tearing away in the road like cheese across a grater. He rolled. He dropped over the edge of the road and bounced down the embankment and stopped with one foot in the black muck beneath the cattails. He stayed that way and listened to the footsteps shuffling above him. When he turned, both men stood looking down at him. One held a pistol, and both wore expressions of amused concern.

"You okay down there?"

"I suspect the tone of this conversation will somehow shift," Joe said and dropped his head on the dirt.

***

Even with his head under the instrument panel of the Lockheed Vega, Frank Deagan heard the car pull in front of the hangar. A flashlight at his side, his feet tangled over the seat cushions. He listened. Three sets of footsteps entered the hangar. They moved toward the Vega. He wiggled his head free and sat up.

"Oh, Francis!" Joe called in a girlie voice. "We have company. I hope you're decent."

Frank stuck his head through the side window. He said nothing but took in the two strangers on either side of Joe. One held a pistol in plain sight, the other moved toward the Vega as Joe was ordered to stop.

"I believe these are the fascists you've told me so much about, Frank. You're right, they are everywhere."

"Shut-up," one said.

"Sorry," Joe replied. "By the way, I didn't catch your names."

"Shut-up."

"Pleased to meet you Mr. Up."

"Can't you shut him up?" the other snapped. Frank had pulled his head inside the Vega and worked his way to the door midway down the fuselage.

"What the hell's this?"

"You Deagan?"

"You FBI?"

Both laughed. "First, we get accused of being Democrats and now Feds. I gotta get a new tailor."

"Could be the shoes."

"If you're FBI, you need a warrant. There's nothing here of interest to you."

"Frank," Joe said. "I don't think they're with the government, anybody's government."

"What the hell happened to you?" Frank asked, seeing the torn trousers and scuffed chin.

"I was defending the oppressed masses."

Frank glanced from one stranger to the other, sizing them up. When he spoke, his voice was cool. "Abner Zwillman send you?"

"Did he?"

"He's got no complaint," Frank said. "We're square with him."

"Are you?"

"Okay, who's Abner Zwillman?" Joe asked and was ignored.

Frank thought for a moment, studying the weak grin on the face before him. The one with gun beside Joe was huge and ugly. He seemed bored. The other was only a few pounds lighter and enjoyed watching Frank. As close as they now stood, Frank smelled his cheap cologne. It reminded him of a police station in Springfield, Massachusetts, just another jail where he'd spent a week after a strike. He tried to remember what that one had been about: glove makers, teamsters, mill workers. He couldn't remember, only the cologne and the split skull in the crowded jail.

"If Zwillman's leaning on us for more money," Frank said, "we could just pull out, because we had a deal, and..."

"Oh, will you forget Zwillman? Do I look like Abner Zwillman?"

"Who's Zwillman?" Joe persisted. "Is he a fascist, too? I seem to be meeting a great many fascists today."

The stranger moved closer to Frank. The smell grew stronger, more like a disinfectant for public toilets than something you'd intentionally splash on your face. "*Longy* Zwillman can shake you turds down for whatever he wants. We don't give a shit, and you can tell him that for me. What you can also tell him, and I mean this most sincerely, is he don't run collections out here without talking to us. It's sort of an affront on our dignity."

"Who the hell are you?" Frank asked.

"Who cares? Call me, Mr. Friendly, because I'm your new friend. Zwillman's your old friend. You used to pay him, now, you pay me."

"It doesn't work that way. Zwillman is the final say; he's got syndicate approval; this is their operation. Are you guys nuts?"

"Oh, you worry so. Look, I say you pay me just what you paid Zwillman, plus ten percent for processing."

Joe waved his hand asking to be called on.

"What, Joe?"

"Frank, are these gentlemen extortionists?"

"Joe..."

"Is this Mr. Zwillman, everyone but me seems to know, also an extortionist?"

All three looked at Joe. The one they knew as Mr. Friendly pointed at Joe and asked Frank, "Does he really work here? I figured you for a classier operation."

"He's new," Frank apologized. "Joe, go sit somewhere."

"Is this a shakedown, Frank? Because if it is I think it falls outside the parameters of my contract." He took a step toward Frank and Friendly. "I specifically requested the chance to fly and to fly against fascists." He spread his arms taking in the two visitors. "Now, these gentleman may be fascists at heart..."

"Will you, please, shut him up?"

"But," Joe continued. "They are not your garden variety, Spanish, monarchist, Franco-loving fascists. Plus, I was retained to shoot said fascists down from aeroplanes, not scrap with them on foot.

"Now, I'm no wizard at geography, but this is not Spain. This is New Jersey, and until I get to Spain, and until I get inside an aeroplane—one with operating machine guns—I am not getting involved with common thugs. No offense, guys, but I will not be a party to illegal activities here in New Jersey. It's just not in my contract. You understand, I'm sure."

Only Frank noticed Joe making his way toward the toolbox while giving his soliloquy. Mr. Friendly had turned his back slightly on Frank who still held the shop flashlight in his hand. The one with the gun followed Joe, but looked to his partner, Mr. Friendly, who stared in disbelief at Joe.

Joe leaned against the toolbox, his hand above an open drawer where he'd set the wrench earlier. "Therefore, Frank," he said. "In lieu of this breech of contract, I consider myself at liberty to give you formal notice, and let these two gentlemen be my witness."

The one with the gun smiled.

The smile was shattered by the twelve-inch wrench Joe snatched from the drawer and slammed into his face.

Mr. Friendly was slow to react, and Frank brought his flashlight across his temple. It was a solid blow but less than needed to take him out. He brought his arm around to catch him again on the back swing.

Friendly, dazed but fuming now, brought his hands up and caught Frank's arm, wrenching it behind his back. Joe, off balance from the blow against the now unconscious and bleeding gunman, recovered his footing and turned in time to hear Frank's arm snap.

A shriek of instant pain, and the flashlight hit the floor, skipped and shattered. Mr. Friendly gave an animal yell almost as terrifying as Frank's when he curled his knee into Frank's groin and brought his doubled fists down onto his neck. The wooden crack told Joe it had snapped. Frank crumpled to the floor, his face pressed to the concrete.

In the time it took Frank to break, Joe had moved the few steps to reach him. The wrench, held in one hand above his head, came down in a short arc aimed at Friendly. The big man turned, his hands barely rising from delivering the blow to Frank. His face, square and twisted in rage, glowered at Joe. His feet tried to shift his weight quickly enough to meet the attack, but Joe had the advantage by a second.

Down the wrench came, three pounds of forged steel moving at the end of a pendulum. When it struck Friendly's skull, to Joe, it felt as though he'd hit a wall of hard mud. Friendly's knees buckled, eyes crossed, and his frame collapsed. Blood ran from his cracked skull onto the pavement. Judging from the rate of accumulation, Joe figured he was still alive and would rise again.

So: The second blow caved Friendly's head in just behind the right eye. The third blow, Joe never saw because he swung with his eyes shut. It struck the now dead man's neck, and the fourth and fifth blows sent sparks off the concrete floor.

\*\*\*

How Joe found himself on Lower Road walking toward the highway he would never be able to completely explain, but at that moment he remembered stumbling through a trench at night dragging his Springfield rifle and frantically climbing to higher ground.

*"Joe!" Daryl called as he ran toward him along the trench, his voice garbled by the gas mask he quickly pulled aside to shout.*

*Joe remembered turning to his name, and Daryl grabbing his arm as something exploded, hell, things exploded all over the place, and the air stank, burned, and Daryl was crying and screaming at him.*

*"They'll shoot you!" Daryl shouted behind the mask. "Deserting, they'll shoot you," and he pulled Joe's gas mask from its pouch, removed his helmet and yanked the mask over his head. "Don and clear!" he yelled, and Joe breathed, sucking in the rubbery canvas air, marginally better than chlorine.*

*Through clouds—memory and gas—Daryl pushed Joe along the trench back toward the explosions, over bodies and helmets, ammo boxes, tin cans, papers—lots of papers—and rifles stuck in the mud and would be a bitch to clean, and there was another explosion, so close, and others much closer, and Daryl, staring through muddy glass eyes, straightened Joe's helmet like his mother adjusting his winter cap before sending him out the door. Then, Angelo appeared and pulled Daryl over the top while screaming at him, "You fuckin' coward!" And there were too many explosions after that...*

It was then, almost 20 years later that Joe realized he'd forgotten his hat and turned back to the hangar.

The airport was still. All the other hangars but Frank's were shut. Rusted padlocks with sheriff notices told their stories of business failed. The dozen or so airplanes parked on the ramp hadn't flown since Joe had been there, and they bore the dust of neglect. Their tires were flat, and one, a Curtiss Robin, had its windshield smashed out. Joe walked toward the hangar.

"Frank's going to need help," he said aloud, then looked at his hand still clutching the bloodied wrench. For a moment, he stared at it, then, frightened, ran to the edge of the parking area and threw it as hard as he could into the marshlands. He listened for the splash. Hearing it, he felt a nauseating fear twist at his insides. He ran toward the hangar.

The Studebaker Dictator was still parked outside with its engine running. He reached inside and switched it off, and then re-thinking, he opened the door, slid onto the driver's seat and restarted the car. He drove into the hangar past the Lockheed Vega, around Frank's still body and into the rear of the building. He jumped out.

Grabbing a tarpaulin from a fuselage, he draped it over the car. "Shit." He ran around the car to catch it as it floated across the roof. He slid it back onto the trunk and pulled it over the rear window. "Need something," he said. "Something...a weight." He looked around. There." He reached for a magneto on a shelf. The tarp slid off the car. "Shit!" He snatched it off the floor and dropped the mag. It cracked but he didn't care. Holding the tarp in place, he grabbed the magneto and tossed it onto the roof.

*BONK*—and then a gentle rumble.

It stayed and pinned the tarpaulin in place. He looked around. "Heh," he laughed and stood back. "That's that," he said and looked back toward the hangar door, wide open with three smashed bodies, two in blood puddles, in full view.

\*\*\*

The hangar doors slid on rollers long since in need of grease. Joe leaned his weight against the door.

"Son—of—a—" The door creaked and moved. Turning, he pressed with his back, the door gradually building momentum and slid toward the stops. Like rolling a stone in front of a tomb.

"Oh," he murmured when finally it shut. He found the latch. The click echoed through the hangar.

His back to the door, he slid to the floor. He drew his knees to his chest and slowly lowered his head while his fingers pressed against his scalp. Fifteen feet away— three bodies formed a bloody circle, and none of them fascists.

A thousand miles away was Daryl, and Joe knew he wasn't the coward.

***

# Chapter 13

# Elizabeth, New Jersey

"**H**ello?" the man's voice on the telephone sounded tinny and suspicious, as in: *Who the hell's calling this number?*

"Yeah, let me talk to Zwill, Zwillman." Joe tried to sound tough, since pleasant hadn't worked with his recent visitors.

"Who's this?"

Joe wiped at his forehead: "Deagan, Frank Deagan."

There was along pause.

"What do you want?"

Joe didn't know what to say. He still didn't have a good idea who Zwillman was, except that he had something to do with the entire operation. "There's been trouble." It sounded like a corny line from a radio thriller—*"Trouble at the old mill..."*—but he couldn't think of any other way to put it.

"Where?"

"Here, the hangar, Elizabeth Airport, Lower Road."

"I know where it is." Another pause filled only with static and the sound of breathing. "Look, there is no one named Zwillman. Got it?"

"Oh," Joe answered. "Sure, I know that." And thought, '*I don't know beans.*'

Another pause.

"You stay put." And the phone went dead.

Joe hooked the earpiece back in its cradle. He looked at the open page of the little phone book tied to a string on the wall. Slowly, he thumbed through the other pages, all were in code, the names merely numbers or combinations of numbers and odd symbols. Starting at the back, where he figure the *Z's* would be, Joe had dialed numbers until someone answered to 'Zwillman.' It had only taken four tries. Joe closed the book, tugged it free of the string and slipped it inside his back pocket. Might need it later.

Except for the sparrows in the rafters, the hangar was quiet. Gray sunshine leaked through the many windows near the ceiling, windows so covered with grime it made the sky look cloudy on the brightest days. Joe walked around the Lockheed Vega toward the three bodies. Passing Frank, he reached down once more to check for a pulse, but the half-closed eyes and slack jaw made it evident the man was dead. Blood clotted in a sticky pool near Mr. Friendly's head, and the third man, the one who had held the gun, lay a short distance away. Surprisingly, he moved.

Like kicking at a presumed dead snake, Joe poked at the man's foot with his toe.

"Hey. You dead?"

He saw an eyelid flicker and stepped back. That's when he spotted the pistol wedged under the Vega's left tire and picked it up. Smith and Wesson Military & Police .38 Special with a snub-nosed barrel. Pleased, he released the cylinder. It fell away, and he checked the chambers—full. In the quiet of the hangar the click of the cylinder locking in place seemed as sharp as an actual shot. Joe saw the man move—first his eyes and then an arm. Joe crept forward, gun at the ready. He drew the hammer back—two clicks. An unmistakable sound.

"Aughh," the man groaned and spit through a broken mouth.

Joe took a length of cord from a workbench. Before the man could move again, Joe lowered the hammer, slipped the pistol into his jacket pocket and squatted to tie the arms behind the man's back.

"What the f...?" the slow voice from a busted mouth asked.

"Steady, partner," Joe said and cinched the cord tight. It bit into flesh.

"Hey! That's tight!"

"Yeah, I know," Joe said. He backed away and pulled the gun from his pocket, double-clicked the hammer and pointed at the man's head. He found another rope on the bench. "Stay on your belly and put your feet together."

"Yer makin' a fugin' mistake, here, pal."

"I make a lot of mistakes, *and* I ain't your pal any more. Put your feet together." He kicked at him, a little harder than required. The two legs scissored together, and Joe dropped on top of them. He poked the gun barrel between the man's buttocks.

"Oooo!" the man with the pistol up his ass exclaimed, because in that situation all other comments seemed inappropriate.

"I saw a man in France take a round in the can once," Joe said and, with his free hand, looped the cord around the ankles. "Took his nuts right off—shnip." One-handed, he looped it again and pressed his knee to hold it in place. "He didn't die too quick, neither." With one hand, he managed a crude knot and pulled it tight.

"Ow! Ya fuck!"

"Sorry." He yanked again.

"Oww!"

Joe pushed clear. "Now, are you listening to me?"

The answer was muffled by the concrete floor, "Yeah...ya fuck."

"You seem to have a limited vocabulary." Joe moved to the man's head, squatted and pressed the pistol barrel against a damp forehead where the receding hairline began. He spoke slowly: "Bearing in mind that your friend's dead, and that I don't like you, plus you're tied

269

up, and I won't hesitate to put a bullet in five different parts of your body before I put the last one in your pea brain—I want you to tell me, please: Who is Zwillman?"

\*\*\*

Maxwell landed the Waco biplane about a half-hour before sunset. Under the belly of her own airplane—really Joe's Travel Air—Kate had been wiping at the oil that streaked back from the engine. Feigning disinterest, she let Maxwell taxi past, and then watched him climb down from the front cockpit. He stood talking to a student for several minutes, his hands animated in a display of whatever maneuvers they'd practiced; stalls, probably, from the way his hand would point up, shudder and drop into a simulated spin. The student nodded his head the way all students nod when they haven't a clue what the instructor's explaining. Then, with a quick smile, Maxwell sent him away with, "See you tomorrow." And he pulled off his leather helmet.

Kate looked up and called as he approached, "Any progress today?"

Max walked around the wing and stooped to his knees in the grass. He wore a white shirt with a plain red tie below an open collar. Despite the heat, he wore a leather jacket. His face was ruddy from the sun and wind of open-cockpit flying, his blond hair pressed flat from the helmet. "He'll solo," he said. She liked his even smile.

"When?" she asked and continued wiping at the oil stains. She inched further down the fuselage on her back. Her blouse, one her mother had given her at Christmas with the warning—*"Now, don't you ruin this around those aeroplanes"*—inched up her back exposing an inviting curve below her ribcage. Maxwell looked too long.

"Soon," he said.

"Milking it?"

"Hey, if I solo all my students too soon, I lose business."

He looked at her, his eyes going directly to the bare mid-section and then to her breasts moving in gentle waves beneath her blouse with the motion of her arms— *like two mounds of Jell-O on a wobbly deck,* he thought. She caught his gaze and, with a slight grin, pulled her blouse and tucked it beneath her belt. He looked aside to show he hadn't been peeking, which, of course he had, and, of course, she knew.

"How was the rest of your day?" she asked. "Fly much?"

"Two lessons; one charter."

"Charter?" Her voice rose.

"Yeah."

"That's good."

"Yeah, I suppose." He plucked a strand of grass and pulled at it with his teeth. He watched the Waco being fueled, and his mind seemed to drift away.

"Can't complain about charters," she said. "Where to?"

"Huh?"

"Where was the charter to?"

"Oh, down toward, ah, down south a ways. Some realtor taking photos, Mr. Sukavati from *Pure Land Realty*. That's all, just another farm foreclosure." He looked at her.

"That's something."

"Yeah, something, but not exactly a run to Chicago." He leaned on his side, the blade of grass between his

271

teeth, his eyes narrow, face relaxed—very Gary Cooper. "I'm wasting my time, Kate."

"Everyone starts somewhere," she said and felt her empty response match her shallow concern. "I'm sorry," she quickly added and reached to touch his knee. He smiled that wan glance he had, the one she'd seen the first day they'd met in the cafe, the one that said, '*Life's funny, when you stop crying.*' She patted his leg and returned to the Travel Air's belly. When her blouse crept up again, she left it alone. Even considered taking it off—wouldn't that cause a giggle?

She worked in silence while long shadows from the orange sunset moved around the biplane. Maxwell chewed grass much as a cow would—unhurried. He watched the fuel truck, and as the gas boy reeled in the hose and pulled the truck back to the shack, he turned to Kate, "Coming over tonight?"

She answered without looking at him, "Third time this week; should I?"

"Yes."

She chuckled. "If you only knew what you were getting into."

"I think I know."

"You know nothing about me, Max." She looked at him.

"Is it because you're older?" he asked. "Should that be a problem?"

"It can be," she said, although, she didn't like hearing, *older.*

"Not to me."

"I don't know, Max."

"Neither do I, but what difference does it make?" He rolled onto his stomach, his waist near her head. She still lay on her back, her hands crossed on her belly, the dirty rag smudging her blouse.

"I'm six years older than you, Max."

"Seven."

Playfully, she poked the rag at his face and then rubbed the fuselage. "I'm not in love with you."

"That's okay."

"I don't want to be in love with you."

"You go to bed with me."

"That doesn't mean much."

"Oh, thanks." He dropped his face into the grass.

"No," she soothed. "I don't mean you." She rolled onto her side and twisted to face him. Being near the tail of the airplane, she had little headroom and had to snake up on him. Her hand reached for his face and found his shoulder. She crawled the short distance. "You are wonderful," she said pronouncing the word slowly.

"But meaningless," he said.

"Not meaningless. Just, just not unique."

"Not unique?" He lifted his head. "How do you mean?"

"Well—"

"You mean like, position? A different position?"

"No," she laughed. "Although, I'm always open to variations on a theme." Her eyes narrowed to slits, her lower lip dropped slightly, and her tongue made a quick pass.

"Are you saying I lack imagination?"

"Your imagination seems perfect."

"Are you calling me a pervert?"

"I'd like to," she said and squeezed his ass. He stretched to kiss her. She maneuvered toward him, her hand still on him, her face reaching his. He slipped a hand to a breast and gently caressed it. When they kissed it was quick, and then they parted, and he stared at her while his hand still gently fondling her.

She saw the infatuation in his eyes, the look of rapidly developing love. She kissed him again, longer this time, and while her eyes were closed, her hand still holding onto his buttocks, she wished she could fall in love with him. And was grateful she couldn't.

"I'll bet we're giving Louie a rise," she said close to his lips.

"He's too old to get it up anymore." Quick kiss. "There are advantages to being seven years younger than one's mate."

She pulled back. "I am not your mate." Cold.

"Bad choice of words?"

"There's no need to complicate this matter." She tapped him on the butt and squirmed away. Getting to her feet, she adjusted her blouse and glanced west. The sun was below the horizon. Clouds above were brilliant red and silver. "Are you hungry?"

Maxwell pressed to his feet. When he faced her, he was a head taller with his shoulders stooped. He stretched his back and stared into her face.

"I'm starved," she said. "I got paid today."

"Hundreds and hundreds of dollars?"

"Just hundreds."

"Then you buy."

"Fair enough."

They stood for a long pause, their eyes questioning each other. She saw before her a slightly immature man who stirred her sexually without touching her soul except to feel sorry for him and, in so doing, to feel superior to him. "Have I hurt you?"

"No," he answered and stared.

She shifted her weight to one side the way only women can. Her head tilted and she wanted to say something.

Instead, he spoke: "I just noticed something."

"What?"

"Your hair. You've cut your hair."

Automatically, her hand brushed at her head. "Kept getting in the way."

"When?"

"When did it get in the way?"

"No, when did you cut it? I watched you brushing it this morning."

"All tangles," she said with a dismissing wave. "A nuisance."

"No, it was beautiful."

"Took you long enough to notice it gone."

"I loved watching you brush it."

"I've never liked it long."

"Made me feel privileged to watch."

"Its unmanageable," she said. "Besides, I used to wear it short years ago."

"When?"

"In, in California," she said and shifted her weight back to both legs. "I'm hungry," she added to change the topic.

"You never say much about California."

"There's nothing to say. Let's go eat. Feel like Italian, maybe a bottle of wine?" She touched his arm and ran her hand across his chest brushing grass from his shirt. His body was hard beneath the cloth. She gently pushed away from him and said, "Let's go."

They walked a few steps, Maxwell in formation, slightly behind and to her side. When he spoke it sounded as though he were conducting an interview: "I want to know about you, Kate."

"There's nothing to know."

"I know you were somewhat of a celebrity in California."

"So you're only after me for my fame," she quipped the way someone nervous in an interview might. "And all along I thought it was my experience between the sheets that drew you in." Interview over. She reached and took his arm to pull him closer. The gesture should have told him to shut-up, to drop the questions about her past, to quit stabbing at the parts of her she kept well insulated.

"Have you ever thought of getting married?" he asked.

Her answer was quick, "I've more important things to do. Besides, why kill a good thing by marrying it?"

"Were you ever married?"

"Does it matter?"

"Yes."

"Why?"

"Because I want to marry you."

"Oh, Max." They stopped. She shook her head. "Dear, Max. You have no idea what you're saying, no idea whatsoever."

"I've been married before. I think I know what's involved."

"You've been divorced, too."

"And that makes me some kind of leper?"

"You should know better." She gently pulled him toward the car. "Can't you just take things as they are and continue the setup we have?"

"Is that a no?"

"Yes," she said. "That's a no. Come on, hunger's affecting your better judgment."

Arms linked, she led him to the car, where as he reached for her door, she stopped him. "Don't take this too seriously."

He nodded and she stared into his face before saying: "My God, but you're young," and sighed.

"I can't help it."

"This, too, shall pass."

She climbed inside the car, and he closed the door. She watched him walk around, and, when he climbed into the driver's side, she leaned over and kissed his face. Pulling back, she realized it was the first time she'd felt anything like affection toward him.

They drove off.

\*\*\*

As Iowa coal companies went broke the miners dispersed leaving whole towns shriveled or vanished: *Promise City, Lucas, Norwood.* Some miners wandered into farming; some moved to the cities. Slowly these masses of immigrants were absorbed into the rolling Midwest landscape to become Americans.

Luckily, some remained Italians.

"I'm stuffed," Kate said through a dramatic sigh. She sipped at her wine and leaned back in her chair. "Would you be terribly embarrassed if I loosened my belt?

"If you do, Mrs. Vitali will come running over with another pile of lasagna."

"It is good, isn't it?"

"And the wine," he said. They looked across the table at each other. The room was rosy dim, their booth almost dark. Mrs. Vitali, owner of *La Giovine Italia Ristorante*, kept it reserved for those she knew wanted more privacy. Checkered tablecloth, candle in an empty Chianti bottle, and above the table a travel agency poster of Italy (actually Sardinia, but who could tell?). Kate and Maxwell had been to the restaurant several times during the summer. Usually hot inside, an anemic ceiling fan did little more than stir the flies. The food, however, was enough to make up for any discomfort. The wine, mellow and red, put color in Kate's cheeks and made her lean on the table, eyes absorbed by Maxwell who poured the remainder of the bottle into their glasses. It felt good to be a little drunk, she thought.

"To payday," he said and held up his glass.

"To your charter," she replied. Glasses clinked. They drank. "To your newest student and his impending solo."

"You make it sound like a prison sentence."

"I'm beginning to think of flying as just that—a sentence, a curse. Hmm."

"Interesting," he said.

"Interesting or disillusioning?"

"Interesting."

"Then you understand disillusionment?"

"I understand someone becoming tired of her job, and flying is your job."

"It's your job, too."

"Only yours pays more." He drank. "A lot more."

"Okay, Max. What is it?"

"What's what?"

"Are you asking me for a job?"

"No."

"Are you hinting I should be in a different line?"

"Not at all," he said. "It's great you're a pilot. I hope you fly forever."

"But?"

"But, what?"

"Don't *but-what*, me," she said looking across her glass. "There's definitely something bugging you, and I think it has something to do with what I do for a living."

"I don't know what you're talking about."

She leaned closer and, in mock dramatics, said, "I fly for the mob."

"Oh, great. Just spit it out. Tell everyone in here you're a, a—"

"Money launderer, dear. You can say it. Laund*ress*, actually."

"It's dangerous."

"*Flying's* dangerous, and I don't want this conversation. Finish your wine; let's go."

"I love you, Kate."

"That's sweet, now, finish your wine."

"If I finish my wine, will you marry me?"

"Marry the poor boy," a voice boomed from the booth adjacent to theirs. "Yeah," a second voice piped in. "Give the kid a chance."

Kate pulled herself up the seat back and leaned over the divider. "Louie! How long have you been there?"

"Came in after the bread and before the cannolis," Louie said. He calmly twirled spaghetti onto his fork, pushing it back with his spoon. A napkin was tucked into his shirt, and he smiled at her. "The boy's in love with you, Katie. If you don't believe me, ask around." He indicated the other tables where diners had interrupted their meals listening to the unfolding romance.

"You should marry him," one man called.

"Yes," a woman added. "Marriage can be a wonderful affair."

Blushing, "Thank-you all very much," Kate said. "But I don't think I'm quite ready for—"

"Can't wait forever."

"Not getting any younger."

"Thank-you, but I don't believe a little wine and a plate of lasagna should lead to marriage."

"Good a reason as any."

"Try the manicotti, then."

"See?" Louie said. "It's unanimous." He pressed the fork against a bread stick. "If you wait until you're pregnant, it might be too late."

"Louie," Maxwell drawled.

"Well, it's true. Would you marry her if she were pregnant?" he called over the divider.

"Who's pregnant?"

"That girl at the other booth—her, the one leaning over the wall."

"Congratulations."

"I hope it's a girl."

"Thank-you," Kate said and waved.

"There," Louie said. "It's decided. You marry young Maxwell; have babies and live happily ever after."

"Louie," Kate said. "He hasn't the first clue what he's asking."

"So who does when it comes to love?"

"Or marriage," someone else added.

"But," Kate defended herself against the crowd, "He's talking about a whole lot more than just love—whatever that is."

"Oh, harsh words."

"Cynical words."

"He's talking marriage, and that can lead to all sorts of complications."

"Complications I can handle," Maxwell offered.

She ignored him with a grin.

Louie stuffed the loaded fork into his mouth and chewed slowly. After washing it down with wine, he spoke, "I'd marry you, Kate, but then you know that."

"Thank-you, Louie. If I thought you had any money, I'd take you up on that."

"Excuse, me," Maxwell said. "Could I say something?"

"Sure," Kate said and looked at Max.

"Let's get out of here."

"Sounds like a movie line," she said and turned back to Louie. "Well, thank-you for the advice, but I think it's too soon."

Louie shrugged and twirled another forkful as Kate disappeared behind the divider. Max dropped a few coins on the table and followed Kate.

"Good luck, and I hope your first child is a feminine child," Mrs. Vitali said when she rang up their bill. "Picked out a godfather yet?"

\*\*\*

They spoke little during the ride from the restaurant. Kate sat on her side of the seat and watched the road. Maxwell drove with both hands on the wheel. If nothing else, they looked married. It was a warm evening, and Kate enjoyed the breeze coming through the window ruffling her short hair.

As though on cue, they looked to each other. Maxwell looked back at the road, and Kate slid the short distance across the seat. Kissing his neck, she pressed her lips against him and inhaled. "I like the way you smell," she said. "Have I ever told you that?"

He looked toward her and worked his arm over her shoulder pulling her close. She pressed a hand to his chest and with her other hand squeezed the inside of his thigh. Way up the thigh.

"Swing past the airport, will you, please?" she asked.

"I thought we were going to my place."

"We are, but I need something."

"Oh," he said.

"Not curious?"

"I never ask women what it is they're doing when they say they need to get something out of purses, ladies rooms or drug stores. I figure that's their business, and I probably wouldn't understand it."

"How like a man."

"Yes, and that's the way God intended it."

"I thought you didn't believe in God."

"I don't, but there has to be someone held responsible for female behavior, hence, a God, a female God, no doubt."

"Have you tried this theory on Lutherans?"

"I never interfere with other people's beliefs."

"And you never ask women what they carry in their purses."

"The world would become imbalanced if everyone went around questioning the natural arrangement of things."

"Such as purses?"

"And ladies' rooms, yes."

He turned off the blacktop and onto the gravel road leading to the airport. The beacon light flashed in the darkness. "I'll wait in the car," he said when they pulled in front of the operations building.

"You're a silly man," she said and opened her door.

"Yes, but you'll probably still go to bed with me."

"I prefer silly lovers." Shrug.

He watched her disappear into the shadows behind the building. A weak ramp light barely illuminated the few airplanes tied down outside. The Travel Air was nearest the lamp, its cockpits draped in canvas. Dew already collected on the wings outlining the ribs. The Waco was a short distance away, also covered. Behind it, deep in shadow, was another biplane. It hadn't flown in several years and was surrounded by weeds, its engine compartment home to sparrows. Sparrows—the only true survivors in aviation.

"Ready." The car door opened, and Kate hopped inside.

"That was quick."

She dropped a photo album on the seat. Maxwell reached for it. "Later," she said and blocked him. "Do you have anything to drink at your place?"

"A half-bottle of rye."

"Templeton?"

He nodded.

"Any soda?"

"I think so."

"Good," she said and kept her hand on the album. "Let's go."

The drive was short. Maxwell rented a small house two miles from the runway's end. He pulled the car into the garage after Kate had climbed out. She waited in the driveway while he latched the doors. Beyond the elm trees the airport's beacon flashed in even beats.

"Watch your step," he said. "Porch light's out."

"Why don't you fix it?"

"That costs money."

"Well, at least I know what to get you for Christmas."

"Will I still know you come Christmas?"

"You may know me, but things might change." She kissed his cheek. He slid his arm around her waist, and they walked the short path to the door. A radio played accordion music from the neighbor's window just beyond the hedges. A dog barked. Someone started a car, and someone yelled for someone named Betty to get her ass inside. Maxwell opened the door and found the light. He dropped his keys on a side table and hung his jacket on a hook inside the bedroom door.

"You're one of the few men I know who makes his bed," Kate said and took her leather jacket off and hung it over his.

"Still can't get over your hair," he said and touched it. "It makes you look—"

"Older?"

"No, different, maybe older, but mostly different."

She clasped his wrist. "You promised me a drink."

"Oh, yes." He left and called from the small kitchen off the front room, "There's no ice; I don't have it delivered."

"Just a little soda's fine." She sat on the couch, its cushions deep and spongy. Hooking her right toe behind her left heel she pried off her boot and repeated it with the other foot. She kicked her socks across the room and waved her feet to dry the sweat. Maxwell entered.

"I brought the bottle."

"Good thinking."

"It's hot in here," he said and pulled the curtains back.

"Leave 'em closed. The neighbors'll be snooping."

"It'll give them something to talk about in church. Here."

"Thanks," she said and took her drink. "Sit."

"Yes, Ma'am." He sat beside her and leaned to untie his shoes.

"Just kick them anywhere," she said and took a swallow.

"You don't mind?"

"Not at all," she said. "Excessive neatness worries me."

"What's in the album?"

She hesitated. Slowly she opened to the first page, holding the book so he could not see. She flipped two or three pages, her eyes blank looking at the photographs. She lifted her drink and sipped.

"Is this a private viewing, or can anyone jump in?"

"Max, what's important in your life?" she asked and held the album close to her breasts.

"Flying," he answered. "And you, I guess." He thought. "And being free to do what I want."

"Flying's your first choice?"

"I suppose.    But you're quickly becoming a contender."

She propped the album on his thighs. "That's me." She pointed. "At fourteen."

"Cute."

"Fat.  I had fat ankles, but well-developed breasts; really irked my sister." She pointed to another photograph taken on a golf course. "Me, two years later."

"Cuter yet; who's the long drink of water next to you?" He pointed to a teenaged boy with curly hair and an oblong face.  He wore golfing plus-fours and held a cigarette. He smiled big teeth at the camera.

"That's Marty Thorndale; lived down the street from us in Des Moines.  His father owned the Thorndale Iron Works on River Street."

"Never been there."

"This was taken at the Wakonda Country Club after a Juniors' Tournament."

"Never been there either."

"Invitation only; Marty was from a very wealthy family; 'Blue Silk Stocking Presbyterians,' my mother called them."

"Close friend of yours?"

"Not really. I lost my virginity to him," she said and glanced at Max's face—a blank. "Same day this picture was taken.  It hurt, I remember that."

"The picture?"

She ignored the comment.  "I remember, also, how much I wanted it, even when he was done, which didn't take long."

"You probably threw his game off."

"Come to think of it, I did beat him afterwards."

"Did you love him?"

"I was sixteen."

"What happened to him?"

She flipped a page. Filling the center of the page was a studio portrait of a young man in uniform. "War," she said. "He turned 18, enlisted, went to France and I never saw him again."

Maxwell studied the long, yet more handsome face. "Killed?" he asked.

She flipped the page. "Nope. Seems he liked Paris. Stayed after the Armistice. Became a writer. You've read Hemingway, I suppose?"

"*That's* Hemingway? He changed his name to Ernest Hemingway?"

"No. He just thought he was Hemingway, but no one else did. Last I heard he was back at the Iron Works—married, four kids, board of directors at the country club." She pointed to another photograph. "That's Tommy Mishick. I slept with him after high school. He had bad breath. Great legs, though."

She flipped a page. "That's Raymond Senser or Schlenser, I forget which, and that's his brother Jed. Another good Des Moines family. Their father had a Stutz something-or-other, and we'd drive out to this gravel pit and drink liquor Ray used to get from some bootlegger downtown."

"You slept with them?"

"No, just rolled around the back seat a lot—one at a time—I had principles."

She flipped the page.

"I've never known anyone to keep an album of all their conquests."

"You've never known me," she replied. She looked into his face. "Do I shock you?" She drank off her whiskey and held the glass to him to refill. He poured it half full of liquor and walked to the kitchen for the soda. He brought the bottle back and shot a squirt into the glass.

"Shock?" he reflected. "No."

"Disappointed, then?"

"Would you prefer if I were? Disappointed, shocked?"

"You're the one who wanted to marry me."

"So now you drag out your sordid past—"

"*Sordid past*? Sounds a tad hackneyed."

"So does '*tad hackneyed.*'"

"Sit."

He did. She flipped through several pages and came to a series of airplane snapshots: Curtiss Jennies, Standards, a Swallow. She tapped a photo of her seated on the lower wing of an Alexander Eaglerock biplane, looking confident and smiling at the camera. "Then, I learned to fly."

"Who'd you sleep with for that?"

"No one," she said. "Men who fly seem to have trouble bedding someone who can out-fly them— threatens their egos, somehow."

"Strong stuff," Maxwell said. "How do you explain me?"

"You I can't explain," she said and looked at him. "That's what concerns me."

"You're weakening. Besides, who says you can out-fly me?"

"Trust me, I can." She turned to a page loaded with newspaper clippings and snapshots. Several were loose and fell onto his lap.

"Who's that?"

"Howard Hughes," she said.

"Jesus—"

"No, just Hughes. Although, sometimes he thought of himself as—"

"You really knew him?"

"Mmmm, yes."

Another page.

"Hey, that's Lindbergh." Max pointed. "And that's *you* standing beside him."

"And Bobby Trout, Louise Thaden and Amelia Earhart." She paused and they were silent knowing Earhart had vanished months before in the Pacific. Kate flipped a page and pointed to another glossy. "That's Doug Fairbanks, Jr., and this one is Frank Clarke, a stunt pilot. That's Roscoe Turner during the filming of *Hells' Angels*, and—"

"How many of them did you bed?"

"Professional secret. Not Turner, though." She turned the page again. "This one—" she said and paused.

"What about him?" Maxwell asked and stared at a wrinkled photograph of a man standing barefoot on a beach, the unseen photographer stood in the surf casting a shadow that pointed toward the subject. It appeared to be near sunset, and his shadow stretched away, pointing toward the beach houses in the distance. He wore slacks, cuffs rolled up and had a white sweater draped over his shoulders, the arms tied around his neck. He was Hollywood handsome. His smile was timid.

"This was taken on Santa Monica Beach. That's some movie producer's house in the background, and the one at the edge of the picture belonged to some other movie actor, Karl Dane or Malcolm McGregor, I can't remember. They were all movie people along there. Marion Davies had a place, a palace, actually, just up the beach. Paid for by William Randolph Hearst, of course. Everyone called it the Hearst Sand Castle. I think it was over that way, might have been the other way, I forget. What a crowd that used to hold."

"Who's the guy?"

"I think that was Hal Roach—"

"That's Hal Roach, the producer?"

"No, no, I mean the house back there. I think this house was Hal Roach's. We went to some party there—lots of fun. I think that's whose house that was."

"So who's the guy with the dopey grin, here, and no shoes?"

She said nothing and stared at the picture.

Maxwell turned his head and froze seeing the distant look on her face.

"That, my dear Maxwell, was my husband."

\*\*\*

# Chapter 14

# That Same Night

After they made love they stared at each other—two spent cartridges still smoking. Crickets made the hot August night feel darker. Wind stirred the trees, and the breeze washed cool across their damp bodies. Kate pulled the sheet across them and touched his chin.

"Why were you divorced?" she asked.

He sighed. "Wouldn't you rather know why I was married?"

"There's no trick to getting married. Anyone can do that—like falling off a log."

"Felt like a cliff."

"Getting divorced, however, takes talent."

"I didn't think so," he said and rolled onto his back. She ran her hand across his chest, and he said, "You know, you never ask much about me."

"Are you offended?"

"Curious."

"'*Curiouser and curiouser*,'" she recited. "I didn't want to snoop."

"I don't mind."

"Maybe I don't care."

"You're a cruel woman, Katie Strauss."

"And you'd want to marry a cruel woman?"

"I'd want to marry *you*."

"Oh, and what, then—reform me?"

"No."

"Soften me up?"

He looked at her. Weak light showed half her face and one naked breast. The sheet draped around it like a piece of sculpted art on display. When she saw him staring, she slipped the sheet completely off. To him, it spoiled the effect and, perhaps, that's why he asked what he suspected she wouldn't answer: "Why aren't you still married?"

"Does it matter?"

"Well, to an extent, sure."

"Some things you don't need to know about me," she said and caressed him roughly to dismiss the issue.

"I know I still want you."

"Even though I've been married—used goods?"

"Fairly well used up myself," he said.

She brushed the sheet below his waist then completely off his legs. She caressed his chest, stomach and further.

"Hardly used up," she said and leaned toward him, kissed him gently on the lips and moved along his cheek and onto his neck. When she reached his chest, she felt him press his hands against her ribs, lifting her. She slid a leg over.

"You are beautiful," his low voice rose from the pillow.

She arched her back, and he took her breasts in both hands, almost too roughly, and she clasped his arms. His hands slipped down her flanks and pressed at her belly and then took her thighs. She leaned forward and pressed her face to his, their mouths joined, her hands sliding behind his back, her legs squeezing together, and then, because the brain gets lost when the body releases, her thoughts began to shift and fly.

She remembered a cloud somewhere and flying around it. It made her giggle thinking of work when her whole body was taking leave of her control. She thought of Daryl. She moaned and felt a deep thrill deciding Max was better, not feeling it, but deciding. Joe's face raced past. She wanted him, too, and then she forgot him just as easily and wished she and Max were on a beach, Santa Monica Beach, to lie in the surf in the darkness and feel his body rocked by the ocean and be cool and warm. But she couldn't see his face in that fantasy.

She grabbed Maxwell's hands. Together they burst.


\*\*\*


"What time is it?" Max asked from the bed, his voice slower than his thoughts.

"Dark time," she answered.

He pushed onto an elbow, and when he saw her across the room, outlined against the night and wearing only her leather flight jacket, he realized how much he missed her long, unruly hair and said, "You look…" and groping for the exact word that would bring her back to bed said, "good."

Kate turned, walked a few steps and leaned against the doorframe between the bedroom and the front room. She pulled the jacket around her and twisted as though embracing the frame, and then gently rolled her head back and sighed. "Good?"

Maxwell slid both feet onto the floor, and, moving like what he thought was a cat but more closely resembled a coyote, approached her. Stopping at the door, he leaned against the opposite side of the frame leaving two feet of empty night air between them beneath the arch. Kate watched him over her shoulder, the only light coming from a yellow bulb in the kitchen.

"You look cold," she said.

"Is there room in there for two?"

Turning, she spread the jacket. He touched her navel with a fingertip. She shifted her legs, and he approached her, his hands taking her by the hips, his eyes dark slits in the shadows. Kate's face was half-lit from the pale glow. She took him with both hands and pulled him toward her, "You never seem to lose interest."

"How can I with you here? You're a good influence." His hands wandered up her back beneath the jacket, and he worked one hand into a pocket. "I want this forever, Kate."

"You don't want that," she said. "At least not forever."

"Do I detect a change in tone?" He kissed her.

"It's possible," she said.

His other hand slipped inside the remaining pocket and pulled the two jacket halves apart. "How'd you ever become a pilot, if you can't make decisions?"

"Who says I can't?" She gently bit his ear.

"I did." He pulled her close. Her breasts compressed against him. "You have no willpower."

"None," she replied, her voice a breath.

"A pilot needs...*ohh*—"

"Yes?" Teasing.

"I was saying, a pilot has needs—"

"Yes, I can tell, and yours seem to be insatiable."

"Your laundry list," he whispered.

She started to nibble his neck but looked up. "What?"

"Your laundry list." Max pulled a paper from her jacket pocket. "You left your laundry list in your...no, I'm sorry, it's your mail." He held an envelope up to the light.

"That's nothing," she objected and reached for it, a little too quickly.

"Feels like money in there." He shook it playfully just beyond her reach.

"Not nice to read other people's mail," she said and snatched the envelope from his hand. It tore. Something flew out and struck the wall.

"Don't move," he said. "It's caught on my toe." He raised his leg. "What is it, a necklace?"

Kate grabbed the medallion and stuffed it back inside the envelope. "Thank-you," she said, her voice suddenly formal.

"'Thank-you'? The lady says, 'thank-you'? That's all?" He reached for the envelope; she pulled it away. "I practically have my schwantz plugged into you, and—"

"Schwantz?"

"Yes. It's a medical term; means well-tempered clavier. Now, what was in the envelope that's so unimportant you don't want me to see it?"

"I thought you were the one who never looked in women's purses."

"True, but whatever falls out becomes public domain. Now, what was that?" He smiled.

Kate held the envelope containing the St. Christopher medal behind her back. She slowly took it from the envelope and held it up. The medallion dangled on its chain, twirling before Max's chin. He touched it timidly as though it were charmed. When he took it Kate let the chain drape over his fingers.

"Saint Christopher," he said, examining the image in the yellow light. "Patron saint of..."

"Travelers."

He looked at her. "Do you always carry it?"

"No," she said. "Someone gave it to me today."

"Who?"

"Does it matter?"

"Yeah, kind of. Who gave it to you?"

"Oh—" She took the medal away from him and stared at it. She turned. The weak light showed her whole face, now, and Maxwell suddenly thought she looked older. The lines in her skin were deeper, her eyes wide and sad.

Her short hair was mussed and dull. "You don't know him."

"Him?"

Her eyes blinked toward him, her mouth firm with thin creases arced at the corners in parentheses. She nodded. "I've told you before you weren't the only one. I've told you I've been married. There are others."

"I've seen the mug-shot book."

"You're jealous," she said. "That won't do."

"And I told you I don't care," he said. He tried to sound like he didn't care: "Did that belong to him? Your husband?"

"No," she answered. "Maybe it should have." She stared at the medal, before turning it over to read her name. "I don't think St. Christopher medals would have kept him alive."

Maxwell knew it was over. "I'm sorry...you should've said, should've told me..."

"Wouldn't have mattered," she cut him off. "It would've taken a great deal more than Roman Catholic Voodoo to keep..."

"Voodoo? That's harsh."

She turned. Her face was suddenly hard, her eyes cold. Maxwell felt himself recoil. He still held her, although, looser now. "Max, you and I have no business being together." She turned and pulled herself away. "I need the bathroom."

"Back there."

"I know where it is," and she left him standing alone in the doorway, his feet bare against the hard floor, his back suddenly tired and his shoulders heavy. He listened to her run water, followed by a long silence while he wondered what to do.

"What the hell just happened?" he asked himself, the way men often ask after the wreck.

When she returned she walked with the same purposeful stride he'd seen her take when approaching her airplane. It was movement without tenderness, mission-focused, and it left him cold.

"Would you take me back to the airport, please?" she asked in passing.

"Why?" He watched her drop her leather jacket on the bed, then pick her panties from under a chair. Her bra hung on the mirror, and one sock was in a corner and the other draped across the curtain rod.

When she buttoned her trousers, she looked up. "Could you hand me my boot, please. It's on the radiator...thanks."

Maxwell backed into the doorway, watching.

"You'd better get dressed," she said and stamped her foot into the boot. "That car seat's going to be cold on your bottom." She smiled, unsmiled and pulled on the other boot.

"I don't understand you, Kate."

"You aren't required to." She stood.

"Did I do something wrong? You can tell me—"

She approached him, head tilted to one side. She finished buttoning her blouse and tucked it inside her trousers. "I warned you, but you wouldn't listen."

"Warned me about what?"

"I said, don't fall in love with me."

"*But take me to bed*, huh? Is that how it goes?"

"You're good in bed," she said. "No, you're *great* in bed." She pulled on her jacket and rolled her shoulders. "You're too great in bed."

Dressed, she was Kate the pilot, the woman who flew the Travel Air, the woman who made more money flying than any pilot who struggled to survive teaching students or hauling small town bankers between nothing Iowa

296

cities. Kate Strauss, dressed, was as tough as shoe leather. Maxwell, naked, was spent.

***

# Elizabeth, New Jersey

Through a screened window, Joe saw the Packard sedan turn off Lower Road and skid to a stop outside the hangar door. His grip tightened on the .38 Special, heavy in his left hand. It was more like holding a small sledgehammer than a well-machined tool.

"They're here," he said over his shoulder without looking at his prisoner, trussed up wrist-to-ankle beside the Lockheed Vega. "I still don't know who-the-hell this guy Zwillman is, but I get the impression you don't like him." He looked toward the Vega. "Which means, he probably doesn't like you."

Another car entered the lot—a Buick, quickly followed by a Chrysler that parked on the road as though to block anyone from entering—or leaving. Joe walked toward the Lockheed, the pistol aimed more at the floor than toward his prisoner. Before he even reached him, however, he could tell the man was unconscious. Fresh blood flowed from the nose where Joe had smashed it into the concrete floor. "Maybe next time, you'll tell me who Zwillman is."

A door opened and Joe wondered if there'd be a next time for either one of them. Tall square men flowed inside the hangar. Dressed alike in summer gray suits, and hats low across their wide faces, they all held guns, except a small man who entered unobtrusively. Like a bank clerk at a KGB convention, he looked completely out of place. He wore a white short-sleeved shirt, loose slacks and light summer shoes. His tie was almost an afterthought, knotted through an open collar. He looked at the two dead men—Mr. Friendly and Frank Deagan; Frank partially covered by a tarp. He looked to Joe.

"Where's Deagan?"

"Dead." Joe pointed. The clerk nodded.

"You Joe?"

"Me, Joe; you Zwillman?" Very Tarzan.

The look in response from this clerk made Joe lose any trace of a smile. They knew his name and they had many guns; he lowered his one pistol. "I'm a friend of Frank's," he said and for the first time since the fight, felt his voice choke. Grief or terror, he wasn't sure. "I...I *was* his pilot." There was silence, then, "You Zwillman?" Less Tarzan, more Jane.

The clerk looked away from him and around at the hangar as though taking inventory. His voice was strong, yet easy. "No," he said. "Forget the name Zwillman; you don't need to know it." He waved the men behind him toward the bodies. They shuffled forward like furniture movers. One checked Friendly for a pulse. "Dead," he pronounced.

"That's the one who killed Frank," Joe added as if it mattered. He felt his voice strengthen.

The clerk looked at him, surprised to hear him speak out of turn. He motioned for Joe to follow him outside. "I want to talk to you," he said and started through the small door in the larger hangar door. They both had to duck.

"This one's still alive," someone called.

Joe answered back, "I had to hit him—in the nose." It didn't sound as tough as he'd hoped. He turned to the clerk, "Who are they, anyhow?"

"Idiots."

They stepped through the door. The sunlight, although hazy, seemed bright after the dark hangar.

"That's their car," Joe added and pointed back inside at the Studebaker. The tarp had slid away making it look hastily concealed. Two men hefted the unconscious trussed man by his armpits and ankles and dragged him across the floor. Joe watched them open the trunk and stuff him inside. "He's bleedin' all over," one said. "So what," the other answered through a grunt, and the legs were folded to fit. "Heavy bastard—"

"Well, don't lift him like that. I've told you a hundred times—lift with your legs; you'll strain your back doing it your way."

"Oh, yeah—"

"Use up all your sick leave with lumbago, keep doin' that."

Outside, the clerk turned on Joe, "I don't know what you know—"

"*I* don't even know what I know."

"Where'd you get the phone number?"

"From Frank," Joe lied. "Who are you, if you're not Zwillman?"

"Name's Ernie—"

"*Ernie?*"

"Yes, and that's all you need to know. Now, how much did Frank owe you?"

Joe answered too quickly, "About a thousand."

Ernie reached inside his pocket and took a roll of hundred-dollar bills. He peeled off two, paused, and then a third. Folding them, he slipped them neatly into Joe's shirt pocket. "More than you're worth," he said.

Joe took the bills from his pocket and contemplated them for a moment. A thin smile played at his lips. "Hard for an honest flyer to make ends meet in this game."

"Then, you'll do fine." Ernie had to look up to face Joe, but when he did, Joe felt at the disadvantage and blinked.

"You get two hundred a week until we find someone else," Ernie said. "You answer the phone; you take messages. You go where I tell you, when I tell you." Ernie ran a hand across his face and massaged his eyes. "I don't know squat about airplanes," he confessed.

Joe listened.

Ernie looked at the hangar and the ramp. "How the hell we ever got behind this pack of nonsense, I'll never know."

Joe ventured, "Zwillman's idea?" Then, "Sorry—I know, *forget Zwillman*...He's forgotten. Never heard of him—Zwillman? Zwillman-who?"

Ernie looked at Joe. "It was never my idea to get into this, this anti-fascist crusade—"

"Mine neither."

Ernie, the mob clerk, ignored him, talking as though to himself. "Frank was okay, but he was some sort of political nitwit. That, however, was his business."

"His business—"

"Ours is making money. Abner just had a soft spot for a cause, I guess."

"Abner? You mean, Zwill—?" A look from the clerk. "Sorry."

"Those two dip-shits trying to muscle into this were absolute morons." He shook his head. "A couple of clowns."

"SPAM for brains."

"Everyone knows how things work around here. Everyone knows what happens if they don't pay attention and get stupid."

"What happens?" Joe asked, but getting the look his hands shot up, one still holding the gun. It looked like a backwards hold-up, "Hey, I'm not everyone, I don't know how things work 'round here."

Ernie talked past him as though lecturing a small class. "There are no warnings. You get out of line, and you're through." He looked into Joe's eyes. "That one you had tied-up in there?"

"Yeah?"

The clerk's head tilted and Joe looked inside the hangar toward the Studebaker where one of the furniture movers pointed a small pistol inside the trunk. *Pop*—the shot was flat but loud. Joe flinched. The second and third shots were flatter yet—like rivets driven into soft steel—*Pop-Pop*.

"Done," Ernie, the clerk, said. He watched for Joe's reaction but saw a cold look returned. He liked that. "Now, they take that garbage over to Bayonne, stuff it inside about six barrels—hands here, head there—then onto a barge, out to sea and—fish food offa Sandy Hook." He wiped his hands and turned for the Packard. "Stay by the phone. Don't talk to anyone, and forget you ever knew Frank Deagan—"

"Or you?"

A smile. "Do that, Joseph, and you get two hundred bucks a week. Forget that, and—" He shrugged like a tailor who couldn't get sleeves to match, and he slipped inside the car. It started and was gone.

Behind Joe, the furniture movers loaded Mr. Friendly's body into the trunk. It took a little jumping, but they made it fit. The trunk lid shut with a soft click. Studebaker—good latches. The hangar door opened, and the Studebaker Dictator pulled away with a wave from the driver as he passed. Joe returned the wave. The tailpipe scraped the pavement over a bump—weak springs; not designed for heavy trunk loads. Poor engineering on Studebaker's part; some Dictator. Good latches, though.

Thirty minutes later, a hearse pulled into the lot. Two men in black entered the hangar.

"We're here to pick up."

Joe pointed. "There." He watched. No one said more than was necessary to lift Frank's covered body onto the cart and slide him into the hearse like a loaf of bread into the oven. As the hearse left, a police car drove in as though on cue. The lone officer walked past the sand-covered bloodstains and approached Joe. He removed his hat. It was hot. "You, Joe?"

"Me, Joe."

The officer looked tired, the way New Jersey cops get after a while. His blue uniform was stained dark from sweat, and he sounded bored. Hell, he was bored. "I need you to sign your statement."

"Didn't know I gave a statement—"

"Yeah, you did." The cop—face blank—offered a clipboard with a typed form attached. Joe read the report without touching it. Neatly filled-in with a short description of Frank's '*accident*,' it detailed how Frank Deagan— '*an independent airport employee*'— had fallen from a step ladder, struck his head on the toolbox— a diagram was included—and hit the concrete floor, whereupon his neck broke. "Sorry for your loss," the officer said and unscrewed a Schaeffer pen. "Sign at the bottom, near the X."

Joe took the clipboard and pen. "Very efficient police work."

"So kiss my ass. Just sign the statement. I got better things to do, if you wanna know."

"I don't." Joe scrawled his name across the bottom. "Can I keep the pen?"

"Eat shit, pal." The officer snatched the pen back.

"They make those in Iowa," Joe said pointing at the pen. "Did you know that?" Pause. "I used to live there."

The cop screwed the cap onto the pen without taking his eyes off Joe and without betraying any interest in anyone living in Iowa. With a glance, he took in the Vega and the various airplane parts. "You a pilot or something?"

"Or something. Are you Zwillman by any chance?"

The policeman's face held the blank expression, "Do I look like a Zwillman?"

Joe shrugged. "Maybe a little around the eyes."

Returning his pen to his pocket, the cop said, "Sometimes I get tired. Sometimes I just get tired of this shit, if you wanna know." Joe still didn't *wanna know,* and the cop drove away along the side road toward the highway.

Alone in the empty hangar, Joe slowly walked across the floor. Frank's coffee cup hung on a nail over the hot plate in the office. He picked it off the nail and examined the brown stain inside. "'*You should never wash a good cup,*'" he recited. "You told me you should never wash a well-seasoned coffee cup, Frank." He brought the cup to eye-level and studied the mallard ducks on the side and the thin crack in the ceramic glaze. Holding it out at arm's length, he opened his hand. It broke into a million pieces, maybe, a billion. Another *'accident'.*

***

# Chapter 15

# Autumn

"Mornin', Daryl," the voice was hollow through the wall.

"Good Morning to you, Mr. Barcus," Daryl called. He poked his hand into the post office box and, expecting it to be empty, was surprised to find an envelope. He recognized the handwriting. Small and even with little flair, it was hard to tell whether penned by a man or woman.

"Good news, I hope," Mr. Barcus, the postmaster, said. His face was barely visible behind the boxes. He'd been postmaster since the previous century. "Of course, your mail is your business—I don't mean to pry."

"It's from Katie, Mr. Barcus," Daryl shouted because the postmaster was nearly deaf. He turned the envelope over hoping she'd written a return address this time. His heart dropped when he saw the blank reverse. Even the postmark was no clue. Being a pilot, she could have mailed it from any place. The previous letters had all been from different towns, some in Iowa, some Illinois. This one was smudged, but read, Washington, Iowa. It could have been Alaska for all the good it did him.

"How is the girl?" Barcus asked.

Daryl slit the envelope open. Even before doing so, he knew from the weight there would be no letter. He removed a money order for $200. The airfield would be paid off in a few more months. Already, she'd settled the tax bills and other outstanding debts. On paper, *Trans Midwest Air Taxi Service* was in the black, but not through Daryl's efforts. If only she'd come home, he thought.

"Is she well?"

"Huh?" Daryl mumbled and looked through the box. Half of Barcus' face showed, framed. Kindly, old and a little nosy, he wanted to know about Kate. "Sure," Daryl said and slipped the check into his pocket. He rustled the envelope and cleared his throat. Pretending to read, "Ah, she says she's fine, and she's coming home for Thanksgiving—"

"Oh, now, isn't that wonderful?"

"Or Christmas."

"Well, you give her a big hug for me when you write her."

"I will, Mr. Barcus, I will." He started to close the box. The postmaster's hand stopped him. If anyone had walked in, they would've seen Daryl talking to a hand waving from a post box. Even for southern Iowa, that was odd.

"Daryl, I still haven't seen your Bonus Check, yet," Barcus said. "Have you registered?"

"Not yet."

"Everyone else has already got paid—the vets that is. Why haven't you registered? You are entitled, aren't you? A veteran and all?"

"Yeah, sure," Daryl said. "Thank you." He shook the hand, pushed it back inside the box and snapped the door shut.

Stepping outside the post office, Daryl held the door for an old woman who smiled at him adding that Jesus would remember him. He thanked her, and Jesus, and walked down the stairs and onto the sidewalk. The Nash was parked across the street with Brian behind the wheel. He looked proud and Daryl thought he looked older; maybe, just bigger since the summer.

"Morning, Daryl," a man called from a passing car. An arm waved from the window, but the face was hidden. Daryl waved and crossed the street.

The day was cool and bright—a big contrast to the brutally hot summer now passed. A slight breeze moved from the northwest indicating it would be cold by dusk. Already the trees around the square had shown their peak colors, and the leaves dropped to the gutter and blew in dry heaps between the cars.

In front of *Pipers* corner grocery store a clerk swept the leaves into a neat pile and chatted with a pretty girl. She wore green plaid and held schoolbooks close to her body. He wore a white apron around black trousers and a red bow tie at his knobby throat. She giggled, and he stopped to light a cigarette. He said something, and she giggled again. She touched his arm, and then—*Ooops*—dropped her books. They almost knocked heads picking them up.

"Any mail?" Brian asked.

"Something from Kate," Daryl answered and climbed over the passenger door. He'd welded it shut rather than replace the worn latch. "What time is it?"

Brian pushed up his sleeve. He was proud of the watch Daryl had given him for his birthday and admired it before he gave the time, "Eight."

"You've got to be at school by what, eight-twenty?"

"Ah, nuts to school," Brian muttered.

"Ah, nuts to intelligence," Daryl mimicked him. "Drive. You don't want to be late."

"What if I cut gym and come out to the airport?"

"Then you'll be fat as well as ignorant."

The Nash complained as Brian searched for first gear. "I think your clutch is going," he said.

"The way you ride it, I'm not surprised. Drive, you'll be late."

They both whined at once, "Ah, nuts to being late."

It was a short drive to the school. Brian drove the speed limit to delay the arrival. "What'd Kate have to say?"

"Haven't read it yet," Daryl answered and stared at the orange and yellow leaves. "You can see how the drought's muted the colors this year. Of course, the drought ruined them last year, too." He turned to Brian. "How long do you think a drought can last?"

"Until it rains."

"School's not being wasted on you." He watched the trees in silence.

"Why don't you read Kate's letter?"

"Maybe later," he said. "You know, this drought's causing dust storms down south. Walls of dirt flying off the fields and blowing away. I read where they say the whole Midwest could just blow into Mexico if the farmers keep cutting down trees and doing whatever it is farmers do." He turned and faced Brian. "Course, now, I think it's the bankers causing the dust storms. After all, they tell the farmers to grow more corn and wheat and whatever it is farmers grow, and then the farmers have to rip out the trees and chop the land up and—"

"Is Kate ever coming back?"

Daryl looked at Brian's profile. Becoming strong with the inevitable acne damage—the penalty for youth—it was the profile of a boy in transition. Not just a kid hanging around an airport anymore, Brian was becoming a man without passing through the phases in between. "No," Daryl said quietly. "She's gone."

Brian turned off the paved road onto the gravel lot in front of the school. "I'm late," he said and pulled the hand brake.

"Want me to pick you up at three?"

"Naw." He took his books from the seat. "I'll hitch a ride somehow."

"It's no problem."

Brian climbed over the door—it, too, was welded—and onto the running board. The car bounced. "You work on the racer; I'll get there when I get there."

Daryl nodded and slid behind the wheel. Brian waved and walked away. He moved heavily with a rolling gait, one hand in his jacket pocket, his other holding his books. Unnoticed by other students in the yard, he walked alone up the stairs and through the heavy double doors. Daryl drove off.

\*\*\*

Leaves blew across the highway. Angelo turned the Ford off the pavement and onto the dirt lane, where he stopped, got out and opened the lock on the cable strung across the entrance. He then dropped the cable and returned to the car. The tires pressed the cable into the dust, and he shifted into second. It was a short drive up the hill and across the ridge. The trees were full of orange and yellow. The air was dry and cool. He drove with the top up and his window down. He passed the mine entrance; the steam shovel and mine super structure rusted and still. It must have been Benjamin's day off—either that or the rat population had thinned to the point where he had to move on. Angelo turned past the shack and drove, still in second, down the slope to the runway. He stopped and got out of the car. Where the sun had not yet reached there was still dew on the grass. Grasshoppers, warmed by the sun, popped in swarms around his ankles.

"Grass needs mowed," he said to himself. It was the sort of thing Iowans say to themselves. Coming from Chicago, he wondered why he'd said it. He looked again; the grass still *needed mowed.*

\*\*\*

Kate was cold, and on top of that, she was sick. Hunched behind the windscreen, she felt the chilled wind seep around the glass and curl inside the cockpit reaching into her pant legs and under her jacket. She wondered when the hell the winter flying suit she'd ordered would come in. She tapped the oil temperature gauge. "Cold beast," she muttered.

Ottumwa was ahead, the Des Moines River, low from the dry summer, barely moved through it. She stared at the municipal airport, its handful of airplanes parked on the ramp. One hangar was open and a truck drove to a side door. It looked so lonely and dull outside the city, isolated and so far from anything. It depressed her.

Turning away from the river, she flew for another ten miles and then brought power back approaching the bottomland outside Blakesburg. Off to her right a cornfield was being harvested, a horse-drawn wagon driven over the stubble. The field was rimmed by trees and near the road stood a white house. A woman hung laundry on a line. Like Kate, she fought the wind as it snapped the washing back at her and she'd vanish in the white billows. Kate stared at her for a moment and felt her depression intensify. The woman moved her basket as Kate's shadow passed overhead. Without looking up, the woman took another sheet from the basket and tacked it to the line. Kate descended toward the mine. She could see the super structure above the shaft but not the airfield, yet, beyond the river.

\*\*\*

Angelo pulled a weed from the runway, shook the dirt clear and tossed the stalk into the bushes. He walked along and bent and pulled another. He picked up a stone and tossed it, too, to one side. He scanned the runway for badger holes and nudged his pistol beneath his jacket itching to spot one of those bastards.

When he heard Kate's engine, he glanced at his watch. "Good girl," he said and walked back up the runway. He carried his Panama hat in one hand and thought it time to unpack his winter clothes—the dark blue suit with dark gray fedora. Wearing the Palm Beach suit into October, although a major fashion gaffe, even in Iowa, somehow, made summer linger. But winter was coming.

He saw the biplane over the trees. A frail collection of wires at first, the nearer it came the more mass it displayed. Angelo shaded his eyes against the sky. Kate was merely a peg behind the wings, a part of the machine growing as it descended toward the runway. His pace quickened, and he stooped to pluck another weed before clearing.

\*\*\*

The landing was good, no bounce. Kate's head bobbed from side to side in quick turns until the Travel Air had slowed, and she taxied in lazy S-turns toward the car. Angelo leaned against the car door, one foot on the running board, and, when Kate looked toward him, he waved and smiled.

He watched the spinning propeller slow. It took a few turns, the engine clanking, a stray puff of smoke disappearing behind the gear legs, and the prop stopped. Silence.

Kate pulled off her helmet and ran her fingers through her hair, kept short, so from a distance she resembled a man. When she stood, though, and Angelo saw her hips as she climbed over the cockpit rim, there was no mistaking her for anything other than the prettiest woman he'd ever know. He also noticed, now, how she moved without her usual energy. Angelo walked toward her, his hat still in his hand, his jacket open.

"Good morning," he called. "Good flight?"

Kate was slow getting over the cockpit's rim and slow to reach into the front hole. She glanced back at him, her face trying to smile. "Hello, Angie," she said. She wiped her nose on her sleeve. Her face was red, her eyes running, and she shook with a sudden chill. "Cold up there."

Angelo was beside her at the wing. "You don't look so good today," he said. "You been getting your sleep?"

She laughed. "A second mother I don't need."

"So you're not getting your sleep?"

"I'm getting plenty of sleep, Angelo." She undid the seat belt holding the box. "Here," she said and handed it to him. He tucked it under an arm.

"Eating okay?"

"Your concern is touching."

"It's my job to be concerned about employees."

"I'm not an employee," she said. "I'm freelance."

"Then I'm concerned about the contract labor, all right? Jeez, you're a pain in the ass at times, you know that?"

"I've been told," she said and squatted on the wing bringing her knees almost to her chin. Angelo thought how young that made her look, how so like a little girl, and, dressed in the leathers and boots, her short hair wild from the helmet, she could have been a kid playing dress-up, wearing clothes she'd found in the attic. "To tell you the truth, Angie, I feel like hell."

"Get another pilot. Didn't Joe have a back-up pilot just in case?"

She shook her head. "Yeah, but we need the money."

"We? Who's we?" he asked. "I don't know what you see in that bum—"

"None of your business," she replied.

"Daryl's a bum. And you're still supporting him, aren't you? Sending him money, I'll bet. A bum. A true bum."

She looked at him. "How is he?"

Angelo shook his head. "He's good, I guess," he said. "He misses you, though."

"That's sweet."

"What is it about you? About him?"

"Nothing," she said. Her eyes closed, and she seemed to be forcing something to remain inside. "There's nothing about either one of us; we're just us."

"Then why don't you go back to him?"

She opened her eyes and looked around at the empty runway and distant trees. A few clouds blew past. The day was bright and growing colder as she thought about it. "I've gone back to him," she said. "Many times—too many times. I've run out of times."

"He ain't drinking now," Angelo said.

"And he's always 'not drinking now,'" she said. "It's an old scenario. I've seen it played out before. Sometimes a person gets tired of the same old song."

"He misses you."

"You've said that—old song."

"Well, he *does*."

"And I miss being twenty-five, but that doesn't give me the right to demand that time stand still."

"What's that supposed to mean?"

"Who knows?" she said and stood. She pulled a handkerchief from her back pocket and blew a loud raspberry. "What's he doing?"

"We're putting together his racer."

"We?"

Angelo shifted his feet, turned and tossed the money package into the Ford; a $10,000-brick flew through the open window and bounced off the seatback and onto the floor. When he looked at her his eyes were filled with a boyish excitement barely held in check.

"You should see it, Kate. It's looking great! We got the wings all painted up—red, bright red. After Brian and me been sandin' on them. Sanded and sanded, and Daryl, he'd lay another coat of dope on, then we'd sand again, so's it's smooth as a baby's butt. It's looking sweet, let me tell you."

"You sound like you've been in the clubhouse with the other boys playing make-believe." She laughed. Angelo cringed. She looked down at him, an amused smirk playing at her mouth. He suddenly wanted to yank her off the wing and punch her square in the face. Something inside, though, said he wasn't supposed to do that to girls.

"You don't give no one no credit," he pouted.

"Oh, I do so," she replied. "It's just that Daryl's been playing at running an airport, and that's not how the bills get paid."

"He's getting by."

"With my money! Sure, anyone can make a go of a business if there's a continuous flow of cash to smooth over the mistakes—makes it sort of like a government project. You'd think I was the WPA.

"No," she continued, "Daryl's going to have to wake up one of these days and realize he can't be carried by everyone else forever. People get tired of that after a while."

"Like you got tired?" Angelo asked.

"Like me, yes," she said. "Don't tell me you didn't think Daryl was taking complete advantage of you—in France. Isn't that what I've heard?"

"Where'd you hear anything about France?"

"Christ, I've lived with the big lug for too many years. I've learned a little about him along the way—a little about him and Joe and you and all the other war buddies all big-parade comrades from the goddam war. All thick as thieves, all so condescending when it comes to giving anyone else an ounce of consideration."

"You've got no reason to—"

"To what? To be miffed? To be sick and tired of you middle-aged heroes living like the only thing ever happened in the world was that stupid war?"

"You don't know."

"You're damn right I don't know." She found her voice shaking, tears filling her eyes.

"You don't know what went on."

She laughed. "Funny, hearing you defend him."

"I ain't defending him," Angelo said. "I'm just tellin' you that you don't know nothin' about what went on, and you got no reason to be callin' him or me, or anyone any names—not until you've been there yourself."

"Girls," Kate replied, "don't get to fight wars, so we'll never know, now will we?"

"You ain't supposed to know," he said and saw Kate begin to protest. His voice stopped her, "There ain't no one's supposed to know."

He stalked away leaving her staring from the wing. When he reached the car, he opened the door and looked as though he'd jump in and race off. Instead, he stood there holding the door and, with eyes closed, he seemed to be sniffing the wind, the way a dog might. When he spoke, his voice was low, but clear. "Kate, you ain't never gonna know what's inside of the man. You ain't supposed to." He turned. "It's been a lot of years since we was over there, and I suppose it should all be forgotten—the dead, the stink, the stupid shit of the whole thing." He chuckled. "Funny, I can't remember what started the whole thing in the first place, something about democracy, wasn't it?"

"I thought it was about submarines," she wondered and slipped from the wing. "Didn't some duke sink a German ship or something?"

"Titanic?"

"No, Lusitania."

"Don't seem worth it now." Angelo thought for a moment, his eyes focused halfway to nothing. "I suppose we look silly, all fat and gettin' bald and still thinkin' about bein' in uniform and, and carryin' grudges and all."

Kate walked toward him and stopped near the bumper. Angelo set his chin on his fist on the top of roof. "Daryl's a bum," he said. "Don't ever forget it; I can't. You get too close to him, and you get burnt. It happens. Maybe we should do the bastard a favor and shoot him—dump him in a hole and cover it over. We'd all be better off."

"I've considered it," Kate said quietly.

"I know where I could get us a shovel." Angelo pointed over his shoulder at the distant steam shovel. He smiled.

"No," she said. "With him gone, who'd we have to complain about?"

"That's what we figured in the Army, so we didn't shoot him."

"Pity."

"Yeah."

For a while they said nothing. Kate took her handkerchief from her pocket and wiped her nose.

"You ought to be home in bed," Angelo finally said.

"Not me." She pointed toward the Travel Air. "I've got work to do."

"Want me to tell anything to Daryl? Like you said 'Hi' or 'Go ta hell,' or something?"

Kate smiled, thought for a moment, and then, "No. If he asks, just tell him—" She waited but nothing came, so, "Just tell him I have a cold."

"He'll worry."

"I know, and I wish he wouldn't," she said. "I gotta run. Give me a twist?"

"Sure," Angelo said and followed her back to the airplane. He stood near the propeller and watched her climb inside. She was putting on her helmet when he said, "This thing needs a bath. Don't you ever wash it no more?"

"Why bother?"

"I don't know—pride, I guess."

"Not mine. I'll wash it before Joe comes back—whenever that is."

"You ever hear from him?"

"Joe? No, well, just that letter last July saying, *'keep the ship as long as you need.'* Little did he know."

"He won't recognize it when he gets back."

"The way the money's coming in, I'll buy him a new one."

"He's probably makin' so much money, himself, over there in Spain he won't accept."

"Hey," Kate interrupted. "Switch is on. Let me get out of here."

*** 

The Travel Air lifted from the runway and bobbed on the wind as it turned away from Angelo who watched with both hands shading his eyes. He saw her wave, and he waved back. The biplane grew smaller and the engine noise turned to a distant hum, then nothing. Angelo started the car and drove back up the hill, past the mine entrance and down the short road to the highway. When he locked the cable across the entrance, he stood for a while and stared at the empty road feeling its loneliness seeping inside him in a way that made him feel somehow useless. Useless with $10,000 on the floorboards.

*** 

When Kate landed in Davenport, only Louie was there.

"Where's the gas kid, ah, Brad?' she asked coming through the door.

"Brent?"

"Yeah, him," she mumbled, not really caring.

"Home with the flu bug."

"Max?"

"Got himself a charter," Louie answered from behind the counter. It was warm inside the restaurant, and the wind, stronger now, blew against the screen door. "After that, he's heading up to Des Moines; got himself an interview."

Kate started. "Who with?" She sat at the counter. Louie slid a coffee cup in front of her, and she held it to her lips letting the steam rise into her clogged sinuses.

"United."

Jealous, she felt herself slip a notch, to lose ground against her former lover.

Louie detected that and continued as delicately as possible. "United's got some Boeings they run through there. He applied long time ago. I guess they're starting another class for DC-3s, and he's been called for an interview. Didn't he tell you?"

Kate sipped her coffee, acting disinterested. "No," she said. "We don't see each other much."

"I've noticed. He dump you?" So much for diplomacy.

"Nobody dumped anyone," she replied. She looked above his head at the cigarette display. "Give me a pack of Old Golds, will you."

He dropped one on the counter. "Add it to your tab?"

"Please," she said with a weak smile.

"I don't know what it is about you flyers," he said and wrote the charge on a pad and clipped it to a stack with Kate's name attached.

"We're all bums," she said. "Let me have a couple of aspirins, too, please. I'm feeling like hell."

"Bug's been going around," he said and opened a small tin. "Here."

"Thanks." She took two, popped them into her mouth and washed them down with coffee. Louie refilled the cup. "Thanks," she said again. Wind shook the screen door. "Makes it seem colder. God, I feel like hell."

"Here, lean forward." She did and Louie wiped his hands on his apron and pressed his palm to her forehead. "Sweetie, you're burning up."

"It'll go away," she said. "Give the aspirin a chance." She turned on her stool. It squeaked. "Did he take the Waco?"

"Who?"

"Max. Did Max take the Waco to Des Moines for his interview?"

"Yeah," Louie said. "Here." He unscrewed the cap on a small tube. He pulled out a thermometer. "Open wide."

"What?"

"You heard me. Open up, put this under your tongue." He shook the thermometer then held it before her face.

"How do I know where that's been?"

"You don't, but I guarantee it's only been used in the proper end. Now, open—" She moved away. "Kate, you're sick and look like something the cat drugged in. Now, open your mouth, stick this under your tongue. I don't want you spreading germs all over this place and killing off my customers. I got enough trouble keeping them as it is."

Kate took the thermometer, "Well, okay," and placed it under her tongue. *"Unther pwoteft,"* she lisped her protest.

Three minutes of silence followed while the wind snapped at the screen door and dried weeds tapped against the outside glass. She stared at the ramp. It looked cold and empty and lonely. Two Monocoupes rocked their wings like ships bobbing at anchor.

"Here, let's see," Louie said and took the thermometer. Pulling his glasses on, he held it to the light and whistled.

"Top the charts?" she asked and dropped her head on the counter.

"You're a sick little girl, Katie. One-oh-two."

"Fahrenheit or Centigrade?"

Louie was around the counter untying his apron. He patted her back and massaged one shoulder. Her head still on the counter, she moaned slightly and curled her arms around her face. "Can I stay here until tomorrow; I fly tomorrow, you know. I fly every day. That's all I do—fly, fly, fly—" Her voice faded into babble.

"You're coming with me," Louie said and took a sign from behind the door and placed it in the window: GONE FLYING—COFFEE—FIVE CENTS.

"Where?"

"Home."

"My home's in the hangar," she said, and he twirled her around on the stool. "I live in the hangar, remember? The little room in the back of the hangar—one cot, two blankets, no water and all the mice I can catch?"

"You're sick, Katie. Now, take my arm."

"I can walk," she said and stood. Instantly, blood drained from her face, and her knees wobbled. "Oh, my," she muttered. "What the hell is wrong with me?"

Leaning heavily on his arm, she allowed him to guide her outside, where she dropped into his car and folded double on the seat.

Her ears rang, her head swam. Fever made her skin crawl with sweat, and then freeze in jagged chills. All this in the time it took Louie to walk around the car and open his door. "Move your head," he said and gently nudged her.

"Can't," she said. "Not attached anymore." She felt him carefully push her aside, and she marveled at how helpless she was becoming. "Cold," she said.

"Put this over you," he said and draped a musty blanket over her. He started the car. "The heater doesn't work so good, but we aren't far."

Kate tried to say something, but her brain seemed to be on fire. She curled onto the seat feeling small and suddenly wishing she were in her own bed, her bed where she slept with Daryl. The car bounced through the gravel ruts, and she heard the whine of the old transmission through the seat. When the ride smoothed out, she knew they were on pavement and drifted into feverish sleep. "I haven't tied the plane down yet," she said and tried to sit up. Louie's hand, gentle yet strong, pressed her back onto the seat, and she fell asleep.

*** 

Steps, a door, Louie explaining to someone why Kate was there; and then fog and silence and more stairs—these creaked but were muffled by carpet—and a bedroom with a window that looked into the trees. Wallpaper straight out of SEARS ROEBUCK, a repeated pattern of tiny blue flowers on beige climbed the walls and by staring at them, trying to trace each vine, Kate lost all sense of depth perception. She turned. A Bible on a table. More fog. A candle—not lit. A table lamp on a doily—lit. She was standing against the wall, then—as though time burped—she was inside a bathroom leaning over a toilet—cool porcelain—and a woman with a kind voice, said, '...*there, there,*' or '...*here, here,*' or '...*how dare.*' Kate could not remember. She was in a bed now—big and soft, and the room with the SEARS ROEBUCK wallpaper was cold, and the room was hot, and she slept and she woke, and she couldn't make it to the bathroom, and the woman said, '*there, there*—'

Louie and his sister, Geraldine, shared a house that had been in the family since before either of them had been born. Louie kept two rooms at the rear on the first floor while Geraldine kept a large room on the second floor. Kate was in a tiny guest room in the southwest corner of the third floor. Above her room was sky. A narrow staircase led to the second floor below, and a wide curved window gave her an uncluttered view over the elm trees, past the rooftops and toward the airport.

Lying in her bed, damp with fever, her mind unfocused between sleep and consciousness, Kate saw a sunset, then stars, and Geraldine brought her something hot, and she slept, and when she awoke the cup was untouched and cold and the room dark, except for the soft glow of a three-quarter moon.

She slept.

\*\*\*

Sunlight, although bright outside her window, barely lit the room.

"Are you with us today?"

Kate shifted herself under the covers. Cottonmouth from sleep, her eyes heavy, she looked at the round woman approaching her bed.

"I'm Geraldine," the woman sang, and Kate thought it was Louie in drag. "Louie tells me you're a pilot. I think that's so strange." She chuckled as she spoke and required no response from Kate. She spoke like someone used to living alone, someone used to taking both parts of a conversation.

"Louie has gone off to that airport." *That* airport. "He says you took ill after some flight." *Some* flight. "Well, I can believe that. Imagine, a pretty young thing like you going around in those machines on a cold day when good sense says to stay indoors. I ask you—"

*No you don't*, Kate thought as she watched this strange woman set a tray on the night table at Kate's side.

"Can you sit up?"

"I—" Kate's voice came out like putty through a straw.

"Let me get you a pillow," Geraldine said and took a massive feather pillow from a small closet and, without waiting for Kate's response, lifted her head and slipped it behind her. She was strong, and Kate was helpless. She moved herself up the pillow until her back rested against the headboard, and it was then Kate noticed her clothes.

"Where's my jacket?" she asked and looked around. "My pants, shirt?"

"Oh," Geraldine laughed. "Those old things were so disgusting I've sent them off to be cleaned." She set the tray on Kate's lap. Four tiny legs held it above her thighs. "I don't know how you could stand to be in them." She pointed at the tray. "Those are prunes, stewed prunes. Should cleanse you right out."

Kate's stomach recoiled at the bowl of withered lumps floating in what looked like tobacco juice in a spittoon. "I don't think so," she said.

"Ha," Geraldine laughed, sounding almost like a bark. "Louie said you'd say that. Ha!" She turned and headed for the door. "Those will set you right in no time. You just need to cleanse the system out, and all that flu-ish nonsense will flow right on out." Her arms moved with her speech indicating some great wave action of bowels and the gushing of evil humors from Kate's body. "You obviously do not eat right," she noted with a chirp. "Louie tells me you've been eating *his* food, and that just will not do." She sniffed the air, then fearing she may have offended Kate, she laughed, "Yes, ha!" And she turned and exited through the small door. Her footsteps were padded thumps descending the stairs, and Kate heard another door click below.

Kate sat for a long time staring at the bowl of prunes. Slowly, she lifted the tray and set it on the nightstand. The effort almost exhausted her, and she let herself melt back into the covers, her head sinking deep between the folds of the feather pillow. Sleep quickly took her, again, but before it did she peeked beneath the covers inspecting the pink flannel gown that had somehow replaced her black leather jacket, boots and trousers.

Pretty young thing? She never felt so ancient.

\*\*\*

A light forced her eyes open. Kate lifted her head. The window beyond the foot of her bed was all gold. Kate pushed herself onto one elbow and tried to pull the bed covers back. Wind rattled something against the roof, and she saw a bird flit past—a brief shadow in the gold.

Her legs moved slowly, the bedcovers and flannel gown catching between them. She pulled the covers back and sat up.

"Oh," she moaned as a wave of nausea swept through her, and she felt herself slipping back onto the mattress. She let her head drop to the blankets, the quilt's satin edge was cool against her cheeks. It smelled faintly of camphor, and she worked her fingers through the folds, all the while staring at the brilliant gold on the curved glass.

It changed colors—from bright to amber and finally complete blackness. When the moon rose Kate was asleep again.

\*\*\*

She heard it through her dreams. At first, her mind put the sound above the Santa Monica Beach, above the surf and the cool water against their ankles. The sound of an airplane's motor began as a vague intrusion into the warmth and excitement she was experiencing with the man on the beach. She tried to ignore it, to will it away. She tried to see into the man's face, to feel the details of his strong arms and broad shoulders. She knew his face was there, but the airplane's motor kept coming, and with the increase in pitch, her lover faded.

"What?" Kate shouted and sat straight up in bed. The roof shook from the passing blast of an airplane buzzing it. Her feet kicked from under the covers and hit the floor. The room was cold. She threw the covers completely away and lunged for the window. Pressing her hands to the glass, she caught sight of the retreating silhouette of a biplane. She strained to see better and fumbled for the latch holding the window shut.

The frame stuck in the tracks, but with a quick heave the window flew up, the sash weights knocking inside the wall. "Hey!" Kate shouted at the biplane. "Hey! Come get me!" She waved and leaned far out the window, a castaway hoping to be rescued. The cold air against her clammy skin revived her. She stopped waving and watched the biplane—the Waco, Max's airplane—heading toward the airport. Barely over the trees, he rocked his wings, and Kate wanted nothing more than to be in that airplane.

Kate sat on the window ledge, her strength bled, her right leg crooked beneath her left, the gown hitched above her knee. Her hand caressed the warm skin, and she closed her eyes and breathed in the cold air. When she looked again, the biplane was a dot approaching the runway far away. When she could no longer see it, she climbed off the ledge and walked back to the bed. Her legs weakened. She slipped beneath the covers and faced the wall, breathing the clean air from the window and picturing Max's biplane. But not Max.

When it was dusk, Louie entered the room. "It's cold in here," he said and closed the window. Kate was awake, having slept, on and off, throughout the day.

"Are you in the habit of sneaking into a lady's boudoir?"

"Normally, I don't have to sneak. More than likely, I'm turning away the invitations." He looked at her. "How are you, Katie?"

"Better. Tired. What time is it?"

He looked at his watch. "Almost dark."

Kate sat up in the bed. "I must look like hell."

"You do," he said. "And you smell bad."

"Louie."

"Just being honest." He sat on a small chair in the corner. His face was in shadow. "But sick and smelly with a bad haircut, you're still the cutest pilot—"

"Oh, Louie," Kate said. "What the hell have I been doing here?" She looked quickly around the room. "I haven't flown. I haven't made the run...what day is it? Oh, how the hell—"

"Hey, calm down," Louie interrupted. "You're not forgotten. We've covered for you." He lit a cigarette, his face briefly orange in the flame. "Do you think your friends would leave you hanging?"

Kate sighed, "Who?"

"Maxwell," he said and blew smoke at the ceiling. It collected in a small cloud before it vanished in the darkness. "Your old pal, Joe, had a good relief system worked out long before you arrived."

"He never said anything."

"And you never thought to ask, did you?"

"No."

"Saw no need, eh? Thought you could fly every day, never missing a trick."

"Maybe," she said.

"Never occurred to you that you were hired over Max? Took his job?"

"I'm qualified—"

"So's Max." His face glowed bright as he inhaled. "Can't do everything yourself, Kate."

"Give me a cigarette, please." He stretched toward her and shook one from the pack. She took it. A match flared. She leaned toward it and sucked in the hot smoke, dragging it deep into her tired lungs. "Oh, crap," she sputtered and looked at the burning tip.

"Taste bad?"

"Maybe I'm not ready for this yet," she said and looked for an ashtray.

"Give it a try. Your lungs are weak; need to readjust. That burning is a healthy sign; tells you the germs are being smoked out." He inhaled a draw. "Best thing for the lungs, a little smoke." He blew it out in cute rings at the ceiling. "Give it time."

\*\*\*

# Chapter 16

# Chicago Heights

Trucci stayed inside the car and smoked yet another cigarette—the seventh or twelfth since he'd arrived; they weren't getting any better, but it gave him something to do while he waited. After each drag he'd tap it against the dashboard ashtray and then turn the windshield wiper knob to clear away the wet film outside. The ritual went: *Drag, tap, turn the knob*—and repeat.

It was only a light mist against the glass and would have taken several minutes to accumulate enough to block his view of the runway, but Trucci was impatient and absolutely hated to wait for anyone.

Moisture distorted the warehouses in the gloom on the far side of the low hill. He rolled down the window to flick the butt into the wet grass where it hissed and died with the others. He listened to the sky and opened the door.

Pulling his hat low across his eyes, he flipped up his collar, which made him feel like a gangster until that illusion vanished when he carefully tiptoed through the weeds hoping to keep his $20 shoes dry. Once he saw the uselessness in that he walked onto the runway full stride.

All around him was a dripping vapor; silent as snow, and almost as cold, it coated everything without forming puddles. He walked the full length of the runway, his shoes quickly soaked by the wet grass; his trouser cuffs wicked dampness into his socks and garters. He pulled his cigarette pack from his coat and shook one out. He held it between his lips and walked to the end of the runway without lighting it. When he turned, he listened for the airplane engine—still nothing.

"Where is it?" he asked himself. Had anyone overheard him, it would have been assumed he simply spoke to himself—something one might do on a rainy day waiting for an airplane on an illicit landing field in Chicago Heights. Had someone known Trucci, and few did, they may have realized he actually spoke to someone else.

It might sound like praying. He was talking to a friend. Trucci was talking to Lenny. Having purposely ignored his death, he lately found himself seeing Lenny in odd places. At first, it worried him. He felt like his grandmother when she would invoke the saints, Garibaldi and the memory of her long dead husband, God rest him. In moments alone, unobserved, in moments of worry or pain or depression, he'd speak to Lenny, and—this was the worrisome part—he'd listen to his old friend answer.

"Would you fly in this crap?" he asked.

"I wouldn't fly in this crap," he answered.

"Those pilots are fuckin' nuts," he observed.

"Got that right," he agreed.

And so it went as he walked back along the runway and water collected on the rim of his hat and rolled in fat drops onto his coat and into the unlit cigarette.

"She didn't fly in the last few days, you know, Len."

Lenny knew.

"She's sick, I hear from the other guy makin' the run."

"Probably got the flu that's goin' around."

"Yeah, and watch me fuckin' get it standin' out here in the fuckin' rain like a fuckin' shmuck."

"Hope you don't talk like that around her—"

Lenny had a point, but Trucci didn't want to admit it, so he didn't say anything. They stopped and looked at the dull overcast. It remained stationary and settled tiny droplets on Trucci's face. It was cold.

"How high you think those clouds are?"

"Hundred, two hundred feet at the most, maybe. Too low far as I'm concerned."

"I don.'t think she's gonna die or nothin'," Trucci said and began walking again. Lenny didn't answer. "She's pretty healthy lookin', you know." Still, he wouldn't answer—he could be like that sometimes; for a dead guy Lenny could be a real jerk.

Trucci shoved his hands deeper into his pockets and shifted the unlit cigarette from one side of his mouth to the other. "God, I think she's pretty," he sighed. "You know what I mean, Len?" He walked a few more steps. "Course, I don't think she gives a rat's ass about you an' me, you know? Dames like her is all kinda too good for the likes of you an' me, you know?" He walked.

"Hey, you wanna know something, Len? You know what I went and did?" He stopped and bent over, hands still in his pockets. "Jeez, you're gonna shit when I tell ya."

Lenny waited.

"I give her that—Oh, Christ, it was fuckin' stupid."

"What?" Lenny was back.

Trucci stood upright and inhaled, then: "I give her that St. Christopher medal your brother, Angie, brought back from the war. You know the one? Said he carried it all over and never got shot or nothin'. Remember? That was when I asked him to be my sponsor for Confirmation, and you told me I was a fuckin' shmuck for askin' him, and all, but I did, anyhow, so what the fuck, huh?"

Trucci took the cigarette from his mouth and watched a drop of water fall off his hat and soak into the paper. He tossed it away.

"Angelo said he'd do it. Remember? I think you was jealous when he said yes." He listened, then, "Oh, yeah you *was*!

"He gave me that St. Christopher medal, and said it'd bring me good luck." He paused. "I wish he'd given it to you, Len. Honest, I wish'd he had." He walked along the runway, and when he got to the car he opened the door and heard the faint murmur of an aircraft engine. He closed the door and watched the lead gray sky. "Man, it looks ugly up there—"

"Got that right."

"Would you fly in this shit?"

"Not me; would you?"

"You nuts? Not me—"

\*\*\*

Maxwell was scared like never before. Visibility shrank as the ceiling lowered until it was like flying into a fuzzy cone with everything closing in the further he went, and like so many flyers he kept going hoping things would improve.

The Waco biplane felt stationary in the mist—no way to tell up from down, left from right, life from death. The air was smooth, the ground occasionally there, long enough to give him a chance to right his head, level his wings, and then just as quickly, it was gone.

All gray.

He lost control for several seconds along the Illinois River and just as his knees began to shake and his mouth went dry, he saw a road, slick and empty and beautiful below. Already skimming the trees, he pushed forward on the stick and squeezed back the throttle. "Get me down, get me down," he chanted the pilot's prayer.

The road curved between barns and power lines and crossed several railroad tracks. When he saw four tracks converge with a set coming in from the south alongside a busy two-lane, he knew he was on course, and Chicago

Heights was near. *'All railroads lead to Chicago'* Joe had once told him. *'Follow one.'*

His eyes strained through the mist. He leaned his face into the slipstream against the sting of the 90 mile-per-hour water droplets. He was cold but ignored it. He glanced at his map, spreading it with his gloved hand on his lap. Holding it between his thighs seemed to keep the shaking under control and the map from flying away. All in all, he was terrified.

A railroad track led off to the northeast, and he followed. He glanced at his watch and estimated a time. Doing the arithmetic kept his mind from locking with fear, but, still, tiny needles of fear prickled at his scalp. He thought of Kate making this run day after day without incident. "Man, what a stupid woman," he said aloud.

"There!" he said to an unseen co-pilot. "Those power lines, then the road." He looked at the map and the hand drawn details Joe had once left for him, *'...should you ever be called upon to make a few dishonest bucks'*. Fifth run and he was still unsure of the route. Fog didn't help. His finger traced along the route and stopped on the red pencil smudge indicating the field. He knew where he should be on paper, anyhow.

Below, Chicago Heights. Square houses flashed past. Power lines snatched at him, trying to snag a gear leg or clip off his tail. He looked down and saw a woman duck as he appeared out of nowhere and blew past her yard. He saw a dog run behind a bush, and he saw a car stop outside a garage. He dropped the map.

"Baloney—" he muttered and reached for it beneath the seat. His fingers stretched. He lowered his head below the panel, just for a second. He grabbed the map and raised his head long enough for his throat to emit a sound like mashed potatoes forced through an oboe.

\*\*\*

Trucci watched but had no explanation for what he saw. The biplane appeared out of the fog to the southwest. Barely above the buildings it, nonetheless, seemed headed directly toward the far end of the runway. Trucci, looked at his watch—pissed—reached inside the car and took the daily package from the seat and was turning to watch the landing, when he saw the airplane bank toward the warehouses.

It looked silly. A perfectly good runway was just off to the pilot's right, and yet, the pilot seemed determined to fly straight into the buildings on the hill.

Trucci did nothing; there being nothing he could do. It all happened as though in a newsreel against the sky's gray screen.

### CINETONE INTERNATIONAL NEWS ©
### *"News In Brief"*
### *THE AIRMAIL MUST GET THROUGH!!!*

(Music up)

<u>Newsreel Narrator's voice:</u>

"Nine steps to a spectacular arrival!"

"Step One—*Just For Fun*: The biplane's nose pulls sharply up.

Step Two—*What Did He Do*: We hear the engine bark, fart and howl.

Step Three—*Up A Tree*: The Waco's gear legs catch the peak of the warehouse. Hope he's got insurance, folks!

Step Four—*Bar The Door*: The wheels, legs and odd parts from beneath the fuselage stay with the roof.

Step Five—*Man Alive*:  The biplane fades into the haze, nose high, and engine howling.

Step Six—*Pick Up Sticks*:  A loud crunch, like lumber falling off a speeding train, and the Waco drops from the mist striking the adjacent warehouse roof, the nose turns to the right as the right wing shatters into the suddenly exposed rafters and roofing tin.

Step Seven—*Go To Heaven*:  A sheet of rusted siding scrapes past the struts, smashes through the windscreen and slices Maxwell's head off at the chin. Ouch!

Step Number Eight—*Nothing Straight*:  The Waco spins a half turn and drops off the roof.  The propeller, incredibly still turning, chews away more roofing tin, takes the gutters off and throws pieces in a wide arc, and then, nose first, the biplane impacts the ground crushing a Model A Ford coupe and breaking a window in the side of the building.

And Number Nine—*Pay The Fine*:  The police arrive, and they can tell Mr. J. Edgar Hoover, he won't believe this one!"

(Music out; fade to black)


\*\*\*


"I don't know who the hell he is, was," Trucci protested and walked around the twisted collection of tubes and cloth, gasoline and blood.  A county wagon drove away—the same one Lenny had ridden.

A plain-clothes detective, his rain coat stained from the mist, walked ahead of Trucci kicking at pieces of the airplane and occasionally humming a bar from Beethoven's 'Ode to Joy'.  Trucci just thought he was humming.

"What happened to the girl?" the detective asked and pulled a bloody map from what remained of the cockpit. His finger traced a pencil line to the edge of the chart where it ended abruptly in a ragged tear along the Mississippi. "Where is she?" he asked without looking up.

"What girl?" Trucci asked.

The detective slowly turned toward him with a knowing grin on his wide face. "You don't own *me*, Mr. Trucci. You and your partners may own every other policeman, judge, street sweeper and dog catcher in the area, but you don't own me."

Trucci said nothing. The detective walked further along the wreckage. "Made quite the mess, now; quite the mess." He hummed the same 'Ode To Joy'.

"The pilot didn't have the money on him, did he? I'd say this was an inbound flight, dead-heading?" He smiled. "Wouldn't you agree?" He raised a hand. "No you wouldn't say anything without your lawyer—good thinking, good thinking."

More humming. More joy.

"My instincts, Mr. Trucci, tell me that you probably had the money on you. You then beat-feet out of here and stashed it before we arrived, hmm?"

He hummed again—*'Ode To Joy.'* He looked at the sky, still heavy and damp. Moisture rolled off the Waco's rumpled fabric. "I've never seen an aeroplane wreck before; quite the mess, quite the mess, yes, yes, yes—" and he hummed—*Joy, Joy, Joy—*

"Good thing that girl wasn't inside there," he said. He turned to Trucci. "She's a cute little thing, isn't she? Nice ass, wouldn't you say? Off the record?" And before Trucci could react the detective pulled several photographs from his pocket and handed them to Trucci.

"They're useless as evidence, but you might like them for, oh, for a family album." He turned aside humming.

335

Trucci thumbed the pictures; all taken with a long lens, all grainy, but unmistakably of Kate near the airplane, on the field in Chicago Heights. He stared. Just seeing her face made him want her, then fear for her. The detective was walking toward his car and called over his shoulder.

"You can keep those, Mr. Trucci. I suspect this little phase of your operation will shift outside my district. Anyhow, it wasn't her I was after—it's you, Mr. Trucci. You and all your friends in town. I really wanted that boy, Lenny, but he took care of himself all right, so now it's you I want." He smiled and hummed.

"I don't know anything about this," Trucci shouted. "I'm a businessman. I run a warehouse—auto parts. That's all."

"Yes, Mr. Trucci, auto parts," the detective said. "And, now, a few aeroplane parts added to your inventory, eh?" He opened his car door. "It's been fun, Mr. Trucci. I'll keep in touch." He scraped mud off his shoe on the running board, climbed inside and closed the door. The engine started, and he backed away.

Trucci looked at the photographs again and stuffed them inside his pocket. Walking away from the airplane wreckage, he called, "Clean it the hell up," and he went for his own car. He wanted to punch the gas pedal, to kick gravel and speed away, but Trucci operated on a more controlled level. Knowing he was always watched, he slipped the Packard into gear and calmly drove off. All the violence, the anger, the confusion remained coiled inside him. Barely away from the warehouse, he reached inside his pocket and removed the photographs of Kate.

"She's a beauty, Lenny," he said to himself. "Damn, that woman's a beauty." It was then he stomped the pedal and the Packard lunged forward, Trucci's grip squeezing the wheel, his eyes narrowing, his mind flailing for balance.

Topping 70 mph, he passed a junkyard where a dog lay at the end of its chain, its muddied legs stretched before it as though sleeping, and its emaciated face soaked with rain. Crows on the dog's back barely noted Trucci's passing and Trucci took no notice of dead dog or crows.

Once on the open highway, he opened the Packard's throttle and ignored the needle pressing 80. Billboards flew past; telephone poles clicked through his peripheral vision, and he found himself tensing with the excitement of anger transformed into speed.

Through a long curve the Packard floated past a truck. Back into his lane, and he flashed across a short bridge— fast whine of tires on steel grate, gentle thump off the other side. His foot to the floorboards, and still the Packard seemed to want to go faster, to bring more power from beneath that immense hood and transfer it through his fingers on the wheel.

Then, because he was Trucci—not Lenny—he pulled his foot from the pedal, shook his head and licked his lips. His eyes glanced to the needle dipping below 60, and he shook just a little as he spoke to Lenny, "So, I'm a shmuck sometimes—"

He drove for several minutes in silence, before adding, "So are you—sometimes."

\*\*\*

An hour outside Chicago, where a yellow *Shell Oil* sign loomed above the trees, Trucci pulled off the road and stopped beside the tall, white and yellow pumps. A skinny teenager, who resembled a pump in his yellow service cap and white overalls, ran toward him wiping his hands on a rag.

"Fill 'er up for you, mister?"

Trucci was caught off-guard by this cheerfulness. "Yeah," he answered, his voice dry. "And check the oil." The attendant ran to the pump. One of the newer electric kind, he turned a key, snapped a lever and inserted the nozzle in the tank. Up came the side of the hood, and his head disappeared. His moves were quick.

Trucci stepped outside the car and stretched. His footsteps crunched in the loose gravel, and he inhaled the cool air. A car sped by and disappeared over the hill.

"Oil's okay," the attendant called and latched the hood. "Radiator could use some water, and you might want to clean those battery terminals before winter."

"Huh?" Trucci responded.

"Those terminals look as though they ain't been cleaned in a while. A guy should brush them off and put a little baking soda on 'em each time you change the oil." Trucci's blank expression made him continue. "How often do you change it?"

"Change what?"

"Oil." He turned three letters into two long syllables, *"Ohy-yul."*

"Ah, I dunno, ah, every now and then, hell, I dunno. Mechanic does that crap. What the hell do I know about oil?" He laughed. But he didn't want to laugh; he really wanted to pull out his gun and shoot the dumb shit.

"Well, a guy could keep a little book in the glove box. You know, with the records of each oil change." They stared at each other as though speaking different languages. Trucci's bemused smile spread into a wide grin. "A guy could do that," the attendant added nervously then wiped his hands.

"Yeah," Trucci said. "Thanks. What do I owe ya?"

He looked at the pump. "Ah, dollar and a half for the gas."

Trucci reached for his wallet then asked, "You got a map inside there—Illinois, I guess, and one for Davenport, wherever the hell that is."

"Yes, sir, I'll fetch them for you."

He returned with the two maps and handed them to Trucci. "How much for them two?" Trucci asked.

"Oh, no charge for the maps."

Trucci shrugged and handed the boy a two-dollar bill. "Keep the change."

The attendant's eyes widened. "Thank-You, mister." And he saluted. He reached to open the door for Trucci. "Have a good trip."

"Yeah," Trucci said, the grin still on his face. He ducked to slide inside and turned back, "Are you for real, or what?"

"Sir?"

"Never mind," Trucci said, and then before slipping into the car, he chuckled, pulled out a five-dollar bill and pressed it into the boy's hand. "Keep up the act, Kid— you'll go far." He started the car and left a confused attendant behind alternately staring at the disappearing Packard and the five-dollar bill.

***

From a phone booth inside a small store just across the Mississippi River, Trucci called Chicago. "Yeah, collect, that's right...huh? *Trucci*, like it sounds, that's how you spell it, for Chrissake," he growled and looked around the one-room store at the clerk behind the counter and the two older men in bib overalls sitting in cane chairs beside a stove. He closed the door to the booth.

"Hello?" a voice came on the phone.

"Who's this?" Trucci asked.

"Who's *this*?"

Realizing this could run on for several exchanges, Trucci said, "This is Trucci. Lemme talk to Paulie."

There was a pause, then the voice, one Trucci didn't recognize, said, "Just a sec."

Trucci sighed and leaned against the phone booth wall. Holding the receiver loosely to his ear, he waited. The front door to the store opened, and leaves blew across the wooden floor. Muffled hellos followed by chair legs scraping against the floor made him look. A third man had joined the two at the stove. Before he sat, he pointed toward the sky and shook his head. They all nodded their agreement and shook theirs.

"Yeah?" a voice answered the phone.

Trucci's eyebrows wrinkled. "Paulie?"

"Yeah?"

"Trucci, here," he said and something alarmed inside his head. He stopped. The line crackled with the long-distance static, and through it Trucci thought he heard someone humming.

"Mister Trucci, how good of you to call," the voice said, and Trucci knew he was talking to the same detective he'd just left at the crash site. "I'm sorry your friend, Paulie, cannot come to the phone, but, is there a message I could deliver?" Then there was that humming, just like he'd done at the crash—'*Ode To Joy*.'

Trucci held onto the receiver and moved slightly away from the wall phone. Someone laughed inside the store, and the front door opened again. Chair legs scraped.

"Mr. Trucci, are you still there?" the detective asked, obviously amused. "If you're still listening, maybe you'd care to join your friends down at the station? I have some extremely interesting papers with your name on them.

"Now, before you hang-up on me, Mr. Trucci, I know you're saying to yourself right now how silly an inconvenience this all is, raiding your book-making enterprise, after all the insurance money you've paid out, you and your friends...Are you still there? Hello?"

Trucci found himself leaning toward the phone again. He said nothing. The detective continued, "Oh, good, I hear you breathing. You needn't worry, Mr. Trucci, your colleagues will be out before close of business. I believe the attorneys have already swung into action—bail set, bonds posted, judges bribed—that sort of thing. It is such a bother for you, isn't it?"

Trucci wanted to shout, to reach through the phone and strangle the cop. Instead, he said nothing. Balance; it's all about balance—keep it you win; lose it and you're Lenny.

"Mr. Trucci, I must confess something to you." The detective laughed. "This wasn't planned, you know. This raid. You should have seen my captain's face when I waved the warrants at him. I had to go completely outside my precinct to find a judge you fellas didn't already have in your back pocket. Found an honest sort who swore the warrants out quick as a wink. Just between you and me, Mr. Trucci, he, too, is as dishonest as hell, but that worked out fine as those who keep him on their payroll have a grudge against your organization." He laughed and hummed. "Small world, Mr. Trucci. Small world." *'Ode To Fuckin' Joy'.*

Trucci considered the implications of his being on the road with $10,000 in company money in the trunk while the police pulled their first ever raid, or at least the first raid that wasn't staged as a pre-election stunt—the kind where a few clerks—winos hired for the day—are hauled away, hands cuffed, faces hidden in shame, tough cops pressing them into paddy wagons while the local ward boss poses before the cameras.

This, Trucci surmised, was the real thing. Somehow, this detective had slipped through their system and was running amuck. He wouldn't last long, not in Chicago, but meanwhile, he could prove troublesome, until someone augmented his detective's retirement fund. Or shot the prick.

"I must thank-you, Mr. Trucci, for being there when the aeroplane cracked up today. Until then, I had no plans for you, but when I saw you drive off as you did—with all that money—and I lost you heading away from town, well, I just began to do some figuring—"

Trucci slammed the receiver on the hook, pressed his fist against his lips and stared at the floor. *Balance, balance, balance—*

He plugged a nickel into the phone.

*Bong.*

"Operator," the nasally voice whined.

Trucci's voice was low, "Chicago Heights, ah, 'HEights-8-5-6-0-7, collect from Trucci." He waited and fumbled for the pack of cigarettes inside his coat pocket. Only one left, it was bent at a 30-degree angle, but he slipped it between his lips and searched for his lighter—couldn't find it.

Balance slipping.

He looked through the glass. Four men now sat around the stove taking turns pointing at the sky while the others nodded. It was like some kind of religious weather rite.

Someone answered the phone. Trucci was calling the warehouse but didn't recognize the voice.

"Will you accept charges from a Mr. Trucci?" the operator asked.

"Yeah," the voice answered.

"Go ahead, sir," the operator said and disconnected.

"Who's this?" Trucci cautiously asked.

There was silence, then, quietly the voice said, "It's me, Mr. Trucci, Sergeant Manaski. I can't talk, 'cause they brought in a bunch of Feds lookin' over that airplane wreck and all, and they hauled off the whole bunch of your people here. I heard one of them Feds sayin' this busted the investigation wide open—"

"What the hell have I been paying you dickheads for?" Trucci screeched. Eight eyes around the stove stopped evaluating the sky long enough to look toward the phone booth. Trucci barely lowered his voice. "Who the hell is that detective?"

"I don't know, Mr. Trucci. Some kind of special investigator from the D.A.'s office—down state, Republican—out of my—"

"Shut up, Manaski," Trucci hissed. He glanced through the glass at the stove where one man pointed toward him, shook his head, then poked a stick into the fire.

Trucci rubbed a hand across his forehead. "I'd better get back there," he said.

"I don't think that's such a hot idea," Sgt. Manaski warned. "You're in a world of hurt right about now."

"Bullshit," Trucci muttered. "So they pop me in the can for a night. I call the lawyer and—"

"It's not the law you have to watch. It's your own people." There was silence and then, "I don't want to say nothing, but it looks real bad you racing away from here and less than an hour later the whole place gets raided...Hey, I gotta go," and the line went dead.

Trucci carefully set the receiver on the hook and stayed inside the booth thinking. Blood drained from his face. A sharp rap on the glass made him start.

*Jeez!*

"You okay in there?"

Trucci turned and opened the folding door. The bent cigarette clung to his lower lip, and he said, "Yeah, fine." He faced the store clerk.

"You just looked like you was sick or something. Maybe you should set a while. Maybe up by the fire. It's getting nippy outside, and folks is getting the bug's been goin' around, you know. You have a temperature, or something?"

"No," Trucci said and squeezed past.

"Hey," the clerk called before he reached the door.

Trucci turned. The store was silent except for the wind sucking smoke through the metal chimney. "You left a nickel in the phone here." The clerk held the coin so all could see. They all looked to Trucci. High point of their day.

Slowly, he walked back across the floor and took the nickel and placed it inside his pocket. "Yeah, thanks," he said and walked past the crowd and out the door.

The car was parked a short distance away, and they watched him get inside and leave. For the remainder of the day and most of the following week, conversation around the stove centered on '...*that fella come in here the other day in that Packard and shouted like he was crazy or something into the phone. Right over there. Like he was crazy.*'

'*Left a nickel, too.*"

'*Yeah, he did.*'

'*Gave it back, too.*'

'*Yeah, ya did.*'

'*I'd'a kept it.*'

'*Yeah, ya would, too.*'

Laugh. Pause. Repeat.

Trucci drove a short distance before he pulled off the pavement and followed a dirt road. He stopped beneath a stand of trees where he could see a piece of the river. A barge, leaving a wide V in its wake, crawled past. He rubbed his chin. Before he realized what he was doing, he had taken the photographs of Kate from his pocket and fanned them across his lap. One by one, he studied them and realized he wanted nothing more than to be with her.

He thought about the raid.

"What a load of nonsense," he said. "It'll straighten itself out. Christ, there ain't no sense me goin' back there and gettin' popped with the rest. After all, I'm the one who kept them from takin' the day's receipts."

He looked at the pictures once more and placed them back inside his pocket.

"What the hell, Lenny. I'll stay out of sight for a few days, go see your brother, Angelo, and give him the dough. No one's gonna think I'm pullin' a fast one." He started the car, relieved that he'd come up with a plan. "I'll go see your brother. Ang'll straighten anything out." He backed the Packard in a semi-circle and shifted into first.

"So what?" he said. "So maybe I'll see Kate. So what? Is that a fuckin' crime, too?

"Huh—?   Okay, Okay, I'll watch my f..., my language."

\*\*\*

# Chapter 17

## Ottumwa, Iowa

Angelo hung up the telephone. The landlord stood at the bottom of the stairwell pretending to dust the banister. When he heard Angelo hang the receiver on the hook he asked, "Bad news? I hope it wasn't bad news." It was the second call his tenant had received in six months, and that was one too many. Mostly, though, he wanted to know what it was about, and bad news would prove more interesting.

Angelo looked down as though no one was there, and a voice had called from the air. He climbed the stairs to the third floor, stepped inside his room and closed the door.

It was after sunset, and the room was half dark except for a yellow wash from a gooseneck lamp on the night table beside the bed. A copy of *LIFE magazine* lay opened to the page Angelo had been reading when he'd been called to the phone.

He closed the door, pulled the bolt and hooked the chain. Walking around the bed, he closed *LIFE* and dropped it into a wastebasket. He, then, slid the night table one foot from the bed and reached to a small shelf to remove a clean white face towel and spread it open on the table.

Angelo then turned a quarter circle and opened the top dresser drawer where he kept his cufflinks and tie tack. He removed a lump wrapped in a blue rag, which he slowly unwrapped. Inside was a brown leather shoulder holster containing a 1911 Colt semi-automatic, chambered to .38 Super—a potent badger killer. He draped the blue rag over his forearm like a waiter and set the pistol, still inside its holster, on the center of the white towel on the night table.

The ceremony continued, and from a lower drawer he lifted a small metal box wrapped inside another rag, also blue. This rag he spread on the dresser before he opened the box and took out a small bottle of solvent and a can of oil. He swiveled and set one on each side of the pistol like wine and water cruets at mass. He then placed a short spiral brush at the base of the towel, beside the holster, and slipping his suspenders from his shoulders, he sat on the edge of the bed, his back straight, and everything within reach.

A snap released a leather strap and the pistol came away. He set the holster on the dresser and adjusted the lampshade, lowering it until the wide beam narrowed to light the altar, leaving his face in shadow. Although his fingers were thick, they worked the pistol with a familiar gentleness.

The clip came out of the grip. Pressing with his thumb, he popped the stubby bullets onto the towel where they nestled together like pigeon eggs.

Next, he set the clip beside the bullets and snapped the pistol's slide back. Holding it to the light, he inspected the barrel—no round and clean except for a fuzzy sprinkling of dust.

He opened the bottle of solvent. To avoid spilling, he held the bottle with one hand and soaked the brush, carefully tapping it against the lip.

The metal bristles were tight against the barrel and pulled through with a gratifying swish. He held the gun to the light and, again, ran the brush through and, again, held it to the light.

A small wad of cotton attached to a shoestring soaked up the excess solvent and left the barrel shiny and without blemish. He then fished a slightly oily wad through, pulling the string with the dexterity he'd shown when dime-fishing through the sewer grate, and the barrel was done.

Piece by piece, Angelo dismantled, cleaned, inspected, oiled and reassembled the weapon. He did so without moving from the bed and barely moving any part of his body, except hands that reached for items without hesitation. When, finally, he had reassembled the entire piece, except the clip, he picked a bullet from the towel.

Holding it beneath his face, he turned it slowly in the amber light. Smaller than the end of his little finger, he carefully wiped it clean with the rag and set it on the dresser. He took another and repeated the ritual until all were lined like squat soldiers in a row.

He inserted the bullets into the clip and then snapped it into the grip before he returned the pistol to the holster and placed it and the cleaning kit back inside the dresser.

From the bottom drawer, he took a clean set of pajamas—flannel, white with thin blue stripes. Once in bed, he turned off the light and stared at the dark ceiling knowing he would not sleep. Never could before going into action.

\*\*\*

# Chapter 18

## November 1937

Kate sat on the window seat. The sun, through the wide glass, was warm against her face. Clouds raced above the trees, and the few remaining leaves dropped from gray branches. She sipped a cup of tea and looked into a neighbor's yard where a man in a red plaid coat had raked leaves into a pile and set it aflame. He moved to one side, leaning on his rake to watch them burn. Smoke rose in a twisted column, was caught by the wind and blown apart above the trees. Kate opened the window hoping to smell the burnt leaves, but the wind carried it away from her, and she sipped her tea, her knees pulled to her chest, both hands cupping the mug.

A soft knock.

"Come in." The door opened behind her, and she turned. "Hello, Louie," she said and turned back.

He was beside her before he spoke. "All the heat's going out the window. You'll put me in the poor house buying coal."

"I'll pay, if you want."

"No," he said. "Keep it open." He sat beside her, his feet pointed into the room with his back to the window. He had to twist uncomfortably to see her, and when he looked into her face he shivered.

For days she'd been at the window when not in bed. A cold breeze rustled her hair, and she moved a hand slowly to brush it from her cheek. She placed the teacup against her lips and stared across it to the trees and rooftops.

"It's getting colder," she said.

"That happens," he said back, uncertain if she meant the tea or the weather. "Look, Kate—"

349

"Louie, do you like winter?"

"I tolerate it, but I'd just as soon—"

"Did Max say how the interview went?"

Louie sighed and placed his hand on her shoulder. "No."

"I'll ask him," she said. "But not today. He doesn't like me asking him about work and about the interview. He's funny that way." She turned on Louie, her eyes vacant inside her puzzled face. "I think he should take that job with United. Don't you?"

"Yes." Louie's voice a crack.

"I think he should." She raised the teacup to her lips again, the cold tea lapped against them, but she never took any. Just stared.

"Katie," Louie said.

She looked at him. "Yes?"

Louie's insides ached trying to speak. "Do you remember what I told you about Max?"

Head cocked. "Yes," she answered. "Why?"

"Didn't you believe me?"

"Louie, of course I believed you," she laughed. "You wouldn't joke about something like that."

"Kate, the man is dead. Maxwell is dead, Kate—"

"Louie, I know that," she said. "You don't have to treat me like some child."

"Then why, Kate, do you keep asking me about him like he wasn't?"

"I'm concerned."

"About what?"

She looked out the window and, again, brought the teacup to her lips. The stare almost carried Louie with her beyond the bare trees and smoke from the neighbor's fire. "I don't like winter, Louie. I don't like it at all."

"I know," Louie answered softly. He started to move away from her.

"I like being in California, in Santa Monica. Did I ever tell you about Santa Monica?"

Louie nodded.

"I have pictures," she said as she set the teacup on the windowsill and stood. "They're around here somewhere." She turned. "Max brought them over when I was ill." And she kept turning. "They're in an album. I have all my pictures in an album." She stopped and stared through the open window. "Unless I left them with Daryl."

"Kate, maybe you should get back in bed."

"No," she snapped. "I want to show you the pictures. They're from California, of me and, and Bobby Trout, and Charles Lindbergh, and Roscoe Turner and some movie actors—Doug Fairbanks, Richard Arlen...Ah, and there's one of me with Wallace Beery beside his Travel Air 6000. Did you know Wallace Beery had a Travel Air 6000? That's the big monoplane, did you know that?"

"No, I didn't."

"He did, and—"

Kate bent to look under the bed, then stood and glanced around the room as though seeing it for the first time. "I have pictures," she slowly said.

Louie was beside her, his arm across her shoulder. She felt small and frail, and she looked up at him, her eyes now loaded with tears, her chin quivering, and he felt his own face crumble with pity. Enveloping her in his arms he sobbed, "Oh, Kate, I miss the dumb bastard. I miss him, too."

Kate's arms held him. His head pressed against her shoulder. She caressed his scalp and lightly kissed him. When he released his hold it was as though all strength had left him, and he slumped against the dresser, head down, eyes moist.

"Jeez," he managed to say. "I—"

"It's all right," she whispered and sat on the bed.

"I guess that makes me some kind of big dope, now, doesn't it?"

"Something like that," she said. "That makes us all some kind of—" She ran her hand across the bedspread. "Louie, it just wasn't fair, that's all. I shouldn't have been sick."

"Things happen whether someone's sick or not."

"He crashed, he died, because I didn't fly."

"It wasn't your fault, Kate."

"I didn't say it was. But he did take my place, and he did crash, and he did die. That's the sequence: One, two three. I don't take blame, I just know—" She thought. "I know what happened, that's all. Max died, because Max couldn't fly worth a hoot."

"Kate—"

"You want truth? You want to see if I can tell the truth? Crazy Katie, locked in her tower, hidden from the world; can she tell where reality leaves off and fantasy begins?" She laughed and jumped from the bed moving toward the window. "I'll bet you thought I've been losing it here lately, huh?"

"Kate, no one—"

"No one what? No one what, Louie? No one thinks poor
Kate's got all her marbles in one bag? Is that it?"

"You didn't kill Max—"

"I never said I did! Damn it, Louie, get it thorough your thick, damn head; I do not take the blame."

"I don't believe you."

"Then don't," she said and stared through the window. Sunlight crept low through the glass driving a shaft across her face. "You want me to take on this pile of guilt. You seem to want a martyr, someone left behind to wail and gnash her teeth—to beat her breast." She clasped her fists together and pressed them firmly between her breasts.

"You want sin punished and me to repent, to beg forgiveness from your pretentious Midwest morality. You want to bless me with your indulgence and see me drop in line with everyone else."

"What everyone else?" Louie pleaded. "What are you talking about?"

Kate thrust a finger at him. "You," she called. "You are to blame, not me, not me at all. I didn't kill him!"

"No one said you did, Kate." Louie's voice quivered in exasperation. He held two hands out, palms up, begging.

"I can still fly better than anyone of them, Mister." She laughed, the sound distant and flat. "Oh, how they forget that when they see this little girl traipsing across the flight line." She skipped a few steps and stopped. "How they look so smug and so almighty condescending." She turned as though watching herself go past—her face in a sneer. "Have you ever noticed that, Louie?"

Louie shook his head, afraid to speak.

"Of course you wouldn't. They all have this practiced look they give." She brought her hand to her cheek and grinned. *"'Oh, isn't she the cutest thing?'"*

Her expression changed to tough. "But I played their game. Yes, I did. I played it so well I began to believe the rules myself.

"Louie, let me tell you something." She moved closer, her eyes narrow and looking at him from the corners, her mouth in a spreading grin. Louie was afraid of her. She walked out of the light shaft and into shadow. When she spoke it was in a low husky voice, "Max was by and large the best bed fellow anyone could ever hope for."

It was a moment before Louie could form words, "Kate," he said, "I've got to go."

"He was great, Louie."

"Everyone will miss him."

"But he couldn't fly, and he died."

"You should forget him," Louie said and didn't know why.

"I saw him go in," she said.

Louie paused.

"I saw him fall, and fall, and fall," she continued while slowly moving toward the open window. Louie took her arm "And when he hit the water..." She stared. "It was so far out, and the waves just swallowed him. No noise, it was so far."

"What waves?" Louie asked.

"There was a crowd on the pier, and you could hear the cheering when he crashed. I watched a cameraman beside me—CINETONE NEWS—I remember the name on the film holder—CINETONE INTERNATIONAL NEWS."

"What waves?" Louie demanded. "There were no waves. He smacked a building, a warehouse. You weren't there—"

"I ran into the water, and someone grabbed me, and we both fell, and a boat went out to get him, and then more boats, and I went under the water, and I heard his voice under the waves, and someone pulled me up, and I fought with them, and I felt their hands pull me, and when I broke through the surface, and the waves crashed around us, and I saw the boats heading out to get him, and I wanted to stay beneath the waves, and when they pulled me out, and this newsreel cameraman kept cranking, and the crowd on the pier kept cheering—they thought it was part of the show—and more airplanes flew over, and the movie camera—it was CINETONE NEWS—I remember that, and the cameraman kept cranking the handle, and when I looked back, the airplane was gone. He was gone."

Kate's face was blank. Louie stared, and silence crushed the room upon them. The light shifted, leaving them in the weak darkness of late afternoon.

Louie spoke first: "I didn't know."

"It's not important," Kate answered. "He's gone."

Louie moved slowly toward her. His two hands reached for her shoulders, then one slipped behind her back. When he kissed her, it was passionate. And when she kissed back, it was desperate.

***

# Chapter 19

Trucci knew he stood out wherever he went. Always the best clothes, the latest style shoes polished to mirrors. He never went outside without the proper hat, coat and gloves, plus, a splash of cologne. He knew he turned heads. He liked being noticed. He liked being Trucci—handsome, lean and a man every bit in control of his life. But he'd never spent three nights in his car, and he'd never been to Iowa.

"Well, where the hell is she, if she isn't here, you dim-witted corn-picker?"

"I told you, Mister," Brent, the line boy, said, his voice tight with his own kind of control, and his feet planted wide. "She's took sick, and she ain't here. Now, judgin' from your looks, I'd say, you got no reason to know where she might be at." He stuffed a rag into his back pocket and placed a foot on the fuel truck's running board. Nothing would give him greater pleasure than popping this city shit square on his big nose. And was that perfume he smelled?

Trucci sighed, kicked at a weed and turned his back. "Stupid, fuckin' Iowa bull-fuckin'-shit," he muttered, then turned on Brent. "Here," he snapped. "Five bucks says you know where she is."

Brent pulled himself into the truck's cab and closed the door. "You can keep your money, Mister. *I* already know where she's at." He started the motor, and Trucci slapped his hat against the door. Brent engaged the transmission, let out the clutch and pulled away. That felt better than popping the creep. Of course, he still wouldn't mind smacking him just once and really could've used the five.

Trucci stood looking around at the empty airport. Wind blew cold across the runways and ramp. He looked to the sky. "Don't say a thing, Lenny. Just don't say a word—"

He walked slowly back toward the hangars.

***

Louie's car stopped beside the airport cafe entrance. He switched off the motor and sat for several minutes staring at the steering wheel. The morning was cold. Wind scratched at his windshield, and he thought he saw snow.

Beyond the hangars, the fuel truck drove toward a Stinson Reliant monoplane that had come in the evening before. Brent stopped, climbed from the cab and took the stepladder from the back of the truck to set it ahead of the airplane's wing. Louie didn't feel like opening the café, so he rolled his window down and took his hat off setting it on the seat beside him. The cold sting in the wind felt good against his skin, still burning from the embarrassment over the kiss the day before, particularly the way Kate had kissed back and then, as though coming to her senses, gently showed him from the room and closed the door with a dismissive smile that said it'd never happen again.

Exhausted, he leaned both arms in an arc across the steering wheel and gazed absently across the ramp. By now, the fuel hose was stretched from the truck, and Brent lugged it over his shoulder while making his way up the ladder like a fireman in no hurry to put out a fire. He leaned far across the wing, and inserted the nozzle into the tank. One foot dangled, and his other stretched to keep planted on the top step. The filler neck was so far back he had to lie across the wing itself. Briefly, Louie thought it would be funny to sneak up and kick the ladder away and watch him kick and flail, gasoline spraying down the wing, his protests swept away in the wind.

"Hey," a voice snapped at him from behind.

Louie started.

"Hey, you work here?" Some guy in a black overcoat, tie loose, needed a shave. He thumped a hand on the roof above Louie's head and leaned his face toward the open window. Louie smelled stale cologne and suspected he hadn't brushed his teeth. "You the boss? Kid said the boss was comin' in any minute, and he was a fat, bald-lookin' guy, kinda dumpy, drove an old Dodge." Trucci's thumb jerked toward Brent, who was still stretched across the wing, the one foot still dangling. Louie decided it would definitely be worthwhile to kick the ladder out. "Well, you him?" Trucci asked.

Louie opened the door forcing him back. "I'm the owner."

"Of everything?"

"Most everything out here," Louie said and drew himself up in front of Trucci. Toe to toe, they stared eyeball to eyeball. "You want to buy the place? I'll let it go cheap. Financing's no problem."

"What do I look like; some kinda airplane nut?"

"No," Louie said. "You don't at that—not an *airplane* nut, anyhow."

"Yeah, well, hey, listen—"

"All ears."

"You got a dame works here, name of Kate?"

"Are you with the law?"

"Oh, give me a fuckin' chance, pal."

Louie moved faster than Trucci believed the fat man could. Plunging his finger into Trucci's chest, he gripped his lapels with the other hand and said in a barely controlled voice, "You've already used up most of your chances, neighbor. Now, tell us just what it is you want, and maybe I won't put you through the windshield."

It was a fleeting decision, whether to reach for the pistol inside his coat, or wave his hands as he did and say, "Look, pal, I got no beef with you. I ain't no cop, and I just wanna see Kate. I hear she's sick, and all, and I just wanna see her."

Their eyes stared at each other for a moment. Louie relaxed his grip and shuffled his feet slightly looking away.

"You're that guy from Chicago, that one she meets."

"She's talked about me?" Trucci said, more hopeful than boasting.

"Yes," Louie said. "She's mentioned you. Not how I pictured you, though. Are you the one who gave her that medal?"

Trucci was slow to answer, but he could feel himself blush.

"Don't worry," Louie said. "No one knows. I found it in her trousers pocket." He caught Trucci's perplexed look. "She's staying at my place. My sister's watching her. She's been sick—Kate, that is, not my sister. Geraldine's her name; she never gets sick. She's never been married, neither; probably never been laid, too." He laughed, and then looked at Trucci, who didn't know what to make of this.

"Did you come all this way to see Katie?"

"Yeah," Trucci said, embarrassed. "Been sleepin' in my car, nearly froze my ass off."

"Well, if you've come to fall in love with the little vixen, the line forms to the left." Louie turned away.

"What, you?"

Louie turned back, jaw set, chest puffed. "What's that supposed to mean?"

"Nothin', I just didn't think she—"

359

"Oh, piss on you," Louie growled. "Every swinging dick who's been through this place and seen her has fallen ass-over-tea-kettle in love with her. The little bitch kind of grows on a person."

Trucci nodded his agreement and stuffed both hands into his coat pocket. Despite the fancy clothes, he looked more the schoolboy with a crush on the girl next door, than a tough guy from Chicago.

Louie sighed and said, "I can see I won't get rid of you until I take you to her."

Trucci hesitated, then, "We could take my car."

Louie looked toward the Packard and said, "Drive that around where I live, and people will think the bank's coming to foreclose; likely get a load of buckshot through the window. Next thing, the police are asking questions. We'll stick with the Dodge, stuff your car in a hangar." He grabbed Trucci by the arm. "But first you need to get inside and clean up a bit." About the worst insult anyone could say to Trucci who silently let Louie lead him through the café door. "Washroom's round the corner, end of the hall, find what you need in the cabinet, don't use the red toothbrush," Louie said and pointed. As Trucci passed he added, "For a guy who dresses fancy, you don't seem real smart."

Trucci thought, *"Why carry a gun at all if I can't shoot someone for smart-mouthin' like that?"* And he turned the corner and followed the hall.

\*\*\*

Geraldine filled the doorway to Kate's room. "I washed several times, once in naphtha, but those stains on the knees—well, I don't know what to do about them."

"They're fine," Kate said. She pulled one leg over her foot, and, balancing, she poked her other foot in and pulled them up. "Did you see my brassier?"

"It's under the blouse," Geraldine said.

Kate turned for the dresser, where her clothes were neatly piled. Her breasts jiggled, and she caught her reflection in the mirror. "I've lost weight," she said and twisted. "You can see all my ribs." She studied herself, stretching her torso and running her fingers across her skin. "I think my tits have shrunk, too. Oh well."

"Must you talk like one of them?" Geraldine asked. She, too, studied Kate in the mirror.

"Like who?"

"Like those pilots. Foul language and such."

"You mean, 'tits'? I shouldn't say 'tits'? What do you call them?"

Geraldine giggled. "I guess I never call them anything. Who would I say it to? Louie?"

"Sure," Kate said. "It'd probably shock the shit of him."

"You should still be in bed."

"A week is too long, even for crazy people." Kate rummaged through the clothes, found her bra and slipped the straps over her shoulder. "I hate these things," she said and pulled her blouse over her arms.

Geraldine watched silently while Kate did each button, stopping short of her throat. She then tucked the blouse into her trousers and did the belt. Taking a brush from the dresser, she pulled it once across her hair.

"Like brushing a Brillo pad," Kate muttered and worked the brush through. "Time to cut it again."

"You should let it grow out," Geraldine said. She moved closer.

"Just turns into a bird's nest." She ran the brush across her head again and tossed it on the dresser. "That's enough of that nonsense." When she turned, Geraldine was standing close and reaching for a comb.

"Here," she commanded. "You just sit yourself down there." She pushed a small chair in front of the dresser and pressed Kate's shoulders until she sat.

"I should shave my head—like Mussolini."

"You should behave and dress like a lady."

"Can't fly airplanes in hoop skirts."

"Turn around," Geraldine commanded. She worked the comb into Kate's hair. "It *is* like a bird's nest."

"Useless."

"You hush. You've beautiful hair, young lady, and you should take care of it."

"I hate it."

"I would kill to have curls like yours."

"You want them? They're yours. Get the shears."

"Sit! Shush! Put your head forward—"

"Ohh," Kate moaned. The comb yanked at a knot and broke free. "Ow!"

"You are not leaving my house until you look presentable. And I don't care what you do to your hair once you get into that silly flying machine, but you *will* look respectable leaving this house."

Kate's eyes remained shut. Geraldine worked around her head, alternately torturing her with the comb, and then running the smooth brush across her scalp. After a while, it felt soothing, and Kate found herself relaxing, pampered and enjoying the attention.

When, finally, she looked at herself in the mirror, her hair surrounded her face in a swirl of shiny dark curls. It was balanced, even and soft. Kate stared at herself and saw a woman's face she had not seen for a long time. She reached to touch it and expected Geraldine, standing beside her to slap her hand away.

"It's all I could do," Geri apologized. "You should let it grow."

"I'd forgotten," Kate said. "It's been so long since I've bothered."

Geraldine ran the brush across the back of Kate's head and patted the side. "You're a very lucky woman, Katharine," she said, and then looked up suddenly as though surprised to hear herself speak.

"Thank-you," Kate said. She looked up and squeezed her hand.

Geraldine set the brush on the dresser and turned toward the door. "I still think you're too weak to go out, especially in some airplane, but I know no one takes my advice." Kate started to protest. "Now, you just get your things together, and I'll be downstairs to say good-bye. Don't touch those bed covers. I'll strip everything down later. All those sheets and blankets need washed, and I'll take care of all that. You just get your things and come on downstairs."

"Geri," Kate called after her. She wondered if shortening the name would sound too casual. Geraldine turned. "I mean it—Thank-you."

"No need to thank me," she said and looked away. "I won't have you leaving my house looking like a ragamuffin, that's all." She opened the door. "Besides, you have a gentleman visitor waiting downstairs."

"Gentleman?" Kate asked. "Who?"

"I couldn't say, but it's apparent he's no pilot." Geri smiled and left, leaving the door open behind her.

*\*\*\**

Kate stepped down the bottom of the staircase. Trucci moved away from Louie and toward her. Hat in hand, he asked, "Kate, how you doin'?" His eyes roamed up and down her. "You look kinda skinny and all."

"My tits got smaller, too," Kate said and heard Geraldine cackle before leaving the room. "Louie," Kate called, "where'd you find this character?" She descended the last step and, taking Trucci's arm, reached to kiss him on the cheek.

Louie clapped Trucci on the shoulder. "I saw him looking lonely out at the airport, so I took pity on him, fed him breakfast and made him brush his teeth. He says he's running away from home and wants to be a line boy like Brent when he grows up. What do you think? Should we give the kid a chance?"

"He's kind of shy," Kate said.

"And skinny—"

"Dresses and smells funny, too."

"Folks'll think we've hired a mortician to pump gas." He turned on Trucci. "Ever cleaned toilets?"

Trucci looked from one to the other, uncertain where to jump in.

"Definitely too shy for airport work," Kate said. "Maybe he could cook for you, Louie."

"Now, wait a second, here," Trucci said.

"He speaks. *Garbo speaks!*"

"He does kind of look like Garbo, doesn't he?"

"He's got better hips than Greta Garbo," Kate said.

"You realize, of course, Katie, he's in love with you."

Trucci dropped his eyes and looked as though he wanted to bolt from the room, but Kate still held his arm.

"That's okay, Louie, when he discovers I'm no virgin he'll drop me like a hot brick."

"You're not a virgin?" Louie asked.

"Never was."

"Amazing. Must be Catholic."

"Presbyterian, mostly, but don't tell anyone."

"Wouldn't think of letting your secret out," Louie said. "But I don't know if I can trust this fella."

"Can I say something?" Trucci injected.

"Let the boy speak, Katie. I think he's about to deny being in love with you, although that would be a flat-out lie."

"Katharine Marie Strauss," Trucci almost shouted, turning on her. "Will you marry me?"

"Oh, well done, boy!" Louie cried. "Brief, to the point, no words minced, no waffling, no senseless protestations of undying love and devotion, but most important—no fear of the inevitable rejection. I like that in a man."

"Then you marry him, Louie," Kate said.

"Kate," Trucci almost shouted. "I'm serious."

"I know you are, but the answer is no."

"I'll marry him," Geraldine said in passing through the room with an armful of folded linen. She gave Trucci a quick grin and climbed the stairs.

"There," Louie said. "You see? Cast your bread upon the water—your proposal wasn't a complete loss. Although," Louie added in a conspiratorial stage whisper, "I warned you, that one's yet a virgin."

"Not true," Geraldine countered and marched proudly along the hallway and up the stairway toward the third floor.

Three sets of eyes followed her, and then Kate said to Trucci, "I'm not marrying anyone, so—"

"You don't have to answer right away."

"I already did—"

"No, I'll wait—as long as you want."

"I don't want you to wait, the answer's no."

"Think about it."

"I don't have to. Nuh-oh—No."

"She's softening on you, Trucci," Louie said. "By the way, is that really your real name? Sounds like an ice cream flavor."

"Kate, I always get what I want," Trucci persisted, "and I want you, so—"

"Okay, I can see we're not getting anywhere with me saying no, so, yes. I will marry you. How's that? Feel better?"

Trucci staggered.

"Can I be the best man?" Louie asked.

"Sure," Kate said. "You can be the preacher for all I care. Now someone take me to the airport. I got to get the hell out of here." She looked at Trucci. "Ready to freeze your butt on your first airplane ride?"

\*\*\*

# Chapter 20

# Chariton, Iowa

Brian leaned into the crank handle that protruded from the engine cowling where *Honi soit qui mal y pense* was painted in gold script. It moved slowly at first, and then as the flywheel weight began to swing, he brought the crank around, feeling the inertia starter build whining momentum.

Around came the crank. His right foot pressed against the airplane's tire, his left braced on the wing, close to the fuselage just aft of the engine. He brought the handle over the top of the arc and down and up around again, and down again.

"Try it now," Daryl called from the cockpit, and Brian quickly removed the crank and pulled the T-handle just below that, releasing all the pent-up energy: *Phkeeeng...*

And the propeller twitched, and he heard Daryl cussing softly to himself or to the engine.

"Start, start," Brian muttered still pulling the engaging handle.

A short distance in front and a little to the side of the monoplane's nose stood Angelo. He wore a greasy pair of overalls over his suit. His tie, normally perfectly knotted, was loose, and he had a large grease smudge across his cheek. His hands were black and skinned from helping Daryl install a magneto. He'd never been so happy.

He stood now with fists clenched, eyes on the airplane, his lips mouthing the words, "Start, start, start—"

Over went the propeller in a lazy swing, and then once again, when, suddenly a pop, not more than a quick gasp like a drunk waking up in the wrong bed.

The inertia starter whined, and the propeller came around again. Another pop.

Daryl swore—something about Herbert Hoover and the way pigs mate, Generalissimo Franco, the Chicago White Sox and...*POP!*

Brian snapped his head back and felt his foot slip from the tire. Catching himself, he let go of the starter T-handle as the propeller swung into a blur, slamming wind back at him, almost knocking him to the ground.

"Get clear!" Daryl called above the howl of the radial. Brian had already dropped to the ground, and hugging the wing's leading edge, made his way toward the tip.

He tossed the starter crank handle toward the Nash, but missed and it skidded in the dirt. Brain didn't care, because he was watching the racer.

"She's runnin'!" Angelo called over the noise. "She sounds good."

Brian carefully listened to the engine, imagining each piston compressing air and fuel, the plugs exploding it at the exact instant Daryl had set the magneto points to open.

"She sounds good," Angelo repeated, although it almost sounded like a question. Brian nodded. Angelo's hand took his shoulder and shook it, then let go. They stood side by side watching, listening.

Daryl was lost in the engine's rumble. Goggles covered his eyes, and, hatless, his red hair whipped in the prop blast. He looked fast just sitting still and moved his head from side to side to catch every clack and rattle the machine produced. He changed throttle settings. He poked his face into the frigid blast of air over the side of the cockpit and smelled the wind. He felt the gut-shaking vibration through his insides, and he knew he'd produced a flying machine capable of launching Katie into the air-racing world beyond grass strips and low-budget tinkering.

He knew from the vicious hammering of the cylinders that they could take this machine to Cleveland, that they could compete, that she could fly against the big names in racing, names that once knew her in California.

He knew this was what she wanted, and he wanted so much to get her name back into the glitter world of record-breakers, movie stars and newsreel cameras. He also knew they really didn't stand a chance of ever winning, and, realistically, maybe never competing, because there was no money left. The $900 he and Angelo had borrowed against their Veterans Bonuses now screamed in front of him.

Daryl pressed the throttle forward. Watching oil temperature climb higher than he'd have liked, he kept squeezing the knob toward its stop. He glanced at each wing. Although the tie-down ropes were out of sight, he smiled thinking of Brian's added caution, rigging the second set of ropes through the same holes.

"We're not losing this one," he'd said earlier, even after Daryl had kicked the larger chocks against the wheels. That was before Daryl headed for the cockpit and slapped the cowling on *Honi soit qui mal y pense.* And when Angelo asked, "Just what the hell's that Pig Latin supposed to mean, anyhow?" Brian beat Daryl to the answer:

"It's old French."

"French?"

"Yeah, like from Lancelot and Knights of the Round Table. It means *'Shame upon him who thinks evil of it,'*" and he, too, slapped his hand on the cowling followed by Angelo who rubbed it cautiously before slapping it hard as though smacking a horse on the butt or a terrified doughboy going over the top, ordering both to run. And then he smiled at Daryl and walked clear.

369

Daryl, now, looked to Brian and Angelo, side by side, both anxious, Angelo with the bigger grin; Angelo, who knew so little about engines and airplanes, but was so willing to get filthy and so willing to learn—and to forget what went before. He was unwilling to admit that the thought of flying in one of then scared the crap out of him.

Daryl looked at Brian. Almost as tall as Angelo, he was a full-grown man in his mechanic's overalls and wool cap. Both faces were red in the cold air. Both men kept fists clenched at their sides watching.

Daryl eased the throttle until it pressed against the stops. The engine ran great. A review of the instruments, and everything was good, even the oil temp had leveled off. Daryl, wrapped in the pure sound of machinery, felt his command over the whole situation rise in his throat.

Katie could fly, he thought.

Angelo was a survivor, a leader needing only himself.

Brian was young, and there was nothing to compete with that.

Bathed in noise he'd created, Daryl thought of Joe—independent, easy-going Joe. Possibly one of the best pilots, anywhere. Daryl tried to decide who was actually more skilled, Joe or Kate.

It didn't matter, because right then, seated behind a 700-horsepower engine Daryl had virtually created from scrap, he knew he was completely alone within this circle, where he, Daryl, was the best, the only one who could turn lifeless steel and rubber and brass and oil and grease into pure, magnificent power screaming from a radial engine six feet in front of his toes.

This was what Daryl did.

This was what made Daryl unique.

This was when a wrist pin inside the number four cylinder, disintegrated.

It didn't take long. The number four piston, freed from the connecting rod, blew through the cylinder head, taking that whole collection of valves and guides, seats and rings straight through the thin aluminum cowling, through *Honi soit qui mal y pense* and sprayed it in a long arc toward Angelo and Brian.

What didn't go through the cowl went into the crankcase. Jagged bits of hardened steel blasted into the lower bearings, instantly chewing them to trash. The sudden uneven jar in number four, threw other cylinders out of whack and they too wrenched, twisted, cracked, jammed, mangled and ripped apart.

When the cowling broke it stretched toward the propeller where it was caught, ripped, shattered and scattered like so much shrapnel. A crosspiece, Daryl had riveted on to stiffen the cowling, also broke loose. This should not have caused much problem by itself, but in coming loose, it wrapped itself like a lasso around the neck of the carburetor and simply yanked that clear off the studs. That, in turn, ripped the fuel line free from the firewall, and that breach allowed the firewall to twist and lurch forward three inches at one end and an inch-and-a-quarter at the other. It buckled in the middle.

As the firewall moved, so moved the engine mount, although only slightly.

By now, a full second-and-a-half after the wrist pin had gone, the right side of the cowling followed the left side into the propeller. In leaving the airplane, it snatched at the oil tank and sliced a gash into it the size of a rumpled baseball card. That's where the oil came from that hit Daryl in the face as he was leaning around the windshield smelling the prop blast.

This was also when Kate landed.

***

Daryl stayed in the cockpit. By the time Kate had taxied back, stopped, killed the engine and jumped from the Travel Air to run toward him, Daryl felt the exhaustion of utter failure pressing him into the seat.

She stopped running as she rounded the wing tip and slowly walked toward the cockpit, staring at the ruined engine. Daryl stared at his feet still on the rudder pedals.

"You've got a slight oil leak there, Mister," she said and clasped his shoulder.

His head turned slowly, and beyond the oil sliding off his goggles she could see the thicker film of tears in his eyes. He forced a grin. "There's something different about your hair," he said weakly.

"I combed it," she said quietly.

"That's it."

"I thought of shaving it off."

"Oh, don't do that; your head will get cold, and you'll have to wear funny hats all the time."

"Would you buy me funny hats?"

"If I had to."

"Would you build me another airplane? One that looks a little better than this one?"

"Maybe," he said. "If you didn't shave your hair off."

"I'll consider it."

"Good, girl." Daryl smiled and looked past her. "Who's the guy in the suit, looks frozen and doesn't know how to climb out of an airplane?"

The stranger banged his head against the upper wing while getting out of the front cockpit. He seemed to collect himself momentarily before stumbling off the wing and landing knees and hands first in the mud.

"His name's Trucci. He wants to marry me."

"Is there anyone who doesn't want you?"

"Not that I can think of," she said and leaned closer to him. "Except maybe you."

"I'd given up long ago. Decided to devote my life to building exploding airplanes."

"Well, you've succeeded. Now it's time to think about the future."

"You mean there's no market for these things?" He waved his hand toward the mass of oily motor parts dangling from bent mounts.

"There might be, but you'll need a test pilot."

"Yeah, I'm not so hot at that," he said and looked at her. "You know someone?"

"I might."

"Who?"

"Me."

"Nope, can't use you. You look too much like a woman I knew long time ago."

"She dump you?"

"Yup."

"Not a very smart woman, was she?"

"No, but she had a steady income."

"Must not have been a pilot then."

"Funny thing is, she was."

"Well, I don't have any income, but I can fly."

"Can you stand on one foot and wiggle your nose?"

"Whose foot do I have to stand on?"

Pause while Daryl pushed the goggles off his eyes.

"Kate, what are you doing here?"

"I live here, remember?"

"I remember a lot of things."

"Such as?"

"Such as, I once had a friend named Kate, and I managed to completely screw everything up in my life, so she ran off with the circus."

"What'd she do in the circus?"

"Not much, really. Her specialty was stepping into the center ring, and causing every male in the audience to instantly fall in love with her, thereby leading them to do foolish things, such as pronounce their undying devotion. It was really quite an act."

Kate leaned over the rim of the cockpit and gently took Daryl's chin in her hand.

"You'll get your fingers all greasy doing that," he said.

She kissed him.

"You'll get your lips all greasy doing that."

She kissed him again.

"You'll get other parts greasy if you keep doing that— please, please—"

Trucci was halfway between the Travel Air and the racer when he stopped. To his right was Angelo, walking toward him. Trucci's focus, however, was on Kate, or more importantly on Kate kissing Daryl.

A hand clasped his shoulder, and he turned.

"Don't get any closer to her," Angelo warned. "Believe me, you get too close, you get burnt. She does that."

Trucci did nothing. He felt Angelo's hand turn him around and lead him away from the airplanes. When they reached Angelo's car Trucci, his mouth dry, asked, "You get a call? From Chicago?"

Angelo nodded and opened the passenger door on the Ford.

"The money ain't gone," Trucci said. "I got it." He pointed toward the Travel Air.

"It don't matter, Truc. They think you set 'em up. I got the call. You know how it works."

"You gonna shoot me?" Trucci asked. "Here?"

Angelo had the pistol out of his pocket before Trucci saw him reach through his overalls. Trucci stood rigid, eyes fixed. He refused to react, to show fear. He found his balance that had been falling off. He felt a complete sense of control knowing it was all over.

Angelo closed the car door and snapped the release lever in the pistol's grip butt to remove the clip. One bullet at a time, he popped them from the clip with his thumb, and they dropped into the dirt. He then placed the clip into Trucci's coat pocket. He snapped the slide back, and the remaining bullet popped out and dropped with the others. He slipped the empty gun into Trucci's other pocket and turned away.

"Just decided, I don't take phone calls no more," he said walking toward the Travel Air. "Where'd you say the dough was?"

Trucci followed hesitantly, and then joined Angelo and reached past him into the biplane to remove the package of money he'd been carrying since Maxwell's death. He held it for Angelo who took it and ripped it open. "How much?"

"Nine grand, plus" Trucci said. "Maybe ten."

Angelo shrugged. "That ought to be enough."

"For what?" Trucci asked, worried.

"For a new motor on the racer, plus, travel expenses to get them on the race circuit. What'd you think? Wanna come along? 'Course you're gonna need new clothes."

"You can't do that."

"Why the hell not?"

"They'll kill you."

"Somebody's been tryin' to kill me since I was a kid," Angelo said. "Right now, I don't give a rat's ass. Right now, I feel like building an airplane. You wanna help?"

Trucci was dumbfounded. He felt the weight of the dismantled pistol in his pocket. His own pistol was loaded and holstered beneath his jacket. "By all rights I should kill you, Ang," he called after him.

"So what?" Angelo answered and kept walking away. "You kill me, and that won't square it with them. It still looks like you set them up and made off with their dough. You kill me, and you got no allies." He looked back at Trucci and through a grin said, "You stick around here, and I'll keep an eye on you. You got friends here. Granted, we're a bunch of losers, but what the hell. You got somethin' better?"

Trucci looked around the tiny airfield. Two leaning hangars and an old shack with a thin trail of smoke rising from a metal chimney. A rusted Nash and busted up yellow and black-checked biplane parked beside the hangar. A tall skinny kid in mechanics overalls poked around a blown-apart airplane engine where Angelo now stood.

And a woman named Kate.

"What do I do?" Trucci called and saw Kate as well as Angelo look.

"Whatever you want," Angelo answered and shifted the moneybox under his arm. "Right now, I think we need someone to run into town and pick us up something to eat. Place in town makes a good loosemeat." He pointed to the Nash. "Battery's dead, so you gotta crank it. The doors're welded shut, and the brakes don't work so good, so plan your stops in advance. You got any cash?"

\*\*\*

# Chapter 21

## —THE CIRCLE COMPLETE—

Burlington, Mt. Pleasant, Fairfield…Iowa towns flowed past Joe like small memories. The train was delayed five minutes in Ottumwa while the brakeman argued with the fireman outside his window.

"Probably deciding who works Thanksgiving," Joe mumbled.

A door slid open and then shut. The conductor entered his car, making his way down the aisle with the authority he thought his uniform demanded. "Please take your feet off the seat, sir," he said without stopping. He was through the car, and another door slid open, then shut, and Joe replaced his feet on the seat in front of him.

A blast on the whistle up the tracks, steam, and the cars shook. They lurched one way, stopped, and then jolted back the other way. Joe turned his head and watched the Ottumwa station creep by. A square sedan turned a corner and stopped at the crossing, the faces behind the windshield dull and waiting.

Joe scratched his nose and pulled his hat over his eyes. The crossing passed with a Doppler: *ding-dinG-diNG-dING-DING-DINg-DIng-Ding-ding*—then, two blasts on the whistle. Coal smoke rolled gray past the window. The *click/click—click/click, click/click—click/click* of the wheels against the rail joints quickened. Joe mulled his decision to escape New Jersey before he got in any deeper. He liked the hundred-dollar bills, but New Jersey wasn't Iowa, and he knew he was getting in way over his head, way too close to becoming fish food. So, he simply walked away. Literally—one foot in front of the other,

377

thumb out, and caught a ride to his room, packed and walked to the nearest station with a train headed back to the Midwest. Back to his old biplane, to grass fields and—he hoped—his old route between Chicago Heights and Blakesburg. It was time to return. To walk out and pick up a life he assumed would be waiting for him, because everyone waited for Joe. Or so he hoped.

*Click/click—click/click, click/click—*

For the third time that day, he took a newspaper clipping from his jacket pocket and reread the headline:

### VETERANS BONUS

It gave details about how to apply; what to expect; who was eligible. "Starting to look pretty good," Joe muttered. He slipped the article back in his pocket and closed his eyes. "Start all over—" And the steel wheels clicked— "Start all over—start all over—"

Behind the lowered brim of his soiled fedora, beneath his eyelids, he saw Kate. The months had not faded her image. Although, it smoothed out some of the rougher edges, as time and distance tend to do. Nevertheless, it was the same face he saw every time he closed his eyes. It was the image he now saw before him as he listened to the steady tap-tap of the wheels and the creaks in the swaying car.

"Listen, pal—"

Joe peeked from under the hat. The conductor's face was six inches from his own; the bovine eyes above a thick mouth that spoke in a low, tired voice. "I've asked you nice; now, I'm asking not so nice—Get your clod-hoppers off of my seat, or I'll throw you off of my train." No smile. His train.

Joe stared and pulled the hat brim lower on his eyes. "You don't have to get all huffy about it," he said and dropped his feet one at a time to the floor. There was a deep sigh, and he felt the conductor leave.

Funny what didn't scare him.

\*\*\*

"Chariton...Chariton…" The conductor called and the cars bucked and rattled. Joe stood, bracing his leg against the seat. He pulled his battered suitcase from the rack above him.

When he stepped from the train, he glanced along the platform and tried to ignore that vague emptiness that comes from arriving somewhere alone with no one there to meet him. He walked toward the station. The conductor passed him without a nod; the brakeman was arguing again with the fireman, and a small boy pointed a cap pistol at Joe and fired—three rounds, each little blue smoke puffs, each sounded too familiar.

He flinched, and made two fingers to gun the kid down—*Pukew! Pukew!* And for good measure: *Pu-kew!*

The mother grabbed the kid, "Jerad, you know you're not supposed to shoot strangers!" Joe pushed aside the heavy oak door to the station and looked around.

*BONG!* His nickel fell into the black payphone. He pressed the earpiece to his head and dialed the first digit. He dialed another, and then a third and referred to the tiny address book where he'd written Kate's number. It was the same book he had found in the hangar the day Frank was killed, the book with the coded names, the book with the name 'Zwillman' disguised as a series of numerals. It was the book he'd claimed he'd never seen but held onto in case he ever needed to negotiate his way out of a jam.

It had taken him from New York to Albany to crack the first page of code—simple number to letter, minus one. The second page took from Albany to Erie—the code changed by a factor of two numbers up for every vowel and three numbers up for each consonant. Pages three and four reversed the two codes, and so it went until by Gary Indiana, Joe had cracked Frank's entire code. About 60 names exposed; names that started with someone named Anastasia and ended with Zwillman—anarchists and New Jersey gangsters whose circle Joe could not crack without selling his independence.

It was healthier that way.

He finished dialing the Chariton number. The line hummed. Relays snapped. Joe stretched outside the booth and waved toward a trash man pushing his barrel.

"Hey," he called, and the man looked. "One for the FBI files." Joe waved the book and tossed it. It bounced off the rim and vanished amid the gum wrappers and cigar butts. The trash man shrugged and moved on. Joe grinned, "Two points."

The phone rang. Joe slid the wooden folding door shut. A bulb came on above his head as though he suddenly had an idea, but he didn't. The phone rang a second time. He rummaged through his jacket pocket for a cigarette, found only an empty case and slipped it back into his pocket. The telephone rang a third, and then a fourth. On the seventh ring, he leaned against the wall, pushed his fedora back on his head and stared through the grimy window at the trash man sweeping with a small broom and a dustpan on a long handle. He worked methodically, getting every scrap into his pan.

The telephone rang and rang and rang—

Twice the operator came on: "…do you wish to keep trying?"

"What choice do I have?" Joe asked, and she didn't know so it rang and rang—

\*\*\*

Daryl climbed from the racer's cockpit. Kate took his hand and followed him around the wing. Brian joined them at the engine and handed Daryl a rag.

The outside telephone bell on the office rang.

"Reminds me," Daryl said. "Your sister called," and then he pointed at the dripping engine mess. "I can fix that."

"Why would you want to?" Kate asked.

"It'll give me something to do. Keep up the pretense of honest employment, preserve the facade of manhood or the New Deal—take your pick."

"Does this mean I'll still be carrying you?"

"Only financially, socially and morally."

"Don't talk about morals in front of B-R-I-A-N—"

"I can spell," Brian interjected. "And I don't need no lectures on morals from *you two*—" He grinned.

"They grow up so fast," Kate sighed.

And the phone rang, and rang, and rang—

"Maybe that's the truant officer wondering why he's not in S-K-O-O-L." Daryl turned on Brian. "Can you spell that?"

"Yeah, it spells, *BORING*—"

"Well, at least the boy can spell."

Angelo walked up to them and dropped a package of money on the racer's wing. "Your phone's ringing."

"Probably the phone company calling to tell us to pay the bill."

"Don't pay it. Let them disconnect. There's no one other than us you'd want to talk to anyhow." He pushed the money toward Kate. "I brung you some money. Well, Trucci did, actually, but I stole it from him." All four turned on Trucci who looked uncomfortable standing in the middle of the runway fidgeting with his hat.

"Hey, lover boy," Angelo called. "Come tell Katie, here, she can have the dough, 'cause the cops got everything else."

"No more runs?" Kate asked.

Angelo shook his head. "Sorry, Kid. It was good while it lasted, but—"

Kate patted Angelo's arm. "Flying jobs are easy to get." She tapped the money. "But I can't take this."

Daryl: "I can."

Trucci was suddenly with them, inside the circle formed around Kate and the failed racer. "Aw, take the dough, Kate. What the hell? I'm a dead man; Angie's a dead man—take it."

She looked as though she'd say something, but the *ring-ring-ring* made her say, "I'm going to answer that phone." And she ran toward the shack. "Probably my sister."

Brian, Angelo, Trucci and Daryl—a circle with a gap about to close—watched her, each man with his own thoughts, each somehow aware how much he could have, and how much he could only dream. Each was aware how much they all could lose. Because even though the story was over, it was far from—

# THE END

DEDICATED TO THE MEMORY OF TWO
SOUTHERN IOWA PILOTS: BILL DAVIDSON AND
DUANE ENSLOW